He looked into her face, trying to gauge her feelings. "Look at me!" he said fiercely, and he cupped her chin to bring her eyes up to meet his. She seemed fragile, and that surprised him.

Her gloved fingers splayed over his chest. "No," she whispered.

His lips curved. "What are you saying no to?"

What was in his eyes; the way her heart jarred; the sudden realization that she wasn't as immune to him as she thought she was.

His hand moved to her neck, his fingers tightened. She knew she should pull back. Instead, she lifted her face to him. His lips were warm, tasting, not taking. She felt her mouth opening to the gentle pressure of his. She couldn't think, didn't want to think.

ALMOST A PRINCESS

ELIZABETH THORNTON

BANTAM BOOKS

ALMOST A PRINCESS

A Bantam Book/January 2003

ISBN 0-553-58489-8

Published simultaneously in the United States and Canada

Bantam Books are published by Bantam Books, a division of
Random House, Inc. Its trademark, consisting of the words
"Bantam Books" and the portrayal of a rooster, is Registered in
U.S. Patent and Trademark Office and in other countries. Marca
Registrada. Bantam Books, New York, New York.

PRINTED IN THE UNITED STATES OF AMERICA

OPM   10   9   8   7   6   5   4   3   2   1

ALMOST
A
PRINCESS

Prologue

*T*he body was still warm.

Officer Rankin turned up his coat collar to protect his neck from the drizzle that was beginning to turn to sleet. Not only was the weather wretched, but Hyde Park at night gave him the shudders.

He went down on his haunches and held his lantern high to get a better look. In his long career, he'd investigated many murders, but he'd never seen anything like this. The victim was roped to the trunk of a tall oak and had fallen forward at the instant of death so that the ropes sagged with his weight. He'd been shot at close range behind his left ear, and his neckcloth was soaked with blood.

Rankin looked up and beckoned to his assistant, a new recruit to the Bow Street Office, who looked as though he might be sick. This was Willis's first night on the job, and Rankin was wishing that they'd been called out to a housebreaking and not a murder.

After a slight hesitation, Willis sank down beside his superior and stared fixedly at the murdered man. Behind them, crowding a little closer for a better view, were the night watch and the elegant young gentleman who had raised the alarm.

"Nasty," said the night watch. He wasn't squeamish about sudden death. As a veteran of the Spanish Campaign, he had seen much worse than this.

Rankin said nothing. In his mind's eye, he was trying to see how the murder was done. The victim was on his knees, bound at the ankles, with his hands tied behind his back. There were no obvious signs of a struggle, but it was hard to tell in that Stygian darkness. His chin was sunk on his chest, and it was impossible to see if there were other injuries on his face—bruises, broken bones—without raising his head. Mindful of Willis's squeamishness, Rankin decided to leave well enough alone until the police doctor arrived.

He couldn't tell how old the victim was, but he could tell from his garments that he had money to spare. He was well dressed, but not what Rankin would call fashionable, not like Mr. Hastings, the gentleman who had roused them from the warmth of the Watch House to investigate the shot he'd heard coming from the park, just inside the Stanhope Gate.

Rankin got to his feet and turned to speak to Hastings. "After you 'eard the shot, what did you do, sir?"

"I ran to the gate."

"And it was open?"

"Someone had smashed the lock." Hastings was

looking over Rankin's shoulder, staring at the victim as he spoke. "I've never seen anything like it. It looks like an execution."

The night watch answered him. "They did that to traitors in Spain, the partisans, I mean. It didn't matter if you was a man or a woman. And sometimes they did worse, cut out your tongue, or cut off your ears or hands, before they killed you."

Rankin's assistant got up. His young face was pale and pinched. Rankin breathed noisily and flashed a warning look at the night watch. *Stow it,* his look said, *or young Willis won't last the night.*

He spoke to Hastings. "Did you enter the park after you 'eard the shot, sir?"

Hastings shook his head. "Well, that is to say, I may have taken a step inside the gates, but I thought better of it." He laughed nervously. "And I knew the Watch House was just up the road, so I went straight there."

"Did you 'ear or see anything after the shot was fired?"

"Nothing, I'm afraid." He gestured to the distant lights of the Oxford Road. "Well, I'll leave you to it, Officer. I'm having dinner with friends and I'm already late."

"I'm sorry sir," said Rankin as inoffensively as possible, "but I must ask you to go with the night watch to Bow Street to make a statement." Then to the night watch. " 'Ave them send the wagon and the doctor. Stanhope Gate, mind."

Hastings's pleasantly modulated voice suddenly turned fractious. "I'm afraid that's out of the question. I told you. I'm late for an appointment. I really must be going."

Rankin let out a long, patient sigh. He hated

dealing with the upper classes, West-end gents who would no more think of heeding a humble officer of the law than they would their own servants. There was only one way to make an impression on them.

"If you refuse to go with the night watch," he said, in the same inoffensive voice, "I shall be forced to arrest you, sir, and you wouldn't want that. Think how it would look to your friends."

It was outrageous! Rankin's superiors would get to hear of it! And so on and so on. Rankin had heard it all before. He nodded sympathetically, but he held his ground, and with no more than a savage curse, Hastings capitulated.

"Now," said Rankin when he and Willis were alone, "let's take a closer look."

In one of the victim's pockets, they found a bill from a butcher in Bayswater addressed to Mr. John Collier, and a leather purse with a few coins. In the other pocket, they found only a small, round pebble.

Rankin stared at that pebble for a long time. He looked at the body again.

"What d'you think, guv?" asked Willis.

"I think," said Rankin slowly, "that whoever murdered Mr. Collier, if this is Mr. Collier, is sending a message to someone."

It seemed to him that this might well be a case for Special Branch.

Not that the magistrates would agree with him. Special Branch was something new, a unit that was set up to combat terrorism and assist local authorities with difficult cases. Trouble was, those glamorous Special Branch agents always thought they knew best and didn't care whose toes they stepped on. That, as was to be expected, stirred up bad feeling. It was hard to believe sometimes that Bow Street and Special Branch were on the same side.

No. The magistrates wouldn't rush to call in Special Branch.

Sighing, he slipped the pebble into his pocket.

Chapter 1

*I*t was moving day for the members of the Ladies' Library in Soho Square. Their lease had run out, and one of their staunchest supporters, Lady Mary Gerrard, had offered her mansion in the Strand. The house was buzzing as an army of ladies and their helpers set to work to transform their new quarters, room by room, from a palatial residence to a library with lecture rooms, reading rooms, and a bright and airy tearoom.

Caspar Devere, Lord Castleton, better known to his friends as Case, stood just inside the marble entrance hall, taking it all in. He was a harshly handsome man, thirtyish, well above average height, with dark hair and gray, gray eyes that, for the moment, were distinctly amused.

He left his hat and gloves on a hall table and wandered into the main salon. Some of the men who were helping the ladies were known to him, and that made him smile. Not many gentlemen wanted it known that their wives or sisters were members here.

As the Viscount Latham passed close by carrying a chair, Case called out, "Freddie, where can I find Lady Octavia?"

On seeing the earl, Latham registered surprise, quickly followed by amusement. In a stage whisper, he replied, "I won't tell anyone I saw you here, Case, if you don't tell anyone about me." Then in a normal voice, "Try next door. That's where she has set up her headquarters."

Case wandered into another salon, and there she was, the library's founder and driving force, Lady Octavia Burrel. Dressed all in white in something that closely resembled a toga, with matching turban, she directed her small army as they came to her for their orders. Though there was much coming and going, there was very little confusion.

Case was not here to help but for information, and when the crush around Lady Octavia thinned, he quickly crossed to her. He was sure of his welcome because he'd known her for as long as he could remember. She and his great-aunt were close friends.

When she saw him, her chubby face lit up with pleasure. "Lord Castleton," she said. "This is a surprise! I had no idea you were interested in our cause."

As Case well knew, there was a lot more to the Ladies' Library than its innocent name implied. The cause to which Lady Octavia referred was to improve the lot of women by changing the antiquated marriage and property laws of England. It was also involved, so rumor went, in helping runaway wives evade their husbands. In some circles, Lady Octavia and her volunteers were seen as subversives. In the clubs he attended, they were frequently the butt of masculine laughter. But there were others who supported the aims of Lady Octavia and her League of Ladies. His aunt was one of them. He had never given the matter much thought.

"I suppose," said Lady Octavia, "I have your aunt to thank for sending you to help us?"

He avoided a direct answer. "I left her in Soho Square, directing things there. I'm looking for Miss Mayberry. My aunt told me she might be here."

"She's in the pantry. Turn left and take the green baize door at the end of the hall."

As Case walked away, Lady Octavia's gaze trailed him. He was easy to look upon, she reflected, this young man who appeared to have everything. As heir to his father, the Duke of Romsey, wealth, privilege, and position were already his, and it showed, not in arrogance exactly, but in something close to it. But it wasn't unattractive, just the opposite, especially to women. And now that he'd turned thirty and had finally taken up the courtesy title of earl, as befitted a duke's heir, he was even more attractive to women.

There wasn't the woman born, his aunt had told her, who could resist Caspar, more's the pity. It would do him the world of good to taste rejection. Lady Octavia wondered how Lord Castleton had come to meet Jane Mayberry. Jane didn't go into society much. When she was in town, she went to lectures and concerts and the opera, especially the opera. Jane was very fond of music. Maybe that was where she had met the earl.

She frowned when another thought occurred to her. Lord Castleton and his volatile mistress, La Contessa, had recently parted company.

She dithered, debating with herself whether she should go after him, to chaperon Jane, when Mrs. Bradley came up and said that she was wanted in the old earl's library.

This request cleared Lady Octavia's brain. She was letting her imagination run away with her. The poor man was just trying to help.

He found her in the first room past the green baize door. She hadn't heard him enter, so he took a moment to study her. She was perched on a chair, on tiptoe, fiddling with crockery on the top shelf of a cupboard. The first thing he noticed were a pair of nicely turned ankles. Unfortunately, they were encased in blue woolen stockings. He should have guessed. He'd made a few inquiries about Jane Mayberry and had learned, among other things, that she was a very clever young woman. Clever women, Lady Octavia and his Aunt Sophy among them, wore blue stockings as a badge of honor, a kind of declaration that their minds were set on higher things. *Bluestocking* was a derogatory term that had been coined to describe such women, and they wore that like a badge of honor, too.

Her fine woolen gown was a muddy green, "olive" his mistress would have called it, but it was not a color he particularly liked. All the same, it suited the honey-gold hair streaked blond by the sun. The gown was well cut and revealed a slender waist and the long, graceful line of her spine.

He coughed to warn her of his presence, then shifted his gaze when a tawny, bristling mass rose from the floor and positioned itself in front of him with bared fangs.

As she turned from the cupboard, Case said softly, "Call off your dog or I shall be forced to shoot it."

"If you do," she said coolly, "it will be the last thing you do." Then to the dog, "Lance, down."

The dog, of indeterminate pedigree with perhaps a touch of wolf thrown in—and that didn't seem right to Case because there hadn't been wolves in England for three hundred years—sank to the floor and rested its jowls on its immense paws. Its gaze never wavered from Case.

"He doesn't like men," said Miss Mayberry, stepping down from her chair. "Lady Octavia should have warned you. I'm Jane Mayberry, by the way."

It sounded as if Jane Mayberry didn't like men either—a pity, because he found her direct manner and unfaltering stare oddly appealing. She wasn't beautiful but she was anything but plain. She had a strong face, with straight dark brows and large, intelligent brown eyes.

"I'm Castleton," he said. He would have bowed, except that Miss Mayberry turned away without bothering to curtsy.

"Yes, I recognized you," she said. "You're tall, that's what matters. At least you won't have to teeter on the chair."

She had the kind of voice a man could listen to day in, day out, and long into the night. But he'd ruffled her feathers by threatening her dog. If he wanted information, he'd have to tread carefully now.

"You recognized me? Have we met?"

"No. But Viscount Latham almost introduced us once, at the opera. You were late for an appointment, and rushed away."

Another black mark against him, he supposed. He had no recollection of her at all, but then, he wouldn't if she was dressed as she was now. His taste ran to something more flamboyant.

He took the stack of plates she offered him and set them on the top shelf. When he turned back to her, she had another stack waiting for him. He gave her the smile that never failed to make a lady's heart beat just a little faster. He spoke to put her at her ease, but he was interested in how she would answer all the same.

"How did you come to be involved with Lady Octavia's library? I mean, you're not married. You can't have an interest in changing the marriage and property laws of England."

"Your aunt isn't married either," she said. "Why don't you ask her?"

"So you know my aunt?"

"Everyone at the library knows Lady Sophy. She's a dear. Would you mind?" She shoved the stack of plates into his arms. "You can talk and work at the same time."

Case took the plates and turned away to hide a smile. This was a new experience for him—being ordered about by a young, unmarried woman. Young women usually tried to flirt with him, or fawned over him. He could be charming, but he could be cruel when he wanted to be, as any overambitious young woman who had marriage on her mind could testify.

Obviously, this wasn't going to be a problem with Miss Mayberry.

He said, "Lady Octavia is my aunt's closest friend. That's how she became converted to the cause. And you?"

She could avoid questions as well as he. "Last stack," she said, "then we can start polishing the silver."

He was taken aback. "I can't believe the silver in Lady Mary's house is tarnished. She wouldn't allow it."

"Then it won't take us long, will it?"

When she opened a drawer and began to assemble her materials, he decided it was time to come to the point. "Miss Mayberry," he said, "I didn't come here to help you move into your new quarters. There's something I want to ask you."

The change in her was almost imperceptible. He might have dismissed it as a quirk of his imagination if her dog had not lifted its head and whined low in its throat, as though uneasy with some implied threat to its mistress.

She said, "Lady Octavia didn't send you to help me?"

He smiled. "That was a misunderstanding. I don't mind stacking dishes, but I'm hopeless with silver."

When the dog made a movement to rise, she pointed to the floor, and it sank back again. *She's afraid,* thought Caspar, amazed. *What on earth have I said to frighten her?* Not that he could tell by looking at her that anything was wrong. It was the dog that was on edge.

She pushed back a stray tendril of hair. "This is the wrong time to ask me questions, Lord Castleton. As you see, some of us are busy. Why don't you come back later? Thank you for stacking the dishes. Now, if you'll excuse me, I have a silver paste to make."

He didn't know whether to be amused or annoyed. He wasn't in the habit of being dismissed like this. "One question, Miss Mayberry, then I'll leave you to your—ah—labors. Where can I find Letitia Gray?"

Her back was to him and he could see the tension across her shoulder blades gradually relax. "Letty?" she said, turning to face him. "You came here to ask me about Letty?"

He nodded. "I was told that you and she were friends."

"Who told you?"

"Does it matter? All I want from you is Mrs. Gray's direction."

She stared at him reflectively for a long interval. "What do you want with Mrs. Gray?" she asked finally.

"That's between Mrs. Gray and me."

He saw at once it was the wrong thing to say. Before he could soften his answer, she said, as abrupt as he, "I'm sorry I can't help you."

"You can't help me or you won't?"

"I won't help you."

Now his patience was wafer thin. "Do you mind telling me why?"

"Because it's against the library's rules. What I *can* do is ask Mrs. Gray if she wants to see you, or you can write a letter and I'll see that she gets it."

"That could take days! If it's character references you want, ask Lady Octavia or my aunt. They'll vouch for me."

"They'd give you the same answer as I. It's against the library's policy to tell strangers where members live."

"I'm not a stranger!"

"You are to my friend."

"How do you know?"

Her brows rose fractionally. "Because she would have told me, of course. Your name has been in all the newspapers. Your brother-in-law is Col. Richard Maitland, the head of Special Branch, isn't he? You and he brought a murderer to justice. The papers called you a hero."

"An exaggeration!" he declared.

Her lashes lowered, veiling her expression. "I

don't doubt it, but I'm sure my friend would have told me if she'd met the hero of the Maitland affair."

He didn't know how to take her. Was she poking fun at him or was she serious? Both, he decided and grinned.

"You're right. I don't know Mrs. Gray, but I know her brother, Gideon Piers."

"You *know* him? That's odd. Gideon died in Spain a long time ago."

"I mean I *knew* him. We served together in Spain." He realized that his voice had developed an edge and he made a considerable effort to soften it. "This really is urgent, Miss Mayberry, or I wouldn't be badgering you like this."

She seemed to soften a little as well. At any rate, in spite of the rising temperature of their conversation, her dog seemed satisfied that nothing was wrong. Its head was resting on its paws again, and its alert eyes were shifting from Miss Mayberry to him, as if it were a spectator at some play in Drury Lane.

"And I don't mean to be difficult," she said. "I'll tell you what I *will* do, though. If you write a letter right now, I'll see that it's hand delivered, and that I have a reply, oh, shall we say by four o'clock? That's only a few hours away. Surely you can wait that long?"

Stubborn was too mild a word to describe Miss Jane Mayberry, but at least she was gracious with it. She'd learn soon enough that he could be just as stubborn.

"Thank you," he said. "I can't ask for more than that. Now, where can I find pen and paper?"

"Ask Lady Octavia. She knows where everything is." He was almost through the door when she stopped him by saying his name.

"You didn't answer my question," she said. "Who told you that I was Mrs. Gray's friend?"

"I remembered that Piers had a sister who was a teacher at St. Bede's Charity School. I went there yesterday and met the woman in charge." This was the shortened version of events and he saw no reason to enlarge on it. "Miss Hepburn—that was her name. She said that when Miss Piers married and moved away, that was the last they saw of her. But you continued to visit the school from time to time." He grinned. "I got the impression that you were the apple of Miss Hepburn's eye. She told me that any letter addressed to the Ladies' Library would reach you."

"But you decided to come in person."

"As I said, the matter is urgent." And bowing slightly, he left her.

Jane waited until the door closed behind him, then she let out a huff of breath. Her hands curled into fists. There was something about Lord Castleton that rubbed her the wrong way. If he'd been less intimidating, she would have given him Letty's direction. Or maybe she wouldn't. He'd gone to a great deal of trouble to find Letty and that made her uneasy.

He'd been to St. Bede's. She wondered how much Miss Hepburn had told him. Not that the headmistress would have gossiped about her, but she might have let something slip inadvertently.

She'd told him where to find her.

No harm done, Jane assured herself. The earl hadn't come for her. It was Letty he wanted to see, and Letty had nothing to hide.

Letty would have to see him, or course. He wasn't the kind of man one could ignore. She'd known that even before she met him in person. Lady Sophy was very proud of her great-nephew and the man she described didn't know the meaning of defeat, whether he was pursuing his light-skirts or fighting battles.

A plain-spoken woman was Lady Sophy Devere.

Jane wondered how Lady Sophy would describe *her*, Jane Mayberry. A young woman who rarely went out in society but devoted all her energies to the cause? A bluestocking? At twenty-six, a confirmed spinster who went out of her way to avoid men? A lone wolf?

Mirrors reflecting mirrors, that's what these glimpses of someone's character were, not illusions exactly, but not revealing the whole truth either. She supposed much the same could be said about Lord Castleton.

This brought to mind something else Lady Sophy once said about her nephew. The war had changed him, not for the worse, not for the better, but he was different, less open, more prone to moods.

Jane thought about this as she mixed the harts-horn powder into a thick paste. Letty had hoped that the army would be the making of Gideon. She'd never met Letty's brother, but she'd heard enough from his sister to form an impression—careless, selfish, and not above using others for his own ends. Not that Letty saw her brother in that light. According to Letty, Gideon was the victim of circumstances, and when his circumstances improved, he would change. All he needed was another chance.

It was true that he'd had a hard life. The family had fallen on hard times when the father died. Letty had been sent at once to St. Bede's as a boarder, but Gideon and his mother ended up in the poorhouse, where the mother died soon after. The poorhouse wasn't exactly a great builder of character. If he took advantage of people, maybe he had cause.

He had one redeeming quality that could not be denied. He'd been devoted to his mother. If he'd lived, he might have made something of himself.

But Gideon's chances had run out in Spain. He'd been reported as missing and his body had never been found.

She stopped mixing the paste and stared into space. What possible connection, she wondered, could Castleton have with a soldier who had never advanced beyond the rank of corporal?

A whining sound brought her out of her reverie. Lance's watchful eyes were on her. "I'm not sad," she told him. "I'm just in a reflective mood."

She knelt down and scratched behind his ears. "Some help you turned out to be. I thought you had a sixth sense about people. Didn't you hear what Lord Castleton said? He said he would shoot you. *Shoot* is a bad word."

Lance thumped his tail on the floor.

"Well, at least you didn't fawn all over him. Not that he would let you. Mustn't spoil that immaculate tailoring with a few stray dog hairs."

Lance gave her his doggie smile.

She looked down at her gown and made a face. Her skirt was covered in dog hair. "Did I forget to groom you today?"

Lance's response was to cock his head to one side.

She sighed. "I know. I've been preoccupied lately, but not for much longer. We're going home, boy. Just think of it—open spaces, meadows, trees, badgers, foxes. You'll have a grand old time."

But before that happened, she wanted to make quite

sure that she'd shaken off the earl. His lordship was a complication she could well do without right now.

Case went in search of Lady Octavia, but it wasn't to ask where he could find pen and paper. He had not known that Mrs. Gray was a member here until Miss Mayberry mentioned it. Now he saw a way of circumventing her. Not that he would have left anything to chance anyway. Mrs. Letitia Gray would see him whether she wanted to or not.

He found Lady Octavia in the library, overseeing the disposal of a portrait that hung above the marble mantel.

"Lady Mary's father," she said to Case by way of explanation. "The old earl, and a most objectionable man. His treatment of his wife and daughter was reprehensible. We can't have him presiding over our assemblies. He would act as a blight."

To the two footmen who had removed the painting from the wall, she said, "Take him to the attics," then to Case, but this time with a twinkle in her eyes, "There's a lesson for you here, Lord Castleton. Consider how your wife or daughter will dispose of *your* portrait when you're gone."

He answered her with a patient smile.

"Lady Octavia," he said, "I'm trying to find a lady who is a member here, Mrs. Letitia Gray, or perhaps you know her as Letitia Piers. Can you tell me where she lives?"

"We never give out that kind of information," she said. "It's the library's policy."

"But you know me! All I want is to speak with Mrs. Gray. What harm is there in that?"

She regarded him steadily. "We have these policies

for a reason, you know. Experience has taught us that it's safer this way. Anyway, before you try to persuade me to change my mind, let me say at once that no Letitia Gray or Letitia Piers has ever been a member of the Ladies' Library."

"You're sure of that?"

"Perfectly. Our membership list is small, and each lady on it is personally known to me. You've been misinformed."

He'd been misinformed, all right, deliberately misinformed by Jane Mayberry. It had come down to a tussle of wills. There was no doubt in his mind who would win the contest. Then he'd find out why Miss Mayberry was so determined to protect her friend.

"Miss Mayberry," he began, and let the name hang there, inviting a response.

"What about Jane?"

He smiled and shook his head. "She interests me. I don't know what to make of her."

"Oh?"

This was not the response he was hoping for so he took a more direct approach. "How would you describe her?"

Until that moment, he had not known that Lady Octavia's placid, fading blue eyes could pierce like the point of a blade.

"Look away from Jane Mayberry," she said. "She is not for you. You can have any woman you want. Leave Jane alone."

He took a moment to gather himself, a moment to rein in his formidable temper, to assume all the dignity and arrogance of his rank. "You are mistaken, ma'am," he said. "You must be confusing me with someone else."

"Jane," replied Lady Octavia, regarding him thoughtfully, "has not had an easy life since her father died. I think she has found a measure of peace with us. I don't want to see that peace disturbed."

He didn't know where elderly ladies got their gall. It was the same with his Great Aunt Sophy. Once they passed a certain age, they thought they could say anything they liked to anyone.

"I doubt," he said, not quite truthfully, "that Miss Mayberry and I shall have occasion to meet again, and if by chance we do, I shall endeavor to look the other way."

"I'm very glad to hear it."

Gritting his teeth, he stalked off.

Five minutes later, he returned to the pantry with the letter in his hand. Jane Mayberry was assiduously polishing a silver tray. The dog rose at Caspar's entrance, but this time there were no bared fangs, only a bark of welcome.

"Your dog is very intelligent," said Case as he handed her the letter.

"That's a matter of opinion." She pointed to her dog, who then sank to the floor and gazed at her with soulful eyes.

"Till four o'clock then," said Case.

"Four o'clock," she replied.

He bowed. She curtsied. The moment he left the room, however, his smile faded. Whatever had put that maggot into Lady Octavia's mind? And what role did she think he had planned for Jane Mayberry, his mistress or his wife? Either way, the idea was laughable.

Chapter 2

As soon as Lord Castleton left the house, Lady Octavia went to the pantry to talk to Jane. She wasn't a busybody, she told herself. It was just that she wanted to put Jane on her guard. Lord Castleton had that look about him, not smitten, or obsessed, or love-struck, or anything so exaggerated or vulgar. *Arrested* was the word she wanted. Jane had made quite an impression on the earl, but he wouldn't let it rest there. He would be back for more.

In her opinion, men like Castleton were truly dangerous, not because they were predators, but because they had a way with women. Even sensible, level-headed girls like Jane had been known to succumb to the flattering attentions of experienced men of the world. And Lord Castleton was definitely a man of the world.

Of all the young women who volunteered at the library, Jane was the one she was closest to, or as close as Jane would allow. They'd met about four years ago, when Jane arrived at the library looking for a place to stay, having heard that the library occasionally leased rooms to single women in the upstairs floors. She wasn't looking for charity, Jane said. She could pay her way. And it wouldn't be for long. She had acquired a dog and hoped to find a place in the country close to town. Meantime, would the dog be a problem?

Of course the dog was a problem! Lady Octavia had opened her mouth to utter the polite words of rejection and surprised herself by saying the opposite. There was something about Jane Mayberry and her dog that was hard to resist. On reflection, she decided that these two were battle-scarred and it would be unfeeling to turn them away.

In the beginning, Jane kept pretty much to herself, but as she began to spend more time in the library, she became more and more involved. She wrote pamphlets and speeches and made herself indispensable, but she never stayed in town for long. She'd found that little place in the country and that was the life she loved.

It wasn't, however, the life Lady Octavia wanted for her protégée. Jane was too much on her own. She suspected that an unhappy love affair had turned Jane into a confirmed spinster, but Jane never explained her circumstances, except to say that she'd spent most of her life in Scotland and had had to earn her own living after her father died.

Lady Octavia understood Jane's desire to bury herself in the country only too well, or she thought she did. She herself had suffered through two disastrous marriages and had been released from them only when her respective husbands had had the grace to make her a widow. She'd cut herself off from society as well, but when Mr. Burrel, her banker, who had become her best friend, asked her to marry him, she'd known it was the right thing to do. And the last twenty years had been the happiest of her life.

She wanted to tell Jane that not all men were rogues, that hearts could mend, and one day she might well meet a man who would be right for her.

But that man would not be Lord Castleton.

As was her way, she didn't waste words on small talk when she found Jane in the pantry. "Well, Jane," she said, "what do you think of Lady Sophy's nephew?"

Jane replaced a silver tray in its rack before answering. "He's everything his aunt said he was."

Lady Octavia smiled uncertainly. "You like him," she said.

"Oh, I wouldn't go that far." Jane's dimples flashed. "Lady Sophy said that her nephew could be a tyrant when someone stood up to him. And she was right."

Lady Octavia laughed, then shook her head. "Be on your guard. I think he fancies you."

Jane stared, then said slowly and distinctly, "I don't know him. He doesn't know me. We met for the first time not half an hour ago."

"You've never met him before?"

"No."

This seemed to deflate Lady Octavia. "Oh. I thought perhaps you'd met at the opera."

"I've seen him there, but I don't think he has seen me." Once again, Jane's dimples flashed. "I'm not saying his eyes haven't alighted on me, but that's not the same as seeing me, is it?"

"No. And you should be thankful for it. But now he has seen you, so be on your guard."

Jane let out a rich laugh. "I was rude to him. I refused to give him my friend's address without her permission, and, as I told you, he turned nasty. That's all there was to it."

"Maybe that's what piqued his interest. He's not used to women saying no to him."

"I can well believe it, but we weren't in each other's company for more than five minutes. What on earth did he say to you to get you fired up like this?"

"He said very little. It's my intuition—" Lady Octavia observed that Jane was becoming annoyed and she floundered a little. "What I mean is, he'll probably marry a princess or someone who is almost a princess. A man in his position will be expected to marry well."

Jane's voice was cool and controlled. "I'm not interested in marrying anyone."

Lady Octavia quickly crossed to Jane and took her hands. "Forgive me, my dear. I mean no offense. If you had a mother—well, well, I'm not your mother, so it isn't my place to say anything."

After this little speech, Jane's expression softened considerably and she returned the pressure of Lady Octavia's hands. "I will confess," she said musingly, "that if I were almost a princess, I might be tempted. He's very handsome, isn't he? Then again—" She made a face. "Maybe not. He's not my idea of a prince."

Lady Octavia laughed, then, in one of her characteristic, lightning shifts, moved on to something else. "So, Jane, you're going home tomorrow?"

Jane nodded cautiously. "Right after breakfast. I

would stay on to help out if I could, but I'm expecting company. I thought I told you."

"Ah, yes. Now I remember." Her ladyship beamed. "An old school friend. I think that's splendid. And it will do you good to get out of the city. I know you're a country girl at heart. And don't give the library another thought. There are more than enough volunteers to help us get settled. Just enjoy yourself, Jane. Just enjoy yourself."

She left, but returned almost at once. "Do you go to the opera tonight?" she asked.

Dimples winked then went out. "I do," Jane replied, "but I promise not to elope with Lord Castleton unless I have your permission."

Lady Octavia stared, mumbled something about "a silly chit," and closed the door behind her with a decided snap.

Jane shook her head. Lady Octavia was muddled and confusing. She often spoke without thinking. But these were small faults. She also possessed a heart that was as big as the ocean. Her ladyship had helped *her* when she needed help. And there were countless others like her. She could be forgiven for taking a proprietary interest in all her lame ducks. She only wanted what was best for them.

On the other hand, it was a mistake to underestimate her or her devotion to the cause of women's rights. Government ministers had been known to quake in their boots when her ladyship went on the rampage. It helped that she was highly connected. Her brother was a marquess and her husband owned one of the biggest banks in London. Everyone owed him money, even the prince regent, if rumor was to be believed.

Warm breath on her hand brought her gaze to her

dog. Lance looked up at her with bright, intelligent eyes. Jane laughed and scratched behind his ears. "And she loves dogs," she said, "so of course we are among her staunchest admirers. Now, let's finish up here and run that errand for Lord Castleton."

As she polished the last silver tray, a picture of the earl formed in her mind. She remembered the quick flashes of humor in his eyes, the careless smile. The warning from Lady Octavia was unnecessary. His reputation with women was well established. He was a practiced flirt.

Only...her brow knit in a frown, and she stared blindly at her reflection in the highly polished silver tray...only, the odd times she'd studied him at the opera, to his credit, he was an attentive escort. He didn't let his eyes roam from one pretty woman to another as did some gentlemen she could name. His mistress, La Contessa, was just the opposite. She could not be satisfied until every man came under her spell. Maybe that's why Lord Castleton and his mistress were no longer together.

And maybe he'd grown bored, as was the way of men, and his wandering eye had alighted on a better prospect.

She didn't need to be told that he would marry well, but there weren't too many princesses going around, not unless Prince Michael had a sister. He was the man Lady Rosamund had almost married before she was literally swept off her feet by Richard Maitland, Chief of Staff of Special Branch. Prince Michael's courtship of Lady Rosamund was written up in the papers, too.

That was the thing about the Deveres. Their names were never out of the papers. It seemed as though the public could not get enough of them.

Lady Rosamund and her husband, for instance, were in Scotland, visiting Colonel Maitland's parents; the younger son, Lord Justin, was in Italy on a belated grand tour, the war having interrupted his first attempt to take in Europe; and Lady Sophy Devere had come up from Hampshire to attend the opening of the New Ladies' Library in the Strand, and was now residing with her nephew, the duke, in Twicken-ham House, the Deveres' palatial home just outside London.

It went on and on, and dolt that she was, she couldn't get enough of the Deveres either.

What wasn't written up in the papers was the shady side to the Devere men. La Contessa's name had never been mentioned in connection with Lord Castleton, except by word of mouth. Gossip. She knew it was spurious; she knew she shouldn't listen to it, but how could she help it? If people didn't talk about the Deveres, they'd have nothing to say.

Nobody had ever taken any notice of her family, except their own friends. When she was a child, her father had taken a position at the university in Edin-burgh, and that's where she'd spent most of her life. In fact, those were the happiest days of her life, with her mother and father, and the friends who used to crowd into their little drawing room on a Saturday night to talk and play a little music and sing. Not that her father could sing a note. He was tone deaf. But her mother loved music, especially opera, and her fa-ther's pleasure came from indulging his wife.

Her father had been a good man.

She wondered what kind of husband the earl would make. According to Lady Sophy, all the Devere men made the best of husbands—loyal, protective, faithful, and unfailingly kind.

"Just like you, Lance," Jane said. "But it's my belief that a woman is better off with a dog." Unless she could find someone like her father, of course, but in her experience, such men were few and far between.

She gazed into space, remembering...

Suddenly coming to herself, she gave herself a mental shake. She was beginning to feel sorry for herself and that set her teeth on edge.

With a shake of her head, she cleared her brain and began to tidy things away.

Chapter 3

*T*wenty minutes later, Jane left the library with Lance at her heels. She stopped for a moment at the edge of the pavement, glanced quickly from right to left, then entered a hackney that had just let down its passengers. The dog jumped in after her. A moment later, the hackney was bowling along the Strand, going west toward Pall Mall.

Soon after, another hackney pulled out from a side street and made the turn onto the main thoroughfare, following Jane's hackney. It had two occupants, Case and Sergeant Harper of Special Branch.

Although Harper was one of London's most celebrated citizens, having helped solve a number of sensational cases in his work at Special Branch, no one would have known it to look at him. He was in his early forties, stocky, with a crop of grizzled hair. His garments were well made and conservative, but he wore them so casually that he looked untidy.

Despite the difference in their backgrounds, there was an easy camaraderie between Case and Harper. In fact, they had much in common. They'd both served throughout the Spanish Campaign and, more recently, had worked closely together to uncover a conspiracy that had almost destroyed Case's brother-in-law, Col. Richard Maitland. Now they were working on another case—the murder in Hyde Park.

The faintest of smiles touched Case's lips. "I thought she might go in person to warn her friend that I wanted to speak to her. It makes things easier for us. All we have to do is follow the dog."

When there was no response from Harper, Case turned his head and looked at Harper's unhandsome face, baked dry by years of soldiering under the hot Spanish sun. "Why the scowl?" he asked.

Harper shrugged. "It don't seem right," he said, "spying on ladies who probably don't have it in them to hurt a fly. Why, they're the best that England has to offer. They're honest and decent and I don't like deceiving them."

"Neither do I."

"Then why didn't we wait till four o'clock for Mrs. Gray's answer?"

"What if Mrs. Gray refuses to see me? What if she's trying to protect her brother? No, Harper. This is the only way."

Harper merely grunted.

After a moment, Case said, "Why would a lady keep a beast like that in town?"

"You mean the dog?"

Case nodded.

"I dunno. You knows more about ladies than I do."

"Hazard a guess, just to humor me."

"Well," Harper scratched his chin, "could be the dog is an affectation, you know. something to make a fashionable lady stand out from the crowd."

"But Jane Mayberry isn't a fashionable lady. And she wouldn't thank you for that description. She's a bluestocking. Women who pride themselves on their intelligence aren't interested in cutting a dash in society."

Harper considered. "Well," he said; "maybe she loves that dog and can't bear to be parted from it."

"I wonder."

"What?" demanded Harper when the silence lengthened.

"Mmm? Oh, I think she keeps the dog for protection."

"Protection from what?"

"I don't know. But there's something secretive about Jane Mayberry."

"Secretive?"

"Mysterious, not transparent. You know what I mean."

"She's just a young woman with a dog!"

"You're probably right."

"That's the trouble with our business. It makes you suspicious of everyone. And when you're not suspicious, that's when the trouble starts."

"Harper, don't break your heart over it. She's probably everything you think she is."

"I hope so. I sincerely hope so, because the man we are after is rotten to the depths of his stinking soul. I wouldn't want Miss Mayberry to end up like John Collier."

John Collier was the name of the man who had been murdered in Hyde Park. That much Bow Street had discovered before handing the case over to Special Branch: John Collier, former soldier, now a solicitor's clerk, fortyish and as clean as a whistle as far as they could tell.

It had taken the magistrates a month of dithering before they called in Special Branch. It had taken the chief of staff five minutes to decide that his own brother-in-law was the best man to handle the investigation. Case had a vested interest in finding a killer whose signature was a smooth-faced pebble left on or near his victims.

That pebble might as well have been a letter as far as Case was concerned. What it told him was that a man he believed was dead, a man he *hoped* was dead, might well have embarked on another cycle of murder and mayhem.

Gideon Piers. The very name was enough to fill Case with a cold, relentless resolve. Corp. Gideon Piers, deserter turned bandit, had cut a swath of terror throughout the Spanish countryside with his band of desperadoes. *La Roca,* the Rock, the Spanish called him because he left a smooth-faced pebble in his victims' pockets, just so that everyone would know how he dealt with anyone who tried to cross him.

He went too far, however, when he began to attack British convoys and steal British gold. He was no longer an annoying bandit on the fringes of the war, but a major disruption that had to be stopped. Case was given the task of recovering the gold, if possible, but above all, of wiping Piers and his bandits off the face of the earth. No quarter asked or given—those were his orders.

With a unit of hand-picked men and a group of partisans, they tracked Piers and his brigands to their hideout, an abandoned monastery in the hills near Brugos. And that's where they'd perished, every last one of them, or so he'd hoped.

It took a moment or two before Case realized that Harper was speaking to him, and another moment after that for the haze in his mind to clear. He pressed a hand to his eyes. "I'm sorry, Harper. My thoughts were elsewhere. What did you say?"

Harper spoke slowly. "I asked if you wanted me there when you question Mrs. Gray."

"No. Two of us might be one too many, and I don't want her to feel threatened. Keep an eye on the house, and stay out of sight."

Harper nodded. "And what was you thinking when that look came over you?"

Case gave a short, muffled laugh. Tact was not one of Harper's outstanding virtues. The trouble was, he'd allowed him too many liberties. If they got any cozier, they'd be the best of friends, then there'd be no holding him back.

Case said, "It's been a month since Collier was murdered. What is Piers waiting for?"

"Maybe he's come and gone. Maybe Collier was the only one he was after. And maybe we're looking for the wrong man. Piers could be dead, you know, and somebody could be copying his methods."

Case was silent. He'd heard these arguments before. But if Piers was alive, there was no doubt in his mind who his ultimate target would be and that was himself. This wasn't the time for complacency.

All the same, he was left with the same perplexing question. What was Piers waiting for? Why the delay in coming after him?

.   .   .

Jane paid off the hackney outside St. Ninian's church in Hans Town. A light drizzle was falling so she turned up her coat collar to cover the back of her bonnet and entered the churchyard. The vicarage was on the other side of the church, through the side gate and up a steep paved path.

It was an old house, its stone walls embraced by the barren vines of winter ivy. A lamp had been lit in one of the front rooms and the sound of children's laughter brought a bittersweet smile to Jane's lips. Some women were lucky in love, others were not so fortunate. Letty was one of the lucky ones. She'd married a gem of a man and had two darling, mischievous children.

And if anyone deserved to be happy, it was Letty.

Before that train of thought could lead her down a treacherous path, Jane squared her shoulders and rapped smartly with the knocker. A moment or two later the door was opened by Letty's maid-of-all-work. A young vicar with a family to support couldn't afford more than one servant.

Peggy, young, capable, and ever ready with a smile, ushered Jane into the hall. "And you brought Lance! The children will be pleased."

"Where is Mrs. Gray?" asked Jane, as Peggy took her coat and bonnet.

"In the kitchen."

"And Mr. Gray?"

"Gone to Lambeth to see the bishop."

After this exchange, confusion reigned. Two small girls, identical twins, came tearing out of the front room and launched themselves at Jane. "Aunt Jane!" they cried. "Aunt Jane." Then they saw Lance and Aunt Jane was forgotten. Their mother emerged from the kitchen.

"Jane! This *is* a surprise."

Letty Gray was a little older than Jane, tall and slender, with thick dark hair and clear, aqua eyes. Though a few strands of hair escaped their pins and there was a smudge of flour on one cheek, she appeared, on the surface, to be completely self-possessed. Orphans, in Jane's experience, often gave this impression. They'd been raised in institutions and had learned to keep their thoughts to themselves. Jane considered herself truly privileged to have won the friendship of this generous-hearted young woman and sometimes wished she could be more like her.

As quickly as the confusion arose, it subsided. Letty suggested that Peggy and the children dress up warmly and take Lance for a walk. After they left, she led Jane into the front parlor and closed the door.

"Flour, on your cheek," said Jane, pointing.

Letty brushed it off. "I thought we wouldn't be seeing you till after Christmas. What made you change your plans?"

They took the chairs closest to the fire. "What's happened is that Lord Castleton came to see me today, but it was you he wanted to talk to."

"Lord Castleton! Talk to me? About what?"

"He gave me a letter—" Jane cut off what she was about to say when the front door knocker rattled alarmingly.

"Oliver must have forgotten his key again," said Letty, and she went to answer the door.

Jane got up. She heard muted voices in the hallway, then Letty entered followed by Lord Castleton. Her lips tightened. She'd known he was tenacious, but she hadn't expected this.

"Speak of the devil!" she said, her words tossed out like a gauntlet.

"Ah, Miss Mayberry," replied Case easily, "sans wolf, and as charming as ever."

"Jane," said Letty, looking curiously from one to the other, "Lord Castleton is with Special Branch. He wants to ask me a few questions about Gideon, that's all."

"Special Branch?" Jane stared. "You're an officer of the law?"

"I've been invited to help Special Branch with a particular investigation, so I suppose I *am* an officer of the law."

"You didn't mention that to me."

"My business wasn't with you, Miss Mayberry, so I wasn't obliged to tell you anything. Mrs. Gray, is there somewhere we can talk privately?"

"Well . . ." Letty looked uncertainly at Jane.

Jane said, "I wouldn't dream of allowing you to question Mrs. Gray without a witness present."

"I would like Jane to remain."

Case sighed. "Then shall we sit down? This shouldn't take long."

When they were all seated, he kept his eyes on Letty, effectively excluding Jane from the conversation. "We think you can help us in our inquiries, Mrs. Gray. I'm sorry I can't go into details. You may think some of my questions are odd or irrelevant. Just answer them as frankly as you can. Will you do that for me?"

When Letty nodded, he continued, "When did you last see your brother?"

"You're investigating Gideon?"

"We're investigating someone we think may have been close to him at one time, someone who served with him in Spain."

"Oh." She waited for him to elaborate, and when

he didn't, she cleared her throat and said, "The last time I saw Gideon was before he sailed for Portugal, oh, eight years ago, when he came to say good-bye."

As the interview progressed, Jane's doubts about the veracity of the earl's claims vanished. She could see why he would be considered an asset in an investigation. He didn't fire off questions or badger Letty; he charmed her into giving him all the information he wanted. It was all so effortless—effortless and unscrupulous.

The facts were few. Letty and Gideon had seen very little of each other after they were orphaned, and if Gideon had any friends, Letty had no idea who they could be. He was older than she so, of course, he'd never confided in her. They'd seen each other from time to time after he left the poorhouse, and when he'd enlisted, she'd written to him, but his replies were few and far between and, of course, she'd stopped writing when his commanding officer wrote to inform her that Gideon was missing in action and presumed dead.

But Lord Castleton wormed other things out of Letty—how Gideon was forever getting into scrapes, how the only time he came to see her was when he wanted money, and how she'd hoped, prayed, when Gideon enlisted, that the army would be the making of him.

When there was a silence, Case turned to Jane. "Miss Mayberry, can you add anything to what Mrs. Gray has told me?"

"No."

Letty covered Jane's rudeness by quickly adding, "Jane never met Gideon. She didn't become a teacher at St. Bede's until after he went to Spain."

"And that's when you and Miss Mayberry became friends? When you were both teaching at St. Bede's?"

Letty smiled. "Yes, I was heartbroken when—"

Jane quickly cut her off. "Lord Castleton isn't interested in hearing about me. Not unless I'm under investigation, too."

"No," said Case. "Just idle interest on my part." He felt in his coat pocket and drew out the pebble that was found on John Collier. "Does this mean anything to you, Mrs. Gray?"

Letty took the pebble and turned it over. "No. Should it?"

"What about the name La Roca?"

Letty shook her head and gave him back the pebble.

"That's Spanish for rock, isn't it?" asked Jane.

"It is. What about John Collier? Does that name mean anything to you, Mrs. Gray?"

Again, Letty shook her head. "I don't think so."

"Think carefully. Lt. John Collier. He served with your brother in Spain. They were in the same regiment."

Letty looked down at her clasped hands. "I'm sorry. I don't remember. It was all so long ago."

Case got up. "If anything occurs to you, Mrs. Gray, you can always leave a message for me at the Horse Guards."

He paused, looked around him and said, "Do I smell something burning?"

Letty was on her feet in an instant. "My scones!" she cried, and hurried from the room.

Case said, "Now that wasn't so bad, was it, Miss Mayberry?"

Jane got up. She said quietly, "There was no need

to be devious. If you'd been honest with me, I would have taken you to my friend."

Case shrugged. "I wasn't devious. I told you as much as you needed to know."

"You deceived me! I call that dishonest."

"I don't care what you call it." His words were hard and clipped. "I'm investigating a murder." He nodded when her eyes flared. "John Collier was murdered and we believe someone from his regiment was paying off an old score. So, if you know what's good for you, Jane Mayberry, you'll stay out of my way. My apologies to Mrs. Gray. Tell her I could not wait."

"Well?" asked Harper after Case gave the hackney driver the order to move off.

"She doesn't appear to know anything," and Case went on to give Harper a summary of his interview with Letty Gray.

When he finished, Harper groaned. "That means starting over with Collier, and by now the trail is stone cold."

"It may come to that, but first, let's see if I've set the cat among the pigeons."

"You think Mrs. Gray may try to warn her brother that we're onto him?"

"No. I don't think she knows anything, or that Piers is stupid enough to let her know where he is hiding. This is just a precaution. In a day or so, if we're no farther ahead, we'll give it up."

Case signaled the driver to stop, then he pointed to a tavern on the corner of Hans Square. "You can make that your headquarters. I'll send Lennox to relieve you."

"Oh, no, you won't." Harper shook his head. "I has

my orders. I'm to stay close to you. That's what the chief told me before he left for Edinburgh."

"Aberdeen, Harper. Colonel Maitland and my sister left for Aberdeen. Meantime, this is my case, and I'll run it as I see fit."

Harper understood only too well where this was leading. His lordship had never been comfortable with the idea that he, Harper, was to be his bodyguard. The earl knew the risks, was aware that he could be the next target, but he chafed at the restrictions of having to account for his movements as though, he said, he were an infant in leading strings, and he particularly chafed at the fact that his bodyguard was now billeted in his rooms at the Albany. These were the conditions the chief had laid down, otherwise, he said, he'd give the case to someone else.

Harper sympathized, but nothing could induce him to go against his chief's orders. Moreover, Lord Castleton was the chief's brother-in-law. The very thought of having to face his chief in the event that something had happened to the earl gave him the shudders.

Case studied Harper's dogged expression and decided to take a different approach. "Look," he said, treating Harper to a companionable smile, "I'll be at the Horse Guards looking over old records. Then I'll be dining with friends at the Bell. We may or may not go on to the opera. But I'll be surrounded by people I trust. I don't need a chaperon, thank you very much. And how would I explain your presence to my friends? They'd think I was a coward and they'd be right."

"What if I have something to report?"

"You know where to find me, and if I change my

plans, I'll leave my direction at the Horse Guards. Otherwise, I'll see you later at the Albany. Understood?"

"Understood," replied Harper, gazing fixedly at a loose button on his coat.

"Fine. And Harper, don't wait up for me."

Chapter 4

Case's office at the Horse Guards was no bigger than a closet, but he considered himself lucky to be assigned any space at all. He wasn't a regular Special Branch agent, but one of the amateurs who were occasionally seconded to the service because they had particular skills or knowledge that would help unravel a difficult case. No one knew Gideon Piers better than he.

His colleagues were friendly, but not much interested in the investigation. They had their own cases to pursue, and murder of an obscure solicitor's clerk by a man whose field of operations had always been confined to Spain did not strike them with the same urgency as it did Case. The general view seemed to be that an old score had been paid off and that was the end of it. In fact, there was speculation that the murderer wasn't Gideon Piers at all, but someone who was impersonating him and had used his methods to confuse the authorities.

This view was shared by Case's brother-in-law, which was why, Case thought wryly, Richard had not postponed his trip to Scotland. He didn't expect Case to get anywhere.

The file on Piers was sparse. Next of kin: sister, Miss Letitia Piers of St. Bede's Charity School, London; Occupation: shipping clerk; Distinguishing marks: rose tattoo on his left arm. He had been in the first wave of British troops to sail for Portugal. Two years later, he was missing in action, presumed dead or captured by the enemy. This was shortly before La Roca emerged. It was British Intelligence that made the connection, and British Intelligence that briefed him before he'd set out with his small unit of men on that months-long, grueling hunt for a man whose name had become synonymous with savagery.

In its wisdom, British Intelligence never divulged La Roca's true identity, except to a favored few. So Piers's war record was spotless. There was another file, this one on La Roca, which he'd had to beg from the War Office, but it wasn't much help. In the main, it detailed all the British convoys that had been attacked by La Roca and robbed of their gold. Case and his men had torn that monastery apart looking for it, but they found nothing. To his knowledge, that gold had never been found.

Gideon Piers must be a very rich man.

They might not have found the gold, but they'd found Piers, or so they thought. His face was shot off, but he had a rose tattoo on his left arm. So they believed what they wanted to believe. But there had always been an element of doubt in his mind.

There was a third file on his desk with John

Collier's name on it. It, too, was spotless. Maybe British Intelligence knew something that wasn't in the file. They were misers when it came to doling out information.

He tossed the files aside and sighed. There were two ways to go about this. He could begin investigating all Piers's former acquaintances, associates, and employers, and hope to come up with a lead. But that was a monumental task, well beyond the scope of one man. The other way was to wait. Piers, if it was Piers, would not be able to resist baiting him. They'd played this game before in Spain. Sometimes it was hard to tell who was the hunter and who was the prey. The ending would be spectacular, a fitting revenge for the destruction he and his special unit had inflicted at the Monastery of St. Michel. No quarter asked or given.

If Piers could not resist baiting him, why the delay after he'd murdered John Collier? Piers wasn't the sort of man to wait for Bow Street to pull itself together. He'd want him, Case, to know that the game wasn't over yet.

He wasn't any farther ahead than he was when he arrived. After locking up his files, he left.

Dark came early in November, and by the time he walked from Whitehall to his rooms on Piccadilly, lamps were lit and lights flickered from every window. He stayed long enough only to bathe and change his clothes, then he took a hackney to Bell's Hotel, just off Covent Garden, to meet his friends. But even in these congenial surroundings, he could not settle, and before long, he made his excuses and left.

Case went to the opera alone, but he had no intention of leaving alone. A month had passed since he and his mistress had parted company, and in that time, he'd been celibate. He wasn't a libertine; he hadn't bedded half the women he was credited with, but he was a healthy male animal and he understood the reason for his restlessness. He needed a woman. It was as simple as that.

During the first intermission, he made his way to Mrs. Amelia Standhurst's box. Amelia was a wealthy widow who had no desire to marry again. She was beautiful, sophisticated, and had made subtle overtures to him in the last month that he had ignored. Tonight, he was far more susceptible.

He entered her box, and within five minutes they had come to a perfect understanding. The opera was boring. Case would escort the lady home.

In the corridor, they stopped while Case draped Amelia's fur-lined wrap around her shoulders. She said something he did not catch. His gaze was caught and held by a young woman who wore a gown of transparent gauze over ivory satin. The lights from the chandeliers imbued her skin and hair with a glaze of gold.

It was Jane Mayberry, but not the Jane Mayberry he'd met that morning. This woman could have stepped off the pages of *La Belle Assemblée,* except that Jane Mayberry was no mannequin. She was animated, vibrant, and obviously enjoying herself.

As though conscious that someone was watching her, she turned slightly, and her eyes traveled the crush of people, passed over him, then returned with the shock of recognition. He sensed the quick indrawn breath, the tension that gripped her, and her smile gradually died.

Her gaze moved to Amelia, lingered, then returned to Case. The slight inclination of her head acknowledged his presence; the quavering half-smile revealed her complete comprehension of the situation between himself and Amelia.

One of her companions said something and she turned away. Only then did Case realize that her escort was Freddie Latham, whom he'd encountered that morning at the library. Freddie was one of his close friends. His sister was there and another young woman whom Case did not recognize.

Amelia's hand touched his arm. "Are you sure you want to come home with me, Case?" Her eyes were vivid with curiosity. "She's very beautiful. Who is she?"

It was a simple question requiring a simple answer, but for some inexplicable reason, Case did not want to have Jane Mayberry's name come into the conversation. "I met her," he said, "for the first time this morning at the Ladies' Library. She's a member there."

Amelia absorbed his words in silence, then said, "Good for her!" Her eyes trailed Jane until she entered a box at the end of the corridor. "If that's the sort of lady," she said, "who supports the Ladies' Library, perhaps it's time I paid it a visit. I mean, I believe in what they do—what woman wouldn't?—but the members I've met so far seem so earnest and single-minded. She looks . . . different."

Case murmured something suitable, but his mind wasn't on Amelia. Most patrons had returned to their boxes for the beginning of the second act, and those who remained in the corridor were liveried footmen and ushers. One of those ushers had his back to him and was gazing out one of the windows.

"Excuse me," said Case to Amelia. "This will only take a moment."

He strolled down the corridor until he came to the man who was staring fixedly out the window.

"Harper!" he said in a savage undertone. "I take it your presence here means you have something to report?"

Harper turned with a sheepish grin. "Eh...no, sir. But don't worry, Lennox is a good man. He's watching the house, and you can bet that nothing will get by his eagle eye."

"Then if there's nothing to report, what are you doing here?"

"I'm doing my job," replied Harper reproachfully.

This was not the time to argue the point with a stubborn, obstinate, exasperating subordinate who couldn't seem to understand that a man was entitled to a private life. A bodyguard was one thing, but Case would not tolerate being spied upon.

"Fine," he said. "Now that you're here, you can do something for me. I presume you noticed that Miss Mayberry is here tonight, too?"

"Aye." Harper's eyes had narrowed fractionally.

"I want her watched, Harper. I want to know who she sees and whom she talks to. If she slips away, I want you to follow her."

"Miss Mayberry?" Harper's voice had risen a notch.

"Yes, Miss Mayberry. Don't take your eyes off her, and that's an order. Have you got that?"

"Yes, sir."

"And don't wait up for me unless you have something major to report."

Case was smiling when he returned to Amelia, a genuine smile. Not only had he managed to outwit Harper, but he'd also caught Jane Mayberry in his net. Not that she was under suspicion, or critical to his investigation. He was curious about her. Add to that the fact that he'd been remiss in not finding out where she lived, and he was congratulating himself on adroitly solving both problems. She would keep Harper busy, and Harper would discover her address.

When he came up to Amelia, she said, "What was that all about?"

"My man. I sent him home and told him not to wait up for me." His head dipped and his lips brushed her ear. "Now to answer your question," he said softly. "Yes, I'm very sure I want to go home with you tonight and only you."

Amelia let out a low, throaty laugh. "Then what are we waiting for?" She slipped her arm through his. "Now, tell me everything. What were you, of all people, doing at the Ladies' Library?"

Case smiled thinly and embarked on an explanation that bore little resemblance to the truth, but that kept Amelia's inquisitive mind away from the one topic he had no wish to discuss.

When the members of the orchestra started to tune their instruments for the beginning of the second act, Miss Drake, the girl whom Case had seen conversing with Jane, said that she'd better return to her aunt. The viscount insisted on escorting her, leaving Jane and his sister, Sally, alone in the box.

"I think," said Sally, "you made a conquest tonight, Jane." Her eyes were bright with laughter.

"I can't think who you mean."

"Lord Castleton, of course."

Jane turned her head to look at Sally. "Castleton? What on earth gave you that idea?"

"The way he was looking at you. If ever a man was stricken, it was he. What do the French call it, *un coup de foudre?*"

A smile slowly curled Jane's lips. "What about Mrs. Standhurst? They seemed very friendly."

Sally made a face. "Women like Amelia don't count. To put it delicately, a man may have many such women in his past."

Jane said quietly, "Every woman counts. It's not up to us to judge her. Isn't that what the Ladies' Library is all about?"

"Yes. That was thoughtless of me. I'm sorry."

Chastened by Sally's response—Sally, who was one of the kindest souls she knew—Jane said lightly, "Besides, Lord Castleton wasn't *stricken* with me. He was looking *daggers* at me. We met for the first time today and we didn't exactly part the best of friends. So you see, there's no love lost between us."

"Oh? What happened?"

"I refused to give him a friend's address and he thought he could bully it out of me."

Sally laughed. "I could have told him not to bother. You can be a Tartar when your dander is up."

Jane was indignant. "And he can be a tyrant!"

The viscount entered the box just then, and Jane cleared her mind of all distractions as the orchestra struck up and the enchanting strains of Mozart's music filled the theater. Her concentration lasted all of five minutes. Twice in one day, she'd been warned that Lord Castleton was taken with her. She didn't believe it. She knew about men, and he didn't look lovestruck to her. What she didn't understand was why her pulse started to race when their eyes met. It wasn't fear on her part—she knew all about fear. It wasn't attraction. It must be resentment, she assured herself. He was trying to intimidate her with the sheer force of his personality. Well, she couldn't be intimidated, not now, not ever again.

She stewed for a little while, thinking about the earl, but the music filtered into her mind, and when the soprano began her famous aria, Jane's thoughts followed a different path. The street scene on stage faded and became a parlor, and the orchestra was her mother playing the piano, and it was her mother's voice that beguiled her. Though her eyes welled with tears, she was smiling. Everyone was clapping. She could see their faces through her tears. There were always students in her parents' house, of course, but because they changed every other year, she couldn't remember their names. But Mr. Morris was there, and his wife, Dorothy, who couldn't sing in tune, but who could recite Shakespeare as well as any professional actress. They all had to do a party piece after dinner, except her. She was too young and had only been allowed to stay up so that she could hear Mama sing.

Mama gave her a little shake. "Jane, Jane, what's come over you?"

She couldn't clap anymore because someone was holding her hands. She looked up with a start to see Sally, smiling, but shaking her head.

"You always lose yourself in the music," Sally said. "Nobody else is applauding now, or hadn't you noticed?"

From Jane's other side, the viscount whispered, "Why don't they sing in English? Then a fellow might be able to follow the story."

"Hush," said his sister, "and follow your program."

From then on, Jane kept her thoughts focused on the present, and soon, the sadness faded and she was caught up in the music again. When the performance was over, the viscount clapped harder than anyone, but Jane knew it was because he was glad he didn't have to listen to any more "caterwauling" as he would call it. Freddie and opera were not compatible, and she thought more of him for setting aside his own preferences to indulge his sister and his sister's friend. He really was a nice man.

When he delivered her to the new library in the Strand, he told the hackney driver to wait, then walked her to the front door. The porter was on hand to let her in.

Freddie said, "You know Jane, you're welcome to stay with Sal and me whenever you're in town. I don't like to think of you alone in this cavernous house."

"But I'm not alone. There are other single women like me who have rented rooms, and I have the best room of all. It's on the ground floor, with a view of the river, and there's a French door onto the terrace so that Lance can come and go as he pleases. Don't worry, Freddie. There are plenty of footmen about, so we're all quite safe. Besides, I have Lance."

He looked as though he might say more, but when she gave him a sisterly peck on the cheek, he sighed, said his farewells, and left.

When she entered her own room, she went straight to the French door, unlocked it, and stepped outside. A few moments later, Lance came padding in. She caressed his huge head; he licked her hand, then sniffed her gown and wrap while she stood there patiently, waiting for his curiosity to be satisfied. That done, he padded over to the hearth and settled down for the night.

Before undressing, she took one last look at her reflection in the looking glass. The gown was everything she'd hoped it would be. She'd made it herself from a pattern she'd seen in *La Belle Assemblée*, and it had been packed away in tissue paper, waiting for just the right occasion to make an appearance. She was glad she'd worn it tonight, glad that Lord Castleton had seen that there was more to Miss Plain Jane Mayberry than the dowd he'd met that morning.

The stray thought brought her up short. This was dangerous thinking. She hadn't worn the gown because she craved masculine attention, but because she liked pretty things. She had a box of pretty things in Hillcrest, her house near Highgate, and when the occasion demanded, she was happy to wear them. The trouble was, she had few occasions to wear them.

She sat on the edge of the bed, lifted her skirts, and stared contemplatively at her silk-shod legs. This was luxury on a grand scale. Silk stockings cost ten shillings a pair, and she didn't have the funds to indulge in them too often. They represented several hours of hard work at her desk, writing pamphlets, speeches, and articles that various clients had solicited, clients that had come to her on Lady Octavia's recommendation.

She didn't know why she was sighing. She was the luckiest girl in the world. She loved her work, she had good friends, and she was solvent. What more could she want?

Lance was looking at her. She got off the bed. "My trouble," she said, "is that I don't have enough to occupy me when I'm in town. Well, that will all change tomorrow when we go home. We're having company, did I tell you? Miss Emily Drake. I know you'll be kind to her because she's a runaway like us."

As she got ready for bed, her thoughts drifted to Gideon Piers. That's what had brought the earl into her life, his investigation of a murder that somehow was connected to Gideon. It didn't make sense.

Then, of course, the earl wasn't interested in helping her make sense of things.

Her feelings for Letty's brother had always been ambivalent. He hadn't been much of a brother to Letty. On the other hand, his devotion to his mother had been unquestionable. It had always chafed him that his mother had been given a pauper's burial and he'd promised Letty that one day he'd have their mother's remains removed to a proper churchyard with a proper service. He'd kept his promise, but he'd done it posthumously, through his last will and testament.

She and Oliver had arranged everything. It was just too much for Letty who had two babies to look after by this time. But Gideon's gesture had impressed them all. It was more than a gesture. He'd left enough money to cover all the expenses, and the expenses were considerable.

She blew out the candle and crawled into bed. She fell asleep trying to imagine how she would have turned out if she'd been raised in a poorhouse.

In the aftermath of their pleasure, Case felt physically replete and vaguely relieved. Nothing had changed. Amelia had been the perfect solution to his black mood. They'd been lovers once before and she hadn't disappointed him. She had a carnal appetite to match his own. She was just the kind of woman he preferred.

There were no promises on either side when he left her, and that was something else he liked about Amelia. She wouldn't make claims on him any more than she would allow him to make claims on her. And he could count on her discretion. She had a position in society to maintain, and though the whole world might suspect that she had taken a lover, as long as she was discreet, she would still be invited everywhere.

It was different for a man. He could be as indiscreet as he liked and no one would raise an eyebrow. It was unjust, but it was the way of their world. The woman always paid the penalty.

Amelia's house was just off Berkeley Square and only a ten-minute walk to his own rooms in the Albany. In spite of the late hour, there were plenty of people about, and plenty of carriages and hackneys coming and going. This was Mayfair, where the residents rose at noon and idled the hours away in a round of partying until they fell into bed just before dawn.

He waved a hackney away and decided the cool night air was just what he needed to clear his mind. He thought about Jane Mayberry on the walk home and felt a small pang of guilt for having set Harper to watch her. He'd done it on the spur of the moment and now he regretted it. Law-abiding, decent citizens had a right to their privacy.

She's very beautiful. Amelia's words flitted into his mind. *Beautiful* wasn't the word he would use to describe Jane Mayberry. *Uncommon,* perhaps, or *arresting.* Her face had character and intelligence rather than the perfection beauty demanded. Freddie had seemed quite taken with her. He wondered what their relationship was.

He was suddenly as restless as he had been before his encounter with Amelia. For once, he didn't try to trace the source of his irritation. He resolutely put Jane Mayberry from his mind and on the rest of the walk home, concentrated on Gideon Piers, speculating on why it had taken him three years to show his hand again, and finally debating whether everyone else was right and he was wrong. Maybe Piers really *was* dead; maybe the murder in Hyde Park *was* the work of someone impersonating Piers and that would be the end of it.

The porter opened the great iron gates for him, and as Case crossed the courtyard to the front portico of the house, he noted that the windows in his own rooms were ablaze with lights. They shouldn't have been. He'd told his manservant and Harper not to wait up for him. One candle in the hallway was all that was required to light his way.

He took the portico steps two at a time and made straight for his rooms on the first floor up. Ruggles, his manservant, opened the door for him.

As he divested his master of his coat, hat, and gloves, Ruggles said, "It's Harper, your lordship. He was set upon and robbed outside the King's Theater. He suffered a concussion, but that's not all. I think he may have broken a rib. He won't let me send for the doctor."

Case lost no time in crossing to the parlor. Two steps into the room, he halted. Relief washed through him and a smile curled his lips. Harper was wrapped in a blanket and seated in front of a blazing fire, looking as cross as Case had ever seen him.

"It's about time you got here," Harper said. "Now would you mind telling this... this fusspot," indicating Ruggles, "that beef tea is for invalids and not veterans of the Spanish Campaign? There's nothing wrong with me that a wee dram won't cure."

The effect of this little speech was ruined when he suddenly clutched his side and groaned.

Ignoring Harper, Ruggles said, "A lump on the

head as big as a turnip, your lordship, and no one
knows what other injuries he sustained in the attack.
He really ought to see a doctor. He hardly knew his
own name when I questioned him."

Ruggles, red-haired, freckled, and in his early thirties, was a well-bred servant who was unfailingly pleasant whatever the provocation. He was supplied by the
Albany, one of the services the management offered
its residents, and Case was determined that if he ever
left the Albany, he'd take Ruggles with him no matter
how much it cost to break his contract.

"How did he get home?"

"The Watch found him and sent him home in a
hackney."

"Get the doctor."

No protest from Harper this time. He was too busy
trying to find a position to ease the pain in his side.
"Bastards," he said. "They must have kicked me when
they dumped me in the alley."

"I'll get you that 'wee dram,' " said Case.

Harper's beaming smile lasted until Case handed
him a glass with a thimbleful of brandy in it. "I don't
call that much of a reward," he said, "after what I've
been through."

"You'll get your reward after the doctor has had a
look at you. No. No more arguments. Tell me what
happened."

Harper bolted the brandy and licked his lips.
"What happened," he said, "was that I did exactly as
you told me. I kept my eyes on Miss Mayberry. When
she and her little party left the theater, so did I. When
they flagged a hackney, so did I, only when I entered
my hackney, someone poked a pistol in my back and
followed me in. My head exploded and the next
thing I knows I'm lying in the lane behind the Hay-

market with the Watch crouched over me, shaking me awake."

"You were robbed," said Case, more a statement than a question.

"Just the opposite. I said I was robbed so your man would stop pestering me with questions." He held out his clenched fist. "Look what I found in my pocket," he said.

Case held out his hand and stared at the object Harper placed in it. It was a small, round pebble.

Chapter 5

*Y*ou took care of it personally?"

"Hardly. Like you, I've come up in the world, Gideon. I don't get my own hands dirty. But the men I used know what they're doing."

"Fine. Then tell me how it was done."

John Merrick sighed. Gideon Piers was turning out to be a monumental pain in the arse. Everything had to be explained to him in minute detail. "One of my men followed the bodyguard into the hackney. After stunning him, he ordered the driver to stop, saying that his friend wasn't feeling well. Bart was waiting for him in the lane. They made sure Harper would be out of commission for a while, then they left. No witnesses worth mentioning. Everything went according to plan."

Gideon Piers allowed himself a small smile. He was well satisfied with how things were progressing, and after tonight, there would be no question in Castleton's mind that Gideon Piers had risen from the ashes. Good. Let the earl stew. Let him wonder where and when he would strike next.

He looked at the man seated on the other side of the fire. They were in a private parlor in the Rose and Crown on Oxford Street, and though it was very late, there was much coming and going on the street below the windows: wheels rattling over cobblestones, the jingle of harness, occasionally a voice raised to hail a passing hackney. London, it seemed, never went to sleep and neither did the Rose and Crown, which was why Piers had chosen to put up here for the few weeks he would be in town. He could come and go at all hours of the day or night without rousing anyone's suspicions.

"Tell me about Castleton," he said.

Merrick grinned. He was thirtyish, of medium height, stocky, and unremarkable at first glance. A closer look would reveal that his garments were of the first quality and he was fastidious about his tailoring and person. He had expensive tastes and the money to indulge them. Much the same could be said about Piers. He was of the same age, pleasant looking and immaculately turned out, but he wouldn't stand out in a crowd. He was, however, leaner and harder than Merrick, the result of his years in Spain and his devotion to the gentlemanly pursuits of fencing and boxing. Merrick was more often to be found at the card table.

He'd known Merrick for a long time, from their poorhouse days. They had once been partners in crime, petty thieves who'd stolen from the homes of the wealthy in Mayfair to augment their paltry wages as clerks. Their careers as housebreakers had come to a sudden end when they'd killed a wealthy merchant who had surprised them in the act. When the authorities started closing in on them, Merrick had retired to his home in Yorkshire for a time while he, Gideon, decided to try his luck as a soldier.

He had no qualms about Merrick's loyalty, not if the price was right. All the same, Piers revealed as little as possible of his private life. Merrick had no idea that he had established a new identity in Bristol. He was Arthur Ward, a wealthy man of business with an interest in various trading companies around the world. To give Merrick his due, he wasn't overly interested in Piers's new life. He, too, regarded himself as a man of business, and his services and connections did not come cheaply.

Merrick said, "Castleton made it easy for us. Halfway through the performance, he left with a lady by the name of Mrs. Standhurst. His bodyguard did not go with him."

"Who is Mrs. Standhurst?"

"A new light o' love is my guess."

Piers frowned. He'd spent the last month gathering information on everyone the earl was close to. This was the first he'd heard of a Mrs. Standhurst. He didn't like last-minute wrinkles in a plan that he was ready to set in motion.

"What about Harper?" he asked. "Why didn't he follow them?"

"Now this is interesting. By all appearances, he was left to watch the party in Box Twelve, Viscount Latham, his sister, and a female companion."

Piers knew all about Viscount Latham and his sister. They weren't important. "Do you have the name of the companion?"

"Jane Mayberry. Yes, you may well stare. The same

Jane Mayberry that Castleton saw this morning at the library, then followed to your sister's place, and encountered tonight at the opera. What's his interest in her, Gideon?"

Piers shook his head. "I have no idea, unless he thinks she's acting as a courier between my sister and me." There was a pause as he thought things through. "All I remember about the woman is that she taught at the charity school with my sister, and that they were good friends." He looked at Merrick. "She's a bookworm and a dowd. Hardly Castleton's type."

"She didn't look like a bookworm tonight at the opera. She was dressed to turn heads and you'd be surprised how many heads turned to stare at her. Castleton's included."

"Yet Castleton left with this other woman, what's her name?"

"Mrs. Amelia Standhurst. But I saw the look he gave the Mayberry woman, and I'd say there's something between them."

There was another pause as Piers digested this.

"What do you want me to do about her?" asked Merrick finally.

"Nothing. No doubt he thinks she can lead him to me. She's not important. If her name comes up again, then we'll take a closer look at her."

"And the Standhurst woman?"

"What do you know of her?"

"Nothing, so far, except her name."

"Then find out if she's important to Castleton."

Merrick cocked his head to one side, studying the other man. Finally, he said, "It's been two months since you employed my services, Gideon, and apart from that first spectacular kill in Hyde Park, you've had me do nothing more than amass a mountain of information on Castleton, his friends, his associates, and his women. I know Castleton is your target, so why are we holding off? Why not simply eliminate him? What's the point in the delay?"

"Through no fault of mine, my schedule had to be rearranged. Hence, the delay."

"What schedule?"

Piers smiled and stood up, indicating the interview was over. "What you don't know can't hurt you. When the need arises, I'll tell you. But one thing I want to make absolutely clear. No one touches Castleton. He's mine, and I'll deal with him in my own time."

After Merrick left, Piers lit a cheroot from the candle on the mantel, and stood there, in front of the fire, idly smoking it. He was reflecting on Merrick's words: *Why are you holding off? Why not simply eliminate him?*

Because that would be too easy; because he wanted Castleton to know that Gideon Piers was calling the shots. Their positions were reversed. He was the hunter and the earl was his prey. It had taken him almost three years to recover from the debacle in Spain. He wasn't interested in a quick kill. He wanted to savor the pleasure of having at his mercy the high-and-mighty Major, Lord Caspar Devere, who had hunted him from pillar to post and cornered him like a rat in the monastery of St. Michel.

He was, however, a lot more cautious now than he was then. He didn't want to stir up a hornets' nest until after he'd made the kill. No one cared about the murder of John Collier. He was a nobody, a mere solicitor's clerk. Harper, the bodyguard, was different. He was a celebrity, but more important, he was a Special Branch agent. If he'd had Harper killed, Special Branch would move heaven and earth to find the killer of one of their own.

He looked up when the door opened to admit Joseph, his right-hand man. They'd been together now for more than five years, and Joseph was about the only person Piers trusted. Joseph's loyalty was unswerving, largely because Piers had rescued him, a Spanish deserter, from a band of Spanish soldiers who were on the point of executing him. And that's how they'd started out, just the two of them, fending for themselves. And that's how it had ended.

Joseph was a good ten years older than Piers. He had the face of an ascetic and gave the impression of being slow-witted, but that was a false impression. In his native tongue, he could be quite voluble when he wanted to be; in English he frequently had to search for words.

Joseph said, "I watched Merrick leave. No one followed him."

Piers was amused. "You worry too much, Joseph. I'm not expecting trouble. If we'd killed Harper, that would be different, though I can't see how Special Branch could trace us. No, this is between Castleton and me, and he doesn't know anything."

"Trouble comes when you least expect it—isn't that what you English say? And that English milord, he's clever that one, like a fox."

Piers masked his irritation behind a smile. If Joseph had been anyone else, he would have annihilated him with a few well-chosen words. No one praised the Earl of Castleton in his hearing. But Joseph hated the earl almost as much as he did, hated him and was just as eager to see him suffer and pay for his crimes.

"If he was as clever as you make out," he said

pleasantly, "he would have known I hadn't died in
the slaughter at St. Michel."

"How could he? He doesn't know your face."

"Precisely. Poor Halford. I was sorry to sacrifice
him, but he made it so easy. He had to have a rose just
like mine tattooed on his left arm. And so we escaped."

"Dressed as women!" Joseph said scornfully, but he
smiled.

"Chivalry is one of the earl's weaknesses," Piers
replied.

It had been a brutal fight, he remembered, with
the only chance of escaping certain death when Lord
Castleton called a truce to allow the women and children to go free. Piers and Joseph, disguised as
women, had joined the caravan that fled the doomed
monastery. The humiliation of it, his abject defeat
and subsequent flight, still had the power to make
him writhe.

Piers gestured to the bottle and glasses on the sideboard. "Help yourself to cognac and pour one for me."

It was a regular ritual, this sharing a glass of fine
cognac before retiring for the night, a symbol of mutual respect and friendship. But Piers didn't really regard Joseph as a friend. In fact, he didn't have any
friends, didn't want any, though there were many in
Bristol who would have been surprised to hear it.
Friendship implied intimacy, a sharing of confi-
dences, and for all his charm, Piers shared himself
with no one.

They pulled chairs up to the fire and sipped their
drinks for a moment or two in silence, but Joseph's
words were still turning in his mind, still rankling and
he felt compelled to justify himself.

"You credit the earl with too much intelligence.

Collier's execution has him completely baffled, and not only Castleton, but the authorities also. They've had a month to investigate, and it was just as I told you. They don't know where to begin to look for me."

Joseph, no connoisseur, gulped at his cognac as though he were drinking beer. "I wasn't thinking about now," he said slowly. "I was thinking about the past, about St. Michel. He found us there."

"It won't happen this time." Piers's words were clipped, almost angry. "There is no Judas to betray our movements, no John Collier to give us false information."

That's how Castleton had found him. It was a trap. Collier was their spy at headquarters. As he'd done in the past, he alerted them to the presence of a British convoy escorting a wagon of gold to headquarters. There was no gold, only Castleton and his crack unit of killers waiting for them.

Collier maintained his innocence to the end, but it had not saved him. Whenever there was a question of a man's loyalty, Piers always erred on the side of caution. And traitors deserved no mercy.

"What about your sister?" asked Joseph.

"What about her?"

"I don't know. Maybe she knows something."

Piers smiled. "As far as Letty knows, I died in Spain fighting for king and country. I'm sure the thought brings her solace. She will never believe anything bad of me. Besides, what can she say? She knows nothing."

"She knows your face."

Piers let out a long, patient sigh. "We're not likely to come face-to-face, but if we do and she recognizes me, she won't give me away. We're family. That means something to Letty."

In fact, if he came face-to-face with his sister, he wasn't at all sure what he would do, but he knew how Joseph's mind worked, and he knew how to manipulate him. There was nothing Joseph prized more than family. The only real family Joseph had ever known were the "Brothers"—that's what they called themselves, not deserters or bandits, but "Brothers." Anyone who betrayed a brother was beyond the pale, and dealt with accordingly.

The reference to family put Joseph in a nostalgic frame of mind, and he reminisced for a while about the good old days, when the Brothers were warlords in their own domain, until the English milord came among them and spoiled everything. Now there were only two left, himself and Piers, and the souls of the dead Brothers that cried out for blood.

After five minutes of listening to Joseph's rambling, Piers suddenly got up. "I'm going out," he said.

Piers never went anywhere without Joseph, so he got up as well. "Where are we going?" he asked.

"To Twickenham."

Joseph groaned. Twickenham, always Twickenham. "It's late," he said, "and it's miles away."

"The trouble with you is you've grown soft. Go to bed, Joseph. I'll go myself."

Joseph knew better than to accept that offer. He followed his master out.

It was a grim-faced, three-story building with windows in the attics. Originally, it had been a barracks, and the acreage on which it stood was the parade ground, but that was before living memory. Sometime during the last century, it had been turned into a poorhouse, but the name Barracks had stuck. It had stood empty and neglected for a long, long time, but had been recently acquired by Mr. Arthur Ward from Bristol.

He would raze it to the ground, thought Piers, and build a house to rival other grand houses in the area, especially the house just across the river. Twickenham House. The name, the memories, were burned into his brain.

He left Joseph to explain their presence to the watchmen he'd hired to keep trespassers away, and he walked along the riverbank till he came to a gap in the trees. Across the river, the Deveres' stately home was quite visible, though on his side of the river it was as dark as pitch. The Deveres, the high-and-mighty Deveres, had money enough to keep the darkness at bay. Outside lanterns were still lit, and though the duke and Lady Sophy must have gone to their beds long since, lights shone from the upstairs windows. God forbid that a Devere should waken and find himself in darkness.

He couldn't count the number of times he'd stood in this spot, as a boy, and watched the comings and goings of the Deveres when he was supposed to be tending the poorhouse's vegetable patch, or collecting fallen branches for kindling for the fires. He couldn't count the number of times he'd been soundly thrashed and sent to bed without his supper because he'd neglected his work. No punishment was severe enough, though, to keep him away from the gap in the trees and his fascination with the Deveres.

Lord Caspar was obviously the apple of his father's eye. In the school holidays, there would be boating parties with his friends—all the sons of wealthy men—and picnics with pigs roasting on spits, and horse riding and drives with his father in his curricle.

There were two younger children, a girl and a boy, but Piers was not interested in them. Lord Caspar was the favored one, his father's pride and joy, and that's what counted.

The Thames was more than a river. It was an insurmountable barrier dividing two worlds, the blessed world of the privileged, and the unspeakable world of the poorhouse.

In the poorhouse, the older children were separated from their parents and rarely saw them. His mother had died there, and before she was cold, she'd been taken away for a pauper's burial. His world was cold, dark, and dirty, with brutal punishments meted out for minor infractions of the rules. In his world, there were no tantalizing smells of roasted pigs turning on spits. There was black bread and soup, and porridge to fill their empty bellies.

Envy was too mild a word to describe what he felt. He hated the Deveres more than he hated anything.

He would curl up at night in his cold bed and pretend he had changed places with Lord Caspar. The Duke of Romsey was his father and he, Gideon, was the favorite son. He would have an army of servants at his beck and call and do whatever he pleased. But that wasn't his favorite part of the fantasy. He saw Lord Caspar reduced to rags, as he was, and going to bed cold and hungry. He saw the bigger boys coming for him, as they always did with a new boy, and showing him how powerless he really was. There were no real friends in the poorhouse. There were gangs of boys who looked out for their own, and weaklings went to the wall. He was quite sure that Lord Caspar wouldn't last the day, but would be reduced to a sniveling coward taking orders from everyone.

He'd left the poorhouse when he was twelve to go

into service, but he hated it and eventually became a clerk. He'd never forgotten Lord Caspar, never stopped hating him. He might have let it go at that if their paths had not crossed again in Spain.

He'd been a prince among men then, a legend. Everyone looked up to him, or they feared him. He'd had a hundred men at his command, and even the partisans kept their distance. He could almost hear the guns, taste the gunpowder, smell the blood. In his war, there were no rules, except the ones he made.

And Lord Caspar had humiliated him.

He felt the rush of blood, just like the old days, when he contemplated how he would crush a hated adversary. Let him wait, let him wonder...

At the end, he wanted to look into the earl's eyes. He wanted to tell him who he was and how he'd escaped from the carnage in the monastery, and how he'd prospered—not bad for a despised poorhouse boy who could rise no higher than a shipping clerk, eking out a living in London's docks.

Lord Caspar had never had to strive for anything. Everything had been handed to him on a platter. Even his title was there for the asking. Lord Caspar had finally condescended to accept the courtesy title of the Earl of Castleton when he turned thirty. It could have been his long before if he'd wanted it. But what was a title to a man who already had everything?

He wondered what Castleton would think if he could see him now, if he could know how far he'd come since St. Michel. After escaping from the monastery, he'd spent two years in hiding, biding his time until he could collect the gold he'd hidden without fear of reprisal. He'd wanted everyone to think he was dead and they had. Then, when they'd retrieved the gold, he and Joseph had set sail for England where they'd established new identities.

This is where it would end, he thought fiercely, where it had all begun. Everything was falling into place. He had only to wait for the appointed hour.

In the interim, he would amuse himself by playing with the earl.

When he walked back to the Barracks, he was thinking of Mrs. Standhurst and Jane Mayberry.

Chapter 6

*J*ane stood on the front porch of her house, enveloped in a man's greatcoat, with a wool cap pulled down to her eyes, staring intently at the stand of trees that lined the road to Highgate. She was watching for Ben, her stableboy, who had taken the buggy into Highgate to pick up Miss Drake. As each minute passed, her uneasiness grew. They should have been here by now. It would be dark soon, and now it had started to snow in earnest.

With Lance at her heels, she started toward the stable, meaning to saddle Daisy for the ride to the village, when her eye was caught by something on the road. It wasn't her buggy but a lone rider.

When the rider turned into her drive, her pulse began to race. Perhaps he'd lost his way, she thought, and wanted directions. Perhaps, but she had good reason to be cautious.

On that thought, she turned herself around, entered the house, and returned a moment or two later with an ancient blunderbuss cradled in her arms. The blunderbuss was used mainly for scaring off weasels and foxes that tried to rob her hen house, but it had also come in handy a time or two when tinkers and gypsies, thinking that a woman on her own was easy prey, had to be chased off. It wasn't the only weapon Jane kept for her protection. In the dresser drawer in her bedchamber, there was a pistol, ready and primed, in case of housebreakers, and a smaller pistol that she kept in her reticule.

A housebreaker, to Jane, was anyone who entered her house uninvited.

With her blunderbuss at the ready and her dog at her heels, she advanced upon the rider. His garments were covered in a film of snow and ice, and it registered with Jane that he'd been riding for some time.

"Who are you?" she shouted above the wind, "and what do you want?"

"Castleton," he replied, not bothering to hide his irritation.

It had taken Case three days to track her down, three days of being fobbed off by her friends' evasions and downright lies before he'd twigged to what they were doing. No one wanted him to find Jane Mayberry, and he was determined to find out why.

"It is Miss Mayberry, I presume?" he said in the same clipped tone.

In spite of the question and her outlandish appearance, he knew it was she. He'd recognized her voice. Even when it was raised it held a pleasant trace of huskiness. But Case was in no mood to be pleased. He hadn't had his dinner; he hadn't dressed for the weather; and if she didn't put that blunderbuss down, he would forcibly take it away from her.

There was a moment when she couldn't believe what her brain was telling her, then she gasped out, "What are *you* doing here?"

Case smiled grimly. "At the moment, I'd be happy just to get in out of the storm and find shelter for my horse."

She watched him dismount in a daze. The last person she'd expected to encounter on her own doorstep was Lord Castleton.

On that thought, her blunderbuss came up, but when Lance whined, she pointed it to the ground again.

"Thank you, Lance," said Case, "for that vote of confidence." Then less pleasantly, "Miss Mayberry, you can put that blunderbuss away. I'm really quite harmless."

"Have you lost your way?" There were other houses in the area, grand houses, and she could only hope that he'd been on his way to one of those when he was caught in the storm.

He straightened. "Certainly not! I'm here on official business. There are some questions I want to put to you."

"Questions? About what?"

He didn't want to go into long explanations out in the freezing cold, so he said simply, "About the opera last Wednesday night."

It took a moment for his words to register, then she said incredulously, "You came all the way out here, in the middle of a blizzard, just to talk to me about the opera?"

That's how it had started out. He'd interviewed everyone who might have been a witness to the attack on Harper—Freddie Latham and Sally, the night watch, ushers—only Miss Mayberry was unavailable and that made him suspicious.

"It wasn't snowing in town. Look, could we discuss this inside, before we all turn into ice sculptures?"

"How did you know where to find me?"

"I never reveal my sources."

"Freddie!" she said bitterly. "It could only have been Freddie!"

"I don't see what difference it makes. So you live near the village of Highgate, in a house called Hillcrest. Why the secrecy? What are you hiding, Miss Mayberry?"

"Don't be ridiculous! I am not hiding anything. I'm a spinster. I live alone. I'm careful who I give my direction to, that's all. My friends know how I feel and respect my wishes."

It was the truth, but it wasn't the whole truth. He couldn't have arrived at a worse time. She wanted to drive him off, tell him that he should have had more sense than to venture beyond Highgate in a snowstorm, but that was only her frustration goading her. Common decency demanded that she offer hospitality to any traveler who was caught in a storm.

From the porch, a voice said, "Is everything all right, Jane? Has something happened to Ben?"

The speaker was Jane's housekeeper, and before that, housekeeper to Jane's father when they lived in Scotland. Mrs. Trent was in her fifties, small and thin, with iron gray hair and a severe expression that was made more severe by anxiety.

Jane turned with a reassuring smile. "Everything is fine," she said. "This gentleman got caught in the snowstorm, that's all. Go back in the house, Mrs.

Trent, and put on the kettle. I'll send our visitor in as soon as we see to his horse."

Case said graciously, "How do you do, Mrs. Trent. I'm Castleton by the way."

Mrs. Trent looked at Case and slowly nodded. "I read about you in the papers," then to Jane, "What about Ben?"

"I'm going after him just as soon as I saddle Daisy."

When Mrs. Trent went into the house, Case said, "Who is Ben?"

Jane looked past him toward the road. "My stable-boy. Mrs. Trent's grandson. He went into Highgate to fetch my friend. They were to meet at the Gate-house Inn."

"Why are you worried about him?"

"He's late home, that's all." She looked at him anxiously. "When you came through Highgate, you didn't see a buggy on the road or outside the Gate-house Inn? Or anything unusual, anything at all?"

"No."

She looked past him again, scanning the road.

"Miss Mayberry," he said.

"What?" she stared at him blankly for a moment, then said quickly, "I'm sorry. I'll show you where to stable your horse."

As she struck out toward the stable, a large wooden edifice that, to Case's eye, must have once served as a barn, he followed. "You're not thinking of going after him in this kind of weather?" he said, but the wind plucked the words from his mouth, so he held his peace until they entered the barn.

"I don't understand your urgency. Obviously, Ben has the good sense to stay where he is warm and dry."

Jane set her blunderbuss on a bench. "What's all this about the opera?"

Now was not the time to ask her questions. She was too keyed up to pay attention. "It can wait," he said.

"Oh." She waved a hand, encompassing the stable in general. "Help yourself to whatever you need. I've got to go. He's only a boy. Anything could have happened to him."

One part of Case's brain registered that the stable was spotless, with a fenced off area for animals at one end and a space at the other for a buggy and tackle. Another part registered that something was seriously wrong here.

"Miss Mayberry," he began, then more forcefully when she turned away to haul a saddle from a post, "Jane!" That got her attention. "I'll go," he said quietly. "I'll find him and bring him home."

She looked at him searchingly. "Why would you do that?"

Her capacity to irritate him was boundless. "Because I want to!"

A smile flashed, then was quickly gone. She shook her head. "Ben doesn't trust strangers, and then there's my friend. Emily is very timid." She stopped, realizing that her explanation was unconvincing. She drew in a breath, then said, "I'm not going to wait here not knowing what's happened to them. If you want to come with me, I can't stop you. You always do what you want anyway."

"Thank you!"

He wrestled the saddle from her and strode to the pen where a piebald pony was eyeing him warily. Jane was right behind him.

"Daisy won't allow anyone to handle her but me," she said.

Of course, Daisy proved her wrong. A few soft-spoken words, a touch here, a caress there, and Daisy was simpering like a starry-eyed debutante.

When he had saddled the mare and led her out of the pen, he said, "You were saying?"

She took exception to his smirk. "So it's true what they say about you," she said. "You have a way with females."

He stopped, turned slowly, and his gray, gray eyes locked with hers. "If that's true," he said, "then why are you always fighting me?"

A gust of wind rattled the window panes; one of the horses whinnied; Lance sat back on his haunches. Jane forgot to breathe. She could hardly sustain the intensity of his gaze.

It took every ounce of will to drag her eyes from his. She said as coolly as she could manage, "I don't take kindly to people who order me about."

"Is that what it is? I wonder..."

When his hand reached for her, she took a quick step back. "Time is wasting," she said crossly. "Come with me or stay. It's all the same to me."

He wasn't done with her yet. When they were outside, he bent down and cupped his hands to hoist her into the saddle. It was only a step or two to the mounting block, as he must have known. She looked at him, then quickly looked away. She couldn't remember when she'd felt so self-conscious. Dressed as she was, he must think she looked a fright.

What did it matter what he thought?

Once mounted, she called for Lance and set off at a canter. Not once did she look back to see if Case was following her.

It would have surprised her to know what he was thinking. He wasn't thinking about her appearance. He was thinking that this maddening woman was in sore need of protection, whether she knew it or not, and since no other likely candidate was in the vicinity, the job fell to him.

Mounting up, he rode after her.

The two-mile ride to the village turned into an interminable test of endurance as dusk thickened and the temperature dropped. Though it had stopped snowing, a thick blanket of snow covered the road and hedgerows, making it difficult to get one's bearings. If it had not been for Lance, Case would have insisted that they turn back. But the dog ran back and forth, herding them as a sheepdog would, keeping them from straying into the ditch.

There was no opportunity to talk, but Case didn't mind. Any conversation he'd had with Jane Mayberry always ended in a stalemate. His curiosity, however, was as keen as ever. Her anxiety for the boy and her friend seemed out of proportion, and he wanted to know why.

When the lights of Highgate appeared ahead of them, they quickened their pace. Not long after, they entered the village's main thoroughfare. The Gatehouse Inn was the first hostelry they came to. So far, Case had been content to let Jane take the lead, but now, he touched his heels to his mount's flanks and passed her as they cantered through the archway into the stable yard.

He dismounted first, and after throwing the reins to a stableboy, went to assist Jane. He expected an argument, but she slipped from the saddle and into his arms without murmur. She was shivering; her face was pale and pinched with cold.

"I'm an idiot for allowing you to come here," he said roughly.

Stripping off his coat, he draped it around her shoulders. Still no response from her. She was glancing this way and that around the stable yard. It was almost deserted.

Her eyes, uncertain and full of anxiety, met his. "The buggy isn't here."

"Perhaps Ben has gone off to visit a friend. There could be any number of reasons why he's not here. Don't jump to conclusions."

"Ben wouldn't do that. And he would have come here first, not necessarily to the stable yard, but to the inn. He would have waited for Emily outside the front doors. Somebody must have seen him."

She questioned the stableboy, but he was no help. He knew Ben, but said he hadn't seen him since he last came into town for supplies, and that was several days ago.

They left the horses in the boy's care, told Lance to stay, then entered the inn. "You seem more worried about Ben than you do about your friend," said Case as he held the door for Jane.

"Emily, that is, Miss Drake, may have changed her mind. Perhaps she could not get away. I had my doubts—"

Suddenly, she stopped, as though she'd said too much.

"You had your doubts?" he prompted. Her friend's name sounded familiar. Then he had it. She was the young woman he'd seen her talking to at the opera. Freddie had given him the girl's name

"I wasn't sure that she would come. She said it might be difficult to get away."

Yes, he thought, *but there's more to it than that,* and

was surprised to find that he was disappointed because she would not confide in him.

Though there were no coaches in the stable yard, the inn's taproom was doing a brisk business. They could hear sounds of merriment every time the door swung open to admit another customer.

"Locals," the landlord answered to Case's question. "It's always like this on a Saturday night." His eyes narrowed on Jane, studying her critically.

That look brought Jane's scattered thoughts into focus again. She slipped out of Case's coat, handed it to him, and squared her shoulders.

"I sent my servant here to meet my friend, Miss Drake, Miss Emily Drake," she said. "Perhaps you saw him? He's only a boy. His name is Ben. Or perhaps you saw my friend?"

"I didn't see any boy."

"But you saw my friend?" Jane asked quickly.

"Who wants to know?" The landlord's tone was almost insulting.

Jane stiffened. "Have you seen Miss Drake or not?"

Case propped one elbow against the counter. "I'd advise you to answer the lady's question. You wouldn't know it to look at her, but she has a ferocious temper."

The landlord, a big, corpulent fellow with a florid face, almost smiled. "Wait here," he said. "There's someone as wants to speak to anyone who is asking for Miss Drake."

If anything, Jane's face went a bit paler, but she kept her spine straight and her shoulders squared.

Case shook his head. "Jane, Jane," he said. "Why is it I have the suspicion that I'm about to become involved in something nasty? You should have confided in me, you know."

"You're *not* involved," she said. "I didn't ask you to come here. I'm perfectly capable of handling this."

"As you wish," he murmured.

He draped his coat over one chair and draped himself over another, deliberately leaving Jane to handle her own problems. This wasn't pique on his part. Or maybe there was a *pinch* of pique involved, but he didn't really believe there could be anything she couldn't fix herself. After all, how much trouble could a reclusive bluestocking get into in Highgate?

The door to the taproom opened and the landlord appeared with a gentleman whom Case recognized as one of London's most unsavory roués, Lord Francis Reeve. Not that he and Reeve were acquainted. They'd never been introduced, and that's the way Case wanted to keep it.

Lord Reeve was closer to fifty than forty, thin, with a face that might have been considered handsome once, but was now showing signs of dissipation, the natural consequence of his mode of living. He also had an ungovernable temper, especially when he'd been drinking, and Case didn't think that his lordship had spent the last hour or two in the taproom sipping tea.

Case yawned behind his hand, but his eyes were watchful.

Lord Reeve hardly spared him a glance. His gaze fastened on Jane. "Miss Mayberry, I presume?" he said angrily coming up to her. "I didn't believe Emily. I thought there must be a man involved, but there isn't, is there, Miss Mayberry?"

"The only man involved is you," said Jane, "but that won't be for much longer, not if Emily has her way. Now where is she? What have you done with her?"

If Reeve was angry before, now he was furious.

"You bitch! You're the one who put these ideas in her head! She was never defiant before this. She was always a biddable girl until you poisoned her mind against me."

"You did that yourself by bullying her! She's afraid of you! You're not interested in Emily, only in her fortune. And your own conscience should tell you that you're the wrong man for Emily, or any woman, for that matter."

These were fighting words! Case rose, went to the counter, and leaned negligently against it. But Jane and Reeve were intent only on each other.

Spittle was beginning to form at the corners of Reeve's mouth. "Do you know what your problem is, Miss Mayberry?" His eyes made an insulting appraisal. "You're a dried up old maid! Look at you! What man would want you? You're jealous because Emily is young and pretty, and has made a brilliant match."

Things were going from bad to worse. Before Jane could add kindling to the blaze, Case put in mildly, "That's no way to speak to a lady. Mind your manners, sir, or I'll mind them for you."

Reeve's gaze shifted to Case. "Who the devil are *you*?"

"Oh, just an interested bystander."

"Then I'd advise you to mind your own business."

"Now you've hurt my feelings."

Reeve ignored him. "And this is my advice to you, Miss Mayberry. Stay away from Emily. No more private tête-à-têtes at the opera. If you defy me, I'll make you sorry you were born."

Jane cried, "If you've hurt her—"

"Don't be stupid!" Reeve snapped. "Would I hurt the woman I'm going to marry? If I hurt anyone, it was that boy of yours. I hope I broke every bone in his body—the impudent upstart!"

The little color she had washed out of her face. "Where is he?" she cried.

"I don't know and I don't care."

She stammered something, and that was enough for Case. He launched himself at the older man, and with a hand on the back of Reeve's neck, wrestled him to his knees.

Fear for the boy fueled his anger. "Miss Mayberry asked you a question," he said. "Where is the boy?"

"I don't know!" Reeve struggled to free himself. "He's only a servant, for God's sake! He was impertinent. He deserved to be beaten."

Case now had Lord Reeve's arm twisted behind his back. "I'll ask you again," he said, "and if I don't like the answer, I'm going to break your arm. Where is the boy?"

"He took off in his gig, going toward Highgate Hill. That's all I know."

"And Emily?" asked Jane.

"She went back to town with her brother."

Case looked at Jane. "Let him go," she said. "If anyone can find Ben, Lance will." Then to Reeve. "You'd better pray that my boy is all right, or I'll find you and have my dog rip out your throat." On that savagely delivered threat, she turned and made for the door to the stable block.

Case got to his feet and stared at Jane's retreating back. Not a word of thanks for his timely intervention. In her usual pigheaded fashion, she was off again, sailing into the Lord only knew what danger.

This woman really needed a keeper.

At least things were beginning to make sense. It seemed to him that there must be some truth to all those rumors about Lady Octavia and her volunteers helping women in distress. They meant well, he supposed, but he couldn't help thinking that all Jane had achieved was to stir up a hornets' nest.

Shaking his head, he snatched up his coat and went after her.

When the door closed behind Case, Lord Reeve pulled himself to his feet. As he tried to even his breathing, he rubbed the arm Case had almost wrenched from its socket. Then his eye fell on the landlord who was again standing behind the counter.

"You saw him attack me," Reeve said furiously. "Why didn't you send for the constable?"

"I would have if I hadn't heard you say you was betrothed to that young woman. I thought you was her father. And I don't take to bullies who beat boys either. Seems to me you got off lightly."

Reeve's hand fisted and unfisted at his side. He wanted nothing more than to smash his fist into the landlord's beefy face. But the man was built like an ox. It wasn't a fight he could be sure of winning.

It was all Emily's fault, but it was Jane Mayberry who had put her subversive ideas in Emily's head. It was because of them that he'd been humiliated like this, and it was not to be borne.

One way or another, they would pay for it. He would make them all pay.

There were people standing around staring at him. He shoved them out of his way and pushed into the taproom.

Chapter 7

*I*t was a relief to find that she hadn't taken off without him. As he mounted up, he said, "I think you're expecting too much of your dog. He'll never find Ben's scent, not after this fall of snow."

"He's a sheepdog," she replied. "He's used to finding sheep that have become lost in a snowstorm. And it's not Ben's scent he will follow but Razor's."

"Razor's?"

"The pony that's harnessed to the buggy. He's a wanderer, if he gets the chance. Lance is used to tracking him and bringing him home."

"Ah. So what are we waiting for?"

"You," she said, and just when he was feeling flattered by her courtesy, she added, "I have enough on my hands looking for Ben without having to worry about you wandering off by yourself."

He might have told her that he'd learned the skill of tracking as a boy at his father's hunting lodge in Shropshire, a skill he had honed to an art in his years in Spain. He stifled the impulse, swallowed his smile, and meekly trotted after her as she and Lance led the way through the archway into High Street.

Here, they reined in. They'd been sheltered in the stable block, but out here there was nothing to stop the wind whipping itself into a fury as it swept down Highgate Hill, funneled through the red brick houses on either side of High Street, and spent itself on the open fields at the edge of the village. He was tempted to tell Jane to return to the inn and let him take over the search for Ben, but he knew that it wouldn't do a bit of good. Whatever else Jane Mayberry was, she was no hothouse flower.

When there was a sudden lull in the wind, Jane pulled her cap down over her ears, then mistress and dog started forward. Case held onto his hat. They kept their mounts to a walk as they traveled the length of Highgate's main street. Lance disappeared for minutes at a time, but he always returned as though to make sure they were still following him. They were the only travelers on the road, and the few pedestrians they saw were either making for the Gatehouse or hurrying to get in from the cold.

"He's caught the scent," cried Jane.

Just as well, thought Case, because in spite of keeping his eyes peeled, he hadn't noticed one sign or track in the snow that would give him a clue as to which way the buggy had taken. So much for all his years in Spain as a scout in the cavalry! But he wouldn't be scouting in these conditions. It was hard to tell whether it was snowing or not, because the wind was whipping up a fine spray that soon obliterated every track. The dusk had settled into an unremitting gloom and there were no stars to guide their way, only the lanterns that winked from every other porch.

He didn't put much faith in Lance. The hounds at Castle Devere would bay and bark excitedly when they caught the scent of a fox. This dog was silent.

Halfway up Highgate Hill, Jane came to a stop.

"What is it?" asked Case, coming abreast of her.

When Jane dismounted, so did he. Lance was running in circles, whining.

"He's lost the scent," said Jane. "It's too windy. It's all right boy." She went down on her knees and hugged her dog. "You did your best." She looked up at Case. "I suppose we could ask the local constable to organize a search. What do you think?"

She'd asked for his advice! If he hadn't been standing on the ground he might have fallen off his horse. It was nice to be consulted. A woman could be too competent.

Both girl and dog were looking up at him, waiting for his answer. He'd been on the point of agreeing with her, that they should approach the constable, but that trusting look stayed his words. He knew that the constable wouldn't exert himself, not for a servant boy, and certainly not in this kind of weather. He wasn't convinced, himself, that anything bad had happened to Ben. Adolescent boys were notoriously unpredictable.

He couldn't bring himself to disappoint Jane Mayberry or her dog. He looked up Highgate Hill, then looked back the way they'd come. "Let's try something else before we call in the constable," he said.

Jane got up. "What?" she asked, her voice half hopeful, half desperate.

Case caught her with one arm around her shoulders when a sudden gust of wind blew the snow into a mad dervish around them. When she moved closer for protection, both his arms tightened around her. Lance edged closer too, and buried his head in the folds of Case's coat.

When the wind died away, she lost no time in shrugging out of his clasp. He was surprised to realize how reluctant he was to let her go.

Her voice was as erratic as the breeze. "What else can we do?"

The answer that flashed into his mind made him grin. But this wasn't the time or place for banter.

He brought his mind around to the problem of Ben. "I don't think Ben got this far. We're almost at the end of the village, and if he came this far, I think Reeve would have caught up to him. I'm betting that Ben turned off somewhere to hide, maybe along one of those country lanes we passed. Maybe he found an empty barn... what is it, Jane?"

Her gloved hand clutched his sleeve. "The road past Lauderdale House turns into a track. It's a long way round, but eventually it passes the back of my house and comes out on the north road. Only drovers ever use it to drive their animals to market. Do you think Ben might have taken it to get home?"

"Let's find out."

"It's not wide enough for a buggy, leastways, I would never attempt it. But if Ben were frightened, really frightened..." She turned her horse. "It's worth a try."

She had reverted to her usual self—capable and in command of the situation. "Lead on, Miss Mayberry," Case cried, and he followed her down the hill again.

.   .   .

They stopped when they came to the end of the grounds of Lauderdale House. If the drovers' track had not been marked by hedgerows on either side, they wouldn't have known it was there.

Jane said, "Lance has caught the scent again."

"How can you tell?"

"He's impatient. He wants us to hurry."

As if on cue, Lance came racing up to them, nuzzled Jane's hand, then went tearing away again.

"This is hopeless," said Jane, peering into the gloom. "We won't get far without a lantern."

Case nodded. "Don't move till I get back." He mounted up and rode back the way they'd come.

She watched him go in some alarm. What if he lost his way? Then she grew impatient with herself. Of course he wouldn't lose his way. He was a soldier. He was competent. He was probably in his element, while she felt out of her depth in more ways than one.

It was stupid to feel so awkward around him.

She didn't fret for long because the earl wasn't gone for more than a minute or two. "I borrowed it from the front gate of Lauderdale House," he said, holding up the lantern.

It was ridiculous to feel so happy to see him again. "Give me the lantern," she said gruffly, "and I'll lead the way."

He dismounted, but held onto the lantern. "No. Let's go together," he said.

"We'll walk the horses."

He didn't mind giving her the last word.

.   .   .

A mile along the drovers' road, they came upon the buggy tilted perilously to one side, but still intact. There was no sign of Ben or Razor.

"This is crazy," said Jane, her voice beginning to crack. "What could have happened to them?"

Case was examining the tracks around the buggy, almost obliterated now by blowing snow. "Either Ben or someone else unhitched your pony. They'll be around here somewhere." He looked up at her. "Don't worry, Jane. With luck, we'll find young Ben safely ensconced in some farm wife's kitchen or, as I said before, sheltering in some farmer's barn."

They found him, or rather Lance found him, huddled at the foot of a haystack. He was sleeping, but wakened when Lance began to lick his face. Jane quickly knelt beside him. Without thinking, she began to brush the snow from his clothes. She could see that he'd been beaten. His lip was split; one eye was completely closed and there were scratches on his face.

"I knew you'd find me," were the first words out of his mouth.

She kept her voice steady. "I should hope you would!"

"Did you find Razor? When the buggy got stuck, I unhitched him but he ran off before I could get up on his back."

"If I know Razor, he'll be home and warm and dry by now." Then, as Case knelt down beside her, "This is Lord Castleton, Ben. I wish you had seen how he stood up to Lord Reeve. He grabbed him by the scruff of the neck and shook him till his teeth rattled. I thought all his teeth would fall out."

Ben's laugh faded to a moan of pain. "I didn't tell him nothing," he said, rallying a little. "I didn't tell him your name. Miss Drake did that."

"Hush now," said Jane, "we'll talk later."

Case said. "We have to get you up and out of here, Ben. Do you think you can manage if I help you?"

Ben nodded, but as Case tried to ease him up, he whimpered in pain.

"Where does it hurt?" asked Case.

"My arm. I can't move it."

"Hold the light for me, Jane."

As Jane held up the lantern, Case began to test for broken bones. Ben bore it stoically until Case tried to lift his right arm. Then he let out a howl.

Case said to Jane, "I don't think it's serious, but we have to get him to someplace warm and dry so I can see what I'm doing."

It was dark now, and outside the pool of light from the lantern, there was nothing to be seen, no lights winking at them from cottages or outside lanterns. And to make matters worse, it had started to snow again.

"We might as well make for home," Jane said, sounding confident for Ben's sake. "It can't be that far and Lance can show us the way."

Case removed his coat. "Hold my horse steady," he said.

Talking soothingly all the while, he wrapped his coat around Ben and hoisted him into the saddle, then mounted up behind him. Ben's piteous moans and groans had Jane gritting her teeth.

Case looked at her set face and said harshly, "There's no other way. And there's more to worry about than his injured arm. He's been out in the cold too long. His skin feels like ice. So, let's move. Walk your horse and hold up the lantern so that I can follow you."

He'd got the wrong idea. She wasn't finding fault

with him. She was well aware that she couldn't have managed Ben on her own. She'd thank him later, but first they had to get Ben home.

She called Lance. "Home," she said, then the little caravan moved off with Lance in the lead.

It was a journey Jane hoped she never had to repeat. In spite of the lantern, they were walking blind and had it not been for Lance, who kept them together like sheep in a little flock, they would have had to stop.

The lights of home had never looked more welcoming. "Home!" she shouted, or tried to shout, but her voice was hoarse from the cold and she couldn't be sure that she was heard.

When the front door was thrown open and the housekeeper was silhouetted against the light, Jane's eyes welled with tears of relief. They soon dried when the earl came abreast of her and started issuing orders.

"Take care of the horses, Miss Mayberry, while I see to Ben."

At mention of Ben, Mrs. Trent descended the steps. "You found him? Thank God! Come this way, your lordship, come this way."

A moment later, the front door closed, leaving Jane, Lance, and the horses out in the cold. She looked at the weary beasts and her pique melted. They looked to be in worse shape than she felt. "We couldn't have managed without you," she told them, and murmuring nonsense interspersed with endearments, she led them to the stable.

. . .

Anxiety for Ben made her hurry through her chores. She'd been right about Razor. He was in his stall, munching his head off. If she hadn't loved animals and abhorred their ill treatment, she would have whacked him on the nose for leaving Ben in the lurch. In any crisis, or if there was work to be done, Razor could be counted on to look out for himself.

She was drooping with weariness when she climbed the incline to the house. Her shoulders hurt, her legs hurt, her fingers were numb with cold. She was beginning to feel sorry for herself when a piercing shriek from inside the house stopped her in her tracks.

Ben!

All her aches and pains were forgotten. She picked up her skirts, raced up the incline, and burst into the entrance hall. All she could hear now was the low murmur of voices coming from the back of the house. Lance led the way to the kitchen.

A makeshift bed was drawn close to the fire with Ben in it, naked to the waist and propped up with pillows. His complexion was parchment white, and tears stood on the tips of his lashes. Lord Caspar was holding a cup to his lips and pressing him to drink from it. She detected the aroma of Mrs. Trent's "marmalade tea," a medicinal brew, made with equal parts of Scotch whiskey and boiling water, sweetened with marmalade to mask, Jane supposed, the awful taste of the whiskey.

"There you are, lass!" exclaimed Mrs. Trent.

She was at the oven, removing hot bricks with a long paddle, then wrapping them in towels. Obviously they were meant for Ben, to keep him warm.

"Did you find Razor?" asked Mrs. Trent. "I was that worried when he came trotting into the yard, with no buggy and no Ben. I couldna imagine what had happened, but I knew you would all be chilled to the bone when you got back, so I put bricks in to heat and made marmalade tea." She went on cheerfully. "There's marmalade tea for you, too. On the table."

Jane sagged against the door. She wasn't sure what she'd expected when she burst into the kitchen, but not this scene of cozy domesticity. She felt suddenly overwhelmed by the heat. The fire in the grate was blazing like a blacksmith's furnace, as was the fire under the oven. The room was quite small, and someone had closed the window. She couldn't breathe.

"Jane."

She turned her head slowly and met the steady, reassuring gaze of the earl. He saw the strain on her face and quickly got up. "Mrs. Trent," he said, "see that Ben drinks this."

"What?" The housekeeper followed his gaze, noted her mistress's expression, and hastened to obey.

On seeing Jane, Ben cried, "I tried to stop them taking Miss Drake away, honest I did, but they hurt my arm, and Miss Drake said she *wanted* to go home."

Jane gathered herself enough to reply, "You did well, Ben." Then anxiously to Case, "What's this about his arm?"

Case removed her gloves, coat, and cap, led her to a chair at the table, and pushed her into it. His voice was matter-of-fact. "His arm was out of joint. I had to reset it. It was painful, but only for a moment or two. And after a good night's rest, he'll be more like himself. He's fine, Jane, so stop worrying."

Her huge eyes met his, then moved to Ben. He wasn't keen on swallowing the marmalade tea, but he screwed up his face and did it manfully. Only then did his grandmother set the cup aside and pull the covers over him. Jane swallowed hard.

As she studied Ben, Case studied her. He hadn't known that her hair was so long or so fair. Now that he'd removed the hideous cap that covered it, it fell in waves to her shoulders. There was a smudge of dirt on one cheek and her gown was mired in mud along the hem.

It seemed incredible to him now that she'd been attending the opera regularly with Sally Latham, yet he hadn't noticed her until last Wednesday. He felt as though his worldview had shifted dramatically. He didn't know whether she was beautiful or not. What he did know was that fashion plate or country dowd, spitfire or damsel in distress, she was utterly compelling.

He picked up the cup of marmalade tea, curled her fingers around it, and told her to drink. That she obeyed him automatically told him how shaken she was. After a few mouthfuls of Mrs. Trent's elixir, however, she began to show signs of regaining her equilibrium. Her spine straightened, her shoulders squared, she put down the cup.

She looked up at him. "If you hadn't come along when you did," she said gravely, "things could have turned out badly for Ben."

As grave as she, he replied, "I was glad to be of service."

The look in his eyes made her feel self-conscious again so she got up. "Trentie," she said, "we'll put Lord Castleton in the room Miss Drake was to have. The fire needs to be lit, and his lordship will need hot water and fresh towels. I'll tidy up down here and get dinner started."

"You'll do no such thing!" declared the housekeeper,

appalled. "Lass, you look as though a puff of wind would blow you away. Sit yourself down and leave everything to me. There's little enough to do. Everything is ready, or just about ready. Now drink your tea."

She moved the teapot closer to Jane, gave Case a beseeching look, and left the room.

As Jane wandered over to the bed, Case topped up her cup.

She looked down at Ben. He was sleeping now and looked much younger than his fourteen years. She ought to be horsewhipped, she thought fiercely, for giving him so much responsibility. She should have foreseen that there might be trouble. What a muddle she had made of things! Now Emily was worse off than before, and Ben . . .

She passed a hand over her eyes as her head began to swim. A touch on her arm brought her head up.

Case said quietly, "You heard Mrs. Trent. Drink your tea. It will steady your nerves."

She took the cup from him and choked down a mouthful of tea, then another. "This isn't like me," she said faintly. "I don't know what's come over me."

"You're human, that's all. You have a right to be upset. Look, why don't you slip upstairs and take a short nap? Mrs. Trent and I can manage things down here. When dinner is ready, we'll call you." When she shook her head, he said impatiently, "Jane, there's no shame in letting others do for you. Let me help."

She glanced at him sharply. "Don't baby me, Castleton, or I won't know it's you I'm talking to."

He was careful not to smile, though the sudden sizzle in her eyes sorely tempted him. "My friends call me Case," he said.

"What?"

"Case. It's short for Castleton."

"We're not friends."

"You can say that after all we've been through together?"

Her cheeks turned pink. "I told you I was grateful. What more do you want?"

He stroked the bridge of his nose with his index finger. "If I told you, you might hit me."

The pink in her cheeks went a shade deeper, but she gave him back stare for stare. "You have yet to tell me why you're here. Something about the opera, you said?"

"Do you always change the subject when you become unsure of yourself? Ah. Now your temper is showing again. This can wait till tomorrow, you know. It's not urgent."

"It was urgent enough to bring you out here in a blizzard, wasn't it? I'd rather get it over and done with." Then the sooner he would be on his way.

"Fine. Shall we sit down?"

He held a chair for her, and when she was seated, took a chair on the opposite side of the table. He came to the point at once. "Last Wednesday night, when you left the theater, did you see anything unusual? Think carefully. Someone or something that seemed out of place?"

She was still struggling with her temper. Eventually, she shook her head. "No. Why do you ask?"

He gave her the same expurgated account that he'd given Freddie and Sally Latham when he'd interviewed them, that a colleague at Special Branch had been set upon in a hackney outside the theater, and all possible witnesses to the attack were being questioned. Gideon Piers's name never once came

up. Her answers were much the same as the viscount's and Sally's.

After an interval of silence, she said, "And that's
why you came all the way out here, to ask me these
questions about your colleague?"

"It's important, Jane," he said seriously. "But if I'd
known that the weather was going to change, I would
have delayed the interview for a few days."

She shivered. "I'm glad you didn't." Her eyes
strayed to Ben. "I'm glad you were here."

He realized she was hardly aware of what she was
saying. She'd been through a lot today and looked on
the point of collapse. There was no need to question
her further. He had what he'd come for. She couldn't
help him with the attack on Harper, and he had a
very good idea now why Jane Mayberry didn't advertise where she could be found, and it had nothing to
do with Gideon Piers.

When he got up, he was feeling quite mellow.
"Come along, Jane," he said. "It's time for that nap."

She looked up at him in some confusion. "I can't
go to bed. There's too much to do."

"What, for instance?"

Her eyes fell on Lance. "I have to take care of my
dog. He needs to be dried off, and fed. And—"

Patience wasn't working with her, so he raised her
to her feet, cupped her elbow and maneuvered her to
the door. "Whatever you may think," he said, "the
world won't end because you're not here to direct
things. I'll take care of Lance."

He opened the door and gave her a little push.
Lance got up from the hearth, but when Case ordered him to stay, he sank down again. She picked up
a candle from the hall table, and mounted the stairs
with her back straight, but once she entered her own

bedchamber and had shut the door on the world, she allowed her shoulders to slump.

The bed looked very inviting.

A wave of fatigue swept over her. She put down her candle before she dropped it, and stumbled to the bed. She would have that nap she decided, not because the earl ordered it, but because she didn't have the energy to stay awake. After slipping out of her gown and donning a warm woolen robe, she stretched out on the bed and drew the eiderdown up to her chin.

The world won't end because you're not here to direct things.

She huffed a little at that. He seemed to think she was domineering, whereas she thought of herself as capable and independent.

That's how her parents had raised her—to be capable and independent. Of course, there was no money for an army of servants to do for them as the earl had at his disposal, only Mrs. Trent, and she was more like a member of the family. It didn't take money to make people happy.

Her parents had done more than raise her to be independent. They'd encouraged her to read widely, to ask questions and defend her point of view. Her fondest memories were of family dinners, with a few interesting guests, and everyone talking across each other, teasing, laughing. It had never occurred to her, then, that she'd had an unusual upbringing, that not everyone appreciated a woman who had a mind of her own.

Her thoughts drifted, became less pleasant. There was one person in particular who was not impressed with the way her parents had raised her. But that was a long time ago.

She moved restlessly as random thoughts flitted in and out of her mind. Why was the earl here? She knew what he'd told her, but what made him think that she could help him when Freddie and Sally could not? They'd all left the opera together.

He'd helped her with Ben.

She was grateful to him, more than grateful, but he unsettled her and took pleasure in doing it. She didn't like the way he looked at her; she didn't like the way she looked at him.

She never blushed!

The sooner he went back to town to investigate the Hyde Park murder the better. Gideon. How did he fit into it? But Gideon was dead, wasn't he? Then why...

She sighed and slipped into sleep before she could complete the thought.

At that very moment, Gideon Piers was enjoying himself enormously, though he hadn't come to the Ladies' Library primarily to enjoy himself. He was curious about Jane Mayberry, the young woman who, he was almost sure, had replaced La Contessa and Mrs. Standhurst in Castleton's affections. For three days, the earl had been trying to find the elusive bluestocking. Today, he'd succeeded and, thanks to his informant, Piers, too, knew Miss Mayberry's address.

Hillcrest by Highgate—that was where she lived and that's where the earl was now.

"Why are we here?"

Piers looked across the table at John Merrick. They were in the tearoom, after catching the last ten minutes of a dreary lecture on property laws and the married woman. He didn't think Jane Mayberry would have to worry about property laws if she married the earl. She'd be rich beyond her wildest dreams. And if Miss Mayberry was anything like the sober-faced women—no, ladies—who mobbed the tearoom, it would have to be marriage.

Either Castleton had taken leave of his senses or there was more to Jane Mayberry than he, Piers, had been led to believe.

Not that it mattered, because Castleton wouldn't be around to marry anyone.

"Well?" asked Merrick.

Piers swallowed a sigh. He'd invited John Merrick along tonight instead of Joseph, because Merrick looked the part of an English gentleman. He fitted in. But in other respects, he was a great disappointment. Everything had to be explained to him. Joseph would have understood intuitively that Castleton— his habits, his preferences, his women—had become an obsession with him.

"Whatever interests the earl interests me," Piers answered. "This is where the girl spends most of her time when she comes up to town. I want to take her impression from the company she keeps, and so on, and so on."

"And I," said Merrick sourly, "think we're wasting our time. What difference does it make what she's like? She's of interest to Castleton and that's what matters."

"Yes, but how interested is he? That's what intrigues me."

Before Merrick could add to his annoyance, Piers got up. "We're finished here," he said. "Shall we go?"

It wasn't an invitation, it was an order, and Merrick knew better than to argue with it.

In the hackney that was to take them to Piers's hotel for dinner, Merrick said, "Does this mean that we forget about La Contessa and Mrs. Standhurst?"

"What gave you that idea?"

"If the Mayberry woman is Castelton's new interest, why bother with the others?"

"To make a point. Don't worry about it, John. It's not necessary for you to understand. Castleton will understand. That's the main thing."

"What *is* the point?" Merrick's ill-humor was beginning to show.

"Chivalry." Piers smiled expansively. "Something the earl understands. You know what to do?"

"I know what to do. First La Contessa, then Mrs. Standhurst."

"Leave the Mayberry woman to me."

"Watch out for her dog. He can be vicious."

Piers laughed. "The dog will be the first casualty."

Chapter 8

*I*t was an old, familiar dream. Her parents were at the dining room table, and she was outside, watching them through the window, trying to attract their attention. She was frantic and a little angry. They knew she was there, but they hardly spared her a glance. They were involved in one of their passionate debates, arguing some point or other about the sermon they'd heard at church that morning. That was just like her parents. They forgot everything once one of their famous debates got going. They didn't feel her sense of urgency. Jack was after her. If he caught her, he would take her away then really hurt her. If they would only stop arguing and open the door, she could get inside and be safe.

It was too late. Jack's hand was on her shoulder, but when she turned to fight him off, it wasn't Jack

who stood there, but Castleton. Gray, gray eyes, a
predator's eyes, held her in an unwavering stare.

On a cry of alarm, she hauled herself up. Air
rushed in and out of her lungs. Her heart thundered
against her breasts. Long moments passed before she
came to herself.

It was ages since she'd had that dream. Now, there
was a twist to it. The earl was after her, too. She wasn't
naive. She understood only too well where that
thought came from. It was in the way he looked at
her, the way he spoke to her. He was deliberately trying to make her aware of him as a man. And he was
succeeding.

Damn! Damn! Damn!

She'd learned her lessons with Jack. Men, no matter how attractive or charming, couldn't help being
males. They were hunters. Women were their quarry.
When they caught them, they put them in cages.

She wasn't about to become any man's prey. She'd
escaped from one cage, and nothing could induce
her to enter another.

After several deep, calming breaths, she looked
around the room. The candle was burning low, but
the fire had been lit, giving off a warm glow. On the
hearth sat a porcelain water jug. Obviously, Mrs.
Trent had been here.

The clock on the mantel told her that she'd been
asleep for hours. It was long past bedtime. Her stomach felt painfully empty. Thinking about it, she realized she hadn't eaten since breakfast. She cocked her
head, listening. The house seemed deathly silent. It
was long past Mrs. Trent's bedtime, too, but she
wasn't sure if she could count on the earl going to bed
this early, and she didn't feel up to talking to him.

She wondered how Ben was doing. Her stomach

growled. That did it. She pushed back the eiderdown and got up.

She didn't take time to make herself presentable other than to wash her hands and face and brush the tangles out of her hair. Then, picking up the candle, she opened the door and walked downstairs.

There was a light spilling from under the kitchen door, but that was to be expected with Ben now using the kitchen as a bedchamber. The kitchen was always the warmest room in the house because the coal fire was never allowed to go out.

She pushed open the door and tiptoed in. Ben's makeshift bed had been pushed back to its alcove, and he appeared to be sleeping soundly. Moving as quietly as she could, she crossed to the bed. He didn't look feverish, but just to make sure, she touched a hand to his brow. It was warm, but nothing to worry about.

The lamp on the kitchen table was lit, so she blew out her candle, put it on the mantelpiece, and went to the larder. A few minutes later, she returned carrying a tray with a glass of milk on it, a thick crust of bread, and a slice of cheese. There was leftover game pie and baked ham if she'd wanted something more substantial, but she didn't think she'd get much sleep if she stuffed herself before going to bed. Besides, it was a matter of pride to make sure there was plenty on hand for the earl's breakfast.

When the door opened, she expected to see Mrs. Trent, come to check on Ben, but it was the earl who entered. He was wearing his greatcoat and it was covered in snow. Lance trooped in at his heels, and bounded over to her.

"So, you're awake," Case said, smiling faintly.

Startled, she watched him walk to the fireplace

carrying a huge scuttle of coal. He knelt down and, using the tongs, began to add lumps of coal to the fire.

"Now let me see if I've got Mrs. Trent's instructions right," he said. "To bank the fire for the night, I must add the coal, then the vegetable parings, and finally set the guard in front of the grate." As he spoke, he followed the housekeeper's instructions. "Have I got it right?" He glanced at Jane over his shoulder.

She stared at him wordlessly. An earl didn't bank the kitchen fire with vegetable parings. That was the job of the scullery maid, supposing there was a scullery maid.

"Jane?" he prompted, getting to his feet and throwing off his coat.

She was embarrassed and that annoyed her. "*You* shouldn't be doing this!"

"I told you I would take care of things, and I meant it. Besides, who is there to do it? Ben won't be able to haul and fetch for you for several days, not with that shoulder."

"You should have wakened me. Mrs. Trent and I are used to managing on our own. We don't haul coal in that scuttle. It's far too big and heavy. We use a pail." She raised her head, her eyes unfaltering on his. "You need not worry about Ben. Mrs. Trent and I know how to look after him."

He'd stung her pride, and that was the last thing he wanted to do. But someone had to put this woman right about a few things. "Frankly," he said, "it's not Ben I'm worried about but you. A woman on her own . . ." When her expression changed, he threw up his hands. "All right, all right. It's none of my business. I'm well aware of it. Believe me, I'm not finding fault. In fact, at the risk of sounding perverse, I have to say I admire what you've accomplished here."

And that was the truth. Of course, he knew a great deal more about her now than when he first arrived at her house. From what he could gather from the housekeeper, Jane Mayberry was the sole support of this little household. There had been very little money after her father died, and she'd tried her hand at various things before settling here about three years ago. The housekeeper had been circumspect, but all had become clear to him when he'd walked into Jane's study after dinner, at Mrs. Trent's behest, to fetch the decanter of brandy that was reserved for honored guests.

The papers he'd found strewn around her desk—and, of course, his curiosity got the better of him so he had to look—had astonished him. Jane Mayberry was a writer! There were pamphlets on women's suffrage and women's rights under the law, and articles dealing with a hodgepodge of subjects ranging from the sublime (Is God Female?) to the ridiculous (In Praise of Stays). But it was the piece on the corn laws and free trade that held his interest. He could almost hear Freddie giving his maiden speech in the House of Lords, when he'd astonished his friends with his grasp of a subject he'd never shown any interest in before. And Jane Mayberry just happened to be Sally Latham's friend.

When he made the connection, he'd wanted to laugh out loud. No wonder Freddie had been ill at ease when he, Case, started asking questions about Jane Mayberry. No wonder he'd blushed and protested he hardly knew the girl, much less where she lived. He was afraid of being found out. She'd written Freddie's speech or helped him to write it. That's how she earned her living. She was a professional writer, and a very successful one if this house was anything to go by. The house wasn't large by any means, but it was well kept and, as far as he could see, in good repair. The furniture was comfortable and well used but far from shabby. The coal cellar was well stocked as was the larder. Though he detected a good deal of thrift in how Jane Mayberry ordered her household, they wanted for nothing. It was impossible not to respect and admire her, and impossible not to be irritated by the very qualities he admired. She was too independent and too capable for a man's comfort, and he didn't know why he was smiling.

She cocked her head to one side, her eyes dark with suspicion. "Are you all right?"

"As right as I'll ever be," he replied, erasing his grin. "I think I'll join you." He patted his midriff. "All that hard labor has made me hungry. Would you mind?" He indicated the door to the larder.

"Not at all. Help yourself."

And he did, to the last slice of game pie, a fair chunk of the baked ham, a thick wedge of cheese, and a half loaf of bread. He deposited his plate on the kitchen table and returned to the larder. A moment later he was back with a jug in one hand, cutlery in the other, and a self-satisfied smile on his face.

"Marmalade tea," he told her, setting the jug down, "without the marmalade or tea."

He attacked his meal with all the gusto of a starving man. His hearty appetite made her own appetite fade considerably. Or maybe it was just his presence that made her ill at ease. At any rate, she picked at her cheese and bread, and forced each mouthful down with a swallow of milk.

She was beginning to feel comfortable when he suddenly looked up and pinned her with a hard stare. "Now," he said, "I want to hear all about Miss Drake.

I'm not asking out of idle curiosity. I think I'm entitled to know what I'm getting into."

Her worry over Ben had driven all thoughts of Emily from her mind. She couldn't see any point in evading the question. He must have worked most of it out by himself.

"Emily Drake," she said, "is Andrew Drake's sister. You may have heard of him, Drake and Mills, merchant bankers."

Case nodded. "I've heard the name."

"I don't know Mr. Drake personally," Jane continued, "but I know he's much older than Emily—she's his ward, by the way. He's extremely wealthy and thinks he can improve his social standing by buying into the aristocracy. That's where Emily comes in. He believes that money can buy her a title, and once she's elevated to the aristocracy, his own social standing will improve. Unfortunately, the only candidate to take the bait was Lord Reeve."

"And that's when Emily turned to you for help?"

She sighed and nodded. "Yes. You see . . ."

For the most part, he heard her out in silence. It was just as he thought. Such marriages were becoming more common. It was a business arrangement. He knew several impoverished peers of the realm who had swallowed their pride and married into the merchant classes. That was the trouble with entailed estates. One could live in a castle and be a pauper, and there was no selling off part of one's estates to fill the empty coffers. It was against the law.

Still, Andrew Drake should have done better for his sister than Lord Reeve.

When she paused, he said, "What I can't understand is why she felt she had to run away. Couldn't she simply say no to her brother, and no to Lord Reeve?"

Jane gave a snort of laughter. "I can't believe I'm hearing this! Are you naive or deliberately obtuse? She's eighteen years old. She has no money she can call her own. Her brother is her trustee. And because she's a female, her opinion counts for nothing. How can she withstand such pressure? Her only chance is to break free."

Though he could see her point, her derision was irritating. "I understand all that," he said, "but what I don't understand is how running away from her brother is going to solve the problem. How will she live? Who will look after her?" He looked around the cramped kitchen. "What exactly did you have in mind?"

"We thought that in a week or two her brother would come to his senses and take Emily's refusal seriously, or that Lord Reeve would retract his offer of marriage because he would hate to be made a laughingstock. Then, when everything was sorted out, Miss Drake would return home."

"And what if her brother didn't come round?"

"Then Emily could do what others have done before her—find employment, earn her own living. It would only be for a few years. When she turns twenty-one, she comes into her money."

"Earn her own living?" Gently bred girls didn't earn their own living. He didn't know whether to laugh or remonstrate. What stopped him from doing either was the sudden realization that the young woman sitting opposite him had done exactly that.

He wondered why she had never married.

"What?" she asked, her eyes narrowing suspiciously on his face.

He shrugged, "I suppose," he said, "Lady Octavia is the driving force behind this harebrained scheme?"

She visibly stiffened. "There's nothing harebrained about it! We've done it before and it's worked. As for Lady Octavia, she knows nothing about it, and if she had known, she would have tried to stop us. She can't afford to have the library mixed up in something like this. We might lose some of our influential backers, then we'd never get the laws changed. That's the most important thing—to change the laws. Until that happens, women will never have the right to make their own decisions and choose their own futures."

She gave a little sigh. "It's not that Lady Octavia is unsympathetic, you understand. I mean, there are always women in desperate straits coming to the library for help. We do what we can, but mostly, we just listen. If a woman leaves her husband, she has to give up everything—all her worldly goods and even her children. Few women will go that far, and we don't encourage it. Surely nothing could be worse than losing your children?"

He was interested in spite of himself. "What if there are no children in the marriage?"

"It's not much better. A woman's husband is not forced to support her or return any part of the money that came to him as her dowry if she leaves him. And if his wife finds employment, he can garnishee her wages so that she has no means of support."

"That's iniquitous!"

"True, but that's the law of the land." Eyes glinting, she rested her chin on her linked fingers. "You should come to our lectures, Lord Castleton. I think you'd find them enlightening, and we're always looking for wealthy patrons to support our cause."

He felt as though she had checkmated him, and maybe she had. "I don't need to attend the lectures," he said with a disarming smile. "All I need do is listen to you."

She looked at though she might take umbrage and surprised him by chuckling instead. "I *do* get carried away, don't I? But this work is important."

"So is parting with my money. Why do you need rich patrons?"

"Well, there's the library's expenses, of course, but most of the funds we raise go to support ordinary members of Parliament when they're seeking election. You see, the more members we help elect to the House of Commons, the more chance we have of having our views represented and legislation passed in our favor."

"That sounds like bribery to me!"

"Well, it is, I suppose. But, apparently, that's how the world works."

Her smile did not coax an answering smile from him. He'd always adopted a patronizing attitude to Lady Olivia and her league of ladies, and was just beginning to realize how mistaken he'd been. This wasn't a joke. These women weren't looking for a hobby to take up to pass the time of day. They were in deadly earnest.

He drummed his fingers on the table. "What happens with Miss Drake now?"

She blew out a long breath. "I'll have to let...my friends in town know how things turned out here, but there's not much they can do, except plead with Emily's brother to see reason. And I don't suppose Emily will have another chance to slip away. Short of murdering Lord Reeve, I don't see what else we can do."

He looked at her closely, then looked away. She was joking, of course. No use asking who else was in-

volved in the scheme, but he'd bet his last farthing
that Sally Latham was part of it. Not Freddie, though.
Freddie would never lend his support to anything
that would undermine the stability of a man's domes-
tic life, and he didn't have the imagination to see that
not all women were happy with the status quo. When
he thought about it, he wasn't much different from
Freddie.

He looked at her again. "This isn't the first time
you've done something like this, you say?"

"No, but I'm sure it will be the last for a long time
to come." She lifted her shoulders in a tiny shrug.
"You might say that my cover has been blown away.
Reeve knows my name now. He may tell others. It
won't be difficult to track me down, after all, you did.
No one can hide away here and feel safe. They'll have
to go somewhere else."

He suppressed the urge to ask her who "they"
were. He supposed she was referring to the women in
desperate straits who came to the library for help,
runaway wives, runaway heiresses, and the Lord only
knew who else. He didn't want to know their names
or anything about them in case his conscience
pricked him to do something about it.

The very thought gave him the shudders. He
didn't believe in meddling in other people's lives.
Miss Drake was a different case. It wasn't her youth
that roused his sympathies or the fact that this was to
be an arranged marriage and not a love match. It was
the thought of Lord Reeve that turned his stomach.
No innocent young girl should be paired with such a
vile specimen of humanity.

He spoke suddenly, startling her. "Let me handle
things with Mr. Drake. I think he will listen to reason

when he hears it from me rather than—you'll forgive my bluntness—from a woman."

Her first impulse was to refuse. She was used to fixing her own problems. But he was right. His words would carry more weight than hers. He was an earl and she was a mere woman, a nobody in men's eyes.

"Thank you," she said, and managed a smile. "Just be careful that you don't fill the empty slot that is left by Lord Reeve."

He grinned. "I'm an expert at evading the parson's mousetrap."

She didn't doubt it.

They'd both finished eating. Harmony reigned. It was an excellent time to get rid of him, for in spite of this cozy conversation, she still felt wary in his presence. He made her feel like a woman and that unsettled her.

"I'll see to things down here," she said, getting up. "You've done enough, more than enough. You should turn in for the night."

"No. I'm bedding down here in front of the fire. I promised Mrs. Trent I would watch over Ben. Why don't you leave Lance, to keep me company."

On hearing his name, Lance got up from the hearth and trotted over to Case. "I'd swear," said Case, "that dog understands king's English."

She laughed. "I've often wondered. But like most males, he can be obtuse when he wants to be. I will say that he's an excellent guard dog, and as a sheepdog, he has no equal."

She sounded like a mother extolling the virtues of her favorite son. Amused, Case said, "How did you get hold of him? I mean, why a sheepdog?"

As she spoke, she stacked the dishes and the remains of their meal on a wooden tray. "I was visiting

Scotland, a small place called Aboyne not far from Aberdeen. You've probably never heard of it."

"Well, I know of Aberdeen. That's where my sister is right now, to meet her husband's parents. It's on the coast, isn't it?"

"Yes, but Aboyne is inland, nestled in the hills on the banks of the river Dee. It's a beautiful spot. I was out walking and Lance appeared out of nowhere. He followed me home." Her eyes were on Lance as she spoke and a shadow of a smile touched her lips. "He didn't look anything like he looks now. He was emaciated and had obviously been beaten. A few days later, I heard that a valuable sheepdog had gone missing, and the description fitted Lance. Naturally, my first thought was to return him to his owner. However," she made a face, "when I met the owner, I took an instant dislike to him. He thinks nothing of beating his dogs. In fact, that's how he trains them. So all I told him was that I'd seen a dog fitting his dog's description near the church at Crathie. I left Aboyne the next day, and Lance went with me."

"You *stole* him?"

"I rescued him!"

"I know about sheepdogs and I bet he was worth a lot of money."

"I could hardly offer to pay for him without letting his owner know that I had him. And what if he'd said no? Then he'd have taken Lance away from me and beaten him for running away. I wasn't going to let that happen."

"No," he said slowly. "I don't suppose you would. You seem to have an affinity for runaways."

A flicker of something came and went in her eyes. "True," she said, "and I make no apology for it."

He couldn't put a foot right with this woman.

She'd gone all prickly on him again. As she marched to the larder with the tray in her arms, he got up and went after her. She had to wait until he opened the door for her.

He was still holding the door as she tried to leave. Whatever he was about to say died unsaid. She was looking up at him, the light from the kitchen playing across her face, sculpting her cheekbones, casting shadows on her impossibly wide eyes. When his gaze moved to her lips, they parted. Her skirts brushed his legs; he could feel the warmth of her body, the soft catch of each breath.

His eyes jerked up to meet hers. *What is it about this woman?* he wondered.

One hand cupped her chin. "This was inevitable, Jane," he murmured. "You know it as well as I."

He'd caught her off guard, and before she could brace herself, heat from his hand sent shock waves to every pulse point in her body. She was stunned. She shouldn't be feeling like this. She should be immune. Why wasn't she immune?

As his head descended, her whole body went rigid. "I want you to leave." Her voice was hoarse. She jerked herself free, took a few steps into the kitchen, and turned to face him. "I want you to leave," she repeated. She wished she could even her breathing.

He studied her for a moment, his head to one side, then he said slowly, "You're overreacting, and I'm asking myself why."

She felt a flash of alarm, but managed to inject ice into her voice. "I didn't do anything to encourage you."

"Didn't you? Admit it, Jane. You're as curious about me as I am about you."

The lazy smile made her temper simmer. "I think,"

she said, "that you are confusing me with Amelia Standhurst. Correct me if I'm wrong, but a few nights ago, she was the lady you were curious about?"

She sensed the quick surge of temper. Anger was useful and less to be feared than intimacy. She pressed home her point. "And not long before that, it was La Contessa, I believe."

He arched one brow. "You've been prying into my private life. I'm flattered."

"You don't have a private life! You're a celebrity!" She tried not to clench her teeth. "Everybody knows about you and your women."

When he advanced toward her, she held her ground. His clever gray eyes scanned her face, weighing, assessing. "You're a narrow-minded prude."

She replied coolly, "I'm careful to avoid..."

"Temptation?"

Her voice was sharper than she intended. "Men I don't know!"

Another lazy grin. "Like it or not, we're going to get to know each other very well. As I told you, it's inevitable."

Her voice rose a notch. "You—"

He put a finger to his lips, silencing her. "Hush. Keep your voice down or you'll waken Ben."

She glanced at the bed and saw that Ben was moving restlessly. She looked back at the earl. In a low, driven tone, she said, "I want you to leave."

"I know you do." He smiled faintly. "But I'm afraid it's impossible. What you don't seem to realize is that it hasn't stopped snowing since you went upstairs for your nap. It's a blizzard out there. I don't think I'll be going anywhere for the next little while. So you see, we're bound to get to know each other better."

She didn't bother looking out the window. She believed him.

Before she could annihilate him with a few well-chosen words, he said pleasantly, "I suggest we treat each other civilly or Ben and Mrs. Trent will get the wrong idea about us. They might even think we've had a lovers' tiff."

When she left, she closed the door with a decided snap.

Case waited until her steps had receded before he lit a cheroot and wandered outside to smoke it. Lance went with him. It was still snowing, but the porch gave them some shelter. After blowing out a stream of smoke, Case said, "She did overreact, didn't she? I'm right about that?"

No response from Lance.

"Most women are flattered by my attentions."

Most women, of course, were too easily impressed by his title and wealth. That wouldn't signify to a woman like Jane Mayberry. His eyes narrowed against the smoke he exhaled. After a moment, he smiled. She was direct to the point of rudeness, opinionated, contradictory, argumentative, and passionate about her beliefs. Principles, he supposed she would call them. And, in spite of all that, he was captivated.

What made her so different?

Life hadn't been easy for Jane Mayberry since her father died. Who told him that? Lady Octavia? He might have agreed with her, except that he didn't think Jane considered herself hard done to. She lived with the kind of courage and passion that he found himself envying. The trouble was, she assumed too many burdens for her thin shoulders, burdens he felt oddly compelled to take upon himself. And it seemed to him that she'd been glad to have him along today.

A look came over her, anxious, searching, and he had the strongest urge to gather her in his arms and tell her he would take care of everything.

There was something else that appealed to him. When he was with her, he felt the cynical part of his nature quietly fade away.

He gazed into space, lost in thought. He was remembering Jane as he'd seen her at the opera. That vision did not fit with the young woman he'd met at the library and now here. There was more, much more to this little prude than blue stockings and lost causes. And why had she buried herself out here?

He wanted to know all about her; he wanted to know all her secrets.

Then what? How far was he willing to go? With a woman like Jane Mayberry, it would have to be marriage or nothing.

Pity.

He flicked the end of his cheroot into the shrubbery and let out a low laugh. He was getting ahead of himself. Whatever was between Jane and him would have to wait. He had to focus all his energies on finding Gideon Piers and finishing the job he'd been given years ago in Spain.

No quarter asked or given.

He thought about Spain for a long time.

After a while, he looked at Lance. "Come on, boy. Let's patrol the area and make sure that everything is right and tight for your mistress."

The dog bounded forward, the man following in his wake.

Chapter 9

*T*hough Case was a member of some of the most exclusive gentlemen's clubs in and around St. James, he and his friends preferred to meet in Bell's Hotel. In the taproom, on the ground floor, they could rub shoulders with the theater crowd, and in the upper rooms, they could gamble a little or order a dinner of plain English fare in one of the hotel's comfortable private parlors. It was here that they planned their annual reunion of former Etonians and friends, a reunion that Case's father, the duke, always hosted at Twickenham House. This year, a problem had arisen. The reunion had to be postponed when the guest of honor became gravely ill. Now it was slated to take place the week before Christmas.

After consuming a splendid dinner of soft roes of mackerel baked in butter, Case's group of friends began to break up. Most of them idled their way to the gaming rooms just across the hall, leaving a committee of three, comprising Case and two companions, to make all the arrangements for the reunion.

Case listened to his friends' suggestions with one part of his mind, but another part was occupied with thoughts of Jane. He'd found a man to help out, but he could only spare a few hours every other day, and he was wondering how she had managed these last few days with Ben to care for and all the chores now falling on her. That last morning, he'd done as much as he could to lighten her load: he'd hauled in coal; taken care of the horses; retrieved the buggy; and seen to Ben's most basic needs. He'd rolled up his sleeves and worked as hard as any common laborer—he, a duke's son and heir! And was she impressed? Of course she wasn't! He hadn't done a damn thing she couldn't do herself.

To be fair though, a look would come into her eyes that gave the lie to her prickly words. Jane's eyes always told the truth, and they told him she was glad that he was there.

He wondered if she understood why she became prickly whenever he came into her orbit.

He looked up when someone tapped him on the arm.

"This isn't funny, Case."

"What?"

"I don't believe you've heard a word I've said."

The speaker was Waldo Bowman, tall and sparse, whose harsh, angular features were softened by a half-smile. The smile was, in fact, the result of a bayonet wound he had sustained at Talavera. Most of Case's friends had served in the Spanish Campaign.

Case stirred himself to respond. "I heard you,

Waldo. Something about inviting Dr. Keate to be our next guest of honor." He looked up with a smile. "As I remember, when I was at Eton, that old scoundrel terrified us boys."

"Only the boys who broke the rules," retorted Waldo, "and you seemed to think that rules were made to be broken."

"Didn't we all at that age?"

Robert Shay, the third man at the table, who was not only Case's closest friend but also a distant cousin, handed round his snuff box. He was as fair as Case was dark, and though not as handsome as his cousin, arresting in his own way. His eyes were his best feature, dark blue, thick lashed, and with a keen intelligence lurking in their depths.

"Let's be honest," he said. "Flogging never hurt any of us. And poor old Keate has dedicated his whole life to the thankless task of educating generations of stupid, ignorant boys like us. He should have been made provost, but as far as I know, there has never been as much as a dinner to mark his long service. Let's do it, and let's throw in a purse as well."

"That settles it, then," said Waldo. "Dr. Keate it is. Case, you'll ask your father if our arrangements will suit him?"

Case said, "I'm sure they will. There's nothing much happening at Twickenham House these days, with Rosamund in Scotland and Justin in Italy. My father always looks forward to these reunions."

"Yes," said Robert, "I believe he does. Even when we were boys, he always gave us a warm welcome. I used to love going to Twickenham House. Speaking of the good old days, where is Freddie?"

"He said he'd be late," Waldo replied. "And Case, if Keate can't make it, find someone to take his place."

"Why me?" asked Case. "Why not you or Robert?"

"Because," said Waldo, "we all have our jobs to do. I'm looking after the invitations, and Robert is looking after the wine list and menu." He looked at Robert.

Robert, who was the dandy of the group and considered a connoisseur, gave an exaggerated bow. "I wouldn't trust that task to anyone else. You Philistines—"

"Yes, yes, we know," said Waldo pleasantly. "We Philistines don't know the difference between piss and port. I had a sergeant who used to say much the same thing, only with him it was that we greenhorn officers couldn't tell the difference between our elbows and our arses."

"Your sergeant," said Robert, "sounds like my valet. Everything worth knowing, I learned from Dobbs."

Case shook his head and Waldo laughed. Robert Shay was one of their few close friends who had not served with them in Spain. No one held it against him because he was the only surviving son, and if he died, the title would die with him, a catastrophe that no blue-blooded family could possibly accept. Duty to family came before everything,

It wasn't Robert's way, however, to brood over things or chafe at the bit, or even to explain himself to friends or strangers. If anyone asked him pointedly why he, a young man, had not done his duty to king and country by serving with Wellington, he invariably replied that he would have done so gladly if he could have taken his valet along with him. He simply did not know how to dress himself.

It was all posturing, this pretense of being a dandy. It always amused him, Robert said, when people took him seriously when he didn't take himself seriously.

In the real world, however, Robert took himself very seriously. He was a highly successful barrister, and in a court of law, he became a different man entirely.

Waldo got up. "If we're finished here, I think I'll try my luck at the gaming tables."

As Waldo limped awkwardly to the door, Robert called out, "And stay out of trouble, especially the kind that comes in petticoats!"

Waldo laughed. "Can I help it if the ladies adore me?"

After Waldo left, Robert said, "It must be hard for him. There wasn't an athlete like him at Eton or Oxford."

Case shrugged. "I can't see that a lame leg has made much difference to Waldo except that he doesn't cut a fine figure on the dance floor now."

"That's not what I mean. The war has changed him. He disappears for a month at a time, drinking himself into oblivion, then suddenly turns up as though he's still the same old Waldo."

"That's the thing about war," said Case. "It changes people. No. I don't want to talk about it, except to say that it was a brutal, vicious business and I'm glad to be out of it."

When Case said nothing more, Robert reached for the brandy decanter and topped up their glasses. After a moment or two, he said, "Yet feeling like that, you stayed on for the duration of the war when you might have sold out and come home."

"True, but I became attached to my men and that would have been tantamount to deserting them. Besides, I was a good soldier."

"You liked the discipline?"

"Good Lord no! I liked winning."

Robert laughed and relaxed into his chair. "That

sounds like you. I suppose that's why you're so determined to pursue your investigation of the Hyde Park murder. How are things progressing, by the way?"

The progress was all in his mind. He was, however, beginning to develop a theory. Planning the reunion tonight had given him something to think about. They'd postponed the reunion when their guest speaker fell ill. He wondered if that had made a difference to Piers's plans. He hadn't understood why Piers had taken so long after killing Collier to come after him. The attack on Harper proved the game was on again. Was it changing the date of the reunion that made the difference? Is that why Piers had held off? Because he'd started the game too soon? How long could he sustain a game of cat-and-mouse?

If his theory was right, then he knew the day and the hour Piers would strike.

It was only a theory, unsubstantiated, and too farfetched to share with a skeptic like Robert. Robert, like Freddie, was of the opinion that the murder of John Collier was an isolated act of revenge by someone who knew Piers's methods. He hadn't told them about the attack on Harper. And he wouldn't until he had more to go on. Waldo was different. He'd taken him into his confidence because Waldo had been a member of the crack unit that had tracked Piers to his lair in St. Michel. At least Waldo kept an open mind on whether or not Piers was alive and bent on revenge.

"We're still at the stage of gathering information."

Robert snorted. "Spoken like a typical Special Branch agent. In other words, it's none of my business. I'm not offended. As an officer of the court, I've used those words, or words very like them, on more occasions than I care to remember. So, there's no progress. That doesn't surprise me."

Case was saved the trouble of a reply, when a burst of laughter from across the hall had both men turning to look at the open door.

"Waldo seems to be enjoying himself," Case observed.

"There's a new girl at the Hazard table and he's taken a fancy to her." Robert shrugged. "You know Waldo. He becomes the life and soul of the party when there's a pretty girl to be won. Which reminds me—" A smile played about his lips. "What's this my grandmother has been telling me, that she and your aunt are to sponsor a young woman in society? Who is Emily Drake, and what is she to you, Case?"

The question surprised Case. He'd talked to his aunt about Miss Drake only that morning, giving her the essential facts of the girl's predicament, and inveigling her help in enlarging the circle of Miss Drake's friends. This was the strategy that he and Jane had agreed to before he left Highgate, supposing his aunt was willing to take the girl up. The idea was to persuade Mr. Drake that his sister would meet eligible young men who would be more to her taste than Lord Reeve. Case hadn't anticipated that he might be counted as a possible suitor.

No wonder the girl's brother had accepted his offer with alacrity.

"You can take that smile off your face," he told Robert. "I've never met the girl, nor do I wish to," and he went on to explain the situation as he'd explained it to his aunt.

When there was a silence, Robert said, "I don't see how a Season in town will help Miss Drake's situation, not if her brother is determined to marry her off to Lord Reeve."

"Her brother," said Case, "has had a change of

heart. A very reasonable fellow is Mr. Drake. I saw him yesterday, and when I explained the situation, he grasped my point at once."

"Mmm. What threats did you use to get him to turn his back on a title?"

"I'm not so uncouth as that. And quite honestly, I think Mr. Drake's motives have been misunderstood. As I said, he seems a reasonable fellow."

Robert picked up his snuff box, looked at it, and put it down again. "Filthy habit, snuff taking," he said. "Can't think why I indulge in it."

"Keeping up appearances?"

"Quite. Every self-respecting dandy knows his snuff. Can you spare one of your thin cigars?"

When they were smoking companionably, Robert said, "I hope Mr. Drake isn't superstitious."

"Oh? Why?"

"I would think that would be obvious. First La Contessa, then your latest conquest, Mrs. Standhurst." Robert's eyes brightened with laughter. "Don't look so surprised. You didn't think you could keep Mrs. Standhurst a secret for long? Too many people saw you leave the opera with the beautiful Amelia on your arm. And now Miss Drake. As I said, I hope her brother isn't superstitious."

Case wasn't interested in bandying words with Robert. A shadow had touched him and he frowned. "First La Contessa, then Mrs. Standhurst—what are you talking about, Robert?"

"You mean, you haven't heard? Where have you been these last few days?"

"Highgate. The Horse Guards. What haven't I heard?"

Observing the change in his friend, Robert said seriously, "I thought you knew. La Contessa's house was broken into. Nothing was taken, but the thieves terrorized her and tortured her cat in front of her eyes. Then last night, thieves broke into Mrs. Standhurst's place. She wasn't there, and the only thing they stole was her lap dog. It hasn't been recovered yet. I'm sorry I spoke. My joke was in bad taste."

Case was on his feet. "Excuse me," he said. "There is something I must do."

When he got over his shock, Robert jumped up and went after him. "Hold on, I'm coming with you."

They met Waldo in the corridor. "What is it?" he asked.

"All I know is we're going to Highgate," said Robert.

Waldo turned around and went after his friends.

Something jerked Jane awake. She lay for a long time, ears straining, listening. "Lance," she whispered.

The cold night air came through the open window and ruffled the muslin drapes. Outside, the wind sighed through the branches of the fir trees close by the house. Other than that, nothing.

Something had wakened her. And why had her first thought been of Lance?

Alarmed now, she got out of bed and crossed to the window. Lance had the freedom of the house and yard. He could come and go as he pleased by means of the old coal shaft in the disused cellar under the kitchen. Tonight, he'd been restless. He hadn't wanted to come inside. She'd thought he'd caught the scent of a fox or badger, and once he'd chased it off, he would return to the house. If that was the case, he'd be in her room, or scratching to get in.

What had she heard that alarmed her? A howl? A moan? Where was Lance?

On that thought, she opened the window wide, meaning to call him, but a door banged off to her right, the stable door, and she was distracted. She'd shut that door herself before retiring for the night. Then who had opened it, and why wasn't Lance barking an alarm? Then she smelled smoke, and her fear turned to dread.

"Ben!" she yelled. "Ben!"

She got her pistol from the dresser, checked it, then raced into the corridor. Ben's room was at the top of the stairs. His voice came to her out of the darkness. "What is it?" He sounded groggy.

"Get dressed and get the blunderbuss."

"Why?" He was instantly awake.

"I think we have visitors. Gypsies. Tinkers. And I think they may have hurt Lance."

She delayed at the front door only long enough to don her boots and greatcoat, then she was through the door and racing down the incline toward the stable. It had rained in the last day or two and the snow had turned to a muddy slush, making the path treacherous, but Jane didn't care. Not a sound from Lance, but she could hear her horses whinnying in panic, and their panic as well as the choking stench of smoke sent an ice-cold chill along her spine.

She wasn't thinking about gypsies or tinkers or that she might be in danger when she slammed into the stable door. Her one thought was to get her animals out of there. She put her gun in her pocket and used both hands to drag back the door. As air rushed in, flames enveloped one wall and licked along the roof. The horses went wild. On the floor was Lance, in a pool of blood.

As Jane started forward, she was hit from behind, and fell to her knees. A hand covered her mouth, muffling her scream, and she was yanked back on her heels. The voice that came from behind her did not belong to the man who was restraining her.

"It would have been better for you, Miss Mayberry, if you'd slept a little longer. Put her out of her misery, but don't hit her too hard."

The man who had spoken began to close the door she'd opened. Rage and terror engulfed her, just as the fire engulfed another wall. She sensed the blow coming and bit down on her assailant's hand, on the fleshy part of his thumb. He wasn't wearing gloves and she tasted his blood. When he yelled and relaxed his grip, she tore out of his grasp and rolled clear.

As she came up, with her pistol in her hand, several things happened at once. Ben, who had stopped halfway down the incline, yelled to the men to be gone or he would blow their brains out. The stable door burst open and Razor charged out with Daisy at his heels. If the men who had attacked her hadn't jumped clear, the horses would have run them down. Smoke billowed out of the stable.

It was now or never.

Screaming at Ben to keep the men covered, she pocketed her pistol, dropped to her hands and knees, and began to crawl toward the spot where she'd last seen Lance. The heat was intense. In those few, agonized seconds it took her to find him, she heard the blunderbuss go off. Someone yelled out a stream of curses in Spanish, then nothing. Her hair was scorched, her eyes and lungs burned. There was no air to breathe, so she held her breath. She didn't know where she got the strength, but she gathered her dog in her arms, not knowing whether he was alive or dead, and she dragged him outside, well clear of the stable that was turning into an inferno.

She stayed as she was for several moments, crouched over Lance, gulping air into her lungs. When she could breathe again, and her eyes cleared, she saw Ben, sitting up as she was, with Mrs. Trent helping him to rise. She couldn't see her horses, but she could hear them whinnying beyond the stand of firs. There was no sign of the thugs who had set the stable on fire.

Eyes tearing, she looked down at Lance. His thick, tawny fur was matted with blood from one shoulder to his chest. She choked back a sob, then another and brushed the tears from her eyes with the sleeve of her greatcoat. The next sob stuck in her throat. Was she imagining things or had Lance moved?

"Lance?" She put her bare hand on his side. "Lance?"

A shudder ran through him, then another. He exhaled a wheezy, coughing breath, but his eyes did not open.

A moment before, Jane did not have the strength to rise. Now, she jumped up and stripped off her greatcoat. "Lance is alive!" she cried out. "Help me, Mrs. Trent. Help me carry him into the house. We'll use my coat as a stretcher."

Chapter 10

*T*hey could smell the smoke when they entered Highgate. Though it wasn't long after midnight, there were few lights at any of the windows. The residents evidently kept country hours, so there was no one about to tell them where the fire was, and no telltale streak of red lighting up the horizon. Not that any of this mattered to Case. Fire or no fire, he knew where he was going.

He did not slacken his pace, and Robert and Waldo, sensing his mood, exchanged nary a word as they rode after him. All they'd been told was that they could well be closing in on Gideon Piers, so they should expect trouble.

When they left Highgate behind, a fine ash wrapped around them like a North Sea fog, unsettling the horses and making Case and his friends turn up their coat collars to keep the worst of the fog out of their lungs. It was a treacherous ride, but the farther they got from Highgate, the more lights they saw winking at windows, and they could follow the road by following the lights.

Suddenly there were lanterns everywhere, and men with kerchiefs covering the lower half of their faces, forming a line from the well to the smoldering ruin that was once the stable. They were passing buckets of water from hand to hand to douse the embers. Case called out to the man who seemed to be in charge.

"Where is Miss Mayberry?"

"Up at the house. She's had a fright, but she's fine."

Case let out a long, pent-up breath. "Are you the constable?" he asked.

After a quick appraising look at Case, the man in charge seemed to realize he was in the presence of a gentleman of rank. "Constable John Turnbull," he replied respectfully. He was a square, thickset man who was also, he told Case, steward of the Lauderdale estate. "Everything around here belongs to the estate," he said, "even the men I've brought with me. It's too bad about the barn, but by the time we got here, it was too late to save it. The horses got out, so that's something. We have Miss Mayberry to thank for that."

Case hadn't realized that Jane rented the house. He'd just assumed that she owned it.

"And the dog?"

"He looked in a bad way to me. Miss Mayberry can tell you." He shook his head. "I never saw such a fuss about a dog."

"How did the fire get started?" asked Waldo.

"Gypsies most likely," replied Turnbull. "Or young bucks from town with nothing better to do than set fire to barns and terrorize innocent people. If I catch them . . ." He left his words hanging in the air and ran to help a man who seemed to have fainted.

"Have a look around and see what you can find out," Case told his friends.

As Case walked his horse to the hitching post, Robert edged his mount closer to Waldo's. "Who is Miss Mayberry?" he asked quietly.

"I haven't the faintest idea. What I'd like to know is how Case knew that something was about to happen here tonight."

Robert thought back on the conversation he'd had with Case at the Bell. La Contessa. Amelia Standhurst. Emily Drake. "It was something I said. So it's true. This Piers fellow really is out for revenge."

"We'll talk later," said Waldo.

Case halted at the kitchen door and took in the room at a glance. Ben was in a chair and looked to be in a bad way. His face was screwed up in pain as a gentleman, the doctor most likely, bound the arm his patient had dislocated only a few days before. Jane was sitting at the kitchen table, hands extended, palms up, while Mrs. Trent anointed them with a salve. Her ministrations seemed to give more pain to the housekeeper than to Jane, for it was Mrs. Trent who winced and sniffed back tears.

"Jane," he said softly.

At the sound of his voice, she turned her head, and when recognition dawned, gave him a look that belied her tart words. "I didn't expect to see you again."

She was wrapped in a woolen dressing gown that was blackened by ash; her hair was scorched, her face was daubed with soot. She would have to be the one, of course, who entered the blazing building to rescue her animals. His sympathy began to waver until he remembered her dog.

"What happened to Lance?"

Maybe he spoke too harshly, or maybe she sensed his change of mood, for the welcoming look vanished, and she said without elaboration, "He's under the table."

"He's not dead!"

His shocked expression softened her considerably. "No. The doctor gave him poppy juice."

Mrs. Trent choked back tears. "Oh, your lordship," she said, her voice cracking, "thank God you're here."

The doctor was looking at Case curiously. "The dog will be fine," he said, "though he'll need constant care for the next little while. A nasty knife wound." He patted his shoulder to indicate where Lance had been stabbed. "I'm Dr. Harvard, by the way."

"Castleton," said Case. "How do you do?"

The doctor inclined his head in acknowledgment. He was a robust man of perhaps fifty, with ruddy cheeks and strong, capable hands. He looked as though he smiled a lot.

Case sank to his haunches and examined Lance. The doctor had shaved the fur around the wound, but beyond that, there was little to see. A bandage covered his handiwork, and where the fur hadn't been shaved, there were singe marks and the unavoidable soot.

He got up, dusted a film of ash from the chair opposite Jane's, and sat down. "He's a very lucky dog," he said.

The doctor was still regarding him speculatively.

Realizing that some explanation of his turning up in the middle of the night was necessary if Jane's reputation was to be safeguarded, Case said, "My friends and I were dining in Highgate when we heard about the fire. Since I'm acquainted with Miss Mayberry, through my aunt, I decided to come and offer my assistance." He looked at Jane. "Now tell me what happened. The constable seems to think that gypsies were responsible."

"They were *not* gypsies," she said. "One of them spoke Spanish, though the constable is sure it must have been Romany, and the other had a..." she paused, trying to bring the memory into focus, "not a cultured accent, but...I know it sounds strange... but no accent at all."

Case knew why she was puzzled. In England, one couldn't open one's mouth without betraying one's origins. Jane had an educated accent with just a hint of Scotland in it. Mrs. Trent and Ben had the Scottish monotone, in their case uneducated, that placed them firmly on the east coast. There was no doubt in his mind that the doctor had been educated at one of the better public schools. His own accent would best be described as cultured. It was an intolerable state of affairs, but a man's accent could well be the deciding factor in whether doors opened for him or were firmly shut in his face.

"What did he say to you?"

"He knew my name, and that surprised me. And he said it was a pity I hadn't slept a little longer. Oh, yes, and he told the other man, the one who cursed in Spanish, to put me out of my misery, but not to hit me too hard." She positively bristled. "I didn't think of it at the time, but now I see that it was Lance and the horses they wanted to kill, not me."

The doctor said, "It's a strange business. Gypsies would steal horses, not kill them."

Case nodded. "Would you recognize these men again?" he asked Jane.

"No. Everything happened too quickly."

"Start at the beginning," he said gently, "and leave nothing out."

It took Jane, Mrs. Trent, *and* the doctor to flesh out the story for him, with Ben occasionally rousing himself to add a few words. No one mentioned a pebble. There was no need. He understood that there would be no more pebbles from now on, only a tide of rising violence, shades of the past when Piers played his tricks to demonstrate how vastly superior he was to any man.

She'd been lucky, he thought, damn lucky. If the horses hadn't bolted, and if Ben hadn't let off that shot...He looked down at the burns on her hands, now beginning to blister, and he unconsciously took a long swallow of marmalade tea from a cup that someone must have put in his hand without him noticing.

The doctor was speaking. He'd been out at a deathbed watch, he said, and was returning home when he saw the fire. No, he didn't see the men who started it. He'd wakened a neighbor and sent him to get help.

He got up and said he had to go. "Wear white cotton gloves at all times," he told Jane. "And don't use your hands till those blisters have healed or they could turn septic. As for you, young man," to Ben, "ah, he's fallen asleep. I'm worried about that arm. It took quite a wallop when the gun went off." He looked at Mrs. Trent. "Don't let him use it until I say otherwise. Would you mind showing me out?" And bidding everyone a cheery goodnight, he left the room with Mrs. Trent.

Case, who'd risen at the doctor's exit, sat down again. He watched in silence as Jane struggled to pull a cotton glove over the fingers of one hand, then, when she winced, he took the glove away from her.

"These gloves are no good," he said. "Look at them! They're smeared with soot."

"They're clean on the inside, and that's what matters."

She would have started over, but he took her wrists in a loose clasp and pulled her hands toward him. She didn't struggle, but sat there passively as he examined the burns and blisters she'd sustained when she'd dragged Lance from the barn.

"These look painful," he said softly.

"Well, they are, though at the time, I didn't feel anything."

He looked up. Their eyes held. She'd never been closer to weeping. Then his expression changed and he let her wrists go.

"You could have died in that inferno." Just thinking about it stirred the incipient fear—and anger—making his voice harsher than he knew. "I know Lance means a lot to you, but no animal is worth a human life."

"I didn't debate whether I should save him. He was there, just a few feet inside the door. How could I leave him? I didn't think about it."

He got up and began to pace. "Oh, no, you wouldn't leave Lance, but you left a frightened boy all alone with those fiends. They could have locked you in the barn and turned on him and on Mrs. Trent too." Just thinking about it made him want to yell at her.

"What would you have had me do?"

"What any normal woman would do. Back off and—"

"Don't be ridiculous," she interjected, as angry as he. "Ben was armed. I told you the men scattered when the horses came thundering through the doors. Lance was only a few feet away from me. I had to save him. But that's not why you're angry, is it? You knew something was going to happen. That's why you're here. I don't believe the story you told of dining with friends in Highgate. You know who set fire to the stable, and you feel guilty. Who was it? Who?"

She was right up to a point. He did feel guilty. But that's not why he was angry. This woman didn't seem to be afraid of anything, and that could be fatal with someone like Gideon Piers. But, of course, she hadn't known whom she was dealing with, or how vicious he could be. If Piers ever began to think of her as an enemy...

He breathed deeply and turned to face her. "I think the man without an accent is Gideon Piers. I think he started the fire. The message wasn't for you but for me." He paused, studying her. "You don't look surprised."

Her brow was knit in a frown. "I *am* surprised, but I'm not shocked. I've been wondering about Gideon ever since you questioned Letty about him. He was missing in action, that's what the letter said, but his body was never found. Is he La Roca?"

"I'm afraid so."

"But why would he want to hurt *me*? That's what doesn't make sense. Couldn't it have been someone else?"

He sat down again. "I know it was Piers," he said, "because you're not the only victim connected to me."

He knew she was too quick to accept evasions, so he told her about La Contessa and Amelia, then worked back to Spain when he and Piers first crossed paths. He told her how he'd tracked Piers for months before finding his hideout. "I'll spare you the details," he said, "but our cat-and-mouse game evolved into..." he smiled fleetingly, "a duel, you might say, between the two of us. Honor could only be satisfied with the death of one or the other. I thought Piers was dead until Collier's body turned up in Hyde Park with a pebble in his pocket."

When she stared at him mutely, he went on. "He likes to play games, Jane. That's all this was tonight, an elaborate game to punish me."

She heaved a sigh. "I'm too tired to take this in. It seems so far-fetched."

"Jane," he said gently, "believe it. Why do you think I knew to come here tonight?"

When she shook her head, he said, "From now on, I want you to be on your guard. This man is truly dangerous." And to drive home his point, he told her about the attack on Harper. "He might have killed Harper or you or the others."

"Why didn't he?"

"I don't know, but I do know that so many deaths would have galvanized Special Branch into combing the country for him. That wouldn't suit Piers, not until he's won and I'm dead. Oh, don't look so stricken. It won't happen. He's not nearly as clever as he thinks he is."

There was something in his tone of voice, something in his expression that she found chilling. But at last he'd convinced her. It must be Gideon. As her focus shifted to Piers and the attack on her, the memory of her terror and sense of helplessness filled her with rage.

"What is it, Jane?"

She looked up at him. "I used to feel sorry for Gideon, but no longer! I had a clear shot at him tonight, and I hesitated. Well, I won't hesitate to shoot him if he tries to terrorize me again."

He had been lounging in his chair, but at her words, he straightened. She sounded as though she meant it. "You'd be dead before you pulled the trigger. I mean it, Jane. You were lucky tonight."

"Well, I don't feel lucky, and I bet La Contessa— what a silly name—and Mrs. Standhurst don't feel lucky either. I almost lost Lance." She put a hand down to touch her dog, remembered the burns on her hands, and pulled back a little. "And I would have lost my horses if it hadn't been for Razor. You might say he saved the day." She was becoming maudlin and sniffed. "He always looks out for himself, you know. And Daisy, well, she's just a follower. That's what saved her. I shall never complain about Razor again."

He smiled. "Yes, he did well tonight."

"But what I can't understand is why Piers chose me. I mean, I can understand why he chose your mistresses, but why me?"

"He must know that I've spent a night or two here, and he's drawn his own conclusions."

She let out a huff of breath. "Every man and his dog knows you spent two nights here. There are no secrets in the country. They know about Lord Reeve and Emily too. The vicar came to call the day after you left. They think I'm a fallen woman."

He suppressed a smile. "What did you tell the vicar?"

She made a face. "I told him the truth, but I don't think he believed me."

"Leave it to me. I'll make him believe you."

She sucked in a breath. "Anything you could do would only make matters worse." She stared directly into his eyes. "And your coming here tonight hasn't helped. Heaven only knows what my neighbors will make of that."

His shrug was barely perceptible. "Don't lecture me about gossip. I've lived with it all my life." Now it was he who stared directly into her eyes. "Don't be too quick to believe all you hear."

There was a challenge in his eyes, but she was too worn out to respond to it. "Gossip is the least of my worries right now," she said.

"What will you do?"

She looked around the kitchen—at Ben's sleeping form, at Lance, who was now snoring softly, and finally at her blistered hands. "We'll manage. We always do."

The words were hollow. She didn't see how they could manage with only Mrs. Trent to do all the work, and that was out of the question. Her housekeeper was old and frail. She did too much as it was. They couldn't stay here under these conditions.

Whatever happened, she wasn't going to abandon her housekeeper or Ben. She owed Mrs. Trent too much. When her mother lay dying, slowly wasting away from some disease no doctor had ever diagnosed, it was Mrs. Trent who was there to help her, changing bed linens, washing down her mother's frail body, taking turns in the sickroom, giving a young adolescent girl, as she was then, the courage to face the inevitable. Her poor father was no help. He couldn't look at her mother's wasted frame without breaking down in tears.

It had been a dark day when she'd had to let Mrs. Trent go, and a dark day for Mrs. Trent as well. She couldn't find work, so she'd gone to live with a married daughter. It hadn't worked out. Their roles were reversed, and Mrs. Trent hadn't taken kindly to being treated as a child. When she'd turned up on Jane's doorstep with her grandson in tow, Jane had welcomed her with open arms.

But it was a precarious existence. They'd had some setbacks, but nothing like this. Her trouble was that she constantly overestimated her capacity to handle things or change things or make a difference. She'd let Emily down. It was the same with the library. So much energy expended with nothing to show for it! The laws of England would never be changed in a woman's favor.

And now this. Another wreck to add to her list of wrecks.

She looked at the blisters on her hands. They were beginning to sting like the devil. What would she do now? She knew what she wanted to do. She wanted to crawl into a nice, clean bed and sleep for a hundred years.

Mrs. Trent's voice roused her from her apathy. "I found these upstairs in your dresser." She crossed to Jane in slow, plodding steps and held out a pair of white cotton gloves that were only marginally cleaner than the ones on the table. "There isn't a room in the house that's been spared. Everything smells of smoke or is covered in ash. The good doctor says we canna stay here." Her voice cracked, but she went on staunchly, "But dinna fash yourself, lass. Our neighbors will take us in."

"Oh, Trentie!" was all Jane could say.

When Mrs. Trent was deeply troubled, she invariably lapsed into a broad Scottish dialect. Jane stirred herself, wracking her brains for a different solution.

She didn't want to go to her neighbors because she didn't know them that well—her own fault, of course—and she didn't want to be beholden to any of them, or to be looked at askance because they suspected she was Lord Castleton's mistress. Besides, they would have to split up. No one would take in three people, two of them invalids, not to mention a dog that needed constant care.

She and Mrs. Trent could put up at the Ladies' Library, she supposed, but Ben certainly couldn't. And how would she manage to take care of Lance?

It was only for a week or two. Then what? Her thoughts ran on.

It was at this point that Case voiced the thought that had been turning in his mind, ever since he'd walked into the kitchen and grasped the situation. In fact, he'd been wondering how he could broach the subject without getting his nose snapped off. But the droop of Jane's shoulders and the worry in Mrs. Trent's eyes convinced him that now was the time to speak.

He got up. "It's because of me you're in this fix, so I'm the one who should make restitution. You're coming with me, all of you, tonight, just as soon as I make the arrangements, and I won't take no for an answer. In a week or two, when you're on the mend, and I think it's safe to return, then well see."

Jane said, "You think Piers may come back here?"

"No, I don't. He's made his point. But I've been wrong before now, and I want you all to be safe. Mrs. Trent, do you think you can pack a box—with essentials only, mind—for Miss Mayberry, yourself, and the boy?"

Mrs. Trent was staring at him as though he had

spoken to her in a foreign language. "Mrs. Trent?" he prompted.

"Aye," she said, blinking rapidly, then, as his words sank in, "Yes, your lordship. At once."

"Good."

When he made to follow the housekeeper out, Jane called after him, "But where are you taking us? Surely not to the Albany?"

"The Albany?" He kept on walking because he didn't want to give her the chance to argue with him. "Oh, no. The Albany is for bachelors only. I'm taking you to my sister's house. Woodlands. I may have mentioned that she's in Scotland right now?" And to quash any protest, he added, "Lance will love it."

Jane endured the next few hours in a blurred haze—another interview with the constable, Mrs. Trent washing the grime from her face and dressing her because she couldn't do for herself, selecting a change of clothes, then wandering like a wraith from room to room, and gingerly plucking things from shelves and dressers she couldn't bear to leave in case thieves broke in in her absence—her mother's pearls, the Egyptian cameo her parents had given her for her fifteenth birthday, her father's walking stick with its distinctive silver stag's-head handle, her pistol, and other odds and ends. Finally, she scooped up her notes for various projects she was working on and hoped to sell to augment her dwindling savings.

The constable returned to lock up the house and chided her gently for her habit of leaving all the bedroom windows open at night. If she'd kept them closed, he said, most of the ash would have been kept out of the house. Then it was time to leave, and true to his word—not that she'd ever doubted him—Lord Castleton had arranged everything.

They left in two coaches—she'd no idea where he'd found them—Mrs. Trent and Ben in one, and herself and Lance in another. Lord Castleton and two of his friends—she couldn't remember their names— were on horseback, escorting them like a guard of honor. Lance was awake now, but not making a sound. When she put her face close to his, he licked her cheek.

"You're going to be fine, boy," she crooned. "We're all going to be fine," and she tried to believe it.

Maybe, if she hadn't been so tired, she would have thought of all the good reasons she shouldn't be accepting the earl's charity or taking up residence in his sister's house, especially when she wasn't there to object. But the swaying of the carriage had a calming effect. She moved closer to Lance. He put his head on her lap. They both slept.

She awakened momentarily to find herself in a strange bed. A female voice made soothing, clucking sounds and pulled lavender scented sheets up to her chin. She knew that scent.

"Mama?" she murmured, and slipped into a deep, untroubled sleep.

Chapter 11

Twenty-four hours went by before Gideon Piers discovered where Jane Mayberry was hiding. On the second day, he went to Woodlands in person to make sure that it *was* she, and not some decoy set out to entrap him.

He and Merrick were in the woods bordering the pasture and had a good view of the front of Woodlands and its stables. Joseph was at the top of the rise, out of sight, looking after the horses. In the last hour, they'd seen two coaches pull up and disgorge a dozen or so footmen or groundsmen before taking off again. Now, the Duke of Romsey's carriage had arrived.

Gideon collapsed his telescope and got to his feet. "The duke, himself," he said. "Now why am I not surprised?"

"Who is the lady with him?" asked Merrick.

"The venerable Lady Sophy." Piers gave a low, rich laugh. "I presume she'll be the girl's chaperon."

"We'd better get out of here," said Merrick. He pointed to liveried servants who had left the house and were beginning to fan over the property. He was annoyed but managed to keep his irritation from showing. When he accepted a job, he liked to be in charge. He liked to know what he was doing. He didn't know what in Hades he was doing here, spying on Jane Mayberry. A week ago, she wasn't that important. Suddenly, Piers was interested in her every movement. Something must have happened when Piers went out to Highgate to burn her barn, but whatever it was, Piers wasn't saying.

Piers was in no hurry to leave. "No sign yet of Castleton."

"You think he'll come?"

"Oh, yes, he'll come, if not today, tomorrow."

"You sound very sure of yourself."

Piers turned a piercing gaze upon Merrick. "You're not the only one working for me, John." He gave a ghost of a smile. "I have spies everywhere. Castleton will come."

A movement caught his eye, and he adjusted his telescope to focus on the stable. "Ah, there goes Harper with her dog. She almost died saving that dog."

He couldn't help admiring her. She'd almost bested him. He'd been too complacent, too sure of himself. When they'd cornered her outside the barn, he hadn't expected her, a mere woman, to fight back. He'd expected her to be more like his sister, Letty. He wouldn't make that mistake again.

Merrick was stamping his feet on the hard-packed earth, trying to keep warm. "So what do you want me to do now?"

Piers either ignored the question or did not hear it. "Is the dog a problem?"

"No. He is only allowed out to relieve himself."

"I think she loves animals more than she loves people."

Merrick was silent, hoping Piers would say more, give him a clue as to what had happened at Highgate. When his companion did not satisfy his curiosity, however, Merrick said, "You won't get to the dog. Harper never lets it out of his sight."

Piers adjusted his telescope and put it in his pocket. "What did you do with Mrs. Standhurst's dog?"

"What?"

"Mrs. Standhurst's lapdog. What did you do with it?"

The question threw Merrick onto the defensive. "I gave it to my mother. She always wanted a dog. She lives in Wimbledon, so it's unlikely that anyone will connect the dog to Mrs. Standhurst."

"I want it back. Go to Wimbledon, right now, and bring it here. I'll wait for you at the Barracks across the river. And tell Joseph I'll be along in a minute."

Merrick could hardly suppress a shudder. He wasn't thinking of the dog, but of his mother when he told her she was going to lose her new pet.

When Merrick left, Piers leaned against a tree, and gazed at the scene below him, taking everything in. Woodlands did not impress him one whit. Lady Rosamund was a duke's daughter, and *this* was the best she could do? His own property in Bristol was far superior to this. And no one gave him anything, no wealthy relatives in the wings to set him up and ease his way in the world. Everything he had achieved had come to him through his own daring and genius.

He could hardly contain his contempt.

Groundsmen were beginning to patrol the perimeter of the property. It was time to go, but he would be back. Castleton thought he was so clever, making out that his aunt and the Mayberry woman were friends and that was why he'd brought her here. They were treating the girl like royalty. Castleton must be besotted.

His lordship, he thought scornfully, was in for a surprise. He would send him a message that he couldn't mistake. There was no escaping retribution.

And he'd teach Jane Mayberry a lesson into the bargain, a foretaste of what was to come.

With a low laugh, he turned and went after Merrick.

The dining room was snug and cozy; the dinner, however, was an ordeal that Jane could hardly wait to end. There were only four of them, Lady Sophy, Jane, the duke, and Castleton, but the Deveres possessed *presence*, and Jane felt as though she'd shrunk.

Part of the problem was that the Deveres were all so tall—tall, graceful, and handsome, even Lady Sophy, in spite of her advanced years. Like the duke, she possessed a thick head of hair, but while the duke's hair showed very little silver, Lady Sophy's mane was snowy white, and was shown off dramatically by her black taffeta gown. Jane could imagine them as a troupe of actors—The Dashing Deveres.

There was something else that made her feel awkward. She didn't know why the duke and Lady Sophy were here. She knew what she'd been told. His aunt, the earl said, insisted that Jane could not stay at Woodlands unchaperoned, and her ladyship would be more than happy to take on that role.

Servants, it seemed, even her own, dear Mrs.

Trent, did not count as chaperones. Such were the ways of the rich.

The duke had not bothered to explain his presence, and his son and heir, who had arrived late, contributed almost nothing to the conversation except the occasional inanity. Would this interminable dinner never end?

Case was highly conscious, if Jane was not, of the veiled glances of his aunt and father, glances that were acutely aware of every nuance and change in his expression, and Jane's. No fool Lady Sophy or His Grace! He was annoyed that his father had insisted on coming along. His feeble excuse—that he wanted to visit his old friend Harper—fooled nobody. For Jane's sake, Case was saying nothing to arouse their suspicions, but he was listening intently, and if either of them dared make Jane feel uncomfortable, he was ready to act.

Lady Sophy had been telling His Grace how she and Jane had met. "So you see," she concluded, "Jane is one of the leading lights at the Ladies' Library, and is an inspiration to us all."

The duke seemed unimpressed by this tribute and ruthlessly diverted the conversation to what most interested him. "I once knew a family called Mayberry," he said. "The Devonshire Mayberrys. Military people. Are you any relation to them?"

Case threw his sire a withering look, but before he could intervene, Jane spoke. "No, Your Grace. Not to my knowledge. My family came from Derbyshire. My father was the only son."

His Grace opened his mouth to pursue the subject, but Jane cut him off. "Devere. That's an uncommon name. Are you related to the Deveres of Oxford, by any chance?"

"The Deveres of Oxford?" echoed the duke.

"The *earls* of Oxford," Jane elaborated. "Though I believe they spell their name a different way. Capital *D*. Capital *V*. A scholarly family. My father taught one of the sons."

"They're a cadet branch of the family," said the duke. "We don't have much truck with them because we fought on different sides..." He stopped. "Well, that's old history."

"I think it's sad," said Jane, "when old quarrels keep families apart, don't you?" She speared a Brussels sprout and popped it into her mouth.

Caspar bit down on a smile, Lady Sophy pressed her lips together, and the duke made a harrumphing sound.

After an interval of silence, Lady Sophy said, looking at Jane, "You've been through a dreadful ordeal, my dear, but it's over and you're not to worry about a thing. You're under our protection now and shall make Woodlands your home until this ruffian is caught and dealt with."

Jane smiled warmly. "Thank you. I appreciate your concern, but I must return to my own home soon. There's so much to do, so much to think about. Then there are my friends at the library. You must see that I can't stay here for long." She looked at Case. "And I understood the danger was over."

"That's my considered opinion," he said, "but it's only an opinion."

"Well, well," said Lady Sophy, "it will be some time before your house is ready for occupation, so we don't have to decide things right now. In the meantime, we'll make a little holiday of your stay. You can join all the little outings and soirées I've planned for your protégée, Miss Drake. I'm really looking forward to it."

Jane had already thanked her ladyship profusely for her promise to introduce Emily to society, but she'd never had any intention of being part of it. Dismayed, she looked at Case. "What's this about my house?"

Her ladyship smiled benignly. "Don't give it another thought. Caspar is taking care of everything. Tell her Caspar."

Case said, "I'm taking care of everything." He raised a hand to call over a footman. "This mutton is delicious. Would anyone like more?"

A half hour later, dinner was thankfully over, and when Case asked Jane to take him to see Lance, she agreed with alacrity. There were things she wished to say to him, questions she wanted answered.

His Grace and Lady Sophy made no move to leave the table. The covers were removed and the decanters were brought out, brandy for the duke, sherry for her ladyship.

When the duke had dismissed the servants, he said, "I think you must be wrong, Sophy. I could see no sign of partiality on Caspar's part or on Miss Mayberry's either."

"Well, what did you expect," demanded her ladyship, "with your eagle eye trained on them as though they were plump pigeons? You promised me you'd be on your best behavior."

"I behaved with the utmost discretion."

"Do you call it discreet to start probing into the girl's bloodlines when you've only just met her?"

The duke made a scoffing sound. "I don't know why you want to protect your little fledgling. Miss Mayberry gives as good as she gets."

Her ladyship smiled. "It served you right. It's not often I see you get a set-down."

"At any rate," said the duke, "I'm entitled to probe if she's going to marry my son."

"That is by no means certain. It's obvious that Caspar is taken with the girl, but—"

"He hardly looked at her! And if he's so taken with her, why haven't I met her before?"

"Because he doesn't want to rush his fences."

"Rush his fences?" The duke was dumbfounded. "What are you talking about, Sophy? Caspar is the most eligible bachelor in England. I've yet to meet the woman he couldn't have if he wanted her."

Lady Sophy shook her head. "If I'm not mistaken, you have met her now. I don't think Jane has the least notion of marrying anyone. I think Caspar knows this, and hopes to change her mind."

After a long, reflective silence, Lady Sophy took up the conversation again. "What do you make of this La Roca business?"

The duke shrugged. "Only what Caspar tells me, that these attacks are meant to make him give up the investigation into the Hyde Park murder. He won't, of course."

"I didn't suppose he would. But isn't it strange that he knows this brigand from Spain?"

"Not at all. That's why Richard turned the case over to him."

"And he never mentioned this La Roca to you before last night?"

"No. Never. Then Caspar rarely speaks about the war."

He took a sip of brandy, then a long swallow as he lapsed into his own thoughts. Something had happened to Caspar during the war, something that he could not share with his own father. War was like that. One could not dwell on its horrors or one would go mad. Still, he missed the closeness he'd once had with his elder son, before he'd gone off to war. It was more than closeness. There was an affection there that he'd seen very little of since his son came home.

If only Elizabeth were here to advise him. He'd been a widower for over twenty years, but not a day went by when he did not think of his wife.

He looked at his aunt. "You never married, Sophy."

His words startled her. After a moment, she smiled, "No. My father, your grandfather, wouldn't allow me to marry the man I loved. He wasn't good enough for a duke's daughter, you see. But my heart was taken, and no one else would do for me. You know, Romsey, you're not a bad old codger. I was proud of you, very proud, when you allowed Rosamund to marry her soldier."

Faint, faint color tinted the duke's cheeks. He said gruffly, "You know, Sophy, you're not a bad old girl yourself. You'll have another sherry?"

"Only if you'll have another brandy."

The duke reached for the decanters.

"Will you wait up?" A stiff breeze fought with the folds of his coat as Case tried to do up the buttons. Jane was striding ahead of him on the path to the stable. "Jane, what's got into you?"

She did an about-face and took the few steps back to him. "Our understanding was," she said, "our understanding was that I'd stay here for a few days, a week at the most, until my hands had healed, then I'd return to my own home. Your aunt seems to think I'll be here for a month, if not longer."

Since she hadn't bothered to button her cloak, he took the liberty of doing it for her. "A month? No, not that long." In contrast to her heated tone, his was calm and pleasant. "You don't realize how much damage the fire has done to your house." He pulled up the hood of her cloak to protect her from the wind. "Don't you like it here?"

"Of course I like it. The house is a gem. But that's not the point."

"What about Lance? Isn't Harper doing a good job?"

"You know very well that he is."

"And I know Mrs. Trent and Ben are happy because I spoke to them before dinner. In fact, I'd say they're in their element. So what's the problem?"

"The problem is I feel as though I'm taking advantage of you."

His hands were still on the edges of her hood. It took very little pressure to bring her face close to his. Grinning, he said, "Take advantage of me, Jane. I won't object."

With a little hiss, she batted his hands away, winced, then set off again at a spanking pace. Case took the opportunity of glancing around. Lanterns were winking at key points along the perimeter of the property. The groundsmen were out in force, as ordered. Well satisfied, he strode after Jane.

In contrast to the tranquility Jane had encountered when she'd visited Lance these last two days, the stable was now a hive of busyness. Every stall was taken and there were grooms currying horses or feeding and watering them. They found Harper in the coach house. He was polishing Lady Rosamund's carriage, keeping up a flow of one-sided conversation with Lance as he worked.

Lance greeted Case like a long lost friend, then, as

if remembering all his grievances at being deserted, held up his paw like a broken wing. It had the desired result. Case made a fuss of him.

Harper put down his polishing cloth. "He's a born actor, that one," he said. "You should see him when the doctor comes calling."

"He's a malingerer?" asked Case.

"Not a bit of it. He prances around as though he's as fit as a fiddle so old sawbones won't change his bandage."

Case laughed. "How are you, Harper?"

"Mending slowly, like Lance. Was that the duke's carriage I saw leaving?"

"It was, but it's only gone to the local hostelry because there's no room here. His Grace is still up at the house. He gave me a message for you. He wondered if you would like to join him for a wee dram of brandy."

Harper rubbed his hands together. "A wee dram. So His Grace hasn't forgotten! You'll look after Lance till I get back?" When Case nodded, Harper went on, "I'll just tidy myself and wash my hands."

When he went into the tack room, Case said, "Harper was our head coachman for a time. You might say he and my father are kindred spirits. Coaching is in their blood."

"Coaching?" said Jane, her brow wrinkling.

"And coach building. When those two get together over a wee dram, they can bore the ears off a deaf man." He gave her a clear-eyed stare. "When His Grace heard that Harper was here, he insisted on coming along."

After thinking this over for a moment or two, Jane said, "I think that's sweet."

Case lounged against an upright post and waited

for Jane to come to the point. He didn't have long to wait.

"What's this about the damage to my house?" she said. "It was the stable that burned down, not the house."

"I asked the constable to make an inventory," Case replied easily. "You may remember he is Lauderdale's estate agent. Just before dinner, I received his reply. It's smoke damage that's the problem, Jane."

As he reeled off a long list of what was necessary before the house was habitable, Jane's spirits plummeted. She hadn't thought beyond sweeping the house out and washing everything down. According to the agent, the inside of the house had to be painted from top to bottom; upholstery and drapes had to be cleaned or replaced; the debris from the barn had to be carted away—the list was endless.

Who was going to pay for it? Her landlord, she hoped. It was his property, and she wasn't responsible for what had happened. If her landlord was true to form, however, it would take him forever to make a beginning.

She shot Case a sharp look. "What did Lady Sophy mean when she said you were taking care of everything?"

He spread his hands. "As I told you before, I feel responsible for what happened. So, I'm sending a team of men from Twickenham to set the place to rights. They should be there tomorrow. But these things take time. You can't expect them to complete the job in less than a fortnight."

She pressed her fingertips to her temples. An ugly suspicion was worming its way into her mind. Before she could voice it, Harper returned, wearing a fresh jacket and with his hair neatly combed.

"Half an hour, your lordship," he said. "That should do it," and off he went.

Jane looked at Case. "Castleton," she said, "I can't be bought. I'm not for sale. Just as long as we understand each other."

He was still lounging against the post, but his pleasant manner evaporated. "If you knew anything about mistresses," he said, not mincing words, "you would know that they don't come that cheaply. You may take my word for it. The going price is a house in town, her own carriage, a box at the opera, and the clothes and jewels to make her the envy of her peers."

"Sounds to me," she said, "as though you'd be better off getting married."

He was charmed by the laughter in her eyes. "Are you offering?"

Her laughter died. "I told you, I'm not for sale, whether it's for the position of mistress or wife." Before he could say something else to discomfit her, she went on, "What about La Contessa and Mrs. Standhurst? Are you going to pay for the damage to their property too?"

"I would have if it was necessary, but the damage to their property was minimal. I visited them before I came on here. That's why I was late."

It was foolish to be deflated by his answer, but she couldn't help what she was feeling.

He cocked his head to one side. "Jane, are you pouting?"

Her eyes blazed. "Certainly not. What I am is amazed that you can't see what an impossible position you've placed me in. I don't like being the object of gossip. I don't want my name mentioned in the same breath as La Contessa's. And that's another thing.

Doesn't the poor woman have a name? 'La Contessa' makes her sound like a pretentious half-wit."

He wasn't the least put out by this tirade. In fact, it quite encouraged him. Striving for gravity, he said, "Her name is Maria Angelo, la Contessa di Pavia e Modena. She really is an Italian countess, Jane. The count left her penniless when he died, and she came to England because she had friends here."

"You being one of them," she added churlishly. "No, don't answer. It's none of my business and I don't want to know. All I care about is my own good name."

He took the one step that separated them and cupped her shoulders. "Now, you listen to me. I know you think I'm a complete degenerate, but I'm not lost to all sense of decency. I have never introduced my mistress to my father, or asked my aunt to chaperon her, or invited her to take up residence in my sister's house. It's just not done. Trust me. Everyone will think exactly what we want them to think, which is more or less the truth: that your house isn't fit for habitation, so your great friend and admirer, Lady Sophy, invited you to be her guest at Woodlands."

He looked into her face, trying to gauge her feelings. "Look at me!" he said fiercely, and he cupped her chin to bring her eyes up to meet his. She seemed fragile, and that surprised him.

Her gloved fingers splayed over his chest. "No," she whispered.

His lips curved. "What are you saying no to?"

What was in his eyes; the way her heart jarred; the sudden realization that she wasn't as immune to him as she thought she was.

His hand moved to her neck, his fingers tightened. She knew she should pull back. Instead, she lifted her face to him. His lips were warm, tasting, not taking. She felt her mouth opening to the gentle pressure of his. She couldn't think, didn't want to think.

He felt an odd tenderness uncurl inside him. He had never kissed a woman like this. It wasn't a passionate kiss. He knew that Jane wasn't ready for that kind of intimacy, not yet. She was inexperienced. She kissed as though she'd never been kissed before. But there was passion there, banked, and just waiting for the right man to unleash it. She might not know it yet, but he was that man.

Needs she had never experienced before warmed her skin, stole her breath. It was madness to give in to what she was feeling. She couldn't allow this. She was playing with fire.

In an act of self-preservation, she deliberately clenched her hands. The pain was just what she needed to bring her to her senses. She gave a little cry, and the next moment she was free. She was wise enough not to back away from him or run. She looked at her hands.

"I hurt you," he said.

"No." Her eyes met his in a level stare. "But I think you will, if I let you."

"No," he said quickly.

"Or *I* might hurt *you.*"

He folded his arms across his chest. "I'm willing to take that chance."

"I'm happy as I am. Don't spoil things for me."

"Are you happy, Jane? Are you sure of that?"

No, she wasn't happy, but she would have been if he had not come streaking into her life like a comet.

"Oh, what's the use!" she said angrily. She stalked to the door. Lance went with her. "Stay!" she commanded. "Stay!"

Lance turned to look at Case, who shrugged, and when Lance turned back to the door, it was to find that his mistress was gone. He put back his head and howled.

"I know the feeling," said Case. He snapped his fingers and after a moment Lance hobbled over. There was a bench against one wall and Case lowered himself onto it. Lance put his head in Case's lap.

"I'm making progress, don't you think?" said Case.

Lance licked his hand, as if commiserating with him. Case returned the favor by stroking Lance's head.

"Did you notice how her eyes turned green when I said I'd already visited La Contessa and Amelia? Not that she has any cause for jealousy there."

He hadn't gone alone, but had invited Waldo along just so that his erstwhile mistress would know that he wasn't interested in a reconciliation. Or maybe he'd taken Waldo along to make sure that La Contessa kept her legendary temper in check. She was still angry with him for ending their affair, and was quite likely to break a vase over his head. That's why he'd ended the relationship. Her ferocious temper, the scenes, the hysterics had become a crashing bore, and no amount of the lady's skill in bed could make up for it.

He'd questioned her, discreetly, without mentioning Piers's name, but she hadn't told him anything useful. Two men who wore masks had locked her servants in the cellar. They hadn't stolen anything. Their one aim seemed to be to terrify the wits out of her, and they'd succeeded. She'd been so afraid that they were going to do to her what they'd done to her poor little cat.

When Case suggested that it might be a good idea

for her to get out of London for a while, she'd told him with an arch smile that that was already taken care of. Lord Gracey had invited her to spend Christmas with him in Brighton, and if she liked it there, she might never return.

He'd left Waldo consoling La Contessa. Gracey might be her new protector, but the lady was a born flirt. The same could be said of Waldo, so it was no hardship for them to be left alone together.

When he called on Amelia, she'd greeted him with an open-mouthed kiss, but she must have sensed his reserve because the kiss was short-lived. There was no embarrassment, no hurt feelings. That was one of the things he liked about Amelia. She didn't demand more from a man than he was willing to give.

Because he knew that he could count on her discretion, he told her more than he'd told La Contessa, but not much more, only that he suspected her housebreakers were warning him off the investigation into the Hyde Park murder, and that she wasn't the only one to be singled out like this. She hadn't been in the house when the men broke in, so she summoned her butler and had him tell the story. Once again there were two men. While one held the servants at bay with a gun, the other, after learning that Mrs. Standhurst was not there, had gone on the rampage, smashing vases and mirrors and breaking chairs. When they left, they took her little dog with them.

It was the loss of the dog that was most upsetting to Amelia. Scamp was old; he had arthritis; he needed looking after. What could these villains possibly want with her dog?

When Lance looked up and whined, Case said, "No, Lance. They could never carry you off. Scamp was so small that one could carry him under one's arm. I once mistook him for an orange muff."

He'd told Amelia that the dog might have run off and been taken in by strangers. He doubted it, but it was too cruel to rob her of all hope. The one thing he could not do was persuade Amelia to leave London. Now that she understood the danger, she said, she would take precautions, but nothing and no one was going to chase her away from her home. Besides, she wanted to be here in case Scamp came back.

He left her house wondering why she couldn't stir his softer feelings the way Jane did. The only thing he wondered about La Contessa was what maggot had persuaded him to keep paying her astronomical bills when he got so little satisfaction from the relationship. But Amelia was different. In some respects, she was not unlike Jane. She valued her independence. Add to that, she knew how to dress and make the most of her looks. She had a certain panache and went out of her way to please men.

He didn't want Jane to go out of her way to please men, only one man, himself.

Lance stirred, lumbered to his feet, and sniffed the air.

"No. She's not coming back," Case told him, "so settle down." After a moment, he reached in his pocket, found a cheroot, then remembered that smoking was absolutely forbidden anywhere near the stables, so he put it away again.

Lance was now prowling restlessly. Case wasn't paying attention. He was still occupied by his own thoughts. Jane had been single so long that she couldn't see a man fitting into her world. And the Ladies' Library wasn't exactly kindly disposed toward men. It wasn't much of a life in his opinion; she had her writing, her little acreage in the country, and the Ladies' Library.

Passion—that's what was missing from her life. She didn't know how it could make her ache, how it could become like a physical pain.

Patience, he reminded himself. If he wanted to win her, he had to move slowly. But patience didn't seem to be working.

His thoughts broke off abruptly when he became aware that Lance was scratching at the door, not the door to the stable, but the outside door to the yard.

Case got up. "What is it, boy?"

There was something wrong here. Lance was growling menacingly, and his hackles were beginning to rise.

Case looked around, found a leather strap, and hooked it to the dog's collar. "All right. Show me."

When he opened the door, Lance drew his lips back and showed his fangs. Injury or not, he was desperate to get going. Case wrapped the leash around his wrist and with his other hand, pulled his pistol from his pocket. "Easy boy," he said. "Easy."

But Lance didn't want easy. He wanted to go. The muscles in his shoulders and back were tensed for action. Case had to use all his weight to control the dog. They made for the front of the house, but before they reached the front steps, Lance veered to the right, and came to a stop in front of a stand of leafless poplars. He sat back on his haunches and alternately growled and whined. Case could see nothing.

He looked around for help just as the bootboy came out of a side door. "Get Harper," Case shouted. "He's with His Grace."

A few moments later, Harper descended the front

stairs. "Get a lantern," Case said, "and bring it over here."

Before Harper could do as he was bid, Case saw what had distressed Lance. On a branch, not far above his head, a ball of fur was swaying in the wind. It looked like a fox cub.

"What is it?" asked Harper, coming up at that moment with a lantern.

"Hold Lance and don't let him go," said Case.

It took him only a moment or two to climb to the branch, then he slid his army knife from inside his boot and cut the rope that bound the small stiff body. It fell to the ground with a soft thud.

"My God!" said Harper. "Poor wee beastie!"

Case dropped to the ground. Lance inched forward and sniffed the orange fur, then began to whimper.

"They hanged it," said Harper. "The bastards hanged Mrs. Standhurst's little dog, didn't they?"

Case nodded. Scamp's eyes were bulging, his little tongue was swollen, and his body seemed grotesquely out of shape. "He's been dead for some hours. They must have done this somewhere else then brought him here."

"We'd better not let Miss Mayberry see this," said Harper.

"No." Case stripped off his coat and wrapped the little dog in it. "We'll bury him on the other side of the perimeter wall."

"Shouldn't we make a search?"

"In the dark? No. Besides, they're gone. Lance would tell us if they were still here. He'd be gnashing his teeth to get at them."

"But why did Piers do it?"

"Just a brutal reminder that in spite of all my precautions, he can come and go as he pleases. He's not finished with me yet."

Case gazed at the woods at the edge of the pasture as though sensing that his mortal enemy was still close by. Under his breath, he murmured, "I'm counting on it, you bastard. I'm counting on it."

He looked at Harper. "From now on, I want Lance to stay in the house with Miss Mayberry, and if the housekeeper objects, send her to me. Now, give me a hand with this poor creature."

Chapter 12

*T*he closing strains of the Irish melody lingered momentarily, then the guests at Lady Sophy's informal soirée burst into applause. Miss Emily Drake, the performer, got up from the piano and dipped a graceful curtsy. A gentleman from the back of the room shouted, "Encore!" Someone else took up the refrain and Miss Drake sat down at the piano and began to play again.

Jane and her good friend Sally Latham were standing at the back of the small audience, at the entrance to the sunroom, drinking punch from crystal glasses. Behind them, a table was laid out with tiny sandwiches and other delicacies to take the edge off one's appetite until supper was served. There were few gentlemen about. As the musical program had progressed, they slipped away in ones and twos to congregate in the library where gentlemen could smoke and a footman was on hand to dispense something more invigorating than pineapple punch.

Two gentlemen who had not slipped away were Waldo Bowman and Freddie Latham. Waldo was turning the pages of Miss Drake's music and Freddie was hovering.

"Like a cursed hummingbird," said his sister wrathfully. "Has he no pride? All she wants is a title, and now Case is in her orbit, a mere viscount counts for nothing. How could we have been so mistaken in her?"

Jane's gaze traveled over the assembled guests. There was no sign of Case. He'd been one of the first gentlemen to make his escape. She spoke without much enthusiasm. "We can hardly blame the girl for making the most of her opportunities. That's why Case...Lord Castleton...persuaded Lady Sophy to launch her in society, wasn't it, so that she could meet eligible young gentlemen and enlarge her circle of friends?"

"That doesn't alter the fact that she deceived us! She made us believe she was a little mouse of a girl, and that her brother was an ogre who was forcing her into a distasteful marriage. I think she had her eye on Freddie all the time. When I think of it, she was reluctant to stay with you in the country. She thought I'd invite her to stay with Freddie and me in town. We were hoodwinked, Jane. That whole business with Lord Reeve was an elaborate plot to drag Freddie into her net."

"I wouldn't go that far," Jane replied, because if Sally was right, she would be tempted to give the spoiled beauty the shaking of her life.

Another thought flitted into her mind and she looked at Sally. Her friend had taken a great deal of trouble tonight with her appearance. The ivory muslin gown did wonders for her red-gold hair, now set in tiny curls to frame her face. Even her freckles seemed to have faded, and Jane wondered if she'd gone to all this trouble for Waldo Bowman. He'd been a frequent visitor at Woodlands this last week, as had Sally.

He was, thought Jane, the kind of man that would appeal to women. He was tall, had a spare, athletic build, and a face that was fringed with crisp, coppery waves that brushed his collar. His bones were elegant, his smile disarming, and oddly romantic. But there was a vaguely dangerous air about him, something in his dark glances that defied description. There was more to Mr. Bowman than met the eye.

Leastways, that's how he appeared to her, and it made her wary. He was not the kind of man she would choose for Sally.

She tried to recall what she knew of him. Not very much. He had black spells that would suddenly come upon him, then he'd withdraw from his friends, withdraw from society, until he was over them. No. Definitely not the kind of man she would choose for Sally.

Sally edged closer. "She slighted Lady Octavia. She made fun of the library and that's why Lady Octavia has stayed away."

"No, Sally. Lady Octavia had a prior engagement. That's why she's not here."

"And what about the duke?"

"What about him?"

"Why isn't he here?"

"Possibly because he lives in Twickenham."

Sally shot Jane a fulminating look. "I don't know why you're defending her. She hasn't a kind word to say about either of us, and after all we tried to do for her!"

That was true. It was nothing obvious, just snide innuendo coated with sugar. The trouble was, Emily looked upon her, Jane, as a rival for Case's affections. It almost had her feeling sorry for the girl, almost but not quite.

"Sometimes I want to slap her!"

Jane couldn't argue with that.

They drew apart as a footman entered the sunroom to replenish someone's glass. When he returned to the salon, Sally said, "It's Mrs. Drake I feel sorry for. She's a nice, decent lady and is embarrassed by Emily's antics. The brother should know better, but just look at him. Emily can do no wrong in his eyes."

Jane agreed. Mr. Drake was puffed up with pride as he watched his sister. Mrs. Drake looked as though she would rather be anywhere than in that lovely salon listening to the third piece her young sister-in-law had been persuaded to play that evening. As Jane watched, Lady Sophy, resplendent once again in black taffeta, leaned over and said a few words to Mrs. Drake, who smiled, nodded, and visibly relaxed.

Lady Sophy really was a remarkable woman, Jane reflected. She was genuinely interested in people and went out of her way to make them feel at ease. It was too bad she'd been saddled with a vixen like Emily, and it made her cringe inside to know that she had nobody to blame but herself. She didn't know how she could have been so mistaken in the girl.

The piano went silent; there was a round of applause, then a footman announced with all the vigor of a town crier that supper was served in the dining room downstairs. Jane and Sally wandered into the sunroom and helped themselves to more punch. A few moments later, they were joined by Miss Drake, flushed with her triumph. Waldo and Freddie were right behind her.

Once again, Jane was struck by the change in Miss Drake. She wasn't mousey in a pretty way. She was quite a beauty. Her dark curls were threaded with white ribbons to match her gown. Her skin was flawless. But her eyes were her best feature, wide set and vividly blue.

"You play very well," began Jane, but was waved to silence by a gesture from Miss Drake.

"I thought Case might be here," she said.

"No," said Jane. "As you see, we're quite alone."

"Lord Castleton," corrected Sally, "cannot abide amateur musicales. It's quite possible he's gone home."

The snub was lost on Miss Drake. "To the Albany?" She let out a silvery laugh. "I hardly think so." Her eyes fastened on Jane. "He promised to take me in to supper."

Freddie said quickly, "Miss Drake, allow me to get you a glass of punch while we wait for...ah...Lord Castleton."

"Lord Castleton?" Miss Drake pouted. "That sounds so formal. No. I shall continue to call him Case. After all, he calls me Emily."

As Freddie moved to the punch bowl, Waldo picked up a tiny sandwich and popped it into his mouth. His eyes were alight with amusement. Sally maintained a stony silence. Jane was wracking her brains for something to say, but all she could come up with were words to the effect that if Miss Drake didn't behave herself, she'd send her to bed without any supper.

Miss Drake said, "I see you've left off your white gloves, Jane. Does this mean your hands are better?"

Jane looked at her hands. "Much better, thank you."

Miss Drake took the glass of punch from Freddie and sipped delicately. "In a way, I'm sorry," she said.

"Sorry?" Jane repeated blankly.

"I know how much you miss your home in the country and now that your hands have healed, I assume you will be eager to get back to it."

This was exactly how Jane felt. Oddly enough, she found herself saying the opposite. "But Woodlands feels like the country, and Lady Sophy is a charming companion. No. I'm not in any hurry to go home."

"No, indeed," said Sally, her expression animated. "Jane could not possibly desert Lady Sophy when she is bringing you into society just to oblige Jane."

Miss Drake's cheeks flooded with color and, for a moment, it seemed that she had been finally put in her place. Then her chin came up and she said coolly, "I understood that Miss Mayberry was a guest here only because she had nowhere else to go and Lady Sophy took her in out of the goodness of her heart."

Sally let out a hissing sound. Jane didn't know whether to laugh or stamp her foot. Here they were, three gown women at an elegant party, dressed to the nines, and circling each other like spitting cats. Someone had to do something before they drew blood.

It was Freddie who rose to the occasion. "Dash it all!" he said. "What could be keeping Case? If we don't go in to supper, there won't be anything left. Tell you what, we'll keep a place for him, shall we? Come along, Miss Drake. You too, Sally. No, I'm not taking no for an answer. Waldo, you'll bring Miss Mayberry?"

He didn't wait for Waldo's reply, and he didn't give Miss Drake or his sister a chance to wriggle out of his clasp. With a hand cupping each lady's elbow, he propelled them from the room.

Jane looked at Waldo. "At least you seem to be enjoying yourself," she said.

He touched a hand to his lips. "Ah, no. This is an old war wound. I always look as though I'm smiling."

"Mr. Bowman, your eyes give you away."

He looked at her hard, then chuckled. "Ah. I see I've been found out. I shall have to watch you, Miss Mayberry."

She had that oddly disturbing feeling again, that there was more to Waldo Bowman than met the eye. A thought occurred to her. "You *are* watching me, aren't you? You and Freddie and Robert Shay and Harper? And there's someone else. A footman with red hair."

"That would be Ruggles," he said.

She had half expected him to deny it, and stared, thunderstruck.

"We're being cautious, Miss Mayberry, that's all."

She shook her head. "I thought the danger was over. Something must have happened. What is it?"

He shrugged. "Nothing that I'm aware of." When she looked skeptical, he went on, "It's not wise to underestimate our enemy. He doesn't like to lose face, and you made him lose face. That's all."

She looked at him closely. "It sounds as though you know him well."

In spite of his smile, his expression hardened. "I was in at the kill, you might say. Only, he slipped through our fingers. Now we're prepared for any eventuality."

His face cleared and he became his usual, urbane self. "Miss Mayberry, may I have the pleasure of taking you in to supper?"

His lightning changes of mood confused her. She wanted to ask him about Gideon Piers, but his long dark lashes veiled his expression and she knew, sensed, the subject was now closed.

She placed her fingers on his proffered arm. "I should be delighted, Mr. Bowman," she said.

At the entrance to the dining room, they halted. Freddie saw them and waved them over to his table. He was sitting with Robert Shay and Sally. Emily Drake was not there.

Jane's eyes skimmed the crush and found Emily sitting next to none other than the earl himself. Case did not look up, but Miss Drake saw her and flashed one of her insufferable smiles of triumph.

As the evening wore on, no one would have known what it cost her to appear unaffected by Miss Drake's trilling laugh. She wasn't jealous. She credited Case with more taste than most. Emily Drake didn't stand a chance.

Careful, she told herself. *This is dangerous thinking. Don't get too attached to him. One day the right girl will come along, and then he'll marry and live happily every after.*

The thought set her teeth on edge.

The evening became more informal as guests finished eating and began to move from table to table to greet acquaintants. When Miss Drake was reluctantly carried off by Lady Sophy, Waldo and Robert idled their way over to Case.

"She's on to us," said Waldo at once.

As Waldo took the chair Emily had vacated, Robert took the one opposite. "All is discovered," he said. "So what do we do now?"

Case smiled. "I warned you she was sharp. Not that it makes any difference. In fact, it may make things easier."

"I don't know about that," said Waldo. "She wanted to know what had happened to make you decide she needed our protection. No, no, I didn't tell her about the dog. I just impressed upon her the fact that you-know-who is a devious, dangerous character and we're not taking any chances."

Robert said, "Is he really so dangerous?"

"Lethal," replied Waldo.

Their conversation was interrupted when they were joined by a well set-up, military-looking young man who exuded affability. Capt. Harry Fellowes was well known to them as a former Etonian and a veteran of the Spanish Campaign.

"Well, well, well," said Fellowes in his hearty way, "what have we here? You look like conspirators. Not interrupting anything, am I?"

"Not at all," said Robert, feeling in his pocket for his snuff box. "Sit down, Harry. We were just discussing..." He looked helplessly at Waldo.

"Our annual old boys' reunion," supplied Waldo. "I hope you'll be there, Harry."

"Wouldn't miss it for the world. Why haven't I received my invitation?"

"It had to be postponed," said Robert.

As his companions began to discuss plans for the reunion, Case got up and excused himself by saying that he had duties to perform as host. He was well aware that many eyes were watching him closely, so he made a point of exchanging pleasantries with every pretty girl in the room. He was doing it to deflect any unpleasant suspicion that might arise if he paid Jane undue attention. That was in public. There were other times, when he arrived at Woodlands unannounced, and managed to get her alone. He had always something to tell her—about the progress of the work on her house, or about the investigation—and she could hardly refuse to see him. They went for walks, or they'd go riding; he would flirt with her, but he never went too far. He wanted her to feel comfortable with him, but not too comfortable.

She was standing alone. He brought his conversation with Miss Booker to an abrupt close and made for Jane. No one would think anything of it. In fact, not to speak to her would arouse everyone's suspicions.

Robert and Waldo were surreptitiously watching Case's progress through the room. After offering his snuff box to Waldo and helping himself to a pinch, Robert said, "You know, Waldo, I've been thinking that if this fellow Piers is as lethal as you say he is, maybe we should drop the idea of holding our reunion this year."

"You think he may try to blow up Twickenham House?"

"The thought had occurred to me."

"Well, you're right. That's exactly what he's up to."

"How do you know?"

"Gunpowder. We found it in the wine cellar, the coal cellar, and even under the floor of the picture gallery." Waldo's gaze was still trained on Case and Jane.

Robert's jaw was slack. "G-gunpowder?" he stammered.

"Oh, don't worry. It's not there now. Case wants to talk to all of us after everyone goes home. He'll bring you up to date."

"But what made you think in the first place that Piers would attack Twickenham House?"

"It was the delay."

"What delay?"

"After Collier was murdered. We all thought Bow Street was incompetent. And they were, of course. But if Piers wanted to, he would have found a way to let Case know he had risen from the ashes. Something must have happened to make him hold off."

"And what was it?"

"Our speaker fell deathly ill and the reunion had to be postponed."

"That's circumstantial evidence and very flimsy, if you want my view."

"That's what we thought, but we changed our minds when we found the gunpowder."

With elbows on the table, he leaned toward his companion. "Tell me frankly, Robert," he said. "What do you think my chances are with Miss Mayberry?"

"Nonexistent," snapped Robert, who was still reeling from the shock of Waldo's words. "Case wants her for himself."

Waldo sighed theatrically. "Yes, that's what I think, too."

As Jane opened the door to her chamber, Lance brushed by her and entered first. He had the run of the house, as Case had promised, but Lance wasn't comfortable with crowds, so mostly he found a quiet spot where he would not be disturbed. He smelled of wind and rain, and Jane knew that Harper must have taken him out for his nightly ramble.

When she was ready for bed, Jane did not blow out the candle. She donned her robe and sat at the window, listening to the sounds of the house settling in for the night. Her room had a view of the front of the house, and she could see lights in the gatehouse at the entrance to Marylebone. Lance sat beside her, alert, sensing that something was going on, but betraying no impatience.

When Jane's head lifted, so did his. The soft thud of footsteps passed, going along the corridor. Jane picked up the candle and made for the door. Lance followed.

In the corridor, she found Ruggles, the red-haired, freckle-faced footman. Although he was obviously surprised to see her, she wasn't surprised to see him.

"Miss Mayberry," he said, "is something wrong?"

She had her pretext ready. "No, no. I could not sleep and thought I'd go to the library and find a book to read."

"I'll come with you."

"That isn't necessary. I can find my own way."

For a moment, he seemed nonplussed, then he said easily, "It's no trouble, and I doubt that Lady Sophy would be pleased if she knew I'd allowed you to wander around the house in the dark."

Jane smiled at this and allowed a moment or two of silence to fall as they navigated the stairs. "It's Mr. Ruggles, is it not?" When he nodded, she continued, "I thought I recognized you. You're Lord Castleton's man."

There was only the briefest hesitation before he acknowledged that he was, indeed, Lord Castleton's man. "You might say I'm on loan to Lady Sophy for as long as she needs me."

He was good. Very smooth. He should have been an actor.

Having discovered what she wished to know, that she was, indeed, under guard, she lost no time in choosing a book and returning to her room. "Is everybody in Castleton's pay?" she demanded of Lance, tossing her book on the bed.

As soon as the word *Castleton* was out of her mouth, Lance pricked up his ears and began to sniff the air. "Castleton," she repeated, testing him, and his tail began to wag. He looked hopefully at the door.

"Not you as well!" She shook her head. "So that's why he's given you the run of the house. You're guarding me too."

She threw off her robe and picked up the book she'd thrown down. *"Pride and Prejudice,"* she said aloud. "Elizabeth Bennet is my favorite character of all time. But as for Darcy," she made a face. "I shall never understand what she saw in him."

She put the book down and scratched Lance's ears. "She would have been better off with a dog, just like me, don't you think?"

The familiar joke had lost its savor. Her shoulders sagged.

Suddenly straightening, she blew out the candle and climbed into bed.

Chapter 13

*E*vidently, it was Harper's turn to watch over her, for when she descended the front steps with Lance and climbed into the waiting hackney, he held the door then climbed in right after them. They were on their way to Letty's house in Hans Town. So much had happened in the last little while that it seemed easier to tell Letty about it face-to-face than write it all down in a letter. Besides, she hoped to find out something about Gideon Piers that would give them a clue to his whereabouts, though it didn't seem likely that she would succeed where others had failed.

"We should have taken the coach," said Harper.

"Nonsense," said Jane. "We'll only be gone for about an hour or so, and why put the grooms to the bother of hitching the horses when they'll only have to stand outside Mrs. Gray's house while I visit with her? It's too much of an imposition, Harper."

That was the crux of the matter. She didn't want to impose any more than she had to. If Lady Rosamund had been her friend, she wouldn't have minded borrowing her carriage. At least she didn't have to borrow her clothes. Nan, the maid, had aired out a box of garments that she'd kept in the attic of her house in Highgate, garments that she'd taken with her when she'd left Edinburgh all those years ago, and she was now fitted out in a pink velvet coat with matching bonnet and reticule.

The air was crisp, the sun was shining, and just for a little while her time was her own. In the afternoon, an outing was planned to Twickenham House, where His Grace would entertain Lady Sophy and her guests.

Neither of her companions seemed to share her enjoyment of the moment. Harper's brows were down as he scanned vehicles on the Marylebone road before their hackney crossed it, and Lance was sulking because she'd made him wear the loathsome coat again, and no amount of gnashing of teeth on his part, or baring of fangs had persuaded her to change her mind.

"Good dog," she said now, and patted him on the head.

His response was to growl and curl his lip, but she only laughed at him.

When they came to Letty's house, Harper paid off the hackney driver. They'd soon find another, he told Jane, when her visit with her friend was over. Meanwhile, he and Lance would take a little walk, to exercise their stiff joints. She smiled and nodded, knowing they wouldn't go far.

The maid opened the door to her. Peggy's bright smile faded. "Oh, Miss Mayberry," she said, "the mistress took the children to Green Park because it's such a fine day. They've only been gone about ten minutes."

"I must have passed them on my way."

"Mr. Gray is home. Shall I tell him you're here?"

Before Jane could reply, Oliver Gray himself came out of a door at the foot of the staircase. "Jane," he said, "I thought I recognized your voice. You look different. What have you done to yourself?"

It was the pink coat. She never wore pink now because she thought it was too girlish for her. "I hope that's a compliment, Oliver," she said.

He laughed. "Of course it's a compliment. You've never looked better. Come in, come in. I suppose Peggy has told you that you've missed Letty and the children? Will I do instead?"

Oliver Gray was about forty, and looked as though he could have stepped out of the pages of a Gothic novel. He would have had to be the hero, because he was the soul of courtesy and grace. Courtesy and grace, in Jane's experience, were not true indications of what might lie below the surface, but in Oliver's case, they went bone deep. He really cared for people. It was no wonder that all the ladies' groups in his little church were flourishing. She liked him immensely.

The study he showed her into was comfortable though a little shabby. It reminded her of her father's study and that was another mark in Oliver's favor. His desk was strewn with tightly written pages of text, some of them smudged, others with lines scored out or blotted. The wastebasket was overflowing with screwed up balls of paper. She remembered that he was writing a commentary on one of the gospels.

"I see," she said, "you've hit a dry patch."

He laughed and motioned her to the chair on the other side of his desk. "As a writer, you would recognize the signs. I was hoping for an interruption, and here you are, a godsend! You couldn't have come at a better time. Peggy, Miss Mayberry and I will have a cup of tea."

When they were seated, Oliver said, "What brings you to town?"

Without wasting words, Jane gave him an account of the events at Highgate and her subsequent invitation from Lady Sophy to stay at Woodlands.

"Lady Sophy," he said, frowning. "Not Lady Sophy Devere?"

"Yes. Do you know her?"

"I know she's Castleton's aunt, and I know Castleton came here to question Letty about her brother. He questioned you, too. What's going on, Jane?"

He had the knack of seeing through evasions and half-truths to the heart of a matter. She thought it was an excellent trait for a vicar, but not very comfortable for the person who was sitting on the other side of his desk. She considered her choices for a moment, heaved a sigh, then told him as much as she knew.

"So you see," she said finally, "no one knows anything for sure. It might be Letty's brother who is behind these attacks, but there's no real proof."

"If it *is* true," he said, "Letty will be devastated. She's taken some comfort from believing that her brother turned himself around and died for a noble cause. I hope Castleton is wrong."

He looked so grave that she was moved to say, "You don't think Letty is in any danger, I mean, from her own brother?"

"No."

He lapsed into a reflective silence. After a moment or two, she said quietly. "You don't like Gideon Piers, do you, Oliver?"

He looked up with a smile. "I never met him."

"Neither did I, but I formed an opinion from what Letty told me, and he sounds like a thoroughly unpleasant character. Oh, not that Letty said very much, and nothing to his discredit. But . . . I can't put my finger on it, except to say that it's hard to believe they were brother and sister."

"Half-brother and sister," he said. "He was born out of wedlock. It's a common story. His mother was in service and was turned off when it became known that she was with child. A year after Gideon was born, she married Letty's father who gave the boy his own name. Then Letty came along. A few years later, when the father died, they all ended up in the poorhouse."

This part of the story Jane knew well. In the poorhouse, children were separated from their parents. It was traumatic, of course. Letty had had the good fortune to be sent to a Charity School. But not Gideon. And when the mother died, all she got was a pauper's grave. It said a lot for Gideon that this so weighed on his conscience that he'd scrimped and saved to have his mother's remains removed from her unmarked grave to her final resting place in the parish where she was born.

"Why didn't Gideon go to the Charity School?" she asked.

"There aren't too many places available, for one thing. They depend on the generosity of wealthy benefactors. However, he had the chance, but he wouldn't take it. He'd become used to the poorhouse and that's where he wanted to stay."

She was feeling it again, this ambivalence toward Gideon. If he'd turned out bad, who was to blame? And did it matter? He couldn't be allowed to run amok. She supposed, if he were her brother, she would see things differently.

Oliver sat back in his chair and studied her. "What are you thinking, Jane?"

"What I think is that if a dog turns rabid, it should be put down."

"If Lance turned rabid, would you put him down?"

"It would break my heart, but yes, I would do it."

"That's the difference between you and Letty. She never could."

Peggy arrived with tea and cakes at that moment and the conversation moved on to other things.

On the way home, they stopped off at Green Park, but there was no sign of Letty, so Jane ordered the hackney driver to take her to her bank in Bond Street. Harper's brows climbed. He had never heard of a lady of quality doing her own banking. When the hackney stopped, Harper made to go with her, but Jane wouldn't allow it.

"I'm quite capable of doing my own banking," she said in a voice Harper was coming to know only too well.

Resigned, he sank back against the banquette and held onto Lance's collar while Jane stepped down and walked back the few steps that took her to the bank's entrance.

She had very little business to transact, only a withdrawal to keep her in stockings and gloves with something left over for gratuities for the servants when she finally went home to Hillcrest. Five minutes later, she left the bank, but she didn't go straight back to the hackney. Next to the bank was a bootmaker, and her eye was caught by a pair of flimsy pumps in lavender kidskin with ribbons to match. Next door to the boot-maker was a milliner's, and next door to that was a draper's with bolts of muslins, silks, and satins laid out in the window to tempt ladies of fashion to enter the shop.

And there were many ladies of fashion doing just that. This was Bond Street, the most expensive and luxurious shopping district in London. The street was lined with carriages on both sides of the street, and elegant ladies and their escorts were promenading, admiring the displays in all the shop windows.

Bond Street was just around the corner from the Albany on Piccadilly, where Case had his rooms, but Jane didn't expect to run into Case. He was at Twickenham House, planning some school reunion or other.

She was enjoying herself enormously and was seriously considering parting with some of her hard-earned money to buy something frivolous, just for the fun of it. She found what she was looking for in the shop next door to the draper's—a perfumery with a display of fine English and French soaps in its front window. She couldn't afford the lavender pumps, but lavender soap wouldn't bankrupt her.

She looked over her shoulder toward the hackney with Harper inside and was surprised to see how far she'd wandered from it. She was debating whether she should go back and tell him where she was when a gentleman in the height of fashion stepped in front of her, obscuring her view of the hackney. He was tall and broad-shouldered, and the fair hair showing beneath his curly brimmed beaver looked as though it had been carefully combed to frame his handsome face. His look of shock was quickly congealing into a mask of pure dislike.

It was a face she'd hoped never to see again, the face of her long absent husband, James Campbell. Though she kept her face impassive, her heart was racing as though she'd just seen a ghost.

He spoke first. "How does one greet one's errant wife?"

There was a time when the deliberately controlled voice would have sent shivers of dread along her spine. She still feared him, but she wasn't the defenseless, lonely girl she had been when she was in his power with no one to turn to. She had friends now, powerful friends. She had Harper and Lance in a hackney not far away, and most reassuring of all, she had her pistol in her reticule.

More than anything, she wanted to reach in her reticule for that pistol, but he was too close for her to even attempt it. Besides, in spite of the little lecture she'd given herself, her hand was shaking so badly, she didn't think she could handle a pistol. The thought that he could still make her cower made her angry with herself.

She tried to keep her voice level. "Hello, Jack. What are you doing here? I thought you'd be in Edinburgh for Christmas and New Year."

He laughed. "I'll just bet you did. Doesn't this remind you of something? The first time we met? It must be fate."

The first time they met, she'd been shopping in Edinburgh's Princes' Street. Jack had taken one look at her and followed her home. What a romantic fool she'd been then!

He was studying her face so she was careful not to let her fear show. "Do you know," he went on, "I'd given up hope of ever finding you again? I lost your trail in the Highlands of Scotland. But that's what you wanted, wasn't it, Jane, to lay a false trail so that you'd never have to answer to your husband for the wrong you did him?"

"How did you find me?"

"I didn't. You found me. A book, Jane, with my name and direction in it. That was careless of you. A kind gentlemen found it on the banks of the Thames and sent it on to me. So I knew you were in London. I've been looking for you everywhere these last few weeks to no avail."

She remembered losing the book. It was a biography of Sir Thomas More, and she'd spent an afternoon in Chelsea trying to visualize how the village must have looked when Sir Thomas lived there. But that was months ago.

All the books she'd taken with her from Edinburgh had Jack's name stamped in them, though the books were hers. He liked owning things. She knew she'd pasted her own bookplate over his name to obliterate all reference to him. Somehow, it must have become detached.

He was edging closer and she couldn't keep her fear in check. Her voice was hoarse. "I'm not going anywhere with you, Jack. Let me pass."

He laughed and shook his head. "Jane, Jane, you have no say in the matter."

He had a way of hovering just before he struck, mesmerizing her like a cobra with the intensity of his gaze. She was prepared and dodged out of his way just as he reached for her.

She was going the wrong way! Jack was between her and Harper and Lance. A quick look around showed her that pedestrians were looking at them askance and keeping their distance. And if anyone tried to help her, all Jack need say was that she was his wife and they would turn her over to him. It had happened before.

When he reached for her again, she darted into the road, meaning to go around a stationary carriage and race back to her own hackney, but he was too close. Without looking to the right or left, she hared across the street and, at the last moment, threw herself clear of the flailing hooves of horses that had been suddenly reined in by their cursing drivers. Jack was not so reckless as she and that gave her a head start. Picking herself off the pavement, she raced into the narrow street behind Burlington House.

Harper could stand it no longer. Because the hackney was stationed on the left side of the road, he was forced to look out the little window in the back of the vehicle to keep his eye on the bank. He was getting a crick in his neck. Telling Lance to stay, he opened the door and stepped down.

No harm in waiting outside the bank, he decided, and advising the hackney driver to wait, he walked to the bank entrance. *No harm in going inside,* was his next thought. He knew Miss Mayberry wouldn't take kindly to someone looking over her shoulder, so he would do no more than take a quick peek to assure himself that everything was just as it should be.

A quick peek, however, did not reassure him. There was no sign of Miss Mayberry. On applying to one of the bank clerks, he was told that she'd left a good five minutes before. He was alarmed when he left the bank but not panicked. Bond Street had the finest shops in England, and he'd yet to meet a female who could resist the lure of pretty things.

In quick succession, he entered the bootmaker's,

the milliner's, the draper's, and had his hand on the doorknob of the perfumery when he noticed something lying at the side of the road. He picked it up and turned it over in his hand. It was a lady's reticule of embroidered pink velvet and it belonged to Miss Mayberry. Her pistol was still inside it.

He ran back to the hackney to get Lance. After tying a leash on Lance's collar, he let him sniff the reticule. "Find her, boy," he said. "Find her."

Lord Francis Reeve was at his usual table in the front window of the King's Arms in Vigo Street. He'd lost a good deal of money at the gaming tables the night before and was in a foul humor. He'd already complained to the waiter that the steak-and-kidney pudding he'd been served wasn't fit for pigs, but since he'd eaten every morsel, the waiter refused to take the meal off his bill. A gentleman asked if he might share his table and he snarled him away.

As he munched on the last slice of toast and washed it down with coffee, he reflected on his future. Everything had been going well until Jane Mayberry poked her long nose into his affairs, and now the girl who was to save him from debtors' prison had been taken up by Castleton's set. Little Miss Emily Drake, he'd heard, was fast becoming the toast of the *ton*.

It galled him. It damn near choked him. He hadn't forgotten the indignities he'd suffered at Castleton's hands, egged on by that prune-faced Mayberry woman. They'd made a grave mistake. He didn't know how it could be done, but he'd promised himself that one day he would make them pay for it, and by damn he would!

He was staring idly out the window when the subject of his reflections came into view. For a moment, he thought he was imagining it. Jane Mayberry didn't look a bit like the dowd who had accosted him in Highgate. She was wearing a rose colored coat with a bonnet to match. But nothing could disguise the set of those slender shoulders or the proud tilt of that chin. He wished he could smack it.

Maybe this was his chance to teach her a lesson. Vigo Street wasn't exactly a busy thoroughfare. It was no more than a lane behind the grand mansions that lined Piccadilly. All he could see from the dining room window were high brick walls to protect the gardens from prying eyes. That could be to his advantage if Miss Mayberry were alone.

He got up, then sat down again when he saw that she wasn't alone. She had turned to face someone who was running to catch up with her. Reeve's gaze shifted to take in a good-looking man in his thirties whose garments were far more fashionable than his own. Obviously the stranger did not suffer from a lack of funds.

It happened so quickly that he was frozen with shock. One moment the stranger was talking pleasantly to Miss Mayberry, and the next moment he had shoved her to the ground. She pulled herself to her knees and got up, and the stranger felled her with a blow to the stomach.

Reeve looked around the dining room, but no one else seemed to have noticed the drama that was unfolding out front, and he certainly wasn't going to raise the alarm. He turned back to watch the spectacle.

The stranger was helping Miss Mayberry to her feet. She could barely stand, barely hold her head up. It wasn't surprising. She had just been felled by a man

who outweighed her by four or five stone. He wished
he were in the stranger's shoes and wondered what
his connection might be to Miss Mayberry. He meant
to find out.

As before, it happened so quickly that he was
frozen in shock. Seventy pounds of savage, snarling
wolf—fangs bared, ears back—came out of nowhere
and charged the stranger, forcing him back against
the brick wall. Miss Mayberry said something, a command to the wolf, Reeve thought, but it didn't have
much effect. It stood there, hackles raised, fangs
bared, ready to pounce if the man moved an inch or
Miss Mayberry gave the word.

Miss Mayberry spoke again and the wolf changed
into something that was closer to a dog. Only then
did Reeve notice that its back was protected by a flan-
nel coat. It left the man, and trotted over to her, rubbing against her legs, licking her face when she
petted it.

Reeve swallowed, remembering that she'd warned
him if he'd hurt her stableboy, she would have her
dog tear his throat out. He'd thought she was exag-
gerating. Now he believed her.

The stranger saw his chance and took it. While the
dog's attention was distracted, he bolted for the front
door of the King's Arms. The wolf-dog broke away
from Miss Mayberry and went after him. Reeve didn't
wait to see more. He hurried to the front door and
opened it just as the stranger reached it and hurled
himself inside.

She leaned against the wall as her stomach began
to heave, but all that came up was a little bile. She

couldn't move without crying out, but pain or not, she knew she had to get away before Jack came back.

"Lance," she called, and he was there, whining, nibbling at her gloved fingers.

Steadying herself with one hand against the wall, she began to retrace her steps. She hadn't gone far when Harper turned the corner into Vigo Street. The sight of that solid body and unfriendly scowl brought more tears to her eyes. She'd never been happier to see anyone in her life.

His pistol was in one hand, her reticule in the other, and he was panting from running to keep up with Lance. Having ascertained that there was no immediate danger, he stuffed her reticule in his waistband and went to help her. "What in blazes happened?" he demanded, fear making him sound angry. "I let you out of my sight for a few minutes, and now look at you."

He supported her with one arm around her shoulders. "I was attacked," she said. "I'm not really up to talking. Please get me away from here, Harper."

He could see that she couldn't go far. He was in no condition to carry her and he couldn't leave her in the state she was in to fetch the hackney. By a stroke of good fortune, however, the back gate into the Albany, where Lord Castleton had his rooms, was only a few steps away in Burlington Gardens, and the key to the gate was in his pocket.

"Where are you taking me?" she asked when he opened the gate.

"To Lord Castleton's rooms. You can rest there till I fetch the hackney to take you home."

"I thought the Albany was on Piccadilly."

"This is the back way in."

He questioned her about the attack again, but

gave up when she answered him vaguely. He wasn't suspicious. All he thought was that she would tell him everything when she was more herself. On one point, however, she was able to reassure him. The man who attacked her was not one of the men who had set fire to her barn.

When Harper shut the stout wooden gate and locked it, she felt that she had entered a fortress. The garden wall must have been about eight feet high. It was a good feeling, but she knew it wouldn't last. Now that Jack had found her, he wouldn't give up. He would soon come looking for her again. If there was one thing she did not doubt, it was that Jack Campbell would not give up.

Ruggles was there, pressing his master's clothes, and she found his friendly face as comforting as Harper's dour one. There was something about red hair and freckles that inspired trust. He looked so sane and ordinary.

After Harper left, Ruggles put a glass of brandy in her hand, but the first sip made her stomach heave, so she set it aside. He was full of questions, too, but she told him no more than she'd told Harper: that she was attacked by someone who must have seen her come out of the bank, and when she ran, he gave chase. It was a lame story, but unless he was willing to call her a liar he had to accept it, and until she had spoken to Case and Lady Sophy, that was all anyone was going to get out of her.

As Ruggles went off to make her a cup of tea in lieu of the brandy, she pressed her fingers to her temples. She had a searing headache. Her stomach was still heaving, and each breath seemed more difficult than the last. When Jack lashed out, he didn't hold back his punches. She'd been lucky. He'd only hit her once. But he knew how to make a blow count. He'd punched her in the stomach, and she still couldn't draw a deep breath.

Lance put his head in her lap and whined softly. That small sound of sympathy brought fresh tears to her eyes. "Don't go all sappy on me," she said, "or I'll never manage to pull myself together. There, there, I'm all right. If it hadn't been for you, I'd probably be on my way back to Scotland right now." The thought made her shudder.

Harper had left her reticule on the table beside her chair. She reached for it and drew out a smallish, pearl-handled pistol, the smallest in what was fast becoming an arsenal. Because of its size, it was ideal for hiding in a lady's reticule. Too bad she'd dropped the reticule. That was the thing about ladies' clothes. There were no oversized pockets to stuff things in, as men had.

She leveled the pistol and pretended that Jack was coming at her again. There was no doubt about it. She possessed the killer instinct in full measure.

"Isn't it funny," she said sadly, "how things turn out?"

When she'd first met Jack, she'd been swept off her feet. At eighteen, she'd been impressed by his gentlemanly manners, his charm, his good looks. So had her father. James Campbell must have seemed like the answer to a prayer. He was distantly related to the Dukes of Argyll. His father was a baronet. He had a fine house in Edinburgh's New Town. He loved Jane and she loved him.

So her father had given his blessing and they were married.

It soon became clear that her husband's courtesy and charm were only skin deep and reserved for his friends and acquaintances, not for his wife. She had assumed that her marriage would be much like her parents'. There would be teasing, and debating, arguing, and laughter. Laughter especially. What a foolish idealist she'd been then.

Jack wanted something different. He wanted to dominate her; he wanted to possess her entirely.

In the beginning, she'd made allowances for his fits of jealousy and sudden bursts of temper. She was spoiled, he said, and she knew there was some truth in that, so she tried to become what he wanted her to be. She stopped making allowances for him the night he walked into her bedchamber and, without warning, knocked her to the floor with a backhanded blow. Her crime, he said, was contradicting him in front of his friends. They had been married for less than two months.

Things only got worse. The smallest offense on her part would incite him to fury. She wasn't sure which she despised more, his violence or his protestations of love afterward and his pathetic attempts to make amends. For the two years she had stayed with him, she'd accumulated a coffer of expensive trinkets with which he'd tried to buy her forgiveness. When she left, she took the trinkets with her. To her way of thinking, she'd earned every one of them. Of course, there was no sentiment involved. In fact, she sold every piece before she left Edinburgh. She needed the money to start a new life somewhere else, somewhere far, far away from Jack Campbell.

She might have stayed with him longer if her father hadn't died. That was a turning point. She wanted Jack to offer Mrs. Trent a place with them, but this he refused to do. He'd pinched her cheek, kissed her on the lips, and said words to the effect that they already had more servants than they knew what to do with, and Mrs. Trent should have retired a long time ago. She had a married daughter, didn't she? Let her go to her.

That wasn't the reason he wouldn't offer Mrs. Trent a position. It was because he was insanely jealous. He knew how much Mrs. Trent meant to her. She was like family, but he didn't want her to have any family or close friends. He wanted her all to himself.

She remembered thinking at the time, as she stared into his smiling face, *Stand up for yourself, you sniveling little coward! Don't let him browbeat you like this!* But in spite of his smile, she saw the watchful look in his eyes, and her nerve deserted her.

She made a sound that was not quite a sob. In retrospect, she didn't know where she'd got the courage to leave him. By that time, she was frightened of her own shadow. She had no friends—Jack had seen to that—no family, no one to help her. But by damn, she'd done it, and she'd never looked back.

In London, she'd found a job as a teacher at St. Bede's under her maiden name. She'd made friends. She'd loved working with the children. She was happy. After three years, she felt confident enough to write to her father's solicitor in Edinburgh, asking if Jack had made any move to divorce her, and the solicitor passed her letter onto Jack's solicitor, who straightway gave it to Jack.

This time, she had friends to turn to, and when Jack came storming in the front door of St. Bede's, they delayed him and helped her slip out the back. These same friends, Letty and Miss Hepburn, arranged for her to go into hiding, and she eventually ended up in Scotland, in the little cottage her parents used to rent for holidays.

That's where she found Lance, or he found her.

That was another turning point. They became inseparable. They were both runaways and that forged a bond between them, or so it seemed to her.

She'd made up her mind that Jack Campbell wasn't going to steal her life. She couldn't go back to St. Bede's, not now that she had a dog, and she had no intention of giving up Lance. They'd start over, she and Sir Lancelot, and find a place where they would both be welcome. And so she'd stumbled upon Lady Octavia and the Ladies' Library.

She'd made up her mind about something else. The next time Jack tracked her down, she would be ready for him. She wasn't a fool. She wasn't going to advertise her whereabouts or grow careless. But the next time, she would stand her ground.

"And what did I do?" she asked Lance with a shaky laugh. "I dropped the blasted reticule with my pistol inside it and ran for my life. Lucky for me you came along when you did."

And now she had to face Case—she was done with calling him Lord Castleton in the privacy of her own thoughts—and make a clean breast of things.

She thought about this for a long time. She supposed it was too much to ask that they remain friends. Something had happened between them that shouldn't have been allowed to happen. Now, perhaps, he would understand.

Chapter 14

On reflection, Jane decided not to tell Lady Sophy about the attack. She didn't want anyone to call in the authorities, or a doctor, or make a fuss, because she wanted Case to be the first to know, and she wanted him to hear it directly from her. So she swore Harper to secrecy, at least until she could speak to Case in person, then she washed the dirt from her hands and face and after dusting off her clothes, sallied forth as though she'd done nothing more dangerous than spend an interesting morning visiting a friend and doing a little shopping.

Evidently, she didn't play her part very well, for the carriage had gone no farther than Hyde Park when Lady Sophy's spate of chitchat faltered and finally died away.

After an interval of silence, her ladyship said, "Are you well, Jane?"

"Oh, quite well," Jane hastened to reply.

"I ask because it seems to me that you're not your usual self."

Jane allowed that she was fighting off an incipient headache.

Lady Sophy nodded. "That would explain why you appear to be so...unsettled."

She wasn't unsettled so much as preoccupied, trying to imagine how Case would respond when she told him the truth about herself. It wasn't a prospect she was looking forward to.

Her ladyship gave her attention to the passing scenery. "Have I ever told you about Caspar's mother?" she asked.

"You've told me that she was vivacious and liked to shock society," Jane answered, wondering where this conversation was leading.

"She was and she did," Lady Sophy replied approvingly. "And we all loved her very much." She gave Jane one of her Devere clear-eyed stares. "Her marriage to Caspar's father rocked society and, I'm happy to say, it rocked my pompous brother as well. He was the duke then. Elizabeth wasn't one of us, you see. That was my brother's view. Her father was only a country squire, and that did not sit well with the duke. They married in spite of him. Of course, there was an estrangement between father and son. My brother never relented, not even after Caspar was born."

"That's sad," said Jane, not knowing what else to say. It was an interesting story, but the question she was loath to ask was: *Why are you telling me this?*

Lady Sophy answered her in the next breath. "Caspar's father would never deal with his own children as his father dealt with him. I know he can appear intimidating, and I'm the first to admit that he is a little stuffy, but at heart, he really is a dear. All he wants for his children is for them to be happy, as he was happy with his Elizabeth. Look how he gave his blessing to Rosamund when she wanted to marry her Richard."

There was no confusion now in Jane's mind. She knew exactly what Lady Sophy was implying. She was much more direct than her ladyship. "There is nothing between your nephew and myself," she said, then added belatedly, "except friendship."

"Oh, Jane," said her ladyship, and laughed. "Oh, Jane."

Case recognized the Devere coach as it emerged from behind the stands of trees that bordered the small lake. A moment or two later, it rolled to a stop in front of the stately portico of Twickenham House. He was looking out an upstairs window, in the billiard room, and behind him were his friends Waldo, Robert, and Freddie. They'd been discussing the reunion that was just one week away.

"Less than a week," said Robert Shay significantly.

Case was watching Harper open the coach door. His aunt stepped down first, then Jane with Lance right behind her. Jane conferred with Harper who nodded, and a moment or two later, having put a leash on Lance, he turned and made for the stable block with the dog trotting happily beside him. Satisfied, apparently, with the arrangements she'd made for Lance, Jane entered the house.

Case's lips curved. The idea for the visit to Twickenham House had come from him. He wanted Jane to see that the Deveres did not live on a grand scale. They were ordinary people, more or less. He'd planned everything down to the last detail—the guest list, the menu, the informal party—to convince Jane that she could fit in without any awkwardness. In fact, she'd be an asset.

Of course, there was Castle Devere to consider, but that could wait. His father hadn't taken his mother to Castle Devere until long after they were married. It was a point worth noting.

There was another reason for the reception, a more compelling reason. He wanted Piers to think that all was normal at Twickenham House, that nobody suspected anything. The last thing they wanted was to convey the impression that they were preparing for a siege.

"Did you hear me, Case?"

Case let the muslin drape fall and turned back to his companions. "Yes, I heard you, Robert." He took a chair by the fire. "You think we should cancel the reunion and turn the investigation over to Special Branch and let them deal with it."

"I do," said Robert.

"And what will Special Branch do that we're not doing?"

"They'll undertake a massive investigation and ferret Piers out."

"But we *have* ferreted him out. This is our best chance of getting him. He won't scare off. He may go underground for a while, and when he surfaces again, we'll be back at the beginning, not knowing where he intends to strike next."

There was a long silence, then Freddie said, "Well, I'm not a soldier, but I think Piers would be a fool to attack Twickenham House, and he doesn't sound like a fool to me. He's bound to know it's well guarded. Impregnable, in fact."

Case sighed. "Freddie, it had better not be impregnable, or we'll never catch Piers."

"Oh. Yes. I see."

Robert said, "You're very quiet, Waldo. What do you think?"

Waldo was lounging against the billiard table. "I agree with Case. But that doesn't make me complacent. As Freddie said, Piers is no fool. If plan A fails, he'll switch to plan B. We should be prepared for anything."

"What about the gold he stole?" asked Robert. "Where is it now?"

"It was never recovered," answered Waldo.

"I think it was," said Case. "Not by us, but by Piers. It's probably sitting in some bank vault. He must be a very rich man."

They fell silent when a footman entered with a fresh pot of coffee. "Just leave it on the table," said Case.

When they had topped up their cups, Robert said, "Piers seems to be lying low right now." He looked at Case. "Do you think he's still playing games?"

"Playing games?" Case took a swallow of coffee. "That's one way of putting it. The short answer is yes. I think he's enjoying himself enormously. He's taunting me, daring me to find him before he tires of the game. And so far, he's winning. What's worrisome is what he'll try next."

There was a profound silence, then Robert said, "Why does he hate you so much, Case?"

"I suppose," said Case, "because I commanded the unit that wiped out his men. They refused to surrender, so there were no prisoners."

Waldo added, "And Piers has never forgiven us for it."

Robert nodded, but he was far from satisfied with their answer.

"And now, gentlemen," said Case, "His Grace is waiting for us."

Luncheon was served in the long gallery with its beautiful vista of the river Thames. Though there must have been about forty guests, the gallery could quite easily have accommodated three times that number. Long, damask-covered tables were laid out with platters of every kind of delicacy, and guests were encouraged to help themselves, picnic-style, then seat themselves at one of the smaller tables that were set out at intervals around the room.

"I think," said Sally in an undertone to Jane, "that the informal manners are for Emily's benefit, you know, to make her and her family feel more comfortable. If we sat down to eat in the dining room, the rules of precedence would apply and poor Emily would find herself at the wrong end of the table."

"Next to me," Jane replied dryly.

Her eyes searched the knots of guests until she found Emily. Once again, she was flirting outrageously, but Jane didn't recognize any of the young men who were hovering around her.

It was, thought Jane, a most agreeable group of people. She already knew some of them, from the Ladies' Library. All the same, she wasn't enjoying herself, couldn't enjoy herself. She was rehearsing in her mind what she would say to Case, how she would explain about Jack.

She'd made up her mind that she wasn't going to apologize. She couldn't change the past and she couldn't change what she was. If she'd taken everyone into her confidence, Jack would have learned where she was, and that was the last thing she'd wanted.

No. She wasn't going to apologize. She was proud of what she had done with her life these last several years.

Then why did she feel guilty?

Case wasn't just anybody. He'd been a good friend to her. The best. That's where she had made her mistake. She should have kept him at arm's length.

But how did one keep the incoming tide at arm's length?

As if on cue, Case and his father suddenly appeared at the glass entrance doors. There might as well have been a fanfare announcing their arrival, because the room instantly fell silent and everyone who was sitting got up.

Sally giggled. "So much for informality," she whispered. "Poor Romsey. Poor Case. It's not their fault if people treat them like royalty."

Jane wondered about that. They made a striking pair, the duke and his son. Their resemblance was so close that no one could have mistaken the relationship. But it was the way they held themselves that made the deepest impression. Here were men who were sure of their place in the scheme of things.

Case said something to His Grace, whose face immediately broke into a pleasant smile. He threw up his hands. "Welcome to Twickenham House," he said in a deep, booming voice. "We're all here to enjoy ourselves, so no standing on ceremony. Carry on! Carry on!"

"And that's an order," whispered Sally.

It was an order no one seemed inclined to obey. People just stood there, darting uneasy glances at each other from the corners of their eyes, willing someone else to make the first move. Case stepped into the breach. He snapped his fingers and a small group of musicians in one corner of the gallery began to play. Then he led his father to a knot of people where they stayed to chat.

A collective sigh went up, and gradually people went back to doing what they'd been doing before the duke arrived. Jane kept a surreptitious eye on Case, but he was never alone, and the time never seemed right to approach him. He didn't ignore her, though. She and Sally shared a table with Lady Octavia and her husband and Case stopped to speak to them, then he moved on, and coward that she was, she felt relieved. This wasn't an interview she was looking forward to.

In fact, the thought of it filled her with dread.

After luncheon, the guests were free to wander over the house or bundle up and go outdoors for a brisk walk. A concert was planned for late in the afternoon, excerpts from Mozart's *Don Giovanni,* to whet everyone's appetite for the gala premiere in England that was to take place in March.

Jane wasn't up to walking far, so she joined the group that Lady Sophy was taking round the conservatory. This was obviously Lady Sophy's domain, for at every bank of exotic flowers, she went into minute detail on the cultivation and propagation of the species. After a while, Jane found herself yawning, so she dropped back and found a wooden bench where she could rest and meditate in silence.

When a shadow fell over her, she looked up. "Case," she said, "I've been thinking about you."

"Well, don't look so fearful. I'm not going to bite you."

He was studying her face, so she made an effort to smile. Gathering her courage, she finally said the words she was dreading saying. "We must talk. There is something particular I want to say to you."

She made room for him on the bench. "What is it?" he asked her.

Two young women had stopped nearby when they saw Case, and were now examining the bark of a gnarled old palm tree as though it were gold-plated. This was not the time for confession.

"You have a beautiful home," she said lightly.

Grinning, he picked up one of her hands and held it casually. There was nothing casual about her reaction. She stopped breathing.

"That doesn't tell me much," he said. "I want to know whether you like it or not."

His boyish eagerness made her smile. "I don't think I've been in a house I like more."

"You haven't seen the grounds yet. Get your coat and bonnet, and we'll go for a drive."

He held out his hand and helped her to rise. When they were out of earshot of the two inquisitive hoverers, she said quietly, "We must talk."

He turned to face her. "I'm listening."

"Not here. Somewhere—"

They were interrupted by a young man in a blue coat whose name Jane forgot as soon as it was mentioned. He wanted to ask Case about the reunion, and whether or not he'd remembered to invite another young man whose name Jane also forgot.

When his friend sauntered off, Case said, "You see how it is. I'm at everyone's beck and call. Just for a little while, I want to please myself. I want to be with you, Jane."

The tension in her neck spread to her spine. She had to stop this before it went too far. A vain hope! It had already gone too far and she had no one to blame but herself.

Someone else hailed Case and he said quickly, "Get your coat, and meet me at the front door. And be quick about it or we may never get away."

She'd already made up her mind that this wasn't the time or place to make a clean breast of things. Driving a curricle was too much of a distraction. She didn't have his full attention. Better by far, she decided, to wait until they were away from Twickenham and all the duties that occupied him as host. She'd tell him when they got home to Woodlands. And if he didn't go home to Woodlands with them, she'd invent some pretext to get him there.

Her logic was faultless, and it was all a lie. She shrank from saying the words that would change things forever between them.

He reined in his team when they came to the summit of the rise.

When she looked up at him, her heart cramped. Right from the beginning, she'd been prejudiced against him. Now that she knew him, she could see below the surface. There was more to him, far more, than good looks, a title, and wealth. He was proud, but he wasn't conceited. He was generous to his friends, generous, open-minded, and as straight as an arrow. When he said something, he meant it.

How could she hope to make him understand?

"Now," he said, "what is it you want to say to me?"

She felt the quick rush of color to her cheeks and quickly looked away. "What I want to say can't be said in a few minutes. Will you call on me tonight after we get back to Woodlands?"

"Jane, let me see your eyes."

When she turned, he studied her face. "It's about us, isn't it?"

"Yes," she said simply. "It's about us."

He gave her a long, searching look, then slowly smiled. "I suppose my aunt has been talking to you?"

"Yes. No. It isn't that."

He bent his head and swiftly kissed her. It wasn't a passionate kiss, nothing more than the brush of his lips on hers, but everything inside her melted with longing. Her fingers fisted in the lapel of his coat.

"Oh, my," he said when he drew away. His breathing was audible. "It doesn't matter what you say, your eyes speak volumes. Jane, don't look so stricken. I promise my intentions are honorable." And he laughed in that careless way of his.

When she made to reply, he shook his head. "As you said, we'll talk at Woodlands. Now this is what I wanted to show you."

Following his gaze, she looked down on Twickenham House and its extensive grounds. The sun was low in the sky, and its wintry rays were caught and reflected back by the many small-paned windows of the three-story house. The stable block was twice the size of her own house, and below the stable block, where the turf ended, she could just glimpse the river with the odd boat floating on its surface. The whole scene was picture-book perfect.

"It's beautiful," she said, trying not to sound as wooden as she felt.

They did the circuit twice, to exercise the horses,

he said, and each time he pointed out something else of interest—the folly, the man-made lake, the rotunda, and the infirmary, which turned out to be the old coach house where His Grace pursued his hobby of rebuilding broken-down coaches. He assumed that this was her first visit to his home and she let him go on thinking it because he was enjoying showing her everything.

She smiled and laughed in all the right places, but there was no joy in it, only an ocean of regret.

As guests filed into the music room and took their places for the concert, Case kept his distance from Jane and stationed himself in one of the window alcoves at the back of the room. He wanted to sit beside her, but he knew that if he did, it would be tantamount to a declaration of his intentions and Jane wasn't ready for that.

He had a fair idea of what she wanted to say to him. She'd want to point out the vast disparity in their social standing, she had no fortune, his family would expect him to make a brilliant match, and so on and so on. Just thinking about it made him want to yawn.

Or she might try another tack: how she was settled in the single life and wanted everything to go on as before. If he couldn't laugh her out of it, maybe he'd kiss her out of it.

It could be, of course, that she'd fling his past in his teeth as she'd done once before. But things had changed between them since then. All the same, she might have some serious reservations about committing herself to a man whose name had been linked to a string of highflyers. The thought made him wince.

The odd thing was that in spite of his less-than-saintly past, he felt as though he were coming to her as a new man. For the first time in his life, he wanted more than passion from a woman. He wanted intimacy, in the fullest sense of that word. He wanted to share his life with her and he wanted to share her life, too.

The musicians took their places and began to tune their instruments. Observing Waldo sitting off by himself, Case went and joined him.

"You look windblown," he remarked.

"So would you if you'd spent the last hour or two walking Miss Mayberry's dog."

"Where was Harper?"

"Where do you think? In the infirmary with His Grace, resurrecting some ancient relic that, in my opinion, deserves a decent burial."

Case laughed. "Just as long as someone is watching my father's back."

"Don't worry, we've got him covered."

The opening strains of the overture had hardly begun when a footman approached Case and told him he was wanted in the vestibule. When Case left the room, Waldo went after him.

A porter from the lodge handed Case a note. "Two gentlemen," he said, "wanted to talk to you. They said it was urgent, but their names wasn't on the list, so we wouldn't open the gates. Not very pleasant they was, if you don't mind my saying so, your lordship. They left this note for you, then went off in quite a taking."

Case opened the note and quickly scanned it.

Sir,

If you wish to save Miss Mayberry and yourself from public disgrace and humiliation, I suggest you

meet me in the Saracen's Head in Twickenham.
I shall give you until eight o'clock.

Your servant, sir
James Campbell

"Who the devil is James Campbell?" Case demanded.

No one could answer him.

"What was the other man's name?" he asked the porter.

"Reeve," replied the porter. "Lord Reeve, it was."

Reeve! He'd forgotten about Reeve, but he shouldn't have. Reeve had been humiliated. He'd lost Miss Drake and, of course, he blamed that on Jane and himself. If Reeve thought he'd let him embarrass or hurt Jane in any way, he would soon learn his error.

When Case thrust the note into his pocket, Waldo said, "Is this our friend Piers up to his old tricks?"

"No," said Case. "This is a personal matter, but I'd like you to come with me."

"Where are we going?"

"Twickenham. We'll take my curricle. We should be there in ten minutes."

Chapter 15

She delayed going to bed for as long as she could, but eventually she had to face the fact that Case wasn't coming and all she was doing was keeping the servants from their own beds. She wasn't alarmed, but she was puzzled. He'd left her without a word of explanation, no note or message with one of the footmen. All Harper would say was that something had come up and his lordship had gone into Twickenham with Mr. Bowman. But Harper hadn't offered her the information. She'd had to ask.

"It's doesn't mean anything," she told Lance as they began to climb the stairs.

Ruggles was already in the corridor, not far from the door to her chamber, and she caught him off guard. He was sitting beside the table with the lamp on it, munching on a sandwich. There was a pistol on the table and a tankard of ale. At sight of her, his fair skin went a guilty red.

"Miss Mayberry," he stammered. "I thought you'd gone to bed."

"No, don't get up. You look as though you should be in your own bed. You can't be on duty morning, noon, and night, you know. I said sit down, Mr. Ruggles."

He sat, but he didn't look comfortable. "I'm not on duty all the time. Mr. Harper or one of the other footmen usually relieves me early in the morning. Then I sleep." He grinned sheepishly. "Or I try to, but I'm not used to going to bed when the sun comes up."

Lance had trotted over to him and was now sniffing at one of his pockets. "Oh, not you, too, Mr. Ruggles," she said.

Another sheepish grin. "Mr. Harper advised me to keep a bit of bacon in my pocket in case I came face-to-face with your dog when you weren't there. May I give it to him?"

She nodded. "He's not savage, you know. He doesn't attack without provocation. You might say his bark is worse than his bite."

Ruggles laughed. Lance took the proffered bacon in one swallow. "Good dog," said Ruggles, and patted Lance, but he did it gingerly.

"You're not used to dogs." It was more of a statement than a question.

"There's no place for dogs when you're in service. And in the houses where I've worked, the dogs are kept outside, so I've never had much truck with them. But one of these days, I'm going to open a nice little tavern. Then maybe I'll get myself a dog."

What he left unsaid, but what Jane picked up right

away, was that he might also get himself a nice little wife and a nice little family. There was no place for children or pets when one was in service, and every footman she had ever known dreamed of saving enough money so that he could start his own little business. A few achieved their ambitions, but only a few. She hoped Ruggles would be one of them.

She nodded to the pistol. "Do you know how to use that thing?"

"Not so you'd notice," he said, and they both laughed. "But Mr. Harper is giving me lessons."

He hadn't touched his sandwich since she'd appeared on the scene and she knew he wouldn't until she was gone, so she bid him goodnight and entered her chamber.

She'd told the maid not to wait up for her, but she had left a candle burning on the mantel. The fire was banked for the night and the bedclothes were turned down. The pitcher of water on the washstand had cooled in the interim, but it was still warm. Sighing, she began to disrobe.

When she was naked, she examined herself in the long cheval mirror. There were no bruises or marks to show that she'd been assaulted. That was the thing with Jack. He was such a gentleman. He took good care to make sure that he never left any bruises to mar her beauty. Occasionally, he misjudged his blows, but not very often and not this time.

It was humiliating. She hated this feeling of helplessness. One of these days she'd have to do something about Jack before he killed her. It wasn't the first time she'd had that thought, but she had never done anything. Perhaps it was time.

She went to bed with her little pearl-handled pistol tucked under her pillow, and with her dog on the hearth. It didn't stop her from tossing and turning. Thoughts came and went. Where was Jack and what would he do now that he knew she was in London? Where was Gideon Piers? When would she see Case and what would she say to him?

Where was Case, and what was she going to say to him?

After ten minutes of turmoil, she pushed back the bedclothes and got up. She lit the candle from the fire, wrapped herself in her warm woolen robe, then looked around for a book to read. Her attention changed direction when Lance got up and with one of his purring sounds of pleasure bounded to the door.

She heard the low murmur of voices, then someone knocked on her door.

Although she was sure it was Case, after that morning's events, she wasn't taking any chances. When she opened the door, she had her pistol in her hand. Lance bounded forward.

"Good boy," Case said. "Yes, I'm glad to see you, too. But you're going with Ruggles right now for a little walk." Then to Ruggles, "Give me the leash." He hooked the leash onto Lance's collar. "Wait for me at the stable block," he told Ruggles. "This shouldn't take long."

When he entered the room and shut the door, Jane had no doubt that he was gripped by powerful emotions. His face was set, and his hands fisted and unfisted at his sides. She could smell the brandy on him. Just as fear began to rise in her, he pushed past her and walked to the fireplace. With his arm resting on the mantel, he faced her across the width of the room.

He made a slashing movement with one hand.

"Put that damn thing away. I'm not going to hurt you."

She'd forgotten that she was holding her pistol. She set it on top of the dresser but kept her distance from him. In spite of his reassuring words, he'd been drinking; he was also a powerful male animal in the grip of strong emotions and that made her doubly wary.

This anger couldn't be the result of Harper telling him about Jack's attack, she was thinking. His next words electrified her.

"Well, don't stand there staring, *Mrs. Campbell.* Come into the light so I can see the face of the lying jade who deceived me. Deceived us all, in fact."

He wanted her to protest that there was some mistake, that Campbell must be confusing her with some other woman, but that was sheer wishful thinking on his part. Besides, her face betrayed her. Her skin went parchment white and she gazed at him with large, fear-bright eyes.

He didn't like Campbell. Two minutes after meeting the man he'd summed him up as a vain, swaggering braggart. If their positions were reversed, if he were married to Jane and he thought Campbell was her lover, he would have called him out. In spite of his bluster, Campbell was pathetic. His wife had deserted him. He'd had no word from her in years. Then he discovers her in London, meets her by chance in Bond Street, and all is forgiven. He realizes he still loves her.

And that was what rankled; that was what galled him. She'd worked the same siren's spell on him. Even knowing how she'd tricked him, deceived him, he still loved her.

Her voice was no more than a whisper. "How did you find out?"

"Campbell found me. With the help of that toad, Reeve. Seems Reeve saw you set Lance on your erstwhile husband this morning in Vigo Street, and afterward made his acquaintance, with, I need hardly add, one object in mind—to gloat at my expense."

He hurled the words at her. "Why didn't you tell me? Why did you lead me on?"

And here was something else that rankled. He'd organized the whole day to make her realize how easily she would fit into his life and all the time she'd been concealing the one compelling reason that could have stopped him before he made a complete and utter fool of himself. He didn't care what others thought of him, but he despised himself for being so completely taken in by her. She'd played with him, uncaring of how true and deep his feelings went.

Guilt made her look away. "I tried to tell you, but the moment never seemed right. There was always someone with you or with me. That's why I asked you to come here tonight, so that I could tell you about Jack."

"If you had one ounce of integrity, you would have told me long before now."

The unjust words had the effect of making her temper blaze as hotly as his. "I didn't tell you because I thought I was entitled to my private life."

When he advanced on her, she held her ground, and when he stopped only inches from her, instinct made her hold up her head and keep her eyes steady on his. In a low, calming voice, she said, "From the very beginning, I tried to make it plain that I was happy with my life just the way it was, that I didn't need or want a man in it. You wouldn't listen."

Her composure only made him angrier. "Oh, no," he said. "From the very beginning, you've drawn me into your life, if you can call it a life. No, you didn't ask for my help, but your eyes, your *lovely* eyes, speak volumes. And I was there when you needed me."

Tears clogged her throat. She couldn't deny it. He'd taken her part against Lord Reeve; he'd rescued Ben; he'd helped her with Emily and taken her in when she'd nowhere else to go. "I didn't know. I didn't understand. It wasn't supposed to happen." She stopped when her voice cracked.

He gathered her hair in his hands. "Didn't know what? That I was falling in love with you?"

"No," she said, making a moan of the word. "That I was falling in love with you."

For long, endless moments, he stared at her, and the fury in his eyes gradually dimmed. She thought he was going to kiss her, but he let go of her hair, turned aside, and went back to the fire. He spoke with a kind of weariness. "You've done nothing but tell me a pack of lies from the moment I met you. But all that is over and done with. Campbell is ready to forgive and forget if you'll only go back to him."

Her mind was numb, then it was awash with fear. She had to swallow the dryness in her throat. "What did you tell him?"

"Oh, I didn't say much. I suppose I was too shocked to think straight. Campbell did most of the talking. Can you believe he still loves you and wants you back? He mentioned an heir. Seems his father would like to see his line continued. In fact, he's insisting on it."

She was aghast. "I'll never go back to him!"

"If you don't, he's going to instigate divorce proceedings against you."

"On what grounds?"

"Adultery."

The breath she exhaled was the only sound in the room. "With whom?"

He said savagely, "Whom do you think? With me, of course."

"But we haven't done anything wrong!"

"Maybe not, but it won't be hard for Campbell to find witnesses to testify that I've stayed the night at your house in Highgate, and here at Woodlands. You're the one who warned me that your neighbors had the wrong idea about us." His jaw tensed. "If I'd known there was a husband waiting in the wings, I would have taken care not to get caught in the trap we're now in."

His tone of voice, his expression, assaulted her like hammer blows. As in a daze, she felt her way to the bed and sat down. There was a loose thread on the cover and she stared at it, trying to put her thoughts in order. She spoke slowly, as the thoughts occurred to her. "I don't care if he divorces me. In fact, it would be the answer to a prayer. But I can't believe he'd give me up so easily. There must be a catch in it somewhere."

He was suddenly looming over her and she involuntarily flinched away. "The catch is *me,*" he said viciously. "He has caught a big fish in his net and he won't let me go."

When she looked at him blankly, he went on, "I'm talking about punitive damages. You remember Uxbridge, don't you? He had to pay the wronged husband twenty thousand pounds in damages for stealing his wife's affections or whatever they call it in legal terms. Frankly, Miss Mayberry, you're not worth twenty thousand pounds to me."

She remembered the divorce action against Lord

Uxbridge very well. It had rocked society. He'd paid another ten thousand pounds to get out of his own marriage. Now everybody was happily married to someone else.

She wanted to laugh; she wanted to cry. She looked up at him. "But you can avoid paying punitive damages if—what?"

"If you leave my protection. If you go back to him."

There was a roaring in her ears and her heart lurched. He didn't know what he was asking of her. But he should have known. If he truly cared for her, he would have taken her part.

His eyes were searching her face. Before he could see just how much he had hurt her, she surged to her feet and sent him staggering back. She made straight for the closet where her box was kept. She dragged it into the center of the floor, and began to pack.

"What in blazes do you think you're doing?" he demanded. He put a hand on her arm but she shook him off.

"Don't touch me!" Her voice was brittle, on the point of shattering, and she made an effort to control it. "What does it look like I'm doing? I'm leaving. As you said, I'm no longer under your protection. I never wanted your protection anyway. I know how to take care of myself. I have my dog and my pistol. They're much more reliable than people."

She finished emptying the drawers of one commode and would have started on the tall dresser if he had not blocked her path. "You can't leave here at this hour of the night. For God's sake, Jane, get a grip on yourself. I'll have someone take you wherever you want to go in the morning."

"Well, it won't be to Jack Campbell! I'll never go back to him."

"I'm not saying you have to stay with him. If you can't patch up your quarrel, that's up to you. But unless you make a genuine attempt at reconciliation—and that's the advice of my attorney—he can still bring an action against us."

"You talked to an attorney?" she asked incredulously.

"I talked to Robert! After I talked to Campbell, I decided I needed legal advice."

And a stiff drink, then another, to wash the bitter taste of betrayal from his mouth. Robert's advice had gone farther—he should cut all ties to Jane Mayberry at once and let Robert act for him. But this he could not do. He had to come to Woodlands to see her one last time and confront her with her lies.

Now, as he looked at her white, stricken face and the panic in her eyes, he began to waver. "Jane—" he began.

"Go back to your attorney and tell him..." her throat was thick and she was forced to swallow, "and tell him that I mean to fight it. I won't give in. And nothing on God's earth could induce me to go back to Jack Campbell, not even to save you twenty thousand pounds."

An awful suspicion was beginning to take root in his mind, but it was so ugly, he didn't want to believe it. "Jane," he said softly, "why did you leave Campbell?"

A fierce trembling shook her whole body and she had trouble articulating the words. "You're so clever, you work it out."

He knew what Campbell had told him, that it was largely his own fault that Jane had left him. He hadn't made allowances for her youth and upbringing. She'd been a straitlaced girl, and he'd been too much the other way, overindulging in gaming, drinking, and, he'd admitted sheepishly, wenching. But he still loved her and wanted her back. More to the point, his father, the baronet, was pushing for a reconciliation so that the title and fortune could pass to the next generation.

He hadn't been thinking straight. He'd been so numbed to discover that she'd deliberately misled him, that he'd sat there like a block of ice. Even his mind was frozen, but it had thawed soon enough when Campbell had pointed out that if Jane didn't return to him, he'd be forced to divorce her so that he could marry again and produce the heir his father so badly wanted. That was when he'd raised the subject of punitive damages.

Now that he *was* thinking straight, he was seeing things in a different light. He was remembering how difficult it had been to track her down, first at the Ladies' Library, then at Highgate. Only a few close friends knew where she lived. She rarely went out in society unless it was to the opera. Her life revolved around the Library and few men ever entered its holy portals. He was one of them, but she'd given him short shrift until she had felt she could trust him. But she hadn't trusted him enough to tell him about Campbell. Something else occurred to him. She trusted her dog and her pistol, and that was all.

"Jane," he said again, "why did you leave Campbell? I have to know."

She couldn't tell him; she couldn't tell anyone. She didn't want to be seen as a pathetic, beaten-down creature who'd been scared of her own shadow. She'd taken back her own name, she'd taken back her life, and she'd made something of herself. That was how she wanted people to see her. Especially Case . . . especially Case.

All the pent emotions she'd kept at bay for so long suddenly overwhelmed her. It all seemed so hopeless. All the lies she'd told, the evasions, never being able to trust anyone. In the end, none of it had worked. Jack had still found her. As his wife, she was still his chattel. That was the law. She'd never be free of him.

Great, convulsive sobs shook her whole body, and she clapped a hand over her mouth to stifle the sound. When he took a step toward her, she backed away, shaking her head violently. He put out a hand in a placating gesture but she recoiled from that too. If she could have found her voice, she would have told him to go away. She just wanted to be left alone.

He'd seen wild things with the same desperate look in their eyes before the hunters moved in for the kill. He ached to see her like this, and he damned himself for being so blind. She was panic-stricken at the thought of returning to Campbell, Jane, who wasn't afraid of anything, who'd stood up to Lord Reeve as well as any man; who'd taken on Gideon Piers and won, then crawled into a burning barn to save her dog. What kind of man had the power to put that look in her eyes?

She wouldn't want pity or an easy sympathy. She wouldn't want him to know how vulnerable she really was. Not Jane.

But now he knew that her life with Campbell must have been intolerable. She was terrified of him. Now he understood why she worked at the Ladies' Library and was so passionate about promoting the rights of women.

His outrage and hurt pride seemed like pinpricks in the face of her anguish. Everything that had seemed difficult was now so simple.

He paid no attention to what he could read in her

eyes but gathered her in his arms, not crushing her, but not giving her a chance to push him away either. She squirmed, she tried to push him away, but his arms only tightened and eventually the sobs died away and she sagged against him.

When she began to sniff, he found his handkerchief and offered it to her. She wouldn't look at him, but that didn't surprise him. He'd said some unforgivable things to her tonight. They'd get to that later.

She took the handkerchief from him and blew her nose.

He said quietly and as contritely as he could manage, "You don't have to tell me anything about your life with Campbell if you don't want to. It's over now. He'll never hurt you again."

She looked up quickly and read in his eyes his complete knowledge of the terrible secret she'd tried to keep from him. Fresh tears welled up. Her sobs had taken a toll on her voice and her words were hoarse. "He is a cruel, brutal man and that's all I'm going to say about him."

He drew her closer, his hands running ceaselessly up and down her spine, comforting her, gentling her of the tension that gripped her. "You foolish girl," he said. "Do you think I would judge you for his sins? Someday, when you feel ready, we'll talk about it, but only then. What's in the past is over and done with. But I promise you, he'll never hurt you again."

"You say that because you don't know him. He doesn't love me, whatever he says. He's obsessed with me. He wants me in his power. He'd rather see me dead than go to anyone else."

He said quietly, "Circumstances change. People change. No, I'm not saying that he's a better man, but

I don't think he's stupid. When he sees he can't have you, he'll have no choice but to accept it."

"He'll make good on his threats."

"So will I."

She frowned. "What threats? What are you saying?"

"I'm saying that if you go back to Campbell, I'll come after you. I mean it, Jane. And if you run away and go into hiding again, I'll find you and chain you to my side. So he'd better make good on his threats or we'll be living in sin for the rest of our lives."

"I'm talking about divorce," she cried. "I'm talking about twenty thousand pounds."

"So am I. No, listen to me. When I came here tonight, I didn't know, I didn't understand. I thought you'd deliberately led me on, knowing that I could never have you. I was crazy with jealousy, and my pride, of course, was cut to shreds. There's no excuse for me, but there's every excuse for you. You would do anything to keep your whereabouts hidden from Campbell. I understand that now."

There was a heartbeat of silence, then she shook her head. "I wish there was another way. What will your father say, and Lady Sophy? Your name will be dragged through the mud."

He smiled at this. "I hate to shatter your illusions, but my family's history is littered with rogues and scoundrels. Of course, we don't mention them in polite society, but without them, the Deveres would be a very dull lot."

His attempt at humor failed to win a smile from her. "Twenty thousand pounds is a great deal of money," she said.

"I don't know why you're shaking your head. He's not giving us a choice, is he? Either you go back to him or the divorce goes forward. I'll pay the twenty thousand pounds and think it cheap at the price. Then you'll be free of him for the rest of your life."

She said in an anguished whisper, "Case, I can't go back to him."

His arms locked around her and he said something soothing in reply, but behind the soothing words, a white-hot rage was building inside him. He was thinking that if only he'd known then what he knew now, he would have beaten Campbell to within an inch of his life.

After a while, he held her at arm's length and looked steadily into her face. "Jane," he said quietly, "I'm taking a lot for granted. What I mean is, you will marry me, won't you, when Campbell divorces you?"

"It's what I want more than anything," she said.

His smile was oddly grave. "Only one more question. Did you mean what you said earlier, that you've fallen in love with me?"

"I didn't want to. I tried not to—"

He gave her a little shake. "Did you mean it?"

"Yes," she whispered.

"That's all I need to know."

He walked to the door, locked it, and on the way back to her, dispensed with his jacket and neckcloth. Her eyes were wide and very dark as she looked up at him, and a fine trembling that had nothing to do with fear had taken hold. She could see where this was leading, and he had taken her completely unawares.

"Case, is this . . . wise?"

He smiled into her eyes. "Very wise. I'm doing the opposite of what Robert advised me to do. Campbell wants a divorce. We're going to make it easy for him. He'll have more witnesses than he'll know what to do with."

When she was silent, he went on seriously. "He'll need evidence, Jane, and that's what we're going to give him, beginning tonight. When I don't appear at the stables, eventually Ruggles will come looking for me. He'll be able to swear under oath that we were alone together, in your bedchamber, for some time. If there was another way, I would take it, but short of killing Campbell, I don't know how else to protect you."

"You're not thinking of a duel?" she said quickly.

Smiling, he replied, "No. He might kill me, and then where would we be? This is the only way."

He gave her a moment to push him away, to protest, to say it wasn't what she wanted, but when she leaned into him with a soft sigh, he began to breathe again. He tipped up her chin and pressed whisper-soft kisses on her brows, her cheeks, her lips.

She could feel her heart beating all the way into her throat, but it wasn't only his kisses that moved her. She was thinking of all the beautiful, experienced women he had taken to his bed; she was remembering her own ineptness, and how she'd always turned to ice whenever Jack walked into her bedchamber.

She put a hand to his chest and drew back so that she could see his face. She spoke simply and with a certain dignity. "Don't expect too much of me, just because I've been married. It wasn't...it wasn't a pleasant experience for me."

He quelled the anger that began to gnaw at him again. This wasn't the time for anger. This was the time for patience, infinite patience, and all the skill and finesse of which he was capable.

"Jane, are you afraid?"

"Of you? Never!"

"No, of this."

He unbelted her robe and slipped it from her shoulders. He was careful to keep his hands on neutral ground, the slope of her throat, her arms, her back. When he drew away to gauge her expression, she smiled into his eyes.

Looping her arms around his neck, she said, "Case, you're not afraid of *me*, are you?"

"I'm afraid of...I don't want to—" He *never* stuttered. So much for skill and finesse. "I'm petrified," he said.

She arched a skeptical brow.

"It's true, Jane." He couldn't resist kissing the dimple that flashed to life at the corner of her mouth. "This is a first time for me. You're the only woman I've ever loved. I feel like a boy again."

A lump formed in her throat. He was a magnificent specimen of masculinity with a body honed to hardness by years of war. It seemed incredible that she wasn't afraid of him. In truth, she felt just the opposite. She'd never been more aware of her own feminine power. With Jack...

"What is it, Jane?"

She immediately distanced herself from thoughts of her husband and said archly, "Is this the man who has been making me silent promises with his bold eyes these last weeks? Not to mention his bold touches and stolen kisses? Well, here I am. Now it's time to make good on your promises."

He took her at her word. She gave a little yelp when he suddenly scooped her up in his arms and deposited her on the bed. They were both laughing when he came down beside her. Catlike, they stretched, rubbing against each other, fingers linked, arms above their heads.

Gradually his expression grew serious. He bent his head and began to kiss her, deeply and slowly. There was no driving need to devour or possess, not yet. He simply wanted to savor the gift she was offering, the gift of herself.

He couldn't have known how much his gentleness moved her. *So this is what it feels like to be cherished,* she thought, and a deep well of joy flooded through her. He made her feel loved. She wasn't shy or afraid. What she lacked was experience. She knew what it was to be the object of a man's passion. But this was different. He was her first lover.

Her hands skimmed over his arms and shoulders, and beneath her fingertips, his muscles tensed and rippled. When he did the same to her, all her muscles went lax. It was so easy, so pleasant, she wondered why she had ever been afraid of him and afraid of this.

As she gave herself up to pleasure, he kept his own needs rigidly under control. He wanted to erase from her mind all the unpleasantness and humiliation she'd endured when she was married to Campbell. More than anything, he wanted her to know that the fault was not in her. She was more beautiful, more desirable than any man could hope for.

There was no fire or urgency in his caresses or kisses. He wanted to tempt and tantalize. And he succeeded. Her blood heated. She grew restless. Her body craved his touch, and he was generous with his touches. But it wasn't enough. She wanted more. When he slipped her nightgown over her head and tossed it aside, she didn't protest. The ways of love had always been a mystery to her. Now, with this one man, this one careful lover, she was ready to absorb whatever he could teach her.

That was what she told herself, but when he invited her to undress him, her confidence wavered. This was something new. Jack had never wanted anything from her but a quick release. He had always taken her in the dark, swiftly and without care. She had no idea how to pleasure a man.

Case sensed what was going through her mind and he didn't give her time to think. Murmuring soothingly, he placed her fingers on the top button of his shirt and helped her undress him.

"It gets easier with practice," he told her.

"As you should know."

"Be thankful that one of us knows what to do."

She laughed. "Oh, I am, Case, I am."

When his shirt and trousers had joined her nightgown on the floor, he stretched out beside her on the bed.

The feel of bare skin brushing over bare skin made her catch her breath. She could hear his heart thundering against hers. His kisses were hot and heady. And she responded. Her mind emptied itself of everything but the sensations he aroused in her. Her breasts were heavy; she could feel the dampness pooling in her loins. She'd known helplessness before, but not this kind of helplessness. She wasn't afraid. She felt liberated.

Case was deliberately prolonging her pleasure, though it cost him more than he anticipated. He'd wanted women before but never like this. But there was something more he wanted. He wanted to erase every memory of Jack Campbell as though he'd never existed. She would never bring the memory of another man to their bed again.

When she began to struggle for breath, his touches became more intimate. He cupped her breasts, stroked them, kissed them. If she'd shown the least resistance, he would have given her time to adjust, but far from resisting, she drew him closer and gave him back caress for caress. When he parted her thighs and probed, air rushed out of her lungs in a low keening sob. Shocked, love-dazed, she stared up at him.

He touched her again. She shuddered once and reached for him. He murmured something—a warning? a caution?—but her need was too great to heed him. With her hands on his shoulders, she urged him to take her.

He rose above her, and just for a moment, watched the play of candlelight over her face. This was what he wanted to see, he thought fiercely. Her skin was love-flushed, her eyes were dark with passion. A memory flashed into his mind—how she'd looked the first time he'd met her, teetering on a chair in the pantry of the Ladies' Library.

"It must have been those blue stockings," he said.

She had no patience for humor. "Case?" she pleaded.

Slowly, carefully, he entered her. He gave her a moment to adjust to his body imposing itself on hers, and another moment to accept the full press of his weight as he came down on her. Her eyes went very wide, and for a moment he thought she might resist him. But another shudder shook her, and she wrapped her arms and legs around him. Only then did he begin to move.

Until that moment, every kiss and caress had been to pleasure her. Now he pleasured them both. Restraint and gentleness were forgotten in the frantic need to possess. When she responded, he thought his heart would burst.

At the last there was no more thinking, only sensation and the frenzied race for release.

A long time later, he braced himself on one arm and studied her face. He wanted a clear look at her, this woman who had turned his life upside down. She looked serene. He wondered if she understood how ferocious the storm would be when it became public knowledge that they were lovers. He hadn't been completely frank with her. It was possible that if they fought the divorce action, they might win. But that was not what he wanted. She'd still be married to Campbell. He wanted her to belong to him, utterly and irrevocably.

She lifted her head from the pillow and pressed a quick kiss to his lips. "Don't think," she whispered. "No regrets. For a little while, let's shut the world out and think only of ourselves."

The knot of tension inside his chest quietly dissolved. She wasn't naive. She understood how cruel the world could be. He would do his best to protect her from the worst of the storm, but he didn't know if his best would be good enough.

"Tell me what you're feeling," he said.

Her lips curved in a complacent smile. "I feel tipsy," she said. "Drunk with my own power." Eyes sparking, she looked up at him. "Do you know, if I'd known that what men and women do in bed could be so wondrous, I wouldn't have remained chaste all these years?" She planted a kiss on his chin. "I would have had a string of lovers to my credit by now."

Her answer delighted him. He brought his lips to hers. "Let's make up for lost time," he said.

·   ·   ·

She was sleeping when the knock came at the door. As he expected, it was Ruggles, come to find out what was keeping him. Lance padded into the room and settled himself in his usual place on the hearth.

When Ruggles saw that Case was wearing only his black trousers, his jaw went slack, and when he looked over Case's shoulder and saw the bed, his eyes went round.

Case said, "Ah, Ruggles. I'd forgotten about you. I'll be out in a minute or two."

He closed the door. On his way back to the bed, he stopped and looked at Lance. "Good dog. You did well today." A thought occurred to him. "You'd better get used to me, Lance, because I'm not giving her up for you or anyone."

Jane said drowsily, "What did you say?"

"I said, my love, the die is cast."

That brought her awake. She looked at the door.

He nodded. "Yes, Ruggles was here. I have to go now. Don't do anything or say anything until I come for you. Do you understand?"

"When will that be?"

"Tomorrow morning." He looked at the clock. "No. Make that later this morning. Be ready for me at, oh, let's say, eleven o'clock."

"Where are we going?"

"To Highgate, to inspect your house." He sat on the edge of the bed and ran his fingers through her hair. He didn't want to leave her. He wanted the right to get back in that bed without having to worry about Aunt Sophy walking in on them. He would never be satisfied until Jane was his wife.

He got up. "But our real purpose is to give Campbell the evidence for his divorce." He kissed her softly. "It's the only way, Jane."

"I know."

When he left her, all the warmth in the room seemed to go with him. She snuggled down and pulled the covers up to her chin.

Chapter 16

Case arrived later that morning to find Jane waiting for him in the front hall. She was wearing the rose-colored coat again but it wasn't the coat that tinted her cheeks a delicate pink. Her skin glowed with happiness. He couldn't resist dragging her into the small waiting room just off the hall. The first thing he did was remove her bonnet and toss it on a chair, then she was in his arms.

His mouth was hot and hungry on hers, and she closed her eyes as the familiar ache spread through her, making her dizzy with love. When he set her away from him, it pleased her to see that she had the same effect on him as he had on her.

He took a deep breath. "I can't think when you look at me like that."

She closed her eyes. "Is that better?"

Of course, he kissed her again, lingeringly, but this

time with less passion. Against her lips, he said, "I was afraid you might have changed your mind. Then, when I saw you there, waiting for me, how could I resist you?"

She smiled into his eyes. "Would you let me change my mind?"

His gray eyes darkened to slate. "No," he said, "not after last night. I'll never let you go now."

Coming from Jack or any other man, those words would have terrified her. But she was coming to know Case and she knew, deep down, that he would take nothing from her against her will.

"Good," she said, "then I don't have to agonize over whether I'm doing the right thing or not, do I?"

"No. It's too late for that."

He fetched her bonnet and tied the ribbons under her chin. "What did you say to my aunt?" he asked.

"That you were taking me to Highgate to inspect my house. She's spending the day at the library anyway, and that's where I'm to meet up with her after we're finished at Highgate. What else are we going to do?"

"We're going to make a convincing case for your husband to win his divorce action."

She felt equal to anything. "And how are we going to do that?"

"You'll see. Shall we go?" He offered her his arm.

The carriage that was pulled up in the drive bore the Devere coat of arms. Harper and his assistant were on the box, in blue and gold livery. Since she wasn't sure what they'd be doing or where they were going, she'd left Lance in Ben's care.

She soon came to see that more was involved than she had realized. Case was laying a trail of evidence to prove that she was a kept woman and he was the one who was paying her bills. They went from one expensive shop to another, the jeweler's, the milliner's, the bootmaker's, the dressmaker's, and everywhere they went, Case spent lavishly. All accounts and merchandise were to be sent to him.

It astonished her that she could accept this course of action without a ripple of conscience. She didn't feel guilty, she felt grateful. At long last, she had found a way of severing all ties to a man she feared and detested. Without Case, it wouldn't have been possible.

She could escape the pangs of conscience, but she couldn't help feeling embarrassed. In the past, she'd looked down her nose at women who sold their favors to men. Now, those shopkeepers were sizing her up and she knew what they were thinking. It took every ounce of willpower to look them in the eye and pretend that she was enjoying spending her protector's money.

Protector. Mistress. Horrible words! In her heart, she thought of Case as her lover. Even when he became her husband, she would still think of him as her lover. She'd had one husband, but no man had ever loved her before.

She balked when their carriage pulled up at the furrier's. "No," she said.

Case looked at her bent head. "Don't you like furs?"

"It isn't that." She looked up at him. "The point isn't to buy me things. The point is to convince the courts that you're paying my bills. I think we've done enough to make that point."

"What?" she said when he chuckled.

"I love spending money on you. It gives me great pleasure. And that's the first time I've ever said those words to any woman."

"And," she said coolly, "I suppose there are many

women you might have said those words to in your time?"

His eyes sparkled. "Dozens of 'em," he replied. "But you're the only one who has ever been worth twenty thousand pounds to me."

They stopped for something to eat at The Gatehouse Inn in Highgate, and dined in the public dining room so, Case said, all her busybody neighbors would have something to gossip about. It was one thing, however, for Jane to return stare for stare with people who were strangers to her. This was different. She had friends in Highgate, people she liked and respected. She kept watching the door, afraid that the doctor would enter, or the vicar, or one of Highgate's leading citizens.

After a few minutes of this, Case got up. "On second thoughts," he said, "I think I'd prefer a picnic."

He had finished his soup, but she had hardly started hers. Puzzled, she gazed up at him. The look he returned was intimate and full of amused understanding.

She spoke to her soup. "I'm not very good at this."

"No," said Case. "I'm happy to say that you're not." He held her chair as she got up. "We'll buy provisions in the local shops and eat at Hillcrest," he said.

She stayed in the coach while Case did the shopping.

There was no barn, only a deep depression in the ground where it had once stood, and there were no workmen in sight.

Case said, "I'm afraid it's going to be some time before the workmen return to build the barn. The ground is waterlogged."

"Well, I hope you're not paying for it," she said. "I'm only a tenant. My landlord should settle the bill."

He smiled at this and, as she walked up to the house, turned to Harper and told him to return in an hour. "You can stable the horses at the Gatehouse if you like, and have dinner on me."

This did not suit Harper at all. In a low, confidential stage whisper, he said, "I'm your bodyguard, your lordship, in case you've forgotten."

Case let out a slow, patient breath. "Suit yourself."

Harper watched as Case followed Jane up the steep incline to the front door. When the young coachman beside him let out a low whistle, Harper turned on him with a ferocious scowl.

"Not a word out of you, Bernie, m'lad," he growled.

"No, Mr. Harper, sir. I wasn't going to say nothing, noways." After an interval of silence, he said, "So what do we do now?"

"We waits," said Harper.

The house looked much the same, although there was the lingering smell of fresh paint. Closer inspection, however, also revealed the lingering smell of stale smoke—on the velvet curtains in the parlor, inside cupboards, on a shawl that was draped over a chair in Jane's bedchamber. She picked it up and put it to her nose.

"What this house needs," she said, "is a good airing. Look at the windows. They're all closed. No wonder the house still smells of smoke."

When she heard Case shut the door, she replaced the shawl and slowly turned to face him. The look in his eyes made her catch her breath. She couldn't look away.

He crossed to her in two strides. She sucked in a breath when he dragged her into his arms, pressing her so tightly against him that her breasts were flattened against the hard wall of his chest. Then he crushed her mouth beneath his.

This wasn't the careful, gentle lover she'd known last night. This was a powerful male animal in the grip of lust. For a moment, she hovered on the brink of fear, then he muttered something hoarse about loving her too damn much and wanting her too damn long, and the moment passed. This was Case. Of all men, this was the one man she *could* trust.

When he pushed her down on the bed, she reached for him and drew him down beside her. Eyes locked, they began to undress each other. This was for him, she was thinking, not for her. He'd outpaced her. But there was joy in giving. There rose in her the desire to please this man, to love him as he'd never been loved before. There was no one like him. He was everything to her.

Suddenly, his ardor became muted, and his caresses gradually stopped. Against her lips, he murmured, "Slow down, you're going too fast for me."

She couldn't help it. She gurgled with laughter. There was laughter in his eyes too. But their smiles disintegrated when he began to touch her intimately, exploiting all her vulnerabilities with a lover's knowledge.

A fire ignited deep inside her. "Case," she whispered. "Case." Her hands fisted and unfisted on his shoulder.

He gave her what she wanted, what they both wanted. As his lean, hard body moved on hers, she held him close, and at the end, when the pleasure engulfed them, she cried out his name.

．　　．　　．

Replete and drowsy, Jane said, "I didn't know it could be like this. I wouldn't have believed it even if you'd told me."

"Like what?" asked Case. Smiling, he cupped her breast.

She brushed his hand away and pulled herself up, bracing herself on one arm as she looked down at him. "That's part of it," she said, "but I never expected to laugh at myself or laugh at you when we were making love. If I'd laughed at Jack—"

When she stopped, he pulled himself up to see her better. "What about Jack?" he said quietly.

She sighed. After a moment, she went on, "I wouldn't have dared laugh at Jack. That's the point. I was too frightened of him, especially when he came to my bed. He believed there were two kinds of women, the kind men marry and the other sort. A wife was supposed to tolerate the intimacies of married life, endure them, in fact. When he wanted pleasure, he went to his mistress."

A pensive look came over her face, and he said in the same gentle tone, "What is it, Jane? What are you thinking?"

The look cleared and she smiled. "I was thinking that I would never have believed I could be happy in an illicit love affair, and now look at me."

His hands closed around her shoulders and he looked directly into her eyes. There was an edge in his voice. "I don't think of this as an illicit love affair. I don't think of you as my mistress, and neither should you. You're the woman I love, the woman I'm going to marry."

"I know. Don't give it another thought. I know I won't."

He knew what had brought this on, and he gentled his tone. "Listen to me, Jane. What happened today is all there is to it. We won't go shopping again. I won't shame you by showing you off in a public place. We've done what we set out to do. We've given your husband evidence for the divorce. Anything else that needs to be done, I can do by myself. Even when it comes to court, you won't have to be there. I'm the one he's suing."

She silenced him by putting her hand over his lips. "I don't care about the shame! All I want is to be free of Jack! All I want is the freedom to choose my own way. And I choose you."

"You *will* be free of him. I promise."

She shivered. "If only I could believe it."

"Look, you told me that his father holds the purse strings and his father wants his line to continue. And he's the only son, isn't he? How can Campbell argue with that?"

"That's true."

When she lowered her head to the pillow, he drew the quilt up to cover them both. "What sort of man is Sir Archibald?" he asked.

"Nothing like Jack," she said at once. "What I mean is, he never tried to be charming. Stern. Intimidating. I don't think I ever saw him smile. I only met him a few times, but I know that when he said something, Jack jumped."

"There you are then. And really, it doesn't make any difference, does it? You're free of Jack Campbell, whether he wants you to be or not."

Her eyes searched his. He met that look with an

unfaltering stare. "Trust me," he murmured. "I'll take care of everything."

As ever, the intensity of his gaze made her breathless. "What happens next?" she asked.

"I see my attorney and give him a new set of instructions." He slid his fingers into her hair and kissed her softly. "Then I see my father. I don't want him to hear about us from anyone else."

"No, of course not. But—"

He stopped her words with another kiss, and soon after, all she could think of was the present moment, and the joy she found is his arms.

Gideon Piers had been feeling rather mellow before Merrick made his call. Everything was falling into place. Castleton didn't know where to begin to look for him. The earl was running in circles, going nowhere. But he knew all about Castleton, about his women, especially Jane Mayberry and the measures he'd taken to protect her; about his friends and acquaintances. Now, he was staring at Merrick, wondering if he'd been too complacent.

"Sit down," said Piers, indicating a chair. "Start over. Tell me again."

When Merrick was seated, Joseph placed a glass of brandy in front of him, then left the two men alone while he went downstairs to act as lookout.

"It isn't necessary," said Merrick, referring to Joseph. "I have my own men with me."

"It makes him happy," said Piers. "He likes to feel useful. Now tell me again about these two men."

"Their names are Lord Reeve and James Campbell. Last night, they tried to enter the gates of Twickenham House. The gatekeepers wouldn't let them pass, but one offered to take a message to Lord Castleton because the younger man, Campbell, was in a foul temper and was threatening to sue the earl and ruin him. At any rate, Campbell and Reeve left, but returned not long after with a sealed letter."

"What was in the letter?"

"We don't know. All we know is that after handing it over, Reeve and Campbell left, and shortly after receiving the letter, Castleton left with a friend."

"Your informant is one of the gatekeepers?"

Merrick grinned. "He is," he said, "but he wouldn't thank you for calling him an informant. He thinks I'm with Special Branch, and we're involved in a secret mission to protect the earl."

"Well done," said Piers. "Go on. What happened next?"

Merrick spread his hands. "If you mean, was there someone hiding in the bushes outside the gates with orders to follow Castleton, then the answer is no. It would be too obvious. The house is fairly isolated. The earl would know he was being followed."

Knowing that Merrick was right didn't soften Piers's annoyance. "So you don't know where they went?"

"I'm afraid not. However—"

"I'm paying you well to gather information!" Piers clamped his teeth together, then after a moment went on more moderately, "Why haven't I heard of Reeve and Campbell before now?"

Merrick was struggling to master his own temper. He couldn't see that this was important. It sounded like a gentlemen's spat to him. But Piers was footing the bill, and it paid him to give Piers whatever he wanted.

As calmly as he could manage, he said, "Because

this is the first time I've heard of them. too. I came here hoping you could tell me something about them, but since you don't appear to know them either, I'll follow up the one lead I have."

Piers's eyes narrowed. "What lead?"

"My informant was able to give me Campbell's direction. He's putting up at some hotel in Dover Street. I was hoping you could tell me which one. Since you can't, I'll be on my way."

"You'll let me know as soon as you hear anything?"

"I'll let you know."

They parted amicably, but Piers's mellow mood had soured. He was remembering that it didn't do to underestimate Castleton. And when he thought about it, the earl wasn't running in circles. Oh, he'd tightened security at Woodlands and Twickenham House, but other than that, he was going about his business as though he, Piers, was nothing more serious than an inconvenience. The party at Twickenham House was a prime example. It was as though the earl was thumbing his nose at him.

The thought was intolerable! When he realized that he was grinding his teeth together, he tried to relax. He'd think of something, he promised himself, to demonstrate that he was still pulling the strings. *Jane Mayberry and her dog.* The earl would be laughing on the other side of his face if anything happened to them.

His thoughts moved on to the problem at hand. Who in blazes was James Campbell and how could he possibly ruin the earl?

He didn't like wrinkles in a plan that was only days away from completion. One thing was certain. Campbell had better not get in his way.

ase's first order of business the following morning was to call on Robert Shay in his chambers and give him instructions on how to proceed in the divorce action that Campbell would undoubtedly bring against him.

"We're not going to fight it?" Robert repeated, dismayed. "But that's tantamount to admitting your guilt. If you follow my advice and sever all ties to Miss Mayberry, Campbell's case against you will almost certainly fail."

"I don't want it to fail."

Robert looked across his desk at his friend's calm expression, knowing that his own face must be mirroring his bewilderment. "But why?"

"Because I'm going to marry her."

For a long interval, Robert simply stared. "You're going to marry her," he said faintly.

Case smiled. "Robert, we're not talking about the end of the world. We're talking about ending a marriage that failed from the beginning and has not been in existence for several years."

The fog in Robert's mind was rapidly clearing. He said heavily, "That's not how the courts will see it. She's still his wife. His possession. I've told you what you can expect in punitive damages if you continue to see her."

"So you did. I'm prepared for it. What I want from you is advice on how we can expedite this divorce so that Jane and I can marry as soon as possible."

Robert could hardly take it in. Only the day before yesterday, he was advising his friend on how to stave off a scandal. Case had been angry then, livid in fact, but his anger was directed against Jane Mayberry. The change in him was astounding. He was relaxed, smiling, happy. Robert felt just the opposite. There was a bottle of brandy in the bottom drawer of his desk and he would have poured himself a generous shot if it had not been so early in the morning.

Jane Mayberry, he thought. Case must love her very much. He'd known he was taken with the girl. A blind man could have seen it. But Case was level-headed. When he found that she was married, he should have sent her packing.

There was no good arguing with him. No doubt His Grace would point out all the pitfalls that lay ahead. He wouldn't like to be in Case's shoes when he told his father.

He tried one last time to make his friend see reason. "Take your time. Think this through before you make any rash decisions. Once you embark on this course, just remember, there's no going back."

"You won't act for me?"

"Of course I'll act for you," said Robert crossly.

Case smiled. "Thank you. Now take me through the steps so I'll know what to expect."

Robert scowled, but finally said grudgingly, "The first thing we must do is write to Campbell informing him that we will not contest his action. All going well, the case should come before the Sheriff's Court in a week, maybe two, then proceed to the Consistory Court of the Bishop of London."

"How long?" asked Case.

"A month, maybe two. But that's the easy part. Campbell will get his divorce and so will your Jane, but that doesn't mean she's free to marry. It will take an act of Parliament to achieve that, and that could take some time."

Case got up. "Then let's not waste time. I want Campbell to know as soon as possible that Jane will never go back to him. I want him to know that she's under my protection. Tell him to do his worst. And put something in that letter that will make him move quickly on this. The sooner the better."

"Where will I find him?"

"Cook's Hotel, Dover Street."

"Where are you going?"

"To break the news to my father."

When Case left, Robert could not resist the temptation. He got out the brandy bottle, poured himself a drink, and took a healthy swallow. He'd never acted in a divorce case before, which wasn't surprising. Divorces were so expensive and difficult to obtain that they were almost unheard of. He'd have to brush up on divorce law. Campbell was Scottish. There must be residency requirements before he could proceed with the divorce. This could take longer than he'd thought.

Maybe, in the interim, Case and Miss Mayberry would come to their senses. It was a comforting thought.

Or was it? He was thinking of the change in Case, his easy smiles, the glow in his eyes, his good humor in spite of the seriousness of what he proposed to do. And then, it struck him. They were lovers! Case and Jane Mayberry had become lovers! The change in Case was so noticeable, it could only have happened after they parted company the other night, when Case went to Woodlands to confront Miss Mayberry about her deception.

He took another swallow of brandy. There would be no turning back now. Case would not have taken this extreme step unless he was absolutely committed to the girl. No wonder he was in a hurry to get this settled. He wouldn't want his first child to be born out of wedlock.

On that horrific thought, Robert drained his glass. Galvanized now, he went to the bookcase, found the tome he wanted, and began to go through it slowly. He soon came to see that divorce law was extremely complicated.

The duke was out riding when Case arrived, so he waited in the library and fortified himself with nothing stronger than coffee. There was a painting of his mother above the mantel, and he stood on the hearth, before a crackling fire, gazing up at it.

He couldn't look at this portrait without smiling. His mother had never liked it. *Don't tell me I look like that woman in the portrait,* she would say. *There's no life in her!*

No portrait painter could have captured his mother's

essence. She was as light in looks and nature as the Deveres were dark. Maybe that's why his father had loved her so much. She'd turned his ordered life inside out and upside down. And when she died it seemed as though all the joy in the world went with her.

It should never have happened. She'd gone riding without a groom, taken a fall, and had not been found till the following morning. Then she developed a fever and had quietly slipped away. She had just turned thirty, the same age as he was now.

He wondered what words of wisdom she would offer him. They wouldn't be the conventional mouthings that passed for wisdom in his circles. Nobody would care if he made Jane his mistress. What would shock them was the fact that he wanted to make her his wife.

He combed his fingers through his hair and took one of the chairs that flanked the grate. He knew what his mother would say. She would want to know what his conscience was telling him, and he could answer, truthfully, that his conscience was clear. He'd never felt more right about anything in his life.

His father would take a different tack. Honor. A Devere's honor was sacrosanct. His word was his bond. He esteemed the virtues of honesty, loyalty, and respect for the weak and underprivileged. He would never dishonor friend or foe.

These were lessons that had been drummed into the three Devere children since they were infants. In a civilized world, his father's code made perfect sense. He'd tried to live up to it. But he'd learned some harsh lessons in Spain. A man's code of honor couldn't protect him from the hard choices he had to make, and in war, honor was often the first casualty.

He couldn't talk about these things to his father. His Grace wouldn't understand. He didn't know if he could make him understand about Jane, either. He wasn't even going to try.

He let out a long sigh. So much was happening at once. The reunion, Jane, Campbell. If the circumstances were different, he would have left the matter of the divorce until after the reunion. He was rushing things for Jane's sake. She was not convinced that Campbell would let her go. She was afraid he would come for her and spirit her away. If she was right, it was imperative that Campbell be made to understand that she had a powerful protector who would come after him if he harmed as much as a hair of her head.

He didn't think Campbell was that stupid.

He should really be thinking of the reunion. He was lucky to have Waldo. Waldo was completely focused. Tomorrow they would all meet here and rehearse, step by step, how this little drama would unfold. No. How they *hoped* this little drama would unfold. No one knew for sure what Piers would do. It was entirely possible that the gunpowder was a feint.

He had to remain completely focused until tomorrow night. Then he'd see Jane.

When he heard footsteps approaching the library door, he got up. The duke entered, a broad smile on his face. "I thought I recognized your curricle," he said. "Was that Harper with you?"

"Yes. I left him in the stables."

The duke nodded and took a few steps into the room. Observing the severity of his son's expression, he halted, and his smile died. "What is it, Caspar? What's wrong?"

"The most damnable thing," Case replied. "The woman I love, Jane Mayberry, is already married."

.   .   .

If ever the duke wished for his wife's counsel, it was now. This hard-faced man sitting opposite him seemed like a stranger. His son hadn't come for advice or to talk things over. It was already decided. Caspar was going to marry Jane Mayberry.

Only she wasn't Jane Mayberry. She was Mrs. James Campbell. From the little Caspar had told him, she had good reason to fear her husband. If there was any justice, someone would have locked him up a long time ago and thrown away the key. But that was beside the point. Marriage was a sacrament. Vows were taken before God. If a husband and wife could not live together, there were other remedies besides divorce. There was such a thing as a legal separation. But that wouldn't suit Caspar. He was determined to marry the girl.

"I'm sorry, Father," said Case.

"I don't think you're sorry at all," snapped the duke.

In the same calm tone, Case went on, "Let me put it another way. I regret causing you pain. I'm sorry for the scandal that is bound to follow. If there was another way, I would take it, but there's not. There are almost no grounds in English law for a wife to divorce her husband. She can't divorce him for his adultery. Jane will be free only if Campbell divorces her."

"What if he refuses to divorce her?" the duke demanded, annoyed by Case's composure. "You said he wanted a reconciliation."

"He'll divorce her. Jane will never go back to him and Campbell wants an heir."

"What about *your* heirs? How will they react at school when boys taunt them about their mother and her shady past?"

He regretted the words almost as soon as they were out of his mouth. His son blazed him a look that was hot enough to reduce him to a cinder.

"I'm sorry," the duke said at once. "That was uncalled for. I suppose I'm in shock. When I walked into this room, I was expecting to hear good news, that you had asked Miss Mayberry to marry you and she'd accepted. I didn't expect to hear that she was already married."

The harsh lines on Case's face softened a little. "Let me get you a brandy," he said.

"Good idea."

While Case drank coffee, the duke nursed his brandy. It didn't help. He regarded himself as a broad-minded fellow. Not only had he let his beloved daughter go to someone who was, in the world's eyes, her social inferior, but at the time, Richard had been a fugitive from the law. He himself had married beneath him, and his father had disowned him. But this was different. They weren't talking about breaking the social conventions. These were vows that a man and woman had made before God.

"Father," said Case gently, "Campbell isn't giving us a choice. If Jane doesn't go back to him, he'll proceed with the divorce."

The duke heaved a sigh. "I know." He looked directly into Case's eyes. "But you could fight it."

"No," said Case softly. "It's too late for that."

That was what the duke had been afraid of. There were convincing arguments that he might still put forward to make Caspar change his mind: that it was Jane who would be ostracized if Campbell divorced her, and marriage to Caspar wouldn't mitigate her position. Even her kindred spirits at the Ladies' Library might well shun her if she turned out to be the guilty party in the divorce. She was the one who would pay the price for being the woman that two men lusted after.

He held his peace because he knew it wouldn't make a jot of difference. When Caspar made up his mind, there was no shaking him. And Caspar had made up his mind about Jane Mayberry.

It reminded him forcefully of when Caspar had made up his mind to join Wellington in Spain. They'd sat in this very room, just like they were doing now, and he'd put forward every argument he could think of to make his son change his mind. He was the heir. He had a duty to his family, and so on and so on. To which Caspar replied that Justin, his younger brother, would have to take on that role.

And what happened with Justin? A few years later it was the same story. Napoleon had escaped from Elba, and off went both his sons to fight for king and country at Waterloo.

Rosamund was no better. He had no objection to her marrying a commoner. But surely a father was right in thinking that his daughter should not marry a condemned man?

He spoiled them. That was his trouble. He'd tried to be both mother and father to them. *Love them,* were the last words Elizabeth had said to him before she'd slipped away. Maybe he'd loved them too well.

He could rant and rave, he supposed, threaten to disown him. But that brought back painful memories of how his own father had treated him when he'd told him he was marrying Elizabeth. He never wanted to be like his own father, a cold and unforgiving man, who didn't know what love was. He loved his son. He didn't approve of what he was doing, but he would never turn his back on him.

He thought about Jane Mayberry and, not for the first time, marveled that she should be the one to capture his son. He'd watched the women who had passed in and out of Caspar's life, some of whom had made him cringe, others who had made him hopeful. They were the kind of women who made men stare. Jane Mayberry was an intelligent, attractive young woman, but not particularly sophisticated or elegant, not in Caspar's usual style. What did she have that other women did not?

He leaned forward in his chair. "Caspar," he said, "why her?"

Case looked down at the cup he was holding, and a ghost of a smile touched his lips. When he looked up, his eyes were unguarded. "Because," he said, "she brings me joy."

It was a joy his father could not share.

He looked at his son and saw a change in him. "What is it?" he asked. "What else do you have to say to me?"

"You know that I'm working on a special assignment for Special Branch?"

The duke nodded. "This La Roca fellow. You're to bring him to justice. What of it?"

"It's only fair to warn you, Father, that I think he is going to make the attempt to blow up Twickenham House."

The duke stuttered, then roared, "Good God, Caspar! Don't you know how to break things gently? What if I had a weak heart? That's two shocks in the space of half an hour. Here, get me another brandy."

When this was done, the duke said, "Blow up Twickenham House? I'd like to see him try. All right. You have my full attention. Now tell me all about it."

·   ·   ·

She was sitting up in bed, propped against the pillows, attempting to read a book, when Case entered her chamber. "Case," she said. "What are you doing here? I thought you were staying the night at Twickenham."

As he approached the bed, he shed his jacket and neckcloth. Lance thumped his tail on the floor, then went back to sleep.

Case plucked the book from her hand and tossed it on a chair. "I can't stay away. It doesn't matter who I'm with or what I have to do, all I think about is this."

His hands were moving gently over her breasts. She pulled back a little. "What about your father? What did he have to say?"

"What?"

"Your father. You were going to tell him about us."

"Oh, that. It's just as I told you it would be. He's not happy about the divorce, but he accepts it. He'll stand behind us."

He was peeling out of his clothes as though they were on fire and he couldn't get out of them quickly enough. She wanted to talk.

"Is that all you're going to tell me?" she asked faintly.

He chuckled. "What more is there to say? Jane, I didn't ride all the way from Twickenham in the middle of the night to talk about my father."

He dispensed with her nightgown and joined her in the bed. "Love me," he said fiercely. "Just love me."

His body was heavy and hard on hers. Her arms went around him, her hands kneading his back, trying to gentle the tension she sensed in him.

"I won't hurt you," he said raggedly. "It's just that I need you so damn much."

"Case," she whispered. "Case."

Suddenly, she wanted him as desperately as he wanted her. She raised her head from the pillow and kissed him long and slowly. The kiss became abandoned, and so did their lovemaking. They moved as one, wildly, gloriously, until they were both spent.

She was still trying to catch her breath when someone knocked at the door.

"Miss Mayberry?" It was Ruggles. "Is everything all right? I thought I heard something."

She looked at Case in horror. "Does he know you're here?"

"No. I didn't think you could go through that again." He rolled from the bed and began to dress. "Get rid of him. Ask him to bring you a glass of milk."

"Ruggles," she crooned, "I can't sleep. Would you bring me a glass of warm milk?"

There was a silence, then Ruggles said, "I'll see to it at once, Miss Mayberry."

They heard his footsteps receding along the corridor.

Case was fully dressed and tying his neckcloth. "Where are you going?" asked Jane.

"Back to Twickenham. My father thinks I'm staying the night. We're having breakfast together early tomorrow morning. Better get your nightgown on."

He tossed it to her and she put it on.

He cupped her face and kissed her softly. "The sooner we marry the better," he said. He found her book and put it in her hand. "We'll talk tomorrow. I'll try to be here for dinner."

He walked to the door, opened it carefully, then slipped away.

It took a few moments for Jane to come to herself. She was sitting up in bed, propped against the pillows, with a book in her hand.

She looked at Lance. "Was Case just here or was it a figment of my imagination?"

It couldn't be a figment of her imagination because her breasts were still tender and there was the familiar stickiness between her legs. Her smile was radiant. There was something deeply satisfying about having a lover who would ride twenty miles in one night just to be with her.

He couldn't have been here for more than ten minutes, she thought.

She got out of bed and went to the washstand to wash the stickiness away. When she looked at the cloth she had used, she saw that it was streaked with blood.

Her courses had arrived.

Chapter 18

She made a pact with herself. She wasn't going to let anyone or anything destroy her peace of mind. She wasn't asking for the world. All she wanted was the chance to make a life with Case. Everyone deserved a little happiness.

No, she thought with a kind of determined defiance, nothing was going to destroy her peace of mind. Besides, she would be betraying everything she'd worked for at the Ladies' Library if she turned craven now. This was the reason the library had come into existence, to give women the same rights as men. Since that hadn't yet happened, she'd allowed herself to become the guilty party.

A month ago, she wouldn't have believed that she could be like this, think like this. But a month ago, she hadn't known that she loved Case and he loved her. It was as though her world had tilted on its axis.

Everything looked different. Everything felt different. She had never known such joy.

She looked at the clock. It was almost time for dinner. She'd hoped that Case would be here by now. She was already changed. She was wearing a long-sleeved blue kerseymere gown that hadn't a frill or bow on it. Now, as she studied herself in the cheval mirror, she thought it made her look like a governess. She was very pale, but she always was when her courses were upon her. She pinched her cheeks. That was better, but there was still something lacking. On that thought, she fetched her mother's pearls and fastened them around her throat. At last she was satisfied.

When they sat down to dinner, her ladyship thought Jane looked very elegant, but as she was the first to admit, she was partial to simplicity. There were only the two of them for dinner, and as the meal progressed, her ladyship took note of other things: Jane's skin seemed more luminous, somehow, as did her dark eyes; a smile flickered at the corner of her lips; and her thoughts were miles away.

Lady Sophy prattled on, mentioning various acquaintances and, when her companion offered only perfunctory replies, her ladyship's eyes began to twinkle. She had a fair idea of what occupied Jane's thoughts. Finally, she could contain herself no longer.

"Jane," she said, "put me out of my misery. Am I to wish you happy or not?"

Hectic color flooded Jane's cheeks and her eyes flared. "I beg your pardon?"

"You and Caspar? I know he went out to Twickenham. Since it's obvious to me that he loves you and you love him, it doesn't take much imagination to infer that you are the reason for the visit."

Jane shook her head. "Oh, no, ma'am. I mean, this conversation is premature."

"Nonsense!" declared her ladyship. "You don't suppose Caspar is going to *ask* for His Grace's permission to marry you? Oh, no. That's not Caspar's way. He'll *tell* his father, not ask him. And do you know, Jane, His Grace will be only too happy to give his blessing. If you'd only known some of the dashers who have chased after my nephew, you'd know why. I think His Grace had just about given up hope that Caspar would fall in love with a nice, decent girl like you. Wait and see. Everything will fall out just as you hoped it would."

In spite of the tide of guilt that rose in her, Jane managed to speak in a reasonably calm tone. "It's not as simple as that. When Case and I have something to tell you, we'll tell you together."

Lady Sophy laughed. "Have it your own way, my dear. I'll say only this, that I couldn't be more delighted with my nephew's choice. Now, shall we have our tea in the sunroom?"

Lord Reeve was highly gratified when he received a note from James Campbell inviting him to dine at Cook's Hotel in Dover Street. He was well aware that it wasn't his scintillating personality that had drawn Campbell to him, but his knowledge of Lord Castleton and his habits. All the same, to be sought after was a pleasant change, and there were other advantages. Since making Campbell's acquaintance, he'd been treated to a case of brandy, some slap-up dinners, and a night of gaming and carousing that hadn't cost him a penny.

He knew it wouldn't last. As soon as Campbell had

what he wanted—the return of his rebellious wife who was in sore need of a thrashing—he would be leaving for Scotland. In the meantime, he, Reeve, was enjoying every minute of this newfound friendship. Campbell treated him with deference, he was open-handed, and he'd hinted that any small service on Reeve's part would be handsomely rewarded.

There was more than this, however, to Reeve's good humor. He couldn't suppress his glee. He was remembering Castleton's face when Campbell told him that Jane Mayberry was, in fact, a married woman, his wife, to be precise. That insufferable air of arrogance had deserted the earl. His face was so set, it was like a death mask.

Jane Mayberry. Reeve shook his head. It was beyond his comprehension. He could not fathom what the earl saw in her. There was no doubt in his mind that the earl hadn't the least notion the girl was married until Campbell told him. He hoped Jane Mayberry was as enamored of the earl as he was of her. Then they'd both be miserable for a very long time.

Campbell's determination to recover his errant wife was more understandable. He didn't love her, but his father was pushing for a reconciliation to en-sure their line would continue.

The smile on his face faded the moment he en-tered Campbell's chamber. The younger man had ob-viously been drinking, and his usually pleasant expression was contorted with fury. He was sitting at a table in front of the window reading a letter. His neck-cloth was askew and his jacket was thrown on the bed.

"What's happened?" Reeve asked, alarmed at the change in Campbell.

"Read this!"

Reeve set his hat, gloves, and cane on the bed and

took the letter that Campbell offered him. "What is it?" he asked.

"You'll soon see! It was hand delivered this morning. The solicitor's clerk even made me sign for it." Campbell abruptly rose and began to pace.

Reeve moved a candle closer to his chair to get a better light. He could hardly believe what he was reading. The letter was from The Hon. Robert Shay, Barrister, who was acting for the Earl of Castleton. It stated, in unequivocal terms, that Miss Jane Mayberry refused to be reconciled with her husband and would remain under Lord Castleton's protection for as long as she desired. That was shocking enough, but the next part was staggering. Naturally, Lord Castleton would claim paternity of any issue of the union.

"You see what this means?" Campbell burst out.

"Oh, yes," said Reeve. "It means that Castleton is out of his mind. His father isn't going to accept this. He's the heir, for God's sake. I wouldn't be surprised if Romsey disowns him."

Campbell ground his teeth together. "He's telling me to divorce my wife! He's threatening me!"

"Well, at least you'll get substantial damages. I wouldn't be surprised if the court awards you more than twenty thousand pounds. You should keep this letter to show your attorney."

Campbell stared at Reeve as though he were an imbecile. "I could have divorced my wife in Scotland if that's what I wanted! Do you imagine I'm going to let her get the better of me? Do you imagine that I'm going to allow myself to be publicly humiliated, to be cuckolded by that . . . that snake in the grass?" He was red in the face and flecks of spittle spilled from his mouth. "He as much as told me that it was all settled, that she would leave his protection at once. If she thinks she'd going to get off scot-free, she can think again."

Reeve was mulling over these words when Campbell pulled up a chair and sat down at the table. "Listen to me, Reeve," he said. "You've told me that my wife is staying with Castleton's aunt at this house in Bloomsbury."

"Woodlands," supplied Reeve, nodding.

"Is Castleton living there, too?"

"Not to my knowledge. He has stayed the occasional night, but he usually goes home to the Albany. If you want grounds for divorce, you'll have to go to Highgate. As I already told you, that's where their love nest is. He's paying to have the place done up."

"You're missing my point."

Reeve frowned. "What's on your mind?"

"I want to know if he's at Woodlands right now."

Reeve thought for a moment. "His curricle," he said.

"What?"

"His curricle. That's how the gossip got started. There's not enough room for it in the coach house, so it's left in the yard. If he's there, his curricle will be there as well."

Campbell stared at him for a long moment, then suddenly slapped the flat of his hand on the table, making Reeve jump. "That's it then," said Campbell, laughing. "If the curricle is there, we do nothing. But if the curricle isn't there, and there's no chance that Castleton will interfere, then we get my wife."

This was more than Reeve had bargained for. "You mean—abduct her?"

"That's exactly what I mean."

Reeve swallowed. "What about the footmen? There are bound to be footmen about."

"They won't interfere when they see that we're armed. Have you got your pistol?"

"Not with me."

"I'll lend you one of mine."

Reeve's brain was working feverishly, putting up blocks to a course of action he could see was fraught with danger. "How are you going to get her away? I don't have a coach and neither do you."

Campbell was on his feet, putting on his coat, adjusting his neckcloth. There was a madness in his eyes and laughter. "We'll make up a plausible tale and bribe a hackney driver to act as our accomplice."

"What about the dog? I hear that she never goes anywhere without it."

"We'll kill it."

Campbell splayed his hands on the table and leaned toward Reeve. "I'll make it worth your while. Shall we say five hundred pounds?"

Reeve's brain stopped throwing up blocks. "Five hundred pounds," he said. "That's very generous."

"I knew I could convince you," said Campbell.

As she sipped her tea and made the effort to converse intelligently, Jane's eyes kept straying to the window. The sunroom was at the front of the house, and she could see lights in the gatehouse and groundsmen with lanterns moving about. She was waiting for Case. When she was with him, everything seemed simple. Without him, her unshakeable resolve began to develop cracks.

She saw groundsmen moving quickly toward the gatehouse. Putting down her cup and saucer, she got up to get a better look. "I think it's Case," she said, and was out of the room before Lady Sophy had a chance to respond.

She flew down the front steps, went tearing over the wet grass, then came to an abrupt halt. It wasn't Case who was surrounded by groundsmen, but her husband. One of the men had twisted Jack's arms behind his back in an effort to subdue him. There was blood on his mouth; his hat had been knocked off and he was struggling wildly to free himself.

"I have every right to be here," he shouted.

"Not when you force your way in at the point of a gun," said one of the porters.

Jack's eyes lighted on her. "Tell them who I am," he yelled.

"I've never seen this man before in my life." She felt very brave surrounded by four burly groundsmen, one of whom had Lance on a leash. He'd obviously been walking the dog when Jack burst in.

Jack's face twisted with fury, then, with a convulsive, desperate heave, he broke free and lunged for her. Lance went wild. It was Ruggles who stepped in front of her and felled Jack with a blow to the stomach. She winced, but she didn't feel the least bit sorry, not even when Jack began to retch.

Ruggles said, "Shall I fetch a Runner?"

"No," said Jane. It was occurring to her belatedly that much as she feared and despised this man, it was in her best interests not to provoke him. "Obviously he's been drinking and has mistaken the house. Show him out."

Jack was hauled to his feet and dragged toward the gates with a porter on either side of him. But he wasn't finished yet. His voice was hoarse and he had difficulty getting the words out. "You can tell his lordship from me that he can rot in hell, and you with

him. There will be no divorce! Let Castleton beget
bastards. Do you hear that, Mrs. Campbell? There will
be no divorce!"

There was more, but so muffled that Jane did not
hear. She stood there as though turned to stone. When
someone draped a shawl over her arms, she turned, expecting to see Lady Sophy, but it was Mrs. Trent who
anxiously searched her face, Mrs. Trent, who knew all
her secrets and had never once judged her.

"Trentie," said Jane, her eyes tearing. Her lips
barely moved.

Mrs. Trent's Scottish brogue was soft with emotion.
"Come away inside, lass. I'll make ye a nice cup o'
marmalade tea. And if that scoundrel comes back,
our Ben will blow his head off."

Only then did Jane notice her stableboy standing
off to one side, with the blunderbuss in the crook of
his arm.

She didn't want to explain things to the groundsmen, and she couldn't face Lady Sophy in the state
she was in. But she didn't know where to go, what to
do, so she did nothing.

Mrs. Trent put an arm around her shoulders and
just like the old days when her mother's illness had
taken its toll on her, she did the thinking for both of
them.

"Come away, lass," she said. "We'll go in the back
way. I won't leave you, never fear."

Ruggles and the two groundsmen escorted Campbell to a hackney that was stationed across the street.
Reeve opened the door to him and gasped when he
saw Campbell's face. Then he saw Ruggles and
scooted to the far side of the banquette.

"I'd advise you," said Ruggles, "not to show your faces in this part of town again. My master doesn't approve of gents who threaten ladies. Don't say you haven't been warned."

The reference to ladies brought Campbell out of his stupor. "She's not a lady," he said savagely. "She's a whore, that's what—"

Ruggles's fist connected with Campbell's jaw and the Scotsman said no more. When they'd tossed the unconscious man into the coach and shut the door, Ruggles told the hackney driver to get the hell out of there. This he did with alacrity.

Lord Francis Reeve was wishing that he was anywhere but here in Cook's Hotel, with a man who seemed to be suffering from a case of dementia. He had wracked his brains for some compelling reason he could offer Campbell so that he could make his escape, but he was afraid of adding to the younger man's fury, so he said nothing.

"She won't get away with this!" said Campbell, the breath rushing through his teeth. "I'd sooner see her dead!"

This wasn't the first time Reeve had heard this, but each time the words were uttered more viciously. He was beginning to realize that he was in over his head. He didn't mind taking Jane Mayberry down a peg or two, and the same went for Castleton, but Campbell seemed to have murder on his mind, and that frightened him.

If only he would stop drinking! He was guzzling the brandy as though it were lemonade.

He cleared his throat. "They'll be expecting trouble," he said. "If I were you, I'd wait for a few days, even a week or two, before I showed my face again."

In a few days, he'd be far, far away in Bath, establishing an alibi, so that if anything happened to Jane Mayberry, no one could point a finger at him.

Campbell rounded on him, and the spit fairly flew from his lips. "She thinks she's got the better of me, but I swear to you she hasn't. I'm not afraid of Castleton. My bloodlines are as good as his, *and* my connections. Do you know who is the head of my house?"

An answer was expected. "Ah, no," said Reeve. "I'm afraid I don't."

"The Duke of Argyll."

Reeve looked suitably impressed, and Campbell nodded. "Yes," he went on, "the Duke of Argyll. He and my father are second cousins."

What this had to do with Castleton, Reeve had no idea. But Campbell's temper could explode like gunpowder, so he prudently kept his thoughts to himself.

He gave a start when someone knocked at the door. Campbell merely frowned, shook his head, and went to answer it.

Two men stood on the threshold, one a little way to the side of the other. "Mr. James Campbell?" the one barring the door politely inquired.

"Who wants to know?" Campbell demanded belligerently.

"I do," replied the man at the door, "Capt. John Cox of Special Branch. You're wanted for questioning, Mr. Campbell." He looked beyond Campbell to Reeve. "And you, too, Lord Reeve."

Reeve wasted no time in retrieving his hat, gloves, and cane. This was the perfect opportunity for him to get away from Campbell. He knew all about Special Branch, though it had been established only in the last year or two. These men were officers of the law. And he had nothing to fear. He was an innocent bystander. Once they'd questioned him, they would let him go.

Campbell said, "And what the devil is Special Branch?"

"We'll explain on the way, sir," said Cox. "Nothing to worry about, but there's a complaint been made against you by Miss Jane Mayberry."

"Oh, there has, has there! Well, we'll soon put that right." Campbell's hands balled into fists.

Cox moved aside the edge of his coat to show that his pistol was tucked into the waistband of his trousers. "I'd advise you both to come quietly," he said.

Reeve needed no second telling. He was first out the door.

Chapter 19

Case arrived at Woodlands to find Lady Sophy in a great state of agitation and Jane in her room with the door locked. "She won't let me in or speak to me," said her ladyship

"What happened?" asked Case.

"I don't rightly know. There was some sort of altercation just inside the gates, a drunkard who'd come to the wrong house by the sound of it. That's what I thought at first. But after Jane locked herself in her room, I didn't know what to think. Do you know who he is, Caspar?"

"I think I should speak to Jane before jumping to conclusions."

"Of course, if she'll see you. Mrs. Trent is with her, but she refuses to see anyone else."

Case smiled into his aunt's worried eyes. With an authority he hoped was convincing, he said, "She'll see me. And don't worry. I'm sure it's a tempest in a teacup. Why don't you send for a pot of coffee and after I see Jane, I'll talk to you."

When his aunt went off, he went in search of Ruggles.

"He called her Mrs. Campbell?" said Case.

"Yes, sir."

"And he said there would be no divorce?"

Ruggles nodded.

"And Reeve was there?"

"Yes, sir. In the hackney."

Case now had a fair idea of what had sent Jane running to her room, and though Ruggles kept his expression neutral, it seemed to Case that he had a fair idea too. "What about the porters?" asked Case. "What do they make of it?"

"They think he mistook the house and mistook Miss Mayberry for someone else. We could smell the drink on him, sir. He was in a bad way."

"Thank you, Ruggles. Consider yourself off duty."

"Thank you, sir."

Case took a few moments to turn things over in his mind. He wasn't sure who was going to be the bigger problem, Campbell or Jane. Either way, he was determined to win.

He knocked at the door. "It's Case, Jane. Let me in."

The door was opened by Mrs. Trent. "She's expecting you, your lordship," she said, then, as she slipped by him into the corridor, "Be patient. That's what she needs most right now."

"Thank you, Mrs. Trent."

Mrs. Trent gave no indication that she'd heard the

edge in his voice. She bobbed a curtsy and hurried away.

He could smell the marmalade tea as soon as he entered the chamber. Jane was sitting in an armchair close to a blazing fire. Lance was curled at her feet, alert, watching Case as though he might turn out to be a wolf in sheep's clothing. It wasn't the welcome he'd been looking forward to.

He said pleasantly, "Was it really necessary to hide in your room?"

She looked at him, then looked away. Her voice sounded strained. "It seemed easier. I didn't know how to explain things to Lady Sophy, and I wanted to talk to you first."

He pulled up a chair close to Jane's and paused when Lance let out a soft growl. Case looked him in the eye. "Thank you, Lance," he said, "but the warning is unnecessary. Mrs. Trent has already spoken to me."

When Lance looked away, Case sat down. "I hear," he said, "that there was a fair amount of excitement at the front gates not long before I arrived."

"My husband," she said, "as I'm sure you know. He created quite a stir."

She was calmer than he'd anticipated, and he glanced at the teapot on the table beside her chair and wondered how much marmalade tea she'd had.

"Go on," he said gently. "Tell me what happened."

Her eyes were very dark, but her gaze was direct. "What happened," she said, "was that I realized that I've been living in a dream world. Jack will never divorce me. I think, deep down, I always knew it." She made a helpless gesture with her hands. "I don't think I ever convinced you that he's a dangerous man. He looks normal; he can be charming, reasonable . . . but it's all an act. There's a touch of madness there. He doesn't love me, not what you and I would call love, but he thinks he owns me. I think he'd rather see me dead than go to anyone else."

"Twenty thousand pounds—" he began.

She stopped him with a slashing motion of one hand. Lance lifted his head and glared at Case.

"Money doesn't matter to Jack," she said. "Pride, losing face—I don't know what to call it, but that's what matters to him. I didn't leave him just because he abused me. I left him because he was insanely jealous, because he was obsessed with me. And nothing has changed."

He knew where this was leading, and his patience began to wane. "I'm sorry," he said, "bitterly sorry that you were subjected to his vitriol tonight. And, if I could change the past, I would. But I can't. The future is all we have, Jane, *our* future. I thought you were committed to it, committed to *me*."

Her words came out in a rush. "What kind of life would we have if he doesn't divorce me?"

His jaw tensed. "A damn good life by my reckoning. You'd have a home, a man who loves you, fidelity, children—"

"Children!" Her lips began to tremble. "That's my point." She got up and took a few agitated paces around the room then came back to the hearth. Her shoulders were heaving. "You're not a fool! You know what I'm saying! Our children would be born out of wedlock. That's what Jack yelled at me tonight. 'Tell Castleton he'll breed bastards.'"

He didn't know whether to comfort her or shake her. Anger won out. The first major hurdle and she'd stumbled. He rose to face her. "It won't be the first time a Devere has fathered bastards—your word, not mine. But if it matters to you. Fine. We won't have children."

She was incredulous. "What about your heirs? You'll have to marry to secure the succession."

"I have a brother. Let Justin secure the succession. And it's a bit late in the day to be throwing this in my face. We've shared a few reckless hours in that very bed. What do you have to say to that, Miss Mayberry?"

Her huge eyes stared at the bed and she bit down on her bottom lip. "We're lucky," she said. She looked up at Case. "My courses came today. I'm not with child."

"Lucky!" He flung the word at her. "Is that what you call it?"

At this point, Lance got up, shook himself off, then padded to the far side of the bed where he plumped himself down, out of sight of the two combatants.

Case combed his fingers through his hair. "Christ!" he said violently, and stalked to the window. With his back to her, he said, "This conversation is pointless anyway. Campbell will divorce you. I'll make him. Then we'll marry."

She sank back into her chair. Her voice was no more than a shaken whisper. "You don't know Jack."

He turned then, his mouth oddly twisted. "No, Jane. You don't know me." Whatever he saw in her face angered him again. "Where do you think I've spent most of my adult life? Spain. Fighting for my country. I was no ordinary soldier. Much of the time, I didn't wear a uniform, and neither did the men in my unit. We were assigned to special duties. We did the dirty work for people like my brother-in-law. I've killed men with my bare hands and thought nothing of it."

He was staring at his hands as though there was blood on them, and she couldn't tear her eyes away.

His voice was more subdued, as though he were speaking to himself. "Some called us executioners, some called us assassins. They were only partly right. But there was no doubt that we were efficient killers. We didn't take prisoners."

When her breath caught, he looked up quickly and their eyes locked. He nodded. "Yes," he said, "we weren't quite civilized. Why do you think Piers hates me so much? My orders weren't to capture him and his bandits but to annihilate them. And that's what we did."

He was breathing heavily, the air rushing in and out of his lungs. "Now, you tell me what Jack Campbell was doing when I was in Spain bloodying my hands. Wining, gaming, and wenching—that's what he told me. And you think he's a match for me? If he knew me, really knew me, he'd be trembling in his boots right now."

She believed him, this man who had a stranger's face.

The silence drew out. He sighed, reached for her, and raised her to her feet. "Don't look at me like that," he said. "I don't know why I told you about Spain. I was a different man then, and it was another life. Don't be afraid of me."

"I'm not," she said quickly, too quickly to be convincing.

"It was war."

"I know. I understand."

His lips flattened. "Good. Then you'll know that Campbell doesn't frighten me. For your sake, I was willing to act like a gentleman. Now I'll play by different rules."

His eyes narrowed as his gaze caught the glint of something on the floor in front of the window, something he hadn't noticed until then. "What in blazes are those?" he demanded, though he was well aware that they were her traveling boxes. His eyes jerked up to meet hers.

"I thought I'd go to Sally's for a few days. We need time to think things through. I need to be alone. I can't think straight when I'm with you."

"You can't leave here!"

Her head came up at that, and temper heated her eyes. "Now, just a minute—"

"No. It's useless to argue with me. I can't let you go. Don't you understand anything? It's not Campbell we have to fear, but Piers. He knows you're under my protection. You're safe here, and here you'll remain until I decide what to do with you."

Lance emerged from behind the bed and bared his fangs at no one in particular. Case pointed a finger at him. "And the same goes for you!"

He stalked out of the room and slammed the door behind him.

Case talked with his aunt, as promised, but he stayed only five minutes, and when he left, her ladyship's mind was deeply troubled. She sympathized, truly sympathized with their plight, but divorce... that was a stigma no woman could escape. Jane would be ostracized.

She'd known better than to try to reason with her nephew. He could not be swayed by anyone's opinion. She toyed with the idea of trying to reason with Jane and rejected it. Casper would never forgive her.

She was not one to pine for the impossible, so she

sat down at the escritoire in her bedchamber and began to write out a list of names, those friends and acquaintances whom she hoped she could count on to see Jane through the scandal that would soon burst upon them. Jane was not going to be cast out of society if she had anything to do with it.

Case came upon Waldo talking to Harper in the stable block. He spoke to Harper first. "Harper. I know you regard yourself as my bodyguard, but there was an altercation here tonight, and I'd feel happier if you kept an eye on Miss Mayberry. Mr. Bowman can look after me."

Harper peered into Case's face, recognized that something serious was amiss, and nodded. "I'll make sure no harm comes to her."

Case waited until Harper was out of earshot. "So, Waldo," he said, "here you are again. What are you—my shadow?"

Waldo let out a theatrical sigh. "I know how careless you are about your safety, and I thought, for old time's sake, I'd keep an eye on you."

Case cocked his head to one side. "Is this my brother-in-law's idea?"

"He may have mentioned something to me before he left for Scotland, but I believe the idea was mine. Now, tell me about this altercation tonight."

"I'll tell you when we get to Cook's Hotel."

Waldo's brows lifted. "Campbell?"

Case nodded.

He had the groom saddle two horses because, he said, his curricle was too obvious. So they left the curricle in the courtyard and were soon swallowed up by the night.

.   .   .

All the landlord could tell them was that Mr. Campbell and his friend, Lord Reeve, had left the hotel some time since with two other gentlemen and had not returned. There was nothing suspicious about it. Everyone behaved naturally, although it did look as though Mr. Campbell had, perhaps, a little too much to drink.

"What time was this?" asked Case.

"Not three hours ago. No. Closer to two, else I wouldn't have seen them. We had just cleared up after dinner when Lord Cadogan asked if he might see over my wine cellar. A very fine wine cellar I keeps here, if I do say so myself, sir, and his lordship—"

"Thank you," said Case. "We'll wait in the taproom, and perhaps you would send up a bottle of your best claret?"

The landlord's crestfallen expression cleared. "Certainly, sir. You won't be disappointed."

When they were settled in the taproom, drinking the excellent claret, Case sketched out the details of Campbell's unwelcome intrusion at Woodlands that evening, and gave a modified account of Jane's reaction to it. Waldo wasn't fooled for a moment.

"You mean," he said, "she's jilting you?" When Cases's eyes narrowed, Waldo said airily, "Well, we can't have that." He lowered his voice. "I take it you're not going to call Campbell out? No, I thought not. That won't solve anything. And if you kill him, even your brother-in-law won't be able to save you. So, it's down to a little gentle persuasion?"

"Only enough to make his hair turn white overnight," Case replied. "You'll have a cheroot?"

They smoked in companionable silence for some

minutes. Finally, Case said, "You know, Waldo, it's always a relief to be with you."

"Why is that?"

"Because you don't keep asking me about the war; you don't keep asking why Piers hates me so much."

"No," said Waldo. He blew out a spiral of smoke and watched it dissipate. "I was there. I know what happened."

"Were we barbarians?"

Waldo turned his head and gave his friend a direct stare. "We saved thousands of lives. Don't expect me to feel guilty for that. And don't become too soft. Piers isn't a barbarian. He's a savage. Remember that."

At the end of half an hour, the claret was finished and they were becoming impatient.

"Let's take a look upstairs," said Case. "It's possible Campbell has come in a back way."

No one answered the door when Case knocked. There were no sounds coming from inside the room. It took them only a few seconds to force the lock. Waldo grabbed a candle from a wall sconce and led the way in.

There was not much to see. It was a comfortable room as one would have expected in an establishment like Cook's. A pile of clothes were on the floor; a bottle of brandy was on the table with two used glasses; there was also a letter.

"From Robert," said Case, quickly scanning the contents.

Waldo had found something on the mantelpiece. "Well, well, well," he said. "Now how is he mixed up in this?"

"Who?"

"Piers."

Case frowned. "What have you found?"

"Pebbles." Waldo dropped them into Case's hand.

They both stared at the two pebbles then looked at each other.

"What the devil does this mean?" asked Case.

Waldo spoke slowly. "I think it means your troubles with Campbell are over."

Case's mind was buzzing with speculation. "But how did he know about Campbell? And why would he turn on him? Campbell means nothing to Piers. I'd think he'd be pleased to know how much trouble that villain is causing me."

"Oh, no. I don't think so. Piers is the only one who is allowed to pull your strings. No one else. As for how he knew about Campbell, we talked about that earlier. He's bound to have his informants in place. We know of the gatekeeper at Twickenham and the groundsman at Woodlands. There may be others. They serve our purpose as well as his. They carry tales that we want them to carry, but we can't stop them tattling on us. I think Piers has had his eye on Campbell from that first night when he tried to breach our security at Twickenham."

"Yes. It wouldn't suit Piers to have Campbell barging in on us at all times of the day and night."

"What do we do now?"

"Nothing. Bow Street will deal with this when the landlord reports Campbell is missing."

"And by the time Bow Street sorts things out, our reunion will be over."

Case slipped the pebbles into his pocket. "This has been a god-awful night, and I have a feeling that things are only going to get worse." He looked at

Waldo. "Let's go home to the Albany and mull things over."

Waldo clapped him on the shoulder. "I have a better idea. Let's go home to the Albany and crack open a bottle of your father's best cognac."

Case couldn't argue with that.

Chapter 20

She had fallen into a light sleep, and the muffled knocking on the door wakened her instantly. Her muscles were cramped because she'd slept, still fully dressed, in the chair beside the fire. A glance at the clock told her that it was long past midnight.

The knock came again, then Ruggles's voice. "Miss Mayberry, are you awake? There are two gentlemen here who wish to speak to you."

At this time of night? Alarmed now, she quickly rose and crossed to the door. Lance was already there.

"Who are they?" she asked when she opened the door.

Ruggles's expression was somber. "Two officers from Special Branch. They asked to speak to Mrs. Campbell, and I thought you would want to hear what they have to say. They said it's urgent, and that's all I know. They're waiting for you downstairs."

"Is Lady Sophy with them?"

"No. We thought it best not to waken her."

"Where's Harper?"

"Harper?"

"I spoke with him for a few minutes last night. I thought he was on duty." If there was bad news waiting for her, she wanted Harper by her side. There was something solid about him, something sterling. *He* wouldn't panic under fire, not Harper.

"He can't be far away. I'll look for him while you're speaking to the officers."

Ruggles led the way to the waiting room just off the front hall, the same waiting room where Case had kissed her before they'd set off on their shopping spree. She'd been happy then, deliriously happy. Now, she was close to panic-stricken. Something dreadful must have happened before two Special Branch agents had come to the house at this time of night. Harper had told her that Case had gone to Cook's Hotel to speak with her husband. What had happened? Where was Case?

The agents' expressions were as somber as Ruggles's. The spokesman who introduced himself as Capt. John Cox, was thirtyish, stocky, but well turned out. The other agent hardly registered with her.

Captain Cox said, "You must prepare yourself for a shock, Mrs. Campbell. It is Mrs. Campbell, is it not?"

"Ruggles, stay with me," she said. Her heart was beating very fast. "Yes, I'm Mrs. Campbell. Tell me what has happened."

"I regret to inform you that a man was attacked tonight in Vauxhall Gardens, fatally attacked. We think it was your husband. There was a letter...At any rate, we'd like you to come with us."

It was some moments before she could get her tongue around words. "Are you saying...was Jack murdered?"

"It looks like it. Would you come with us, Mrs. Campbell?"

"Vauxhall Gardens?" she said faintly. Her mind was in a whirl. She knew Vauxhall Gardens. In the summer months, the gardens were filled to capacity, and the entertainments went on till all hours of the night. In the winter, the gardens were locked up. "But they're closed for the winter," she said.

"A watchman found him. I'm sorry, Mrs. Campbell."

She nodded, acknowledging his words. "I'll get my coat. Ruggles, find Harper."

She met Mrs. Trent in the upstairs landing. The housekeeper was in her nightclothes. Something had awakened her, she said, but she didn't know what, and she'd come to investigate. In a few terse words, Jane told Mrs. Trent what had happened.

As she helped Jane on with her coat, not the dressy pink velvet, but an everyday, serviceable gray worsted, Jane said, "Don't mention Lord Castleton's name. Don't tell anyone...oh, Trentie, just keep him out of this."

"Aye, lass. No one will get a cheep out of me."

Jane snatched up her reticule with her pistol inside, and quickly descended the stairs.

Ruggles was there but not Harper, and the Special Branch agents were not inclined to wait until he was found. Nor would they allow Lance to go with her.

There was a nondescript coach with barred windows pulled up outside the front steps. Ruggles followed her in, then the two agents. Not a word was said as the coach rolled through the front gates. Though no words were spoken, Jane's mind was reeling. She was thinking of Case, recalling every word he'd said to her about Spain and his work in the special unit. She remembered his words. *Some called us executioners, some called us assassins. And now it's time to play by different rules.*

Mrs. Trent watched from the window in Jane's bedchamber until the coach was out of sight. She hoped to God that Jack Campbell had finally got his just deserts. She wasn't going to shed a tear for that scoundrel. Her prayer for the earl was even more fervent. She hoped he was not involved. Miss Jane might think herself well rid of her beastly husband, but it wouldna sit right with the lass if Lord Castleton had anything to do with it.

Sighing, she absently began to tidy things away, then stopped when she realized what she was doing. She should be in her bed. Something had wakened her. What was it? Not voices. Then it came to her. She'd wakened, then she'd heard glass breaking. In the room beneath hers, she thought. She'd been on her way to investigate when she'd heard Miss Jane's voice—shaken, she'd sounded—and that put the breaking glass right out of her mind.

Candle in hand, she walked the length of the corridor and gave a little start when something brushed her legs. It was only Lance. She was glad to have him for company. She wasn't really afraid. She didn't think that robbers had broken in or anything like that, but she'd had more than enough excitement for one day and her nerves were on edge.

The room she entered was an unoccupied bedchamber. She knew she had the right room because a chair had been overturned and the glass in the cheval mirror was shattered. A candleholder and candle were on the floor. She was staring at the mirror when Lance bounded forward and began to scratch at the closet door. Trembling, Mrs. Trent crossed to it. When she opened the door and a body tumbled out, she let out a piercing scream that went on and on and on.

Case was drinking by himself and Waldo was sleeping in a chair when someone knocked insistently on the door. There was no manservant to answer the summons. Case was cursing himself for telling Ruggles he was off duty, but omitting to tell him to go home to the Albany.

He answered the door with his pistol in his hand. It was one of the porters from Woodlands.

"You're to come at once, your lordship," he said. "Mr. Harper's in a bad way and Miss Mayberry went off with two men."

"What is it?" asked Waldo from behind Case.

"Piers," Case said savagely, "pulling my strings. What else?"

Harper sat stoically while Mrs. Trent cleaned the gash on his forehead, the gash he'd taken when he'd keeled face first into the cheval mirror. She'd already doctored the lump on the back of his head. They were in the kitchen. The whole house was roused, even Mrs. Morrison, the head housekeeper, who could be counted on to sleep through an earthquake. She was making sandwiches for his lordship and Mr. Bowman, and anyone else who had a mind to take one.

Harper looked up gratefully when Case put a glass with a small measure of brandy in it into his hand. Mrs. Trent had tried to fob him off with marmalade tea, but he wasn't having any of that.

He'd already told his story once, but now that Lord Castleton and his friend had arrived, he had to tell it again. "It was like this," he said. "I was patrolling the corridor when someone called my name. I looked around, saw that one of the doors was ajar, and as un-suspecting as a newborn babe, I walked into the room. That's when he clobbered me." He touched a hand to the back of his head. "And I went staggering into the looking glass."

"Who?" asked Case, his voice tense. "Who clob-bered you, Harper?"

Harper looked down at his glass. When he looked up, he said, "I don't know, your lordship," but his eyes said something different.

When Case nodded, Harper went on, "And that's all I remember until her ladyship brought me round with her smelling salts."

Lady Sophy said, "But why would anyone do this to Harper? What could they possibly gain by it?" She looked anxiously at Case.

Case and Waldo exchanged a quick glance. They'd already questioned the porters and Mrs. Trent, so they knew all the salient details about the Special Branch agents and Jane's going off with them, and they had a fair idea of why Harper had to be gotten out of the way.

Waldo said, "I'm asking myself the same question."

Before his aunt could probe deeper, Case spoke to

Mrs. Trent. "You're sure they said they were taking her to Vauxhall Gardens?"

"That's what they told her. And that's what she told me."

Case nodded. "Harper, a word with you?"

They went through the door to the back hall. Case said, "All right, Harper. Who was it?"

"Ruggles," said Harper at once. "I saw him in the looking glass before I crashed into it."

"You saw him in the dark?"

"No. I still had my candle clutched in my hand."

"Christ!" Case slammed his fist into the palm of his other hand. "I knew there had to be someone, but Ruggles—I trusted him! But it makes sense. He's usually on night duty, but I gave him the night off. They weren't expecting you to be here. That must have given them a fright."

"Aye," said Harper, " 'cos I knows every agent who works for Special Branch."

"You're lucky Ruggles didn't kill you."

"I don't feels lucky. And who says he didn't try?"

They drew apart when Waldo and Lady Sophy joined them.

"Thank you, Harper," said Case. "Now get your injuries seen to."

"But, sir—"

"Now, Harper, now, and that's an order."

With a disgruntled snort, Harper walked back to the kitchen.

Lady Sophy said, "Caspar, I want to know what's going on."

"We don't know. We're not sure."

"Those men were not Special Branch agents, were they?"

"We don't think so." He waved Waldo on. "Send a

couple of men to the Horse Guards, just in case they're the genuine article. Maybe they did send two agents out here. I'll be along in a minute."

Lady Sophy said, "If they weren't genuine, Harper would have known it. He works for Special Branch." Her eyes went wide. "So that's why he had to be got out of the way. He would have known they were imposters."

"We don't know anything for certain yet."

"Poor Mrs. Trent. She doesn't have a clue."

"And let's keep it that way! There's no sense alarming anyone until we find out what's happened." He studied his aunt's face, then spoke in a more moderate tone. "Do something for me, Aunt?"

"Anything."

"Make sure Harper doesn't come after us. He's in no state to go anywhere. And it wouldn't hurt to have the doctor take a look at his injuries."

"I've already sent for the doctor."

"And try to keep everyone calm."

"Yes," she said. "I can do that." She gave a wan little smile. "Just bring her back to us safe and sound."

Case nodded, then strode toward the front doors.

The cold blast of air was just what he needed to bring him out of the paralysis that seemed to have gripped him. He was never at a loss. He was always in control. What he had to do was forget that Jane was Jane. He mustn't become distracted. He had to slip into his old skin. He was a hunter and his prey was Gideon Piers.

Waldo and several groundsmen, all former soldiers, were already mounted. "Are we taking the dog?" asked Waldo.

Case looked down and there was Lance, right at

his heels. "Yes," he said. "If anyone can find Jane, Lance can."

When Case was mounted, Waldo said, "There are a lot of questions running through my mind—timing, sequence, opportunity. You see what this means?"

"I see what this means," replied Case grimly. "There's a Judas in our midst."

Waldo frowned. "Who is it?"

"Ruggles, my manservant."

Waldo was aghast. "But it can't be Ruggles. Robert checked out his references. They were impeccable."

"I'm sure they were, but money is a powerful corrupter. We'll talk later. Now, let's move."

The coach dropped them at the great portico then drove off. They entered the gardens by a side door. It was much like entering the Albany's gardens with its fortresslike walls, but Jane had taken shelter in the Albany during the daylight hours. This was nighttime, gloomy and foreboding, and the lanterns her escorts carried made little impression on the vast ocean of darkness.

Captain Cox was right at her elbow. From time to time, she glanced over her shoulder, to the men who accompanied her. There were four of them now, including Ruggles, and the light from their lanterns made their features seem like death masks.

To keep her panic at bay, she tried to remember Vauxhall as it was the one and only time she had visited it. She remembered hordes of people, and a full orchestra playing in the Grove. Everyone was happy. They were celebrating one of Wellington's victories in Spain. She couldn't remember which one.

Her ploy didn't work. The ugly thoughts kept intruding. She was here to identify her husband's body. Had Case called Jack out? Was this the result of a duel? That would explain why they'd chosen somewhere deserted like Vauxhall Gardens.

This was all her fault. Oh, God, this was all her fault.

If only someone would speak, break the crushing, protracted silence. But they were all dumb. Her own tongue seemed to have stuck to the roof of her mouth and her throat felt as though she'd swallowed a desert. There was nothing but the crunch of their feet on the gravel and the bare branches overhead soughing in the wind.

They turned off the main walk into another walk, narrower and more hemmed in by trees and shrubbery. The darkness was suffocating. She couldn't breathe. She gave a start when something grazed her cheek. Captain Cox's hand cupped her elbow, steadying her.

"Not far to go now," he said.

When they turned a corner into another walk, narrower still, her steps slowed. There were so many walks in Vauxhall, each running into another, that it was like navigating a maze. She had lost her bearings. If she tried to escape she would not know the way out.

The thought opened a shutter in her mind. These men said they were from Special Branch, but anyone could say that. She had accepted them without question. Why?

Ruggles. He had vouched for them. And Ruggles wouldn't take any chances with her safety. She trusted him.

Captain Cox said, "Here we are."

The shutter in her mind snapped shut. Ahead of her was one of the many small pavilions that were dotted about the gardens, a place of refuge if it suddenly started to rain. The globe lantern hanging from the eaves had been lit, and there was a pale glaze of light spilling from inside the pavilion on to the gravel path. She felt safer where there was light.

"The chief would like a word in private with you first," said Captain Cox gently. "Better leave this with me."

"This" was her reticule with her pistol inside it. She was loath to give it up, but logic won over instinct. These men were from Special Branch. She was here to identify her husband's body. If they wanted to hurt her, they would have done it by now.

She looked back the way they'd come. There was nobody there, no escort and no Ruggles. Her throat froze. Then Captain Cox's hand was on the small of her back, propelling her into the pavilion.

"I'll stand guard outside," he said.

The man inside the pavilion was of medium height, but she couldn't see his face because the lantern was behind him.

"Sit down, Miss Mayberry," he said.

She sat on the wooden bench he indicated. Her stomach cramped when he took the few steps that separated them. He towered over her. Mustering her courage, she said, "Where is my husband's body?"

He chuckled. "All in good time. May I say what a pleasure it is to meet you again, though our last encounter left something to be desired. I had not expected such spirit in a woman."

Instinct and logic fused into one and flashed through her brain like a thunderbolt. This was the man who had set fire to her barn. She recognized his voice—the uninflected accent. There were no Special Branch agents. There was no body to identify.

She'd walked into a trap and fallen right into the hands of Gideon Piers.

If she'd had her gun in her hand, she wouldn't have shot him, she would have shot herself for being so stupid, stupid, *stupid*. She'd better get a grip on herself, better take her bearings and think up a way of getting away from him. *Don't panic! Think!*

Cox was standing guard outside the door. But where was Ruggles? And where were the others? If only she and Ruggles could get away, they could hide in the gardens until they were rescued. In her mind's eye, she measured the distance to the door.

He chuckled. "I don't know what's going through your mind, Miss Mayberry, but you have nothing to fear from me, not unless you get in my way, and if you're wise, you won't do that again."

Her breathing was hoarse and thick, making speech difficult. "Why should I believe you? You murdered that man in Hyde Park." She winced at this further evidence of her stupidity. Now she'd put the thought of murder in his head.

"Collier? He deserved what he got. He was one of the Brothers and he betrayed me." His voice took on a hard edge. "It was because of him that Castleton was able to ambush me."

She was surreptitiously inching away from him, along the bench, toward the door. His justification for killing Collier hardly registered. In another moment—

"I wouldn't try it!" he said sharply.

She froze. A moment of silence went by. All she could hear was her own panicked heartbeat.

He smiled, or she thought he smiled, for when he spoke, his voice was lighter. "Letty told me," he said, "that very little frightens you."

Letty was wrong. Gideon Piers terrified the life out of her. He was so calm, so much in command of the situation, while she could hardly control her breathing.

"Her letters were full of you," he went on. "You were a good friend to her when she needed a friend."

She hadn't a clue what he was talking about, but she wasn't going to argue with him. If he wanted to think well of her, so much the better.

Other things began to occur to her. He didn't seem depraved, or evil, or anything like the monster she'd built him up to be in her mind. Not that that weighed with her. She'd been married to Jack Campbell, and she knew the value of charm. It was a salutary reminder. This man was a cold-blooded killer, capricious, unpredictable. Case had warned her never to underestimate him, and she wouldn't.

On that resolve, she peered up at him, trying to make out his features in that dim light. It was too dark to see him clearly. He must have planned it like this, because the light from the lantern was shining full on her face. It gave him an advantage.

Schooling her features to show nothing, she said, "Why have you brought me here, Mr. Piers? Your man, Cox, told me it was to identify my husband's body. But that was a ruse, wasn't it?"

"I brought you here for two reasons. The first was to pay off a debt I owe Castleton. *Sit down, Miss Mayberry.*"

She wasn't aware that she'd half risen from the bench. She automatically obeyed his command.

"A debt of honor is what I meant," he said.

"Honor?" she stammered.

When he took a step back, she began to breathe a little more easily. "Yes, honor. I don't know how much

Castleton has told you about Spain, but before our last pitched battle, he allowed the women and children to leave. He's not the only one who understands chivalry. One good turn deserves another is what I say. Now he and I are quits. I want him to know it."

She didn't understand a word of this. "And the second reason?" she asked.

"As I said, one good turn deserves another. You were a good friend to my sister. I shall be a good friend to you. You have a husband you don't want. I'll fix that for you. Campbell will never trouble you again. All you have to do is say the word and you'll be a widow. Think about it, Miss Mayberry. You'll be free to marry again. Oh, not Castleton, I'm afraid. I have other plans for him."

He sounded so reasonable, so gentlemanly. He was offering to murder Jack, yet he might have been offering to do nothing more sinister than hail a hackney for her.

One thing was becoming clear, though. She was going to get out of this alive. Her stomach stopped churning. Her nerves steadied.

"Thank you," she said, "but I'd rather not go to that extreme. I have no wish to marry again, not Lord Castleton or . . . or anyone."

"Fine, then I'll kill the other man."

Now she was completely at a loss. "What other man? What are you talking about?"

He shook his head. "Perhaps I haven't made myself clear. Out there are two men whose fate hangs in the balance. One of them will live, the other will die. The choice is yours to make."

Her lips felt frozen. She made them move. "Jack. You have Jack?"

"Yes. Didn't I say so?"

The other man must be Ruggles. He had Jack and Ruggles, and one of them had to die. The words were torn from her. "Why kill either of them? They're not mixed up in your vendetta with Lord Castleton."

His voice was rich with amusement. "My dear Miss Mayberry, I didn't have you brought here tonight so that we could exchange pleasantries. I wanted to give Castleton a message. If I let you walk out of here unscathed, he'll think I've lost my nerve. Don't take too long to decide or I'll kill both of them."

Weak with fear and horror, she watched him leave. He didn't mean it. No one could be that fiendish. Letty said that there was good in him, that all he needed was another chance.

And Case said the opposite.

She struggled to her feet as the lamp outside the door went out. Paralyzed by indecision, she stood there, not knowing what to do. For one moment more, she hesitated, then, snatching up the lantern, she ran outside.

She didn't go far. There was nothing to guide her, no lights, except her own wavering lantern, no sound except the wind in the trees. "Piers!" she screamed. "Piers! Don't do this! Letty—"

The words were drowned out by the blast of a pistol shot. Her head whipped round to where the sound had come from. "Oh, no," she moaned. "Oh, no!"

She steeled herself for the second shot, and when it didn't come, she began to run. She plunged into a thicket of bushes, yanked herself free when she became tangled in thorns, and ran on. Ahead, she could just make out a small clearing. Her steps slowed when she smelled the acrid stench of gunpowder, and she halted altogether when her lantern picked out a grotesque heap on the ground. A moment went by, then another. Finally, she made her feet move.

He was lying on his back, bound hand and foot and gagged. His eyes were still open and a dark pool of blood stained the front of his coat.

It was Jack.

She put out a trembling hand to touch him, then quickly snatched it back. He was dead. She didn't have to touch him to know it.

A sob caught in her throat. Oh, my God! What had she done?

She put back her head. "Ruggles!" she yelled at the top of her lungs. "Ruggles!"

Ears straining, she listened. No response. Then close by her, a twig cracked. Something Case once told her gripped her mind. Piers, he said, liked to play cat-and-mouse games.

Oh where was Ruggles and what had they done to him?

She had to get out of here! She had to get help!

She heard another twig snap and her heart leaped to her throat. Was it her turn next? *Easy!* she told herself. *Don't panic. Don't provoke him into doing anything. Take your time. Slip away. Just get out of here and get help.*

"Ruggles!" she called again. "Ruggles!"

As though she were searching for him, she retraced her steps. Once in the thicket of thorns, she set her lantern on the ground. She was loath to part with it, but to keep it with her was too dangerous. It would only give her away.

Moving as soundlessly as she could manage, she began to flit from tree to tree. Occasionally, she paused to listen, but no one seemed to be giving chase. She knew she wasn't going in circles, because she stayed close to the gravel path. The darkness there was less dense and she used that paler ribbon of shadows to guide her.

Two things happened at once She stumbled over the root of a tree, and another shot went off, far, far behind her. *Ruggles!* her mind screamed. Her nerve broke. She was on her feet in a flash, caution forgotten as blind panic took over. She began to run. She did not look back once. She was aware of nothing but her feet flying over gravel and the need for greater speed if she were to save herself.

Then she head a sound that made her heart lurch, not in fear but with renewed hope. "Lance?" she called out. "Lance?"

He came bounding down the path and fairly leaped at her. Her arms around him, she sank to her knees.

"Jane! Where are you?"

Case's voice. "Over here."

Lanterns flickered through the trees. A minute or two later, Case was beside her. Heaving herself up, she threw herself into his arms. "They've killed Jack," she cried. "Oh, Case, they've killed Jack and I think they've killed Ruggles too."

"It's all right, I'm here," he said. "Now tell me what happened."

Case sent Jane with an escort of men to wait for him at the hostelry across the road. She wanted him to go with her and let constables and Runners look for Ruggles. He couldn't be persuaded. All he wanted from her were directions to where she'd found Jack's body. She wasn't sure, but Lance seemed to have picked up the scent of something. He kept running along the path, then coming back for them as though he wanted them to follow.

As soon as Jane left, Case put a leash on Lance, and after telling the men to fan out and keep their guns at the ready, he set off. Waldo walked beside him, holding the lantern to guide their steps.

Waldo said, "So what message is Piers giving us this time?"

"Same as always. That he's the puppet master and we're the puppets. I'll know more when I speak with Jane."

"This was different, more elaborate."

"I know, which leads me to believe that he's growing impatient. The end of the game is near. He wouldn't stir up so much trouble unless he was ready to disappear into thin air again."

"The reunion?"

"I hope so, Waldo, otherwise we're chasing our tails."

They stopped talking because Lance was now straining at the leash. Case let him have his head and had to run to keep up with him, but when he saw the clearing ahead, he reined Lance in, then snapped out a command when Lance refused to obey him. Lance whined and looked up at Case as if willing him to give a different command.

"Take Lance," Case said to Waldo, "and give me the lantern."

"Be careful," said Waldo. "It could be a trap."

"Then keep me covered."

There were two bodies in the clearing. Case removed his glove and touched Campbell's face. It was cold. He had died some time ago, but rigor mortis had yet to set in. He moved to the other man and found himself staring into the face of Lord Reeve.

There was no shock of recognition. This was what he'd expected to find. Like Campbell, Reeve was cold. It seemed to Case that they'd both been killed somewhere else and brought here.

He got up. He stared at Campbell's face with its hideously surprised expression, but he could not dredge up one drop of regret or pity. If he had any regrets it was that Ruggles's body wasn't lying there too.

Chapter 21

*J*ane shook her head in disbelief. "What do you mean they were cold? That doesn't make sense. I heard two shots. Piers had them shot because I wouldn't choose."

Case went down on his haunches in front of her chair and clasped her hands. She was trembling and her face was white with fatigue and dread. She blamed herself for what had happened to Campbell and Reeve. For himself, he considered the world well rid of them, but this was not what Jane needed to hear right now.

"Listen to me, Jane," he said. "They were murdered somewhere else, and their bodies were brought to Vauxhall. Piers was playing a game with you. You had nothing to do with their deaths."

"You wouldn't lie to me?"

"I swear I'm telling the truth."

"Oh, God!"

A shudder ran through her, then her face crumpled, and she convulsed in tears. Case would have drawn her into his arms, but she shrank away from him. He straightened and looked down at her helplessly. When she began to sniff, trying to stem the tide of weeping, he put his handkerchief into her hand. Lance was pressed against her legs, and she seemed to take more comfort from her dog than she did from him.

They were in a private parlor of the White Horse Hostelry, overlooking the entrance to Vauxhall Gardens, though all that could be seen from the window were its high walls. They hadn't called in the authorities. As far as Case was concerned, Campbell's and Reeve's bodies could stay there, undisturbed, till kingdom come. They'd made a fatal mistake when they'd tried to make Jane their victim. Piers's methods had been more drastic than those he was willing to employ, but the result was the same. Jack Campbell would never trouble Jane again.

Eventually, the authorities would come calling, but later rather than sooner if he had his way. He didn't want them connecting Jane to what had happened at Vauxhall tonight. With luck, they might never get around to questioning her. Few people knew that she was married to Campbell.

Her shoulders gave one last, convulsive heave, she blew her nose, then looked up at him. "Where are Waldo and the others?"

"Downstairs. I sent a man to Woodlands to let everyone know that we'd found you, safe and sound. I found your reticule, or I should say Lance found it and brought it to me. Your pistol is still in it, but it's been disarmed."

She nodded, only half listening. She couldn't make sense of what Case had told her. Ruggles was a Judas. He was one of them. Case had found two bodies, but one was Lord Reeve's. She couldn't get her mind around it all. She remembered her terror when the shots went off. But Jack and Reeve?

"Why?" Her voice was uneven. "Why would Piers do such a thing? What's the point? Why kill Jack and Reeve? What have they to do with anything?"

"Because they got in his way. I'm only guessing, but I think Piers decided they could foil his plans for me, especially Campbell. Maybe he thought I'd call Campbell out or vice versa, and one of us would be killed. Either way, it would take me out of the drama, and Piers can't allow that to happen." *No*, he thought, *he's saving that pleasure for himself.*

"But to lure me to Vauxhall...what was the point in that? Why not leave their bodies in a deserted alley?" The thought had her shivering again.

"Where's the drama in that? The thing you have to remember about Piers is that he's like an actor, playing to the gallery. He feeds on applause."

"I'm not applauding!" she burst out.

He smiled at the outburst, glad to see that she was coming back to herself. "Aren't you?"

"No. I'm lost for words! He's the most diabolical specimen of humanity that I've ever come across."

"And Piers would be delighted to hear you say so."

She stared at him for a moment, then said slowly, "And what would you say, Case? Would you applaud?"

He gave a twisted smile. "Most assuredly. He's shaken me to my very foundations. I didn't know what to expect tonight when I got to Vauxhall."

She was suddenly weepy again, and groped for his

handkerchief to blow her nose again. That done, she said fiercely, "I will *not* turn into a watering pot."

"You're in shock," he said gently. "No more arguments. You're going to drink that brandy."

Her untouched glass of brandy was on the mantelpiece. He reached for it and put it into her hands. Under his watchful stare, she took a sip, then another. He pulled a chair up to hers and sat down.

"More," he said sternly, and she obeyed.

Warmth spread through her and she stopped shivering. Staring at the amber liquid in her glass, she said softly, "I liked Ruggles."

"Didn't we all?" He couldn't disguise his bitterness.

"You don't think," she looked up at him, "you don't think that you could be mistaken about him?"

"Not a chance. Ask Harper if you don't believe me. What?" he asked when she shook her head.

"He must have been passing on information. But how could he? He seemed to be at Woodlands all the time."

"But he wasn't. He divided his time between Woodlands and the Albany. I'm sure he had a system set up to pass on anything of interest. And no one questioned his comings and goings. But tonight his system failed."

"What makes you say that?"

"Harper. Ruggles expected to be on duty tonight. He must have had the shock of his life when I told him that Harper would be taking over. Harper would have known at once that those Special Branch agents were imposters."

She shivered and took another sip of brandy. "He told me," she said, "that he was saving to buy his own little tavern, where he could keep a dog."

He made a small sound of derision. "I'm sure he

thinks Piers will give him the money to achieve his heart's desire."

"But you don't think so?"

He looked at her pale face with its lines of exhaustion and decided not to tell her what he really thought, that Ruggles was expendable. Piers wouldn't leave witnesses behind who could identify him, unless he was sure of their loyalty. That was one thing that eased his mind. Piers had taken a great deal of trouble to keep his face hidden from Jane tonight.

Or was this another ruse to keep him guessing?

She looked at him, waiting for an answer. "I don't really know," he said.

There was a desperate edge in her voice. "When is it all going to end?"

He wasn't going to tell her that he thought it would end on Saturday, at the reunion. He didn't want her to show up uninvited. Above all, he wanted to keep Jane safe and out of it.

He shrugged. "Soon. But not before Piers and I meet face-to-face."

"Face-to-face?" she said faintly.

"It's inevitable. I'm the audience he wants to impress most. He'll want to lord it over me, throw in my face how clever he's been. Don't look so worried. I'm a lot cleverer than he thinks I am."

She took a mouthful of brandy before she was aware of what she was doing, and had to choke it down. She didn't like the sound of this. She had a picture in her mind of two gladiators squaring off in a Roman arena.

"Why do you hate each other so much?" she whispered.

He didn't answer at once, but reaching into his pocket he produced a cheroot and lit it from the candle on the table. "Do you mind?" he asked belatedly, holding up the cheroot.

She shook her head.

He inhaled, blew out a stream of smoke, then stood on the hearth with his back to the fire. "It's not a question of hate," he said, "not for me. It never was. As I told you, in Spain, I was given the task of rooting out a band of men who were worse than savages. I won't go into the details of their crimes. It's enough to know that they were vicious. We were seasoned soldiers, yet our stomachs turned at the sights we saw. And God help you if you were a British officer and fell into Piers's hands. Then he was barbaric.

"Piers thought he was invincible. I proved him wrong. I beat him at his own game using his own methods, or so I thought. Until he turned up in London and murdered John Collier."

"And now he's after you."

"That's one way of putting it. I like to think that I'm the one who is after him."

He walked to the sideboard and poured himself a large brandy. After taking two healthy swallows, he returned to his chair. "Jane," he said, "I know this has been a night of horrors, but do you think you're up to going over your story again? I want to hear it while it's still fresh in your mind. Then I'll take you home."

In spite of all he'd told her, she still had that picture in her mind of two gladiators measuring each other in a Roman arena before the first blow was struck.

"Jane."

She looked up at him with a start. "Of course. If it will help."

"It may."

"The odd thing is," she said, "he seemed quite gentlemanly, oh, I don't mean in his dress, but in his manner and way of speaking. He even spoke of chivalry. He owed you a debt of honor, he said, because you'd allowed the women and children to leave before your last battle. And now you were quits. What did he mean by that?"

"I suppose that he's done the same for me. He proved that he could have killed the women in my life, you, Amelia, La Contessa, but he spared you, just as I spared the women in his camp."

"He has an odd sense of chivalry! I was terrified out of my wits!"

This was better. He liked to see her with her spirit intact. "I know. But he spared you. Even tonight, he spared you."

"And now, I suppose," she said crossly, "with all the courtesies out of the way, you can kill each other with a clear conscience!"

"Something like that." He took a sip of brandy so that she couldn't see his smile, though why he was smiling, he hadn't the faintest idea. It had been a harrowing night. "Tell me about Letty again," he said. "What was that all about, that you'd been a good friend to her?"

"Nothing that comes to mind. We were good friends. He said her letters were full of me."

"But you never met him."

"No. He was in Spain by the time I joined St. Bede's. Letty wrote to him regularly, but he hardly ever wrote to her. Then his letters stopped altogether." She gave a bitter little laugh. "Letty thought he'd died a hero's death."

After an interval of silence, he said, "Go on."

"Then," she swallowed hard, "he said that one

good turn deserved another, and since I'd been such a good friend to Letty, he would make me a widow."

"He lied, Jane. Believe me, he lied. He didn't kill Campbell to reward you for being a good friend to his sister. Piers does everything out of self-interest. Campbell was a nuisance, a liability. That's why Piers killed him. And being Piers, he had to make a spectacle of it. So don't blame yourself for Campbell's death."

That's exactly what she was doing. She couldn't help feeling responsible.

As though reading her mind, Case said, "Do you blame yourself for Reeve's death, too?"

"No. I don't understand why Piers killed him."

"For the same reason he killed Campbell. He got in his way. This charade tonight wasn't for you. It was for me. He wants me to think that he's invincible."

"But you don't think that, do you, Case?"

"No. I beat him once and I'll do it again. Now, go on with your story."

She went through it again and again, but the only thing that stuck in her mind was Piers promising to make her a widow.

They arrived at Woodlands just as the first glimmer of dawn rimmed the horizon. They'd hired a chaise at the hostelry for Jane and Lance, but the men were on horseback. When Case opened the chaise door it was to find both Jane and Lance fast asleep, and none too pleased when they were forcibly removed. His aunt, looking as though she'd aged ten years, was still waiting up for them. Jane did not stir. He carried her to her bedchamber, set her on the bed, and pulled the coverlet over her.

He took a moment to study her. There was still very little color in her cheeks and there were dark shadows under her eyes. She looked as helpless and defenseless as a child.

It would have been better for her if she'd never met him. Maybe it would have been better for him as well. She wouldn't be suffering like this, and he wouldn't be worrying about her.

That wasn't the only thing that gnawed at him. Piers had done him no favors by removing Campbell from the scene. If anything, the reverse was true. Jane felt so guilty, she couldn't bear to have his arms around her. She wouldn't allow him to comfort her. He'd told her he loved her and she couldn't say the words back to him. There was something else. He was wishing he'd kept his mouth shut, wishing he'd never told her about Spain and the kind of man he'd been then. He'd never told his own father, whom he was close to, or his brother. He'd never told Robert or Freddie. So what in the name of Hades had possessed him to reveal that dark and secret part of him to someone as decent and innocent as Jane?

And she was decent and innocent in his eyes. He supposed the world would call her his mistress. Well, the world could go to hell.

All the pent-up frustration inside him gradually slipped away. Jane was exactly as he wanted her to be. He would have been repelled by a woman who jumped for joy because someone had murdered a husband she hated, and if anyone had a right to jump for joy, it was Jane. She was sensitive and felt things deeply. She needed time to adjust, time to come to terms with her feelings of guilt, misplaced guilt, in his opinion. It was the same with her reaction to what he'd told her about Spain. Even he found it hard to come to terms with the man he'd been then. Why should he expect more of Jane? Some women, he knew, were attracted to the dark and brutish side of men, but those women had never appealed to him. To win the love of this woman was something worth striving for.

He pressed a kiss to her brow. "You're the only woman for me," he said softly, "and I'm the only man for you. We'll work things out."

She sighed softly, but did not waken.

But first, he had to deal with Piers. Only one of them would survive this final battle, and he was determined it would be he. He had so much to live for.

On that thought, he went in search of his aunt. He had very little to say to her except that she should put last night our of her mind. Campbell did not come to the house. There was no scene. There were no Special Branch agents arriving to take Jane to Vauxhall. And if anyone called her a liar, she was to refer them to him.

His aunt rose to the challenge. "I'm the daughter of a duke," she exclaimed. "If anyone calls me a liar, I shall refer him to the king."

Waldo met him in the front hall. "Harper was snoring his head off," he said, "and became quite agitated when I wakened him and told him he was hors de combat. He seems to think he's fighting fit and doesn't want to miss the action."

"To which you replied?"

"I told him he was to guard Miss Mayberry with his life and not to let her out of his sight." He cocked his head to one side, studying Case. "But there's no danger to her now, is there, Case?"

"I shouldn't think so." He smiled grimly. "I believe we are entering the lull before the battle is joined."

"What day is it?"

"Thursday, going on Friday."

"And our reunion is on Saturday. I may sleep till then."

"Oh, no," said Case. "We're not finished yet."

He'd had a change of heart. He decided that he couldn't leave Campbell's and Reeve's bodies moldering in Vauxhall until a stray vagabond or caretaker stumbled upon them. He couldn't do it because he knew it wouldn't sit right with Jane. He would speak to Massie, the acting head of Special Branch, and ask him to remove the bodies and inform the next of kin. Then he'd ask Massie to hold off the investigation until after Saturday. He'd give him a full report then. And Massie would do it as a favor to Richard, because it's what Richard would do for his brother-in-law.

It helped to have relations in high places.

Waldo said gently, "Case, the day hasn't even begun. I don't know what you have in mind, but surely it can wait until the sun is up? Now, I'll tell you what we're going to do. We're going to find beds, right here in Woodlands, and sleep for the next few hours."

Case looked out the window. It was still dark. "Fine," he said. "A few hours won't make any difference."

"What day is it, Joseph?" asked Piers.

"Friday. As you know very well."

"Not long to go now. But I don't want Saturday to arrive too quickly. I want to savor every moment of the coming victory."

It was a bright, sunny day, and matched Piers's mood exactly. He'd spent the morning at Angelo's, fencing with the master himself, then he'd gone on to Gentleman Jackson's on Bond Street where he'd mingled with amateur pugilists, men of the first rank, who had accepted him as though he were an equal. And now they were at the Clarendon Hotel, still on Bond Street, within easy walking distance of Cook's on Dover Street, and were enjoying a superlative French meal with champagne to go with it.

Not that Joseph was enjoying the meal as much as he was. He'd chosen the Clarendon because it was the haunt of the Deveres, especially the duke, who rented a suite all year round for the convenience it offered. Twickenham wasn't far away, but it wasn't in the center of things. It was quite possible that His Grace or his heir would put in an appearance, which was why Joseph was keeping his head well down.

Piers put down his knife and fork. "Joseph," he said, mouthing the words, "they don't know us. The Deveres? They can't possibly recognize us. Relax. Enjoy your dinner. It's costing me a fortune."

Joseph gave a surreptitious glance around the dining room to make sure no one was eavesdropping. "You take too many risks. What if Castleton walks in?"

Piers chuckled. "He won't. He'll be running himself ragged, trying to decide what to do with two bodies, not to mention acting nursemaid to one hysterical woman. Then there are all the last-minute details he'll have to oversee for his annual old boys' reunion. Frankly, I wish he would put in an appearance. I'd like nothing better than to look him in the eye and wish him good day."

He suddenly frowned. "Joseph," he said, "use your fork the English way. And straighten your spine. That's better. Now you look as though you belong here."

That was part of the pleasure of being here, this sense of belonging. The Clarendon was only the beginning. There were those exclusive gentlemen's clubs in St. James's. But money wasn't enough to get him through those hallowed portals. He needed sponsors and a suitable background. It was something to work for, a goal to achieve.

Joseph said, "I don't know why you don't simply shoot him."

He couldn't explain his motives to Joseph, so he said simply, "What about the others? Are they to get off scot-free? No. We'll get them all together, just as they got our brothers in St. Michel."

"He'll be expecting us."

"I know. But he'll be the one who is caught in *my* trap."

Of course, there was always the element of chance, but that made the game all the more interesting. He was thinking of last night at Vauxhall, the stakes, the timing. He'd pulled it off perfectly, and two troublesome interlopers who could have ruined his plans for the earl were no longer in the picture.

He wondered if Castleton was rubbing his hands together, thinking he would be free now to marry Miss Mayberry. It would never happen, of course.

"And his manservant?" said Joseph in his slow way. "He's seen my face. What are we going to do with him?"

"Why, Joseph, we'll take care of him on Saturday, when we get to Twickenham House. I think another body turning up right now might alarm the authorities."

Joseph nodded and smiled.

Chapter 22

*I*t wasn't odd, thought Jane. It was bizarre. She'd thought everyone at Woodlands would be bombarding her with questions, but it was just the opposite. They were killing her with kindness. It was as though nothing had happened. Jack had not forced his way in and caused a scene. The villains who had passed themselves off as Special Branch agents had not arrived at the house in the middle of the night and carried her off. Ruggles was not a Judas. Vauxhall might never have happened.

Not that she was going to spill her heart out or be indiscreet. Case had told her to say nothing until they'd had a chance to go over things together. That was before they left the White Horse. Now it was Saturday, and she still hadn't seen him, nor would she before tomorrow. He was hosting that reunion for former Etonians and friends. She wondered what time it would be over. She looked at the clock. It was just going on seven. Maybe he would come to her later.

Lance was prancing at the door, asking to get out for his evening constitutional. The fresh air would do them both good. A terrible lethargy had taken hold of her. She'd slept most of yesterday or what was left of it after she got home and had wakened today feeling as though the weight of the world rested on her shoulders. Maybe that's why they were killing her with kindness. She was acting like an invalid, so they treated her like an invalid—turning away visitors and letting her eat her meals in her room. If she didn't snap out of it, they'd be sending for a priest to administer last rites.

"Harper!" she called when she stepped into the corridor. She wasn't allowed to go anywhere without him.

He appeared almost at once in the doorway across the hall. Poor Harper. He looked as doleful as she felt. What a pair they made.

"Time for Lance's walk," she said.

Harper nodded.

Not a word was exchanged as they descended the stairs and passed the porter who held the door for them. Outside, lanterns were lit and groundsmen were patrolling, but it seemed to Jane, not as many groundsmen as usual. She let Lance off the leash and they set off on their usual circuit along the perimeter of the property.

After a while, Jane said, "Are you feeling all right, Harper? I ask because you seem more silent than usual. If you need to see a doctor—"

"I don't need to see a doctor! It's just..."

"What?"

He shrugged. "I've been thinking it's time I resigned from the service."

She was dumbfounded. "What brought this on?"

"It comes to us all, when we gets old and useless."

"Useless? Harper, your exploits are legendary! What are you talking about?"

He hemmed and hawed, but she finally got it out of him. He felt he'd let them all down. The first time was outside the theater, when someone followed him into the hackney and coshed him on the head. The second was when she was attacked in Vigo Street because he'd been too slow off the mark. And the third was when Ruggles hit him with a candlestick and locked him in the closet.

"No bloody good to anyone!" he said bitterly. "Begging your pardon, Miss Mayberry."

She tried to reason with him, pointing out that he was still recovering from his cracked ribs, and couldn't have been expected to move with his usual agility. She reasoned in vain. His mind was made up.

They walked on. Harper broke the silence this time. "What about you, Miss Mayberry? You ain't exactly chirping like a canary."

She could have fobbed him off, except that he'd been frank with her, and it seemed ungracious to throw up a wall of reserve. No. There was more to it than that. This slightly battered veteran of the Spanish Campaign seemed wise and good and virtuous. If he gave up the service, he should think about taking up Holy Orders.

"I feel as if I'm lost in a fog," she said. "Take Ruggles, for instance. I liked him, really liked him."

"So did I," responded Harper, "until he hit me over the head."

"You'd hardly know it to look at you."

"I suffered from a mild concussion, the doctor said!"

She changed the subject. "And I keep thinking about Vauxhall."

He patted her awkwardly on the shoulder. "You was a very brave lady. Yes, I knows about it. Mr. Bowman told me."

She couldn't bring herself to talk about finding Jack's body and the anguish she'd experienced when she'd heard those shots, but there were other things that fretted, questions she couldn't get out of her mind.

"Did Mr. Bowman also tell you why Gideon Piers hates Lord Castleton so much?"

He said slowly, "We've all wondered about that, but all we can think of is the battle at St. Michel. Piers lost all his comrades. The Brothers, he called them. Now he's out to return the favor."

"So it's not just Lord Castleton he hates?"

"I suppose not."

She was persistent. "He must hate Mr. Bowman and all the other soldiers who were part of that special unit."

"I suppose so."

"Then why is Piers playing these games only with the earl? Why hasn't he picked on Mr. Bowman, or any of the others who destroyed his hideout?"

"Because Major Devere was in charge of the operation."

They walked on, but she was still fretting. Suddenly, she stopped and called Lance to heel.

"What is it?" asked Harper.

"I think there's someone who knows the answers to my questions and I'm going to see her."

"Who?"

"My friend, Letty Gray, you know, Gideon Piers's sister."

"Not without me, you don't!"

"Good. Then we'll go together."

Getting past the gatekeepers at Twickenham House was as easy as picking pockets at the Frost Fair. Gideon showed his invitation and his carriage was waved on. It helped that his companion was none other than the guest of honor, Dr. Keate, and it was his carriage they were traveling in. As far as Dr. Keate knew, his companion was one of Romsey's personal physicians, a man whose sole object was to make sure Romsey was as comfortable as possible and to be on hand in case he suffered one of his troublesome palpitations. Dr. Keate was gratified by His Grace's thoughtfulness. To all others, if challenged, Gideon would pass himself off as a friend of a former Etonian, Lord Castleton's friend, to be precise. He didn't know much about Eton, but he knew all about Castleton. No one could catch him out there.

When they stepped down from the carriage, he told Dr. Keate that he would catch up to him in the gallery where the reception was to be held, then he quietly disappeared into the shadows. He looked toward the river. When the first explosion went off, that would be the signal for Joseph to bring the boat over.

The gallery was filling up nicely. There was no formal reception line. His Grace, with the guest of honor in tow, moved from one knot of gentlemen to the next, exchanging reminiscences and cracking the odd joke. His gaze, however, frequently strayed to his son.

Case was doing much the same as his father, but when Waldo entered the gallery, he excused himself and followed Waldo to a window embrasure where they could talk in private.

Waldo said, "He's in, unless His Grace sent one of his personal physicians to attend Dr. Keate."

"He didn't. Did you get a description?"

"Yes. Mid-thirties, medium build, and nothing to distinguish him from half the gentlemen here."

"How many are here now?"

"Four by our reckoning."

"Don't do anything to scare them off. When the fireworks go off, just keep your eye on me."

"You're sure he'll come for you?"

"Waldo, I'm not sure about anything. How are Freddie and Robert bearing up?"

"They're as nervous as kittens. But they know what to do."

"Good."

Case signaled the groom of the chambers, Mr. Turner, and shortly after, footmen with powdered wigs and blue and gold livery began to move among the guests, dispensing champagne.

Ruggles pulled his coat collar up and looked across the river at Twickenham House. "Looks like they're having quite a party," he said, glancing at Joseph.

Joseph merely grunted.

"What are we waiting for?"

"The signal," said Joseph.

"Then what?"

"Then we take the boat across and pick up our guests."

Ruggles looked across the Thames at the flickering lanterns that moved along the riverbank like ghostly wraiths. "We'll get caught," he said. "There's a patrol on the riverbank."

"There won't be when we cross."

"Why? What's going to happen?"

"You ask too many questions."

A long silence went by, then Ruggles said, "Look here! I've done my job. I wasn't employed to do this kind of work. I want to know when I'm going to get paid."

Joseph smiled. "Soon. Don't worry. You'll be paid in full."

"I don't want a bank draft or anything like that. I want to be paid in gold."

"You'll get everything that's coming to you, Mr. Ruggles."

The fine hairs on Ruggles's neck began to rise.

Lady Sophy was not happy to hear that Jane was going off to visit a friend. She tried to dissuade her, but when Jane was adamant, there was nothing she could do but give in gracefully, with certain conditions attached. They were to go in Lady Rosamund's carriage, and the coachmen were to be well armed. Then Lady Sophy returned to the game of whist she'd arranged with her friends. She couldn't keep her mind on the game and lost every hand she played. Her partner was not amused.

·   ·   ·

On arriving at Letty's house, Jane was shown into the front parlor. As she expected, the children were in bed, and Oliver was in his study, working on his sermon.

When Letty saw her face, she cut off the customary exchange of greetings. "Jane, what is it?" she asked. "What's happened?"

Jane hadn't realized just how tense she was. She'd planned to question Letty gently, knowing how defensive she felt about her brother. But something was nagging at her, a sense of urgency she couldn't understand.

Before they had a chance to sit down, she said, "Two nights ago I was abducted and taken to Vauxhall Gardens to meet your brother. Letty, if you argue with me, I think I will hit you. It was your brother, all right. He knew too much about us, too much about me. We're not going to have a conversation, Letty. You're not going to tell me again how poor Gideon never had a chance. You're going to answer two questions for me, then I'll go. Do you understand?"

Letty swallowed and nodded.

"The first question is this. What good turn did I ever do you?"

"I don't know."

"*Think!* You wrote to your brother. He said your letters were full of me. He said that I was a good friend to you. That's why he let me go. 'One good turn deserves another,' he said. What good turn did I ever do you? If you turn into a watering pot, I'll scream."

Letty blinked hard. One hand fluttered up to her throat. "There's nothing in particular. Just little things. You made me go to lectures. We went for walks together. That sort of thing. I never had a real friend until you came to St. Bede's."

Jane felt strangely relieved. Gideon had lied to her. No one in his right mind would kill a man for a woman merely because she'd been kind to his sister. Case was right. Gideon had murdered Jack for his own reasons.

"Jane?"

She drew in a deep breath. "The second question is this. Why does your brother hate Lord Castleton?"

Letty shook her head.

"Letty," said a voice from the door, Oliver's voice, "you must tell her."

He walked to his wife and put his hands on her shoulders. "Tell Jane about the poorhouse," he said. "Tell her how and why this hatred got started. If you don't, I will. Shall we sit down?"

When they were all seated, Letty said tremulously, "Gideon believes that the Duke of Romsey is his father."

When Jane entered the coach, she told the driver to wait.

"Aren't we going home to Woodlands?" asked Harper.

"I don't know. I don't know."

Her brain was reeling from everything Letty had told her. She didn't believe that Piers was Romsey's son, and neither did Letty or Oliver. But it was what Piers believed that counted. All these years, he believed that he and his mother had been abandoned by the duke to live and die as paupers. His mother had told him so.

All those years growing up in the poorhouse,

watching the comings and goings of the Deveres across the river! Hating them! Envying them! Despising the duke for what he thought he'd done to his mother.

She had not known until today that the poorhouse was so close to the duke's house. She had never asked, and Letty had never told her.

She looked at Harper. "Tell me about the reunion tonight. Who will be there?"

"Just old Etonian boys and their friends."

The same Etonian boys that Piers used to watch from the other side of the river.

"Harper, I don't like the sound of this."

"Now, don't you worry none. His lordship knows what he's doing."

"His lordship knows what he's doing?" She stared at him aghast. "He's expecting Piers to strike tonight. Is that it, Harper?"

Harper shifted uncomfortably. "I didn't say that."

Jane poked her head out of the window and yelled, "Driver, take us to Twickenham House."

The coach did not budge.

"Now just a minute," said Harper, his face as fierce as she had ever seen it. "I has my orders."

She placed a hand on his sleeve, "Listen to me, Harper. Lord Castleton thinks that Piers is after *him*, but that's only partly true. It's the duke Piers really wants. Don't you think we should tell his lordship tonight? Or can it wait till tomorrow?"

"You can't know that!"

"It's what Letty told me. I'll tell you about it on the drive out to Twickenham."

Harper passed a hand over his face. "Bloody hell!" he said. "What time is it?"

Jane looked at the watch pinned to her coat lapel. "Going on eight o'clock."

Harper poked his head out the coach window. "Twickenham House!" he yelled. "And spring 'em!"

The coach lurched forward, gathered speed, and was soon charging along the Knightsbridge Road toward Twickenham.

Case was beginning to wonder if Piers had played him for a fool. It was nerve-wracking. The dinner was over, the gentlemen were lighting their cigars and cheroots, decanters of brandy and port had been set on the tables, and Dr. Keate was glowing from the tribute that had just been paid to him by one of his former pupils. The old boy rose to address the assembly amid thunderous applause. What was Piers waiting for?

Suddenly, the whole building shook. Windows cracked. Plaster fell down from the ceiling. Outside, it sounded as though artillery shells were exploding all over the grounds. Case breathed a sigh of relief. Everything was going to plan. The infirmary, with all his father's precious old wrecks, had just been blown to smithereens. He was sure, if he looked at his father, he would see tears in his eyes.

The few moments of shocked silence turned into a panic.

"Leave the building," Case shouted. "Get out through the conservatory."

Turner had been well briefed. At a signal from him, footmen hurried to open the doors to the conservatory and gentlemen streamed through them. There was no panic now. These were Etonians. Many of them were veterans of the Spanish Campaign.

They had a reputation to maintain. The exodus became quite orderly.

This is it, thought Case. Piers or one of his henchmen would get to him in the conservatory. Beyond that he didn't care to speculate.

He stood riveted when another explosion went off. This wasn't supposed to happen. He sprinted through the conservatory, elbowing everyone out of the way, and burst onto the terrace. On the west wing of the house, the rotunda was in flames.

What else had they missed?

Waldo could hardly get his breath when he came up to him. "Turner can't find your father," he said. "He lost him in the conservatory."

"You take the rotunda," Case said, "and I'll check the infirmary."

Waldo went off at once, but Case stood there, undecided. His Grace wouldn't wander off on his own. He knew what was at stake. Piers must have got to him.

He heard the step at his back but he didn't flinch. It took every ounce of willpower not to fight back. Pain exploded through his head and he slumped to the ground.

There were no porters at the gates when their carriage rolled to a stop just inside the grounds of Twickenham House. Jane and Harper descended the steps with Lance at their heels and stared in horror. Flames licked around one end of the house and smoke and particles of ash billowed everywhere. But the main house wasn't on fire. Lights blazed from the downstairs windows and people were milling around outside in the fog of smoke.

"Why is there so much smoke?" asked Jane.

"That'll be the infirmary," replied Harper. "Poor Romsey."

The infirmary. That was reassuring. There wouldn't be people in the infirmary. Only some broken-down coaches.

"And that's the rotunda," said Harper. "That wasn't supposed to happen. But no harm done. It's not attached to the rest of the building."

Jane didn't have time for chitchat. Nor did she share Harper's confidence that the earl knew what he was doing. It seemed to her that Gideon Piers was always one step ahead of them.

"Let's go," she said, and made for the coach.

Harper had other ideas. He ordered the coachmen to man the gates. No one was to get in or out without his say-so. And they were to stay at their posts come what may.

"We walks," he told Jane. "Have you got your pistol?"

"Right here." It was in her hand.

They didn't walk. They ran. That terrible sense of urgency was like a clamp around Jane's throat. Her breathing was shallow, her heart beating so fast she felt as though her chest might burst. It wasn't that she didn't trust Piers. She trusted him to be true to form: vicious, capricious, and wily. It was Case she didn't trust. Whatever he said, she couldn't suppress the picture of two gladiators in a Roman arena. A fight to the death.

There was so much noise, people shouting across each other, that she could hardly make herself heard. All she wanted to know was if anyone had seen Lord Castleton, or the duke. No one had, but she was the only one who seemed disturbed by that fact.

Harper said, "I'm going into the house. Mr. Bowman is in charge of this operation. Maybe he'll know."

Jane's gaze was flitting from one knot of people to another. She was the only female present. Her gaze moved on, then returned as recognition belatedly registered.

She clutched Harper's arm. "Harper," she said, "I recognize those two men over there. They're the men who said they were Special Branch agents and took me to Vauxhall Gardens."

"You're sure?"

"Positive."

Harper began to idle his way toward them. One saw him coming, tapped his companion on the shoulder, and they began to walk away.

"Halt!" shouted Harper. "Halt, I say!"

The men took off like hares with Harper in pursuit.

"Lance, help him," said Jane. "Lance?"

Lance had disappeared. What more could go wrong? "Lance!" she called. "Lance!"

He came out of the shadows, whining, and brushed against her legs. His coat was wet. Then he was off again, going toward the river. Jane followed. He stopped at the water's edge.

"What have you found?" Jane asked.

He took a few steps into the water and was soon submerged. Then he swam back to the bank, pulled himself up, and shook himself off.

"You want me to cross the river?" said Jane.

Lance whined.

"But what—" She stopped. Of course. She knew what was across the river. Letty had told her. The poorhouse. It was from there that Gideon had watched the comings and goings of the Deveres and where his envy and hatred had taken root.

Had Lance picked up Case's scent?

She walked along the bank, but of course it was too dark to see anything. Why was it you could never find a groundsman when you needed him? She supposed, like the porters at the gates, they had run to the house when it came under attack.

Maybe it was just as well that she couldn't find a groundsman. He could turn out to be one of Piers's men and she wouldn't know the difference.

She had to get help. "Lance," she said, and pointed back to the house. "Fetch Harper!" He was the one person she knew she could trust.

Lance whined, but balked.

Jane crouched down and held his face between her hands. "Now you listen to me!" she said fiercely. "I think Piers has Case. I think he's taken him to the poorhouse across the river." She didn't want to think farther than that. "I can't rescue him by myself. I need help."

She straightened and pointed back to the house again. "Lance, fetch Harper!"

Lance bounded away.

She walked farther along the riverbank till she came to the boathouse. Now that her eyes had adjusted to the gloom, she could pick out shapes and identify them. There was an upturned boat lying on the ground. She perched against it and tried to contain her impatience for Lance's return.

Then she saw it, across the river, a light flickering through the trees. It wasn't moving. There must be a house there, though all she could see was the beacon of light.

The poorhouse.

She jumped up and took a few steps back the way she'd come. "Lance!" she shouted. "Harper!"

Ears straining, she listened. No response. Heart pounding, she returned to the boat. It was just like the little rowing boats the salmon fishermen used on the river Dee.

She was going to get that boat in the water if she strained every muscle in her body.

It wasn't as hard as she expected. She hauled it up with both hands, put her shoulder to it, and toppled it over right side up. Then she fell over something on the ground, something warm to the touch. It was a man's body.

"Case," she sobbed. She couldn't see, she couldn't make out his face. But she could tell by touch that this man wasn't Case.

A slow burning anger ignited deep inside and spread through her veins. This was Gideon Piers's handiwork. She could sympathize with the hard life he'd endured in the poorhouse, but she couldn't condone this. He was like a dog that had gone rabid. Someone had to put him down.

After putting her pistol on the bottom of the boat, she threw a pair of oars in, then dragged the boat into the river, waded knee deep into the water, and jumped in.

Chapter 23

*C*ase woke to find himself tied to a chair, his chin sunk on his chest. He didn't lift his head; he didn't stir. In spite of a blazing headache, he took a few minutes to come to himself and get his bearings. The last thing he remembered was being hit on the head at the edge of the terrace. He also remembered sending Waldo to the rotunda to look for the duke. Not a good strategy when Waldo's job was to keep him in sight at all times.

He lifted his head and stretched his muscles. Piers, or the man he presumed was he, was standing at a window, looking out. He turned and smiled. "So, you're awake," he said.

"What is this place?" asked Case.

"The poorhouse, or it used to be. Now it's just a derelict building."

And none too safe by the look of it. Not that Case

could see much in that gloomy interior with only a
lantern on the table to give them light. But he could
see the ceiling, and the huge dip in the center of it. It
wouldn't take much to bring it down on their heads.

His gaze shifted to Piers. He had always pictured
Piers as larger than life, someone who would stride
into a room and become the cynosure of all eyes. But
he was just as Waldo had described him: medium
height and build, and nothing in that pleasant face
that distinguished him from half the gentlemen at
the reunion tonight.

Maybe that was the secret of his success. He was un-
memorable.

Case said, "Why have you brought me here?"

Piers came to stand in front of him. "This used to
be my home," he said. "I don't suppose you knew it
was here. The poorhouse? Across the river from
Twickenham House?"

"I knew of it. It was one of my father's benevolences."

"Benevolences!" Piers sucked air through his
teeth. "A sop to his conscience! He never visited,
never saw the conditions here, how the children were
separated from their parents and put into the hands
of jailors—the whippings, the beatings. You all lived
like princes on the other side of the river. I watched
you, oh yes, I watched you: your magnificent parties,
your well-fed, well-groomed friends. Well, just watch.
Any moment now, you're going to hear Twickenham
House and all it stands for come tumbling down like
a house of cards."

He went back to the window and looked out.

Case was at a complete loss. He'd expected to be
harangued, but not about Twickenham House. His
focus had been on Spain and the barbarous battle

that had ended Piers's career. He'd expected Piers to gloat about his triumphs and his final revenge. This was revenge, all right, but revenge for what?

He said carefully, "You've hated me all these years, just because you envied me?"

"I hated you," Piers roared, "because you were the favored son, and our father, yes, *our* father, left me to rot in this hell."

There was a moment of paralyzing silence, as Case tried to feel his way out of this maze. Finally, he said slowly, "So this is not about Spain, not about the slaughter that took place in St. Michel?"

Piers laughed. "I cared nothing for the Brothers. You did me a favor when you slaughtered them. Now I can keep all that English gold to myself."

Case had difficulty changing his focus. "Then... you're taking your revenge because you think we Deveres owe you something."

"You could never repay me what you owe me."

"You think you're my brother."

"I know it."

"You fool! You know nothing about the Deveres if you think that. If you were my father's son, he would never have abandoned you. He would have provided for you. That's our way. I don't know who told you this lie—"

"My mother told me!" Piers screamed. "On her deathbed. Here, at the poorhouse. She was in service at Twickenham House. Your father got her with child then cast her out."

In the grip of strong emotion, that unremarkable person was beginning to look and sound as though he had just escaped from a lunatic asylum.

"You will never convince me of it," said Case. "My father would never have dishonored one of my mother's maids." He stopped. Something clicked inside his head. He looked at Piers. He judged him to be a few years older than himself.

"How old are you, Piers?"

"Older than you. What does it matter?"

"It matters, because if you're older than I am, your mother could not have been in service at Twickenham House. It would have been a bachelor establishment and the Deveres have a tradition of keeping only male servants when there is no mistress of the house."

"Lies! Lies! Lies!"

Piers picked up a chair and smashed it against the window.

"When my sister married," said Case, "all the female servants went with her to Woodlands."

"If you don't shut your mouth, I'll gag you."

"You were at Twickenham tonight, weren't you? Did you see any female servants? I know you didn't, because it's a bachelor establishment."

"You would say anything to save your father, *our* father."

A cold dread uncurled in the pit of Case's stomach. When he'd awakened to find that his father was not with him, he'd assumed, hoped that His Grace was still at Twickenham. "What have you done with my father?"

Piers giggled. "He's in the punishment room. Appropriate, don't you think? Tied to a chair, just like you. But under *his* chair, there's a keg of gunpowder. Oh, he won't escape. Joseph is guarding him. When I leave here tonight, I'm going to light the bonfire and then—bang! No more duke, no more favored son, no more poorhouse."

He put a hand on either side of Case's chair and

leaned toward him menacingly. "Then I'll rebuild. Yes. Right here on the foundations of the poorhouse. I'm a very rich man, Castleton. The house I build is going to be far more opulent than Twickenham. I'll join all the best clubs in town, and rent a suite at the Clarendon, for convenience. Then I'll find me a blue-blooded wife and have me some blue-blooded children and live happily ever after. I hope that sticks in your craw."

He went back to the window, but he'd smashed it and couldn't see out, so he took the chair and knocked it out. Cold air blew in, and with it the stench of burning.

"Do you smell that?" Piers asked. "Breathe deeply, Castleton. Let that be the last memory of your life of privilege and power."

Jane could hear the voices when she came out on the landing. It had been a nightmarish ascent, three floors up, her only guide a lantern at the top of the stairs. She'd had to cling to the banister all the way up because some of the steps were missing. This was supposed to be the poorhouse. It had the feel of a prison.

She trod on a loose board and it cracked. Hand covering her panicked heart, she pressed herself flat against the wall. A door opened along the corridor and a beam of light spilled out.

"Joseph!" She recognized the voice. "Joseph!" yelled Gideon Piers. "What are you doing down there?"

"Answering nature's call."

The sullen reply came from the floor below. Jane edged forward a little and through the slats of the banister saw what appeared to be a footman in Devere livery—powdered wig and a blue velvet jacket with gold frogging. Oh, God. She had only one pistol and one shot. How many of them were there?

"Get back to the duke!"

"*Dios!* He's not going anywhere."

"I said get back."

There was some mumbling in Spanish, then a door banged.

Jane took a deep breath. Inch by inch, she crept along the corridor to the room where she could hear the voices. The door was ajar. Painstakingly, every muscle tensing, she eased it open. Her pistol was leveled, ready to blast anyone who challenged her.

The room must have run the whole length of the house. It was immense. *A dormitory,* she thought, *a dormitory for the inmates.* The poor were not allowed privacy or their own possessions. Letty had told her that. At the far end of the room were two men, one standing, one tied down on a chair.

She flitted into the room unseen and keeping as much to the shadows as possible, began to traverse the room's length.

Piers said, "I want you to see this. I'm going to cut you from the chair, but you'll still be bound, so don't try anything. One false move and you're a dead man."

When Case was cut from the chair, he stood up. He'd managed to loosen the bonds tying his wrists together, but not enough to free himself. "Twickenham is only a building, Piers," he said. "By the way, shouldn't my father be here to see it? I would think he's the one you want to impress."

"Unfortunately," said Piers pleasantly, "His Grace put up quite a fight when Joseph tried to abduct him. My man had to subdue him with more force than I would have wished. But, as I said, the duke will pay for his sins against me. A little fire, just like Guy Fawkes night, then...boom."

He was at the window again, fretting. Case choked back his rage and said laconically, "It's not going to happen, Piers. Twickenham House is not going to blow up. We found the gunpowder. My father's workshop and the rotunda? That's all we were willing to give you."

"You lie!"

Case chuckled. "You've forgotten your history. Don't you remember, Guy Fawkes's plot was foiled and he was hanged for his crimes?"

With a roar of rage, Piers backhanded Case across the face, splitting his lip. It was now or never. Jane stepped out of the shadows. "Piers," she said. Her finger, steady and sure, tightened on the trigger.

She was quick, but somebody else was quicker. With a speed and precision that shocked her, Piers's gun was blasted out of his hand. She looked across the width of the room. It was the man who was dressed in the Devere livery. Joseph. How had he managed to creep up on her?

"Don't kill him, Miss Mayberry! We want to take him alive!"

Not Joseph, but Ruggles. Her hand shook and her pistol wavered between Piers and Ruggles. What was going on?

"Keep your pistol trained on Piers!" Case yelled. He was working frantically to free himself from his bonds. Ruggles started forward.

"Stay where you are!" Jane cried.

Piers lunged for her. She pulled the trigger, but the upward thrust of his arm sent the bullet into the ceiling, and the impact of his shoulder on her chest sent her sprawling. She was trying to catch her breath when chunks of plaster and a torrent of dust swept down on them. Her eyes stung, breathing was difficult, and the lone lantern flickered and went out.

Someone made a run for it and hared down the length of the dormitory. It had to be Piers. She knew Case wouldn't run away. Then two other figures were up and running. At least nobody had a loaded gun. She was feeling on the floor for Piers's gun when a shot went off. Her heart leaped to her throat. One of the pursuers went down.

She was on her feet in a heartbeat and sprinting down that long dormitory. "Case?"

"No, miss. It's Ruggles." He grabbed his silver wig and threw it away.

She said crossly, though really, she was close to weeping, "I suppose you're going to tell me you're one of us?"

"Afraid so, miss. I was hoping to get the duke away unseen, when you passed me on the staircase. I couldn't let you face Piers on your own."

"I think I might have managed him. Oh, Ruggles, you should have saved the duke."

From below, there came a great crash, a whoosh, and within seconds, the staircase was glowing from a fire that had burst into life in one of the rooms off the hall.

Ruggles said, "Piers has lit the bonfire." Then more urgently, "We have to get out of here. Give me your arm, miss, and help me up. The bullet nicked my leg. Don't worry, it's only a scratch."

When he was on his feet, he said, "Now get out of here, as fast as you can. I'll be right behind you."

She was torn. She wanted to help Case, but she couldn't leave an injured man. The decision was taken out of her hands. Case appeared in the hall. His shoulders were heaving, and one arm was propped against the door frame.

"Jane," he roared. "Ruggles. Get down here."

When they were outside, in the cool night air, Case said, "Ruggles, where is my father?"

"Two floors up, sir. Right below where you were held. He's in a bad way. You'll need help getting him out. I'll come with you."

"Let's not waste time! You're to take Miss Mayberry in one of the boats and row like hell. Get her away from here. Now!"

"Yes, sir."

"Is there another way in?"

"Staircase in the back, sir."

"Case," said Jane. Tears were streaming down her face. "I can help. We'll go together."

He took her face between his hands. "You're the most precious thing in the world to me," he said, and kissed her. "I'm not giving you up. I'll come back to you. I promise."

Then he left her. Just like that, he left her. There were so many things she'd never told him, how a smile from him could make her heart turn over; how he brought out the best in her; how much she admired and loved him.

And what a liar he was! How could he promise to come back to her when he took the most appalling risks?

"Get in the boat, Miss Mayberry."

"Ruggles," she began, "couldn't we—"

"I said get in the boat!"

He didn't sound like the nice Ruggles she knew. He sounded like a soldier who was used to giving orders.

"Watch your step!"

She drew back, then flinched away. Piers was there beside the boat, facedown in the water.

"Ruggles," she said, "I found a body on the other side of the river. Whose was it?"

"Joseph's, Miss. I had to kill him. It was either him or me."

"I'm glad he's dead," she said fiercely. "I'm glad they're both dead!" Her head lifted. "What was that?"

"Ahoy!" shouted Harper from the prow of a rowing boat. "Ahoy!"

It was hopeless, Case thought. There was so much smoke, he was choking on it, though he'd tied his neckcloth around his nose and mouth to spare him the worst. He couldn't get his bearings. He knew he was on the right floor, but that was all he knew. "Father!" he yelled. "Father!"

Something brushed against him. "Lance?" he said. "Is it you?"

Lance barked.

Then Harper was there, wheezing and coughing. "Up here, Mr. Bowman," he shouted, and Waldo came abreast of them.

Case said, "You do realize that this place could go up at any moment?"

Waldo slapped him on the shoulder. "We've been in tight spots before."

Case had always known that he was lucky in his friends, but his breath caught in his throat and he clapped Waldo on the back.

"We'll find the duke, sir," said Harper. "Never you fear. *Lance, fetch the duke.*"

Lance did not hesitate.

Maybe, thought Case, they had a chance after all. *Lance, fetch the duke! Lance, fetch the lost sheep!* He didn't know whether to weep or laugh.

Ruggles stopped rowing. *"They're out! They're out!"*

From end to end, the ground floor was ablaze, so all they could see against the building were dark figures moving quickly to the water's edge.

"I think they have the duke," Ruggles cried.

"Oh, they'll have him. Case wouldn't leave his father behind."

That was something else she loved about him. Some people thought he was aloof and arrogant, but that's because they saw what they wanted to see. He was scion of a great and noble family. But this noble family had more than blue blood running through its veins. There was deep compassion here, loyalty and honor . . . she didn't know why she loved him. In point of fact, he *was* arrogant and aloof. What he needed was the right woman to soften him. Lucky for him, he'd met up with her.

"Miss Mayberry, they're safe. There's no need to take on so."

"I know. I know." She found her handkerchief and blew her nose.

She caught her breath when it came—an almighty roar, then the whole building went up in tongues of fire. Whoever was rowing Case's boat, didn't stop to watch. The little boat came on steadily.

Their boat touched shore and Robert and Freddie were there to wrap them in blankets and help them. "Don't kill Ruggles," she said. "It turns out he's one of us. He's injured. Someone should help him."

"It's only a scratch," said Ruggles. "I'll take care of it myself."

The riverbank was lined with men, most of them guests, many of them footmen and groundsmen. They had grim expressions and talked in whispers. Jane doubted that they knew what was going on.

When Case's boat came into shore, and everyone could see that he was all right, they started to cheer, but the cheers died away when they saw the duke. There were blankets on hand and one was used as a stretcher.

"Let's get him to the house, *now*," Case said. "Robert, Freddie, tell all these people to go home. They can read about what happened in the papers."

He saw Jane and elbowed his way through to her. He was covered in soot; there were burns on his face. She went on tiptoe and kissed him. "We'll face this together," she said.

"If it hadn't been for Lance—" His voice broke. "Thank you for sending him. Where is he?"

Lance was staying close to the duke, and when the stretcher bearers began to make their way to the house, he went with them.

It was a subdued procession that followed after them.

When they'd scrubbed the dirt from their hands and faces, they gathered in a small parlor off the duke's dressing room, Jane, Waldo, and Ruggles. Case was with his father and the doctor; Robert and Freddie were assessing the damage to the house and making sure the danger was over; and Harper had taken off for Woodlands to fetch Lady Sophy and fresh clothes for Jane. Nobody commented on it; nobody thought it odd. Everybody knew that her place was with Case.

She looked up when Waldo put a cup and saucer into her hand. "Tea," he said. "Drink it. It will do you good."

She took a sip, but she did it to please him. Her thoughts were on the duke, and how still and silent he'd been when they'd laid him on the bed. His face had seemed all angles and planes and shadows. There was a lot of blood. He'd been beaten into unconsciousness. Then she'd looked at Case. He seemed to be suffering torments.

He'd told her to wait in the parlor, and when she'd called Lance, he'd refused to come.

"Leave him," said Case. "I'll send him out if he becomes troublesome."

She'd groped for words to comfort him, but his mind wasn't on her. Before she could find them, he had turned away. "I have to send messengers to bring my sister and brother home," he said.

Waldo's voice broke into her thoughts. "Jane," he said, "do you think you're up to answering a few questions?"

Anything to take her mind off the duke and Case. "About what?"

"About Gideon Piers."

"Gideon?"

"You're one of the few people who has spoken to him. You may be able to help us solve a puzzle."

She looked from one to the other. "Who are you?" she asked.

"You know who I am," said Waldo. "I'm one of Case's closest friends." When she said nothing, he sighed and went on, "We work for a branch of the service."

"What service?"

"The Secret Service, but not Special Branch."

"Does Case know about this?"

Waldo shook his head. "We couldn't tell him, but I'm sure he's figured most of it out by now."

"Let me get this straight," she said. She was looking at Ruggles. "You're just like Special Branch agents, yet you let me go to Vauxhall to meet with that fiend?"

Ruggles had the grace to look shamefaced. "I knew nothing would happen to you," he said. "Or you may believe I would have kept you from going."

"You hit Harper over the head!"

"A tap, merely. He wasn't supposed to be there."

"Why didn't you tell us who you were and what you were up to?"

"Because," said Waldo gently, "that's not how we work in our section. Jane, those questions?"

She pursed her lips, but after a moment, she mastered her temper. "Fine," she said. "Ask your questions."

Waldo said, "Our section head thought, when Piers burst upon the scene again, that this might be our last chance to recover the gold he stole from all those British convoys in Spain. We thought he was dead, you see, and he'd buried the gold in Spain, and we'd lost it forever. But he would never have come home to England without his spoils."

"He never mentioned any gold to me."

"What we're looking for is a hiding place."

"A hiding place? What's wrong with a bank vault?"

Ruggles grinned. "Thieves and villains have been known to rob banks and bank vaults. That wouldn't suit Piers. Besides, there would be too much gold to hide easily. He'd want a safe place that he could get to without being seen."

She shook her head. "I wish I could help you, but I can't."

"It could be hidden in the floor of a church," said Ruggles, "or in the crypt, in the gallery, in the cellars, in a grave."

Again Jane shook her head. "There's his mother's grave," she said. "But Piers revered his mother. He would never desecrate her grave."

"If she died in the poorhouse, she would be buried in the local churchyard, wouldn't she?"

"No. She had a pauper's grave. It was dismal, really. No gravestone, just a numbered wooden marker. It was supposed to be hallowed ground, but it was just a bare patch of land beside a busy thoroughfare in Kensington."

Jane set down her cup and saucer with enough force to make droplets of tea go flying. "At least, that's where she was until three gullible, green-as-grass innocents had the remains removed to a more suitable setting! At her son's behest."

"Where is the grave?" asked Ruggles quietly.

"In a little village called Newbrey, out past Staines. It's supposed to be the parish where his mother was born."

"How will we know the grave?"

"It's in the parish graveyard. There's a stone. 'Sacred to the memory of Sadie Sellars.' "

She looked up when the door opened. Case stood there. She searched his face anxiously and thought it was a little less strained. "How is your father?" she asked.

"It's too soon to say, but the doctor thinks there's hope. Come and see this."

He took her hand and led her to the duke's bedside. Lance was lying on top of the bed, pressed close to the duke. "No, don't take him down, just watch."

Lance whined piteously, then licked the duke's hand. Moments went by, then the duke brushed his fingers along Lance's flank. After a moment or two, they repeated the process.

"I've never seen him do anything like this before," Jane said.

The doctor said, "You have a very intelligent and very valuable dog there, Miss Mayberry. He seems trained for this work. Was he a mountain dog?"

"No. Just an ordinary sheepdog."

"She wouldn't know," Case said. "She stole him."

Oh yes, she could tell that he wasn't nearly as wound up. He sat down on the bed, took his father's hand, and brushed his fingers along the palm. The duke did not return the gesture. His lips moved. "Caspar," he whispered.

Case turned brilliant gray eyes upon Jane. His voice quivered only slightly. "We look like chimney sweeps," he said. "But what does it matter! I can't leave my father, Jane, but I want you here too. Will you stay?"

"I'll sit over here," she said, "as quiet as a mouse."

The doctor excused himself, not to go home, he said, but to go to the room the servants had made up for him. If there was any change, he was to be called at once.

Jane sat silently, huddled into her blanket, and listened as Case talked quietly to his father, childhood memories that gave him pleasure to recall. She found herself smiling, and as his voice droned on, her eyelids grew heavy, and her breathing became slow and regular. Finally, she slept.

Chapter 24

They were married in the parish church in Twickenham on a typical January morning. It poured with rain. Nobody seemed to mind, especially the happy couple. It was a quiet affair, with only a dozen or so people in attendance, among them, and most gratifying to His Grace, his daughter, Lady Rosamund, and her husband, and Lord Justin, who had arrived home in the wee hours of that very morning.

The duke, in an invalid chair, was flanked by Harper and Lance. In fact, Harper and Lance had been His Grace's constant companions since the night of the accident, and in Case's view, had made a great contribution to his father's recovery.

As His Grace watched the young couple kneel before the priest for the blessing, an odd tightness gripped his throat. It seemed to him that he had awakened three weeks ago, on Christmas Day, to find his son a changed man. That wall of reserve that he found hard to tolerate had come tumbling down. He wasn't sure if that lovely young woman was the reason for it or the fact that he'd come to within a hairbreadth of succumbing to his injuries.

He couldn't remember a damn thing about that night, and Dr. Nichols said he might never remember. Most of what he knew came from the newspapers, that a notorious bandit known only as La Roca, who was thought to have died in Spain, had returned to England to take his revenge on Major Devere, the soldier who had inflicted a crushing and humiliating defeat on La Roca and his desperadoes at their hideout in St. Michel. A report from the War Office stated that one of His Majesty's Secret Service units had not only foiled the attempt, but had recovered most of the gold La Roca had stolen from British convoys all those years ago in Spain.

Caspar filled him in as questions occurred to him, but he wasn't terribly interested. He was just thankful that, for once, the Secret Service had not bungled things, or he might not have had his son.

His daughter, Rosamund, who was sitting right behind him, put her hand on his shoulder. "Father," she said, "this must be the happiest day of your life. I know you were beginning to think that Caspar would never marry."

That odd tightness was back in his throat. "No," he said, "the happiest day of my life was when you came back to me after you were abducted from Newgate."

Lord Justin, deeply tanned, a younger version of his brother, said, "Honestly, I don't know why we English don't all move to Italy. It's freezing in here. Isn't there some sort of heating system?"

"I think it's quite warm," said Lady Sophy.

Richard Maitland sighed.

Harper said, "Hush! This is a solemn occasion. I wants to hear what the priest is saying."

All the Deveres sealed their lips.

When the service was over, friends and family, led by the duke, went forward to congratulate Case and Jane. Afterward, the duke had Harper wheel him to the side, but he kept his gaze on his son. He saw him exchange a brief glance with his bride, and noted the blaze of happiness that suddenly transformed Caspar's grave expression. Jane was blushing, as though his son had touched her intimately in a roomful of people.

Life was odd, thought the duke. A few weeks ago, he'd been wishing that his son had never met this woman. But seeing them together, day by day, had made him change his mind. Or maybe it was the realization of how fragile life was that had changed his mind. If anything had happened to Caspar, it would have been some consolation to know that he'd found joy with this woman.

The husband was gone. That made things simpler, of course, but even if Campbell were alive and the awful prospect of divorce still loomed, it would not trouble him now. This was not an infatuation. Caspar and Jane were not young or flighty or romantic. If anything, they were too serious, too responsible. They would not have chosen the route of divorce unless they were convinced of the rightness of their decision.

The details of Campbell's murder were sketchy. Footpads, he thought Caspar told him. He couldn't seem to muster any interest in the details. The doctor said this was not unusual in one who had suffered a severe concussion. In time, he would begin to take an interest in outside events again.

For the present, he was content to enjoy the moment. He had everything he wanted and needed right here, his children and their spouses, his good friend Harper, and Lance.

He wondered at the bond that had formed between himself and the dog. Something must have happened that night. If only he could remember.

He was too happy to think of that now, and his happiness made him realize how lonely he'd been these last months, after Rosamund married and went to live at Woodlands. But all that was going to change. Caspar and Jane were going to make their home with him, and Harper had taken a leave from Special Branch. They were going to rebuild the infirmary, make it bigger and better, and scour the local parishes for broken-down carriages that, with loving care, could be restored to their former glory.

Yes, life was odd. One moment he was at death's door, and the next he was impatient to be up and doing.

Impatient? He wasn't impatient. He was profoundly content. He had raised three fine children. He knew Elizabeth would be proud of them.

It was late in the afternoon before the party began to break up. Freddie wanted to get home before it was dark, so he had one of the footmen order his curricle brought round, then he slipped away to the billiard room to enjoy a cigar with Richard and Waldo. Jane went with Sally to get her coat. She'd ordered Case to stay with his family. They needed this time together, alone with their father, especially as this was Justin's first night home.

Sally said, "Lady Octavia is going to be beside herself with joy when she hears you have married Case."

"I'm not sure about that," replied Jane. "She told me that he would marry someone who was almost a princess, and you know how she hates to be wrong."

"What? 'Almost a princess?' What does that mean?"

"I presume someone on the same social footing as Case."

Sally's frown cleared. "The Deveres are lucky to get you, and I hope they know it. What I meant, though, is that Lady Octavia will be thinking of the Devere connections, their influence and, dare I say, their money?"

"As long as she doesn't expect me to use my influence with the Deveres."

They were descending the stairs to the front hall when Sally took up the conversation where it had left off. "Jane, you're not thinking of giving up your work at the library, are you?"

"Well . . . as a matter of fact, I am."

"You mean, Case is forbidding it?"

Jane laughed. "Oh, no. He knows better than that."

"Then why?"

When they reached the hall, Jane indicated that they should take chairs flanking the grate where a fire burned brightly. "I don't mean to give it up entirely," she said, "but you have to understand how things work with me. When I stumbled upon the library four years ago, it was as though a door opened. I didn't seek it out. It was there in front of me. I could choose to go through it or not. I chose to pass through it, and I've never regretted that decision. In the last few weeks, another door has opened for me. I choose to go through this door too."

"What door?" asked Sally, completely absorbed in Jane's words.

Jane breathed deeply. "Poorhouses, or workhouses, whatever you want to call them. The people who run them. The people who staff them. Orphans. Their care and education. It all comes down to the Poor Law. Oh, I'm not going to take everything on at once. I'm going to start in a very small way."

The porter entered and announced that his lordship's curricle had been brought round.

"Curricle!" exclaimed Jane. "Don't tell me Freddie brought you here in an open carriage?" When Sally nodded, Jane said, "Let me have one of the duke's carriages brought round. Or you can stay the night. That's what Waldo and Robert are doing. Then you can go home tomorrow in Robert's carriage."

"Thank you, but it isn't necessary. It's stopped raining. And I don't want Freddie more upset than he already is."

At this point, Jane sent the porter to fetch the viscount. This was one of the things that was hard to get used to, remembering not to say too much in front of the servants, and remembering that there were servants passing in and out of rooms all the time.

"Is Freddie upset? I didn't notice."

"Well, you wouldn't on your wedding day." Sally sat forward in her chair. "Oh, Jane, something heartbreaking happened at our house yesterday. Emily Drake came to call. She asked to see me, but it was really Freddie she wanted to talk to. The poor girl is completely crushed. Freddie is barely civil to her. He practically ignores her in company. And she is as deep in love as a girl can be. She was never interested in Case. That was only to make Freddie jealous.

It's always been Freddie with her. The thing is, I think Freddie loves her too. But he refuses to see her."

"What was the point of her visit?"

"To make a clean breast of things and ask his forgiveness."

"Sally, stay out of this. It's not your problem."

"But I hate to see him like this. He loves her and she loves him. She only stirred things up to get Freddie moving. Well, you know how slow he is."

"Freddie may love her, but Emily doesn't love him. She loves herself. She's like a child. She uses people, then casts them aside. I'm not thinking only of you and me. There were others she involved in her schemes. Lord Reeve for one. Lady Sophy, Case, Waldo. Even my stableboy. Is that the kind of woman you want Freddie to marry?"

Sally said, "But people change. I think this has been a lesson to her."

"I hope it has. But it may be too late for Freddie. Anyway, they have to work things out by themselves."

They heard Freddie's steps on the stairs, and Jane said, "I'll walk you to the door."

Arms linked, the two friends strolled to the front entrance. "Do you know what I think?" said Jane. "I think, when Freddie's heart has mended, he's going to meet the woman who is right for him, and she's going to be as straightforward and as honorable as he is. Trust me, he's not going to be slow off the mark when he meets the right woman."

"And what about me, Jane? When am I going to meet the right man?"

"I don't tell fortunes."

"I know, it's a game. Indulge me."

"Well," said Jane, "you won't be looking for love. You'll be teetering on a chair, moving crockery around, and a seductive masculine voice right behind you will say, 'Call off your dog or I'll be forced to shoot it.' Naturally, you'll hate this gentleman on sight, and he'll be forced, for the rest of his life, to try to make you change your mind."

Both women laughed uproariously.

Robert had gone for a walk, leaving Richard and Waldo alone in the billiard room.

"So, Waldo," Richard said, "when exactly did the Secret Service come into the investigation?"

Waldo was savoring a very fine cognac. He looked at Richard over the rim of his glass. "I'm ashamed to say, we drifted into it. Like everyone else, yourself included, we didn't take the murder of John Collier seriously. However, because there was a great deal of money still to recover, two of us were assigned to the file."

"You and Ruggles?"

"Well, I was the logical choice."

"You being Case's best friend."

"Do I detect a sneer behind those words? You, of all people, should know that that's what made me invaluable. Come now, Richard, you were in the Secret Service before you transferred to Special Branch. You know how it works. Would you like another cheroot?"

"God, no. One is my limit. I only smoke those things to be sociable. But you can pass over that decanter of brandy you've been hoarding."

Waldo passed him the decanter of brandy.

After topping up his glass, Richard said, "Tell me about Ruggles. When did he become Case's manservant, and how did he infiltrate Piers's outfit?"

Waldo grinned. "I've never worked on an assignment

like this before, you know, when you're only going through the motions because you don't expect results, and you strike lucky every time. That's what happened with Ruggles. The Albany supplies its residents with manservants, if they want them. Case made use of the service. It was easy enough to arrange to have Ruggles assigned to Case. The timing was awkward, coming so soon after John Collier's body turned up, but naturally we provided Ruggles with impeccable references, and Case accepted them."

"Naturally," replied Richard.

"Infiltrating Piers's outfit was our real object, but we thought that was a lost cause. As I said, we were simply going through the motions."

"So they approached Ruggles?"

"After he'd sold a few bits and pieces that belonged to Case. Obviously, he was dishonest and could be bought."

"What about this place across the river where the bandits were camping out?"

"We knew it was there, but not Piers's connection to it. Case's strategy was to do nothing that would scare Piers off. As it turned out, it was a successful strategy."

"Except that the duke was almost beaten to death."

"Yes, well, things always go wrong. We never expected the duke to be a target."

"You were lucky to recover the gold."

"Yes, weren't we?"

"Mmm." Richard gazed into space. "Piers's last will and testament. How did that come about?"

"We're still investigating. There's no mention of it in army records. We think he arranged it privately, through a third party."

They drank their brandies, each lost in his own

thoughts. Finally, Richard said, "That was a fascinating story, Waldo. Highly entertaining, in fact. Now let's have the real story."

"Don't you believe me?"

"Up to a point. But I know it wasn't that simple. As you said, I was in the Secret Service before I transferred to Special Branch, so I know how it works."

"Then," said Waldo, "you'll know that we never divulge our secrets, especially not to Special Branch agents."

After a moment, both men began to laugh.

Richard met his wife in the hall. She had come to look for him, and he was looking for her. He frowned when he saw the pallor of her skin.

"You look tired," he said.

"I am a little," she admitted. "But if you think I look tired, you should see Justin. He's quite shattered. He hadn't realized how ill Papa would be. I told him he's made tremendous strides this last week, but I'm not sure that he believes me."

"Justin was the life and soul of the party. He seemed in good spirits to me. He had us all laughing."

"Yes. Well, that's Justin's way. But that doesn't mean he doesn't feel things deeply. He did have us laughing, though, didn't he? Papa especially. I think Justin is just the tonic Papa needs right now."

His hand brushed her abdomen. "You didn't tell them about the child?"

She sighed and put her head on his shoulder. "No. Too much excitement for one day. Besides, I want to keep it our secret for a little while longer. Just the three of us, getting to know each other."

She raised her head and looked into his eyes. "Do you think I'm being foolish?"

"I don't care whether you're foolish or not. If that's what you want, that's how it will be."

"That's no answer."

"No," he said softly. "I don't think you're being foolish."

Arms around each other's waists, they walked along the corridor. "Where are you taking me, Richard?"

"I'm going to tuck you up in bed so you can have a little rest before dinner."

"Mmm," she sighed.

When she was tucked up in bed, with hot bricks at her feet, Richard sat down in front of the fire to read a book. But he couldn't concentrate. His eyes kept straying to his wife. A few months ago, he would never have believed that he could be this man, in this chair, so deeply happy that he wouldn't care if he never got out of it. Everything that was precious to him was in this room.

The accident happened just after they passed Kensington. The trouble was, the curricle lights had winked out and they were traveling blind. One minute they were on the road, and the next, they were driven into the ditch by a coach and four that came charging out of the dark and tried to overtake them. One of the curricle wheels broke and both Freddie and Sally went tumbling into the ditch.

The coach stopped and a gentleman and one of his coachmen walked back to them.

"My fault entirely," said Freddie, scrambling to his feet. "If there's any damage to your carriage, I'll pay the shot, of course."

"You can be sure of that. Well, we can't leave you here. I suppose you'll have to travel with us. Joe, unhitch the horses. We'll take them with us."

The offer, so grudgingly given, had Sally's temper heating. "You were driving too fast," she declared.

Freddie said quickly, "Very good of you. Thank you. I'm Latham, by the way, and this is my sister, Miss Latham."

"Chalbury. John Chalbury. How do you do?"

Sally kept her lips closed. Freddie helped her to her feet and got her onto the road.

"Well, don't just stand there," said Chalbury. "Take your sister to my coach, then get back here and help us."

"I'll be right back," said Freddie.

When they were out of Chalbury's hearing, Freddie said, "Sal, what's got into you? The man is only trying to help. You're not usually so stiff and starchy."

"He was driving too fast," she said.

"No, he wasn't. And the accident was my fault. I knew those lamps were faulty and should be replaced. I just never got around to doing it. So, be polite. Unbend a little."

But she couldn't. She'd taken an instant dislike to John Chalbury, and nothing could make her change her mind.

Most of the upstairs lights were doused and the ground-floor shutters were drawn when Jane and Case slipped out of the house.

"Where are you taking me?" Jane asked.

"Somewhere private and romantic where I can be alone with my beautiful wife."

"What's wrong with your bedchamber or mine?"

"Justin. He has an odd sense of humor. I wouldn't

feel safe with him loose in the house. I'm not jesting. Frogs and toads between the sheets, bells going off, literally, every time we move in bed. No, this way is better."

He did up the top buttons of her coat then became lost in her dark eyes. He had to taste her lips, had to feel her softness between his hands. Her trembling response and the enforced celibacy of the last few weeks undermined his control. His kisses became urgent, demanding.

With palms splayed against his chest, she pushed out of his arms. "Case, this is madness." She started to laugh. "Let's hurry. Let's get to that private romantic place where we can be alone, then make love to me in earnest."

"I don't make love in earnest. I do it with finesse."

"Shouldn't I be the judge of that?"

He laughed. He seemed so carefree and young in that moment that she was captivated.

"I love to see you happy," she said.

He put an arm around her shoulders, hugging her, and they walked on. "This hasn't been much of a wedding day for you," he said. "The bride is supposed to be the center of attention. But with Justin newly home, and our father so frail, and no one wanting to leave his side..."

"Oh, yes," she said, "I'm quite cast down. Case, I'm not a child. I don't care to be the center of attention, and if that happened, I'd run away and hide in a closet."

Another laugh from him and another hug for her.

"Of course your father is the focus of attention," she said. "If he wasn't, I'd wonder what kind of family I'd married into. And I wasn't lonely. I spent some time with Trentie and Ben."

"Your housekeeper and stableboy." He groaned.

"That's not how I think of them. They're my friends. They were at the church, weren't they? That's how much I think of them."

A little while later, he said, "Your friend, Mrs. Gray, didn't come to the wedding."

She went quiet. "No," she said. "Oliver sent me a letter saying that it would be too much for her. It seems an officer of the law called at their house the morning after Gideon died and asked her to identify the body. So now she knows the truth about Gideon, and she's not taking it very well. Oliver begged me not to take offense, and not to give up the friendship."

"You won't give up the friendship, I know that. But how are you going to mend it?"

She sighed. "I don't really know."

He looked up as the first flakes of snow began to fall. "You know, Jane, you could ask her to help you with a project for the parish poorhouse. She's a vicar's wife. She would feel obliged to do her part. And from what you've told me about Letty, she would have a real interest in that kind of work. Then, who knows."

She clutched his arm. "Case! Sometimes you astound me! That's a splendid idea. I think it might work."

"Yes, I'm quite an intelligent fellow when the occasion demands." He was distinctly amused.

"No. That's a compliment. Most men wouldn't even think of it."

They came out of the trees and climbed a steep incline lined one either side with small cottages. "Workers' cottages," Case told her. "This one is ours."

It stood a little back from the others. When they

entered it, the draft from the door sent sparks shooting up the chimney. It was very snug, with a carpet on the floor, and a table in front of the window and a narrow bed.

"This used to be Richard's cottage," he said, "when he was on the run and hiding out at Twickenham, posing as a coachman. I say 'posing' because he was the worst coachman that ever darkened our doors. This was his idea. The carpet, by the way, was his suggestion. We don't outfit our workers' cottages with luxuries."

"I didn't know your brother-in-law hid out here when he was on the run."

"No. Well, not everything gets reported in the papers."

"No," she said, thinking of the newspaper reports of the night Gideon died. They hardly skimmed the surface, but that was because British Intelligence doled out the information, so Case said, and they wanted the public to know only what they wanted them to know.

"And here," said Case, "is champagne for milady, and a basket of provisions to stave of starvation."

"The champagne will do fine."

She was disappointed. She didn't want champagne or something to eat. She wanted to be in his arms. Her body craved his touch. But obviously, there was something he wanted more. He wanted to talk.

It came to her, then, that that's what she wanted, too. There were things she should have said to him long before now. This was the beginning of their marriage. They had to start with a clean slate.

When they were sitting in front of the fire, drinking their champagne, Case said, "You know, Jane, everything happened so fast after I left you that last time, when you told me we had to part. We never got round to talking about it, and these last weeks, my mind has been full of my father. I can't remember, but I think I may have said some unforgivable things to you..."

"You were hurt," she said.

He studied his glass of champagne. "Yes."

"And I was a fool."

He looked up at her. "You were?"

She nodded. "There is nothing like a life-and-death experience to strip away everything that is not essential. That's what happened to me when I climbed those three flights of rickety stairs in the poorhouse, with hardly any light, guided only by the sound of your voice."

Her voice was low and she spoke slowly. "I learned then that nothing can ever separate us, not the claims of our families, our unborn children, or society, or anything under the sun. Life is too short. Time is precious. I don't want to waste it. I don't want second best. I want you.

"I wasn't going to let Gideon Piers take you away from me, not after all we'd been through to claim our love. I knew in those moments of fear for you that I had to kill Gideon or be killed." She captured his free hand and brought it to her lips. "You told me once you had killed with your bare hands. I understood how you felt then. If I'd had the strength, I would have killed Gideon with my bare hands if I had to."

When she looked up at him, he let out a deep, shaken breath. "You can't know how much those words mean to me."

He plucked the glass of champagne from her fingers, set both glasses on the table, and pulled her to the bed.

"What?" She was laughing at his haste. "Don't I get some pretty words in return?"

He began to undress her. "Yes. I've been meaning to say this to you for some time." His voice rose by several notches. "Don't ever try anything like that again! I damn near died when I saw you creep up on Piers with that silly little pistol clutched in your hand. He could have killed you! Think how I would have felt!"

She looped her arms around his neck. "But my darling, that's precisely my point. I didn't have a choice. And if our positions were reversed, neither would you."

"You're right. But knowing you're right doesn't make me feel any better."

"Is this the finesse you promised me?"

"I don't think of finesse when I make love to you."

She said archly, "Just what do you think of when you make love to me?"

"You. Only you."

"It's the same for me. I want to forget all the ugliness. Help me forget."

Arms wrapped around each other, they sank onto the bed. The last, loverlike words he said to her before coherent speech became impossible were, "I'm going to get you a proper pistol to replace that toy."

She knew what he meant. "I love you, too," she said.

A month later, when they were on honeymoon in Aboyne in Scotland, Jane received this letter from her friend Sally Latham:

Dearest Jane,

    The most amazing thing has happened. I'm engaged to a wonderful man, John Chalbury of Stan-

ton Hall. It happened exactly as you said it would. Who would believe it?

"Almost a princess" doesn't do you justice. You're the most amazing woman, a seer, a prophetess, and the best friend a girl ever had.

I hope you're as happy as I am, my dear, dear countess.

Your devoted friend,
Sally

Author's Note

Special Branch, in my story, comes from my imagination, and is inspired by the real Special Branch (Irish), which did not come into existence until 1883. It was set up in Scotland Yard and was a police force within a police force, established to combat terrorism.

About the Author

Best-selling, award-winning author Elizabeth Thornton was born and educated in Scotland, and has lived in Canada with her husband for over thirty years. In her time, she has been a teacher, a lay minister in the Presbyterian Church, and is now a full-time writer, a part-time baby-sitter to her five grandchildren, and dog walker to her two spaniels.

Elizabeth enjoys hearing from her readers.
If you wish to receive her newsletter, e-mail her at: *elizabeth.thornton@mts.net* or visit her web page at: *http://www.elizabeththornton.com.*

Turn the page for a sneak peek at

Elizabeth Thornton's next spellbinding romance. . . .

Look for it in the spring of 2004!

Prologue

He knew the precise moment that a stray comment from one of the other guests struck a chord in her infallible memory. Something shifted in her eyes, not suspicion, not comprehension. *Speculation* would be closer to the word he wanted. Then the look was gone. But he knew Chloë. She had stored the tidbit of information away for future reference.

He had to kill her before she worked everything out.

He had killed before and would kill again to protect his own. He couldn't afford to be squeamish, and he couldn't afford to waste time, not in this case. She had to be silenced before she broadcast her suspicions to the world.

It was time to go to bed. Footmen were on hand with candles to light the way upstairs. No one lingered. The house party was over. Some guests had already left. Everyone else was packed and ready to leave first thing in the morning.

Once in his bedchamber, he lay on his bed, fully dressed, with his hands behind his neck, listening to the sounds of the house settling in for the night. He waited half an hour, got up and left his room.

After dismissing the maid, Chloë sat down at the escritoire, opened her diary and began to make notes on the dinner just past. She described the menu, the china, the guests—what they wore, how they looked and what they said. There were influential people with friends in high places. There had been quite a bit of name dropping, and she duly noted that too.

One conversation in particular stayed in her mind, something Lady Langston had said. As the memory came back to her, her hand trembled and she put down her pen. Thoughts chased themselves in quick succession through her mind. It hardly seemed possible. Her memory might be at fault. She couldn't accuse anyone without checking on a few facts. But if she was right, she could be in mortal danger.

A moment before, she'd felt quite warm. Now she was chilled to the bone.

Her whole body jerked when someone knocked softly on the door.

"Chloë?"

His voice!

"I want to talk to you. Open the door, Chloë."

Not in a month of Sundays!

Moving swiftly, she crossed to the window and closed the drapes, then she sat down at the escritoire and rummaged in one of the drawers for paper. The box of stationery that she found was of the best quality vellum and had Lord Brinsley's coat of arms stamped on each page. In other circumstances she would have been impressed. The thought wrung a shaky sob from her.

It took her only a moment or two to write what she had to say. She hoped, prayed, that this letter would be redundant, that she'd live to tell the tale herself. She didn't want to involve Jo, but there was no one else she could turn to now.

Lord Brinsley had offered to frank his guests' letters. All they had to do was leave them on the hall table.

Maybe she was panicking for nothing. Maybe she should invite him in to talk things over.

The doorknob rattled. "Chloë, I know you're still up. I saw the light under your door. I'd like to talk to you."

"Just a moment."

Christ Jesus! He must think she was a simpleton!

She locked her diary in the escritoire and left her letter on the mantelpiece, hoping that the maid would take care of it for her. Snatching up her cloak, she glided soundlessly through the door to the servants' staircase.

As she descended the stairs, her mind worked like lightning. If she screamed at the top of her lungs, would anyone hear her? And if they heard her, would they get to her in time? Would they believe her? Where should she go and what should she do?

She left the house by the back door. After a few steps she halted, giving her eyes time to adjust to the dark. Her skin prickled. She wasn't alone.

A shadowy figure stepped in front of her. "Chloë?" he said. There was a smile in his voice.

His hands reached for her throat.

She ducked beneath his outstretched arms and began to run.

Chapter 1

I should have known you would be a woman."

Jo Chesney, publisher and proprietor of the *Avon Journal*, looked up with a start. She was in her office, at her desk, studying the latest edition of the newspaper, hot off the press, and was taken aback by the stranger's presence as much as by his offensive words. This was Friday, the day they got the paper out. She hadn't time for interruptions.

Her first thought was that he was an actor. He had that look—tall, dark and dramatic rather than handsome. He had presence. And this was, after all, Stratford-upon-Avon, Shakespeare's birthplace, and the theater season was still in full swing.

She wasn't unduly alarmed when he took a step toward her. There were plenty of people about, and Mac Nevin, the managing editor, was in his office across the hall, or in Dispatch. All she had to do was call out and someone would come running.

All the same, she was aware that he had her at a

disadvantage. For one thing, he was immaculately turned out and she was dressed in her working clothes. For another, he was looming over her like a great beast of prey. She evened the odds by getting to her feet.

Obviously he was laboring under a misunderstanding. He must have entered the wrong building and mistaken her for someone else. Misunderstanding or no, she took exception to his insulting manner and tone of voice. She was a respectable lady who also happened to run a successful business. No one talked to her like that.

Her gaze as chilly as his own, she said, "These are the offices of the *Avon Journal*. If you've lost your way, I'd be happy to give you directions."

"I haven't lost my way. You are J. S. Chesney, I presume, the owner of this scurrilous piece of refuse?"

She hadn't noticed that he had a copy of the *Journal* tucked under one arm, not until he tossed it on the desk.

Scurrilous piece of refuse. If he wasn't an actor, he must be a politician. No normal person spoke like that. He was trying to be offensive. He couldn't have known how well he was succeeding. The *Journal* was more than a paper to Jo. It was her late husband's price and joy. When John died, it seemed that the *Journal* would die with him. She wouldn't allow it. Against everyone's advice she'd stepped into the breach and kept the paper going. In her mind John and the *Journal* were inseparable.

"Yes," she said. "I'm Mrs. Chesney. I own the *Journal.* What did we do, misspell your name? Give you a bad review?"

"A bad—" His brows slashed together. "You think I'm an actor?"

Obviously not, but since the idea seemed to annoy him, she added fuel to the fire. "You certainly look the part." She studied him for a moment. "You could pass yourself off as the hero if you stopped glaring and minded your manners."

For a moment she thought she'd gone too far. His lips compressed, but only momentarily. He said slowly, "I was right. You don't know me at all, do you, Mrs. Chesney?"

"Should I?"

"You write about me as though you know me ... intimately."

She didn't like his choice of words. But whether the innuendo was deliberate or unintentional was debatable. She decided to give him the benefit of the doubt.

She lifted her chin a notch. "If you have a complaint, I suggest you talk to Mr. Nevin, our managing editor. I'm the publisher. I don't have control of everything that goes in the paper."

"A typical female response! If all else fails, find some man to bail you out of your difficulties. Oh, no, Mrs. Chesney. Your name is on every edition of the *Journal*—J. S. Chesney. You're the one who will pay the toll, unless, of course, you have no money of your own. Then your husband, poor devil, will be held to account for your misconduct."

She wanted to lash out and annihilate him with a few well-chosen words. What stopped her was the sudden realization that he was serious. This sounded like litigation, the courts, punitive damages. She had to hear him out.

"I don't stand in any man's shadow," she said quietly. "I'm a widow, as I'm sure you've already discovered."

"No, I didn't know." He seemed to be hesitating, as though he were about to apologize, but went on instead. "It doesn't make any difference. I want this stopped."

He reached out and flipped the *Journal* over so that she was staring down at the back page. "London Life," the heading blazed. This was fairly new, an unapologetic commentary on the comings and goings of London's rich and famous. Readers, it seemed, even those who lived as far afield as Stratford-upon-Avon, couldn't get enough of these celebrities—what they wore, what they ate, where they lived, what they did.

It was her friend Chloë who had come up with the idea, and Chloë who wrote the rough copy and sent it by express from London every week. She was ideally suited for the job. Though now a widow, Chloë had married well and moved in the upper reaches of polite society.

Polite society, according to Chloë, was anything but polite, except on the surface. Beneath the surface raged dangerous currents, explosive passions, tempestuous liaisons. In short, Chloë said with a laugh, everything that made life interesting. And every week she shared the salacious secrets of the rich and famous with the *Journal*'s readers.

Since the inception of "London Life," the *Journal*'s circulation had soared.

Now Jo understood. The irate stranger must be one of Chloë's glamorous celebrities, and he had obviously taken exception to what Chloë had written about him. But which one was he?

She sank into her chair, rested her linked fingers on the desk and made a slow perusal. She saw an athletically built man in his early thirties, immaculately turned out in a black coat and beige trousers. She couldn't see his boots, but she knew they would be Hessions, possibly with gold tassels, and polished to a mirror shine. His hair was dark, but it wasn't black. There were shades of mahogany in those crisp locks that brushed his collar. On his left cheek, close to his mouth, was a small scar. But most telling of all, and something she *should* have noticed and *would* have noticed if she hadn't felt under attack, was that he was leaning heavily on a cane that had a distinctive silver handle.

"You're Waldo Bowman!" she declared.

When he inclined his head in acknowledgment, the small knot of tension between her shoulder blades gradually receded. He might look reckless and dangerous, but according to Chloë the only thing he was guilty of was taking advantage of the fact that he was irresistible to women. A breaker of hearts, Chloë called him, but she said it without malice. She admired Waldo Bowman.

Chloë had a fondness for rakes that Jo did not share.

He was studying her with as much interest as she studied him. She knew she looked a frump in her work clothes, with her awful red hair swept severely off her face and tied back with a ribbon. She hoped it was a ribbon and not a piece of string. She wasn't going to apologize for how she looked. Getting a paper out was a messy business. There was no reason for her to feel awkward or embarrassed.

There were ink stains on her fingers. She resisted the impulse to wipe them surreptitiously on her dress.

Her eyes jerked up to meet his. "I didn't hear that. What did you say?"

There was a short silence while he regarded her thoughtfully. At last he said, "You don't move in my circles, so I know you are not the author of this scandal sheet." He shook the paper. "Her name, Mrs. Chesney. Give me her name, and you and I shall be quits."

She shook her head. "My sources are confidential. You won't get his or her name out of me."

"It has to be a female."

"Why?"

"Because only a female would be interested in such drivel."

Her only response was to raise an eyebrow.

He splayed one hand on the desk. His eyes had

chilled by several degrees. "Let there be no misunderstanding between us. I won't tolerate having my name bandied about in a second-rate broadsheet that can only appeal to the vulgarly curious. Have you no conscience? Or is your only object to sell papers?"

The reference to her conscience left her unmoved. It was the word *broadsheet* that fanned the flames of her temper. Broadsheets were one-page news sheets and were lurid beyond belief, and generally despised by intelligent people. He had delivered the ultimate insult.

When she rose to confront him, two spots of color burned in her cheeks. He had the foresight to take a step back before she rounded the desk.

Her voice was low and trembling with anger. "I publish the news, Mr. Bowman, and you happen to be news just like"—she snatched the newspaper from the desk and held up the front page—"just like William Hogg, who murdered his wife and buried her body under the floor of his barn. So don't talk to me about conscience. If you had one, you wouldn't appear in my paper."

His eyes narrowed unpleasantly. "You're comparing me to a murderer?"

"Of course not! The point I'm trying to make is that you've developed a following. My readers want to hear about you, just as they want to hear about the Duke of Wellington or the Prince Regent."

"You never write anything derogatory about them."

"I don't publish anything derogatory about anyone, not even Mr. Hogg. I publish the truth."

An insolent smile curled his lips. "The truth as you see it."

She mimicked his smile exactly. "Correct me if I'm wrong. Did you or did you not present your latest flirt with an emerald pendant when you ended the affair?" His jaw seemed to have locked, so she went on deliberately, "And did you or did you not only last week fight a duel with Lord Hornsby in Hyde Park?"

He unlocked his jaw. "If you print that in your paper, I'll sue you for defamation of character!"

"Hah! You'd lose! How can I defame the character of a rake?" She folded her arms under her breasts and stared doggedly into his face, challenging him to contradict her.

He moved his cane to his other hand and studied her face. Gradually the heat died out of his eyes and he began to look amused. "You're not going to print the story of our duel?"

"No."

"Not to save me embarrassment, I'll wager. Then it must be to protect Hornsby. Do you mind telling me why?"

"I wouldn't lift a finger to protect Hornsby."

"Then why—"

She said impatiently, "Lady Hornsby has been shamed enough by her husband's indiscretions. I've no wish to add to her humiliation."

"You don't want to shame Lady Hornsby," he said slowly, "but it's all right to shame my relations?"

"You're not married."

"I have a mother and sisters."

"It's not the same."

"How is it different?"

"The difference is..." she floundered a little, "the difference is..."

"Yes?"

"Oh, you know what the difference is. Your indiscretions can't hurt a mother or sister the way they can hurt a wife."

His voice rose fractionally. "At the risk of sounding rude, may I point out that I'm not married."

"No," she said, warming to her subject, "and that's all to the good. Let's be frank. You're hardly a matrimonial prize, Mr. Bowman. All the same, innocent young girls and others who should know better are thrilled when you make them the object of your attentions. Each thinks that she will be the one to reform you. They're all doomed to disappointment."

"I don't want to be reformed!"

"Of course you don't. Bad boys never do. And if those London debutantes and their foolish mothers would only read the *Journal,* they'd soon come to realize that your case is hopeless."

She didn't think he was angry, but something had darkened his eyes, something quick and dangerous. When he snagged her wrist, she sucked in a breath.

"That sounds like a challenge," he said.

He wasn't wearing gloves, and the heat of his fingers on her bare skin was highly unsettling. In polite society, members of the opposite sex did not touch each other in this intimate manner unless they were closely related.

Intimate! That word again! She shivered for no apparent reason.

"What?" She'd lost the thread of their conversation.

He was no longer amused but frowning faintly. "You're trembling."

"No. I think it's you."

It was a lie, but the best she could come up with to save face. She wasn't going to give him something to laugh about.

It was that thought that kept her from crying out when he tugged on her wrist and brought her closer. He grinned, lethally, and with a will of its own her pulse began to flutter.

He said softly, "If I kiss you, will you write about it in your paper?"

"No," she managed in a credibly calm tone. "I'll shoot you."

He laughed and let her go. "A word of advice, Mrs.

Chesney. If you want to preserve your good name, don't take mine in vain."

She took the precaution of hiding her hands in the folds of her gown. "Are you threatening to spread lies about me?"

"You do have a low opinion of my character, don't you? No. I was thinking of the *Journal*'s good name. If I sue and you lose, your paper will be discredited."

"I won't lose."

His lips quirked. "Is that another challenge?"

They were interrupted when the door opened to admit a young gentleman, also in the height of fashion, whom Jo knew quite well. Henry Gardiner, at thirty-two, was the most eligible bachelor in the county, largely because his father, Sir Robert, *owned* half the county, or so the locals claimed.

"Waldo!" exclaimed the newcomer. "Ruggles said this would only take five minutes. What's keeping you?" He turned to Jo with a smile. "It's a pleasure to see you again, ma'am. I hope you don't mind the intrusion, but our coach is waiting, and the wedding can't go forward without my friend here."

For some odd reason Jo had been feeling that Mr. Gardiner had caught her red-handed. On hearing his last remark, however, she brightened considerably.

"Wedding?" she said, eyeing Waldo speculatively. "Who is the lucky lady?"

A look of amusement crossed Waldo's face. "You're way off the mark, Mrs. Chesney. I'm not getting married."

"Eh?" Mr. Gardiner stared, then gave a chortle of laughter. "I beg your pardon," he said, regaining his composure. "I suppose anything is possible. No, no, ma'am. A mutual friend is to be married today in Warwick, and Mr. Bowman is to be his groomsman. There was a piece about it in last week's *Journal*."

Jo couldn't remember the piece offhand, and she

didn't want to prolong the conversation, so she didn't ask for details. "Warwick?" she said. "That's at least eight miles away. Then I won't delay you." She smiled brilliantly. "Good-bye, Mr. Gardiner, Mr. Bowman. Have a pleasant journey." Jo curtsied, the gentlemen bowed. As soon as they had quit the room, she sagged against the desk, then straightened almost at once when Waldo Bowman reappeared.

"What is it now?" she asked, rattled.

He smiled slowly, as though he knew how unsettling his presence was. "I'll be in Warwick ovenight," he said, "but I should be back in Stratford tomorrow. Perhaps we could make up a party and go to the theater?"

"Why should we do that?"

"If you don't know, I can't explain it."

"No!" she answered emphatically.

"You don't mince words. I like that in a woman. Not the theater, then. We'll talk about this again."

"Oh, no, we won't—"

He put a finger to his lips, silencing her. "Don't rage. Henry is right outside the door. We wouldn't want to give him the impression that we're having a lovers' tiff." He moved to the door and paused with his hand on the doorknob. There was no grin now to set her pulse fluttering. "I meant what I said, Mrs. Chesney. Be careful what you print in your newspaper. Don't go looking for trouble."

She stayed rooted to the spot, scarcely breathing, till she heard the sound of footsteps and voices receding along the corridor, and finally a door closing. She was more than a little confused. One moment he was flirting with her, the next he was threatening her.

He wasn't anything like she expected. Chloë had misrepresented him or, at the very least, underestimated him. He wasn't all charm. When he wanted to be, he could be intimidating. Now that she'd met him in person, she was unlikely to forget that he'd served with Wellington in Spain. That's how he'd come by his lame leg and, she supposed, where he'd acquired a core of steel that no amount of charm could conceal. Such men were used to having their orders obeyed. But not by her, and he would do well to remember it. Besides, the war had been over for two years.

She looked at her wrist. It really, *really* annoyed her to recall how she'd trembled at his touch, not in fear—she could have excused that—but because he'd made her aware of him as a man. She wasn't used to men like Waldo Bowman. The gentlemen in her circle treated her with deference, knowing that she was devoted to her husband's memory.

Don't go looking for trouble.

She wasn't afraid for herself as much as for Chloë. If he sued the *Journal,* he would lose. She published nothing but the truth. If he found out about Chloë, however, and sued her, she could be ostracized by her friends.

No. He would put the blame squarely where it belonged—on the owner of the paper that published Chloë's pieces.

He was making a mountain out of a molehill. Chloë wasn't snide or malicious. If she had a fault it was that she was gushing. She truly admired the people she wrote about. There must be something she was missing, a more compelling reason for Bowman to threaten legal action if his name appeared in the *Journal* again.

She almost jumped when the door opened, but it was only Billy, the apprentice printer, who had brought the post.

"Mostly bills," he said cheerfully, setting the burlap mailbag down on her desk. "And one from your friend Lady Webberley. I recognized her writing."

A letter from Chloë. That was unusual. Chloë's personal letters usually went to the house on Church

Street, not to the *Journal*'s offices. Jo thought no more about it. They never got round to reading the post on Friday. They were too busy. She'd get to it later.

She put a hand on Billy's shoulder. "If we get everything out and away before noon, there'll be an extra sixpence in your pocket."

Billy beamed. He was thirteen years old and his mother's sole support. An extra sixpence would go a long way in their frugal household.

"You're on," he declared.

They moved quicky—through the door, down the corridor and into the room they used for Dispatch. Long tables were laid out with sections of the paper, and everyone who worked for the *Journal*—printers and their apprentices, paper sellers, cleaners, clerks and editors—was involved in either assembling the paper or tying stacks of newspapers into bundles and carting them outside to waiting wagons.

Jo paused fleetingly to savor the moment. Mac Nevin, shirtsleeves rolled up, gave her a cheery wave. He was in his sixties, ruddy of complexion with a thinning mane of silver hair. Some people thought that Managing Editor was too grand a title for the editor of a small, provincial paper. Not Jo. She knew how much she owed Mac. Without him, she wouldn't have known how to begin publishing a newspaper.

At one time Mac had been sought after by every paper in the land. His fondness for the brandy bottle, however, eventually put paid to that. He'd returned to his hometown a shade of his former self. Now he was sober, and the *Journal*, he once confided, had been the saving of him. Jo could have said much the same about herself.

She observed the chaos in Dispatch with a smile on her face. Everything she wanted was right here. She rolled up her sleeves and set to work.